# TROLLEY DAYS

## by Robert T. McMaster

UNQUOMONK PRESS

Williamsburg, Massachusetts

U.S.A.

Trolley Days

Printed in the United States of America.

For information contact
Unquomonk Press, P.O. Box 126,
Williamsburg, MA 01096 USA.

www.TrolleyDays.net


ISBN 978-0-9856944-0-1

Published by Unquomonk Press,
Williamsburg, Massachusetts 01096 USA

Third Printing 2014

This is a work of fiction. Names, characters, places, and incidents
either are the product of the author's imagination or are used
fictitiously. Any resemblance to actual persons, living or dead,
events, or locales is entirely coincidental.


Cover design by Benjamin Christopher Martins

*Dedicated to*

*Robert W. McMaster,*

*my father,*

*who inspired me with his memories of*

*the days of trolleys*

CHAPTER 1

# Two Storms
*November 1916*

Jack Bernard had lived in Westfield most of his life and he felt he knew his town as well as anyone. Every neighborhood, every street, nearly every building brought back memories of his childhood: the imposing brick edifice of St. Agnes Church where his family attended Mass each Sunday; Aucoin's Market on Main Street with its green and white awnings where he and his mother shopped for groceries; and LeClaire's Newsstand where he browsed the latest issues of *Boys' Life* and *St. Nicholas Magazine*.

Almost as familiar were the fields and woods north and west of town: the Dunham Farm on Russell Road where Jack worked on the tobacco harvest one summer; the angular ledges of Mount Tekoa he climbed to watch the Boston and Albany train descending from the Berkshires, its shrill whistle echoing off the rock faces; and the bend in the river where he and Tom Wellington swam on a sweltering August day, the late afternoon sun turning the water to shimmering gold, back when he and Tom were best friends.

But on this ashen November afternoon, those days were only distant, shining memories. A chill wind was blowing out of the northwest, snow was just beginning to fall, and the streets of Westfield were already nearly empty as families withdrew to the comfort of their fireplaces, coal stoves, and down comforters.

Jack once loved days like this, nestled at home with his parents and sisters by the light and warmth of the fire. Their house was small, but it was well-protected from the frigid winds of winter, tucked against a dense row of hemlocks on the north side of town. Behind the house stood a barn and several sheds; beyond was the vegetable garden, its narrow rows of black earth nearly converging in the distance. In early mornings he often paused to gaze across those fields, listening for the sounds of a new day: the raucous cawing of crows, the resonant clip-clop of the muscular draft horses pulling the ice wagon up Southampton Road.

The Bernard farmhouse had white clapboards on the front, weathered cedar shingles on the sides and rear. To the left of the front door was a small parlor with a fieldstone fireplace; to the right a dining room barely large enough for a table and six chairs. At the rear was a kitchen with a soapstone sink, hand pump, and cast iron cooking stove with shining chrome trim that burned wood or coal. A wooden ice box stood against the rear wall next to a Hoosier cabinet where his mother prepared bread for baking. Bathing was done in the kitchen in a large tin set tub filled with boiling water from the stove, adjusted for comfort with cold well water. The small toilet attached to the rear of the house was a recent and very welcome addition.

A narrow hallway connected the kitchen with a bedroom shared by Jack's sisters. Off the hallway was a tiny windowless alcove with a gate-legged mahogany table and cushioned kneeling stool. A white lace runner covered the table; it was tatted by Jack's mémère in Québec almost half a century earlier. Neatly arranged on the runner were two votive candles in red crystal bowls, a family bible, and six strings of rosary beads laid neatly side-by-side. Centered on the wall above the table was a crucifix framed by hand-colored portraits of St. John and the Blessed Virgin. This was the Bernard family shrine.

A steep flight of stairs rose from the parlor to the second floor and two tiny bedrooms with slanted ceilings and small windows. Jack's bedroom, on the left, had a single window that looked out on the back lawn and gardens. On the opposite side was his parents' bedroom with two windows, one facing the rear, one overlooking the row of hemlocks.

On wintry days like these when they were very young, Jack's sisters, Marie, Thérèse, and Claire, would sit on their mother's lap, listening enraptured as their father read to them. Jack sometimes listened, but often he would be reading with the aid of an oil lamp, or just gazing into the flames, lost in his thoughts. From time to time the children coaxed their father into telling them about life in Québec, before he met their mother, before Jack was born. It was a hard life, Charles Bernard would say; winters were long and cold, but families, friends, and neighbors helped each other to make it through until spring. "Family, friends, faith, those were the pillars of life in Québec," he repeated again and again.

Jack wanted nothing more than to be home in the embrace of his family on this cold November day. Of course, it wasn't the same anymore. Marie and Claire were now fifteen and twelve; their dear sister Thérèse was gone, lost to diphtheria at the tender age of four. Their mother had died of influenza just a year-and-a-half ago, when Jack was sixteen. Even today bitter tears stung his eyes at the memory of that March day when Evelyne Bernard breathed her last and gave up her spirit to God.

The happy, innocent days of Jack's youth were gone and in his heart he knew that was so. But knowing that didn't prevent him from wishing otherwise. Still today he loved to be with his family. When his father wasn't feeling well, which was often, Jack felt like the head of the household, and it gave him strength and a sense of purpose that he needed right now. Even at his young age, he had lost too many who were dear to him, and his heart ached to the very core at the thought of them.

As Jack made his way along Elm Street, the broad intersection known as the Trolley Centre at Park Square came dimly into view. But the approaching blizzard was not the only storm he was struggling with that day. Another battle raged within. On one side was his family, at home, by the fire, calling him back. On the other was a sense of duty and friendship that propelled him forward, and duty and friendship were things that Jack Bernard took very seriously.

The trolley stop was empty and Jack stood alone for several minutes until a figure approached out of the swirling snow. It was Mr. Bowen, an old friend of his father and dispatcher for the Springfield Street Railway Company. He was shorter than Jack with a round face, ruddy complexion, and ready smile.

"Jack? Jack Bernard? Is that you? What in heaven's name are you doing out in this weather? There's a blizzard comin', my boy, you should be home with your dad and sisters, shouldn't you?"

"I have to go to Boston, Mr. Bowen, on an errand," replied Jack haltingly.

"Boston? Are you mad, son? It'll take you forever. Can't it wait a few days?" he asked, a smile of both affection and concern spreading across his face.

"No, it can't," replied Jack emphatically. "Are the cars still running?" he asked, referring to the trolley line that ran along Western Avenue from Huntington to Westfield and all the way into Springfield.

"There's one more car coming from the mill in Russell...that's it for today...and probably for several days until the snow ends and they can get the tracks plowed. Better go home, son, and wait out the storm, don't ya think?"

"But I have to get to Boston," repeated Jack, "It's about a....a friend."

Mr. Bowen looked intently into Jack's face, as if trying to discern a possible motivation for the young man's ill-conceived venture. He took Jack's arm, leaned in and spoke softly, his words barely audible above the wind: "That must be a real good friend, my boy, a real good friend. Godspeed to you, son." He turned and walked away, the swirling snow quickly engulfing him.

The wait for the last trolley was long and cold, but at last a single headlamp appeared through the driving snow, sparks flew from the wires overhead, and a clanging bell announced the car's arrival as it shuddered to a stop. The battered wooden door squealed as it slid open and half a dozen riders disembarked, probably workers from the paper mill in Russell who had finished their shift and were headed home.

Jack boarded the car, dropped a nickel into the coin box, and chose a seat at the rear as the trolley lurched forward. He would have been more comfortable sitting up front next to the electric heater, but he was the only passenger and he did not wish to be drawn into conversation with the motorman; he had too much on his mind right now.

The ride to Springfield, normally only forty-five minutes, took well over an hour. By now the snow was accumulating rapidly. At every switch the motorman halted the car and climbed down to inspect the rails to be sure it could pass safely. Finally, it pulled up to the curb on Main Street in Springfield.

"All off, this is the end of the line," announced the motorman loudly to his solitary passenger. "Next stop's the car barn." As the rickety door opened before him, Jack climbed down the two stairs and stepped onto the street.

Springfield looked as deserted as Westfield as he ascended the wide stone stairway to the railroad station two flights above. The station was an imposing stone structure, dark and cavernous within. Jack's steps echoed off the walls and ceiling as he strode resolutely to the ticket window. "One ticket for Boston, please," he said to the clerk at the window.

"The trains are running behind due to the weather, son. It could be hours before the next train for Boston arrives," responded the clerk.

"That's okay," replied Jack, and he produced two dollars and fifty cents, practically his life savings at that moment. He grasped the ticket tightly in his fingers and sat on a worn oak bench next to a coal stove in one corner of the waiting room. Half a dozen other would-be travelers were seated in silence around the same stove. He dug into his rucksack and drew out a book.

Jack sat awkwardly on the hard, narrow bench, trying to read. He was almost six feet tall, remarkable considering his parents were both quite short. His nose and chin were angular, but the blue-gray of his eyes softened his face. His brown hair still showed some lighter streaks that appeared after working all summer long in the family's vegetable gardens. His smile could be infectious, lighting up the hearts of all around him, but he was in no mood to smile right now.

An hour went by with no sign of the train from Albany. Several of the other parties in the waiting room had drifted off, deciding to return home and postpone their travel plans to another day. Jack shifted his position on the hard bench, staring vacantly toward the vaulted ceiling. His reveries were suddenly interrupted by a loud voice from the ticket window. The train for Boston had just left Albany. With luck it might arrive in Springfield in two hours. He looked at his watch; it was almost midnight. He turned the watch over in his hand, his eyes glistening as he read the inscription on the back. He slumped against the armrest of the wooden bench and fell into a restless sleep.

It was nearly two o'clock in the morning when at last a loud voice announced the arrival of the train from Albany. Jack and the few other remaining travelers rose from their seats, hoisted their bags, and exited through large swinging doors onto the platform. There was plenty of room on the train and Jack fell into the first empty seat and slumped against the window, half awake and half asleep, his head filled with memories of him and Tom in happier times.

CHAPTER 2

# Lessons Learned
## 1904 - 1911

Jack was six years old and about to enter grade one at St. Agnes School in Westfield. Sister Marie greeted him and his mother brightly that first morning. She did her best to console Jack as his mother kissed him and departed. He whimpered a little, as he recalled, but quickly became distracted by his classmates and soon was happily occupied with crayons, a big sheet of drawing paper, and a story read by his teacher.

Most of the nuns of St. Agnes were warm and motherly. Sister Suzanne, his grade two teacher, was French-Canadian, and that made Jack feel especially at home. Some of his classmates were also from Québec; several had arrived in Westfield only lately and spoke little English. Others were Irish or Italian, and there were even a few from Lithuania, their faces and mannerisms reflections of another world. Mother Superior, from Montréal, was a stern matriarchal figure and the children avoided her whenever possible for fear she would find some fault in their character and exact a harsh punishment.

Father Lévesque, the pastor of St. Agnes Church, was a frequent visitor to Jack's classes. He was nearly sixty and the lines and wrinkles in his face bore witness to a long career spent ministering to his flock, sharing their joys, bearing their sorrows. He walked with a slight stoop as if carrying the accumulated burdens of his parishioners, his hands clasped behind his back. He had a shock of steel gray hair that was often too long; the sisters in the rectory had to speak to him from time to time to remind him when he was overdue for a trip to the barber.

Whenever Father Lévesque entered the classroom, a hush fell over even the most boisterous students. He would walk down the narrow aisles between the desks, looking at the students' work, complimenting often, reprimanding only occasionally and gently. Before departing he would lead the class in prayer or deliver a short lesson. A frequent topic was sin, a matter he believed was important to children of all ages, and Jack recalled especially Father's words about venial sins and mortal sins. Venial sins were small infractions of God's laws that did little harm and only temporarily damaged our relationship with Him – "little white lies," for example. Mortal sins such as stealing or killing, these were quite another matter, explained Father, his voice dropping, for they separated us from God and his love.

Jack also recalled Father's explanation of "bearing false witness." The words meant little to him as a ten-year-old, but they took on new meaning today as he thought about the past year and the walls that come between friends. At the same time he remembered Father's recitation of a line from the Book of Ephesians: "Be kind to one another, tenderhearted, forgiving each other, just as God in Christ forgave you."

Once in grade four Father Lévesque made a special visit to Jack's class. The father of a classmate had died suddenly while working in the paper mill. The pastor discussed death frankly with the children, answering their questions about the body, the soul, purgatory, and heaven.

"Father, where is heaven…is it up there?" asked one boy, pointing skyward.

Smiling, Father Lévesque reached out, lightly touching the boy's head. "No, my child, heaven is not up there, it is right here among us. When someone we love passes on, we do not really lose him, he remains with us in spirit. We may not see him or hear him, but he is nearby. That is why we must talk to the departed and pray for them daily. Remember that, my child."

St. Agnes School was small and Jack thought of the other students and the nuns as nearly family. His sisters would eventually enter first grade following him and his mother would become an assistant teacher in afternoon Christian Doctrine classes. So school felt very much like an extension of home for Jack. But even in the comfortable confines of St. Agnes School, Jack felt the sting of prejudice. Some of the older children called him "Jacques," his Christian name which he hated, and they taunted him with strains of *Frère Jacques* when no adult was within earshot. "Canuck" was also used derisively behind his back. While he was a mild-mannered boy, Jack feared the day when that epithet would cause him to lose control and do something he might regret.

Jack attended St. Agnes School for seven years. But during the summer before he would have entered grade eight, he began to suspect that his parents had other plans for their only son. He noticed how their whispered conversations stopped abruptly as he entered the room, or the way they avoided his questions about who would be his grade eight teacher at St. Agnes School. Late one August afternoon they returned from what he had been told was a doctor's appointment. Conversation around the supper table was stilted and he suspected that his parents had something on their minds. After supper Marie and Claire were asked to do the dishes.

"Jack," said his mother gently, "Please come into the parlor. Your father and I want to talk with you." Evelyne Bernard was slight with reddish-brown hair worn in a bun at the back of her head. Her hazel eyes were soft, her nose and lips delicate. Her warm smile and gentle manner won her friends wherever she went. Despite her mild disposition, Evelyne was possessed of a steely determination that her children not suffer the pain and hardship of her own childhood.

"You know how proud we are of you and how we want only the best for our boy," she began. Jack had a sinking feeling; this sounded like an ominous opening for a conversation he didn't want to have. "St. Agnes is a wonderful school, and you have done very well. But you are growing up and we want you to have something more than what the nuns of St. Agnes can provide," she continued in what sounded like a rehearsed speech.

"Son, we've enrolled you in grade eight at the Forestdale Grammar School in Holyoke," explained his father. "It's a fine school with excellent teachers. And the principal, Mr. Lataille, is a good man. You'll like him and we know you'll be happy at Forestdale."

That was it, "the die is cast," as his father often said of things that were over, done, and must be accepted. Suddenly Jack's comfortable world had been turned upside down. "But how will I get to Holyoke? That's miles away," Jack protested.

"We'll take you in the carriage the first day. Then you can ride the trolley. It takes only twenty minutes and you can get off the car right in front of your school," his father explained.

"You'll like it, Son, I know you will," added his mother with her infectious good spirit and optimism. And somehow Jack believed her. He loved riding the trolleys, electric cars that ran on tracks along the main streets of nearly every town. The longer "interurban" routes ran across country from town to town and were used mainly by workers going to the mills along the river in Hadley Falls, Holyoke, Chicopee, and Springfield. Jack's father had been riding the trolley to and from the mill in Holyoke every day since they bought the farm and moved to Westfield. The idea of traveling to school by trolley with the grownups appealed to Jack and took much of the pain out of leaving behind his friends at St. Agnes.

Forestdale Grammar School presented many new challenges to young Jack that he could not possibly have anticipated. He found himself in a class of forty eighth graders, many from Holyoke families very different from his own. These were city children with experiences and attitudes that were new to him; that was sometimes good, sometimes bad, sometimes stimulating, and sometimes unsettling.

One thing that Jack looked forward to at Forestdale was leaving his French-Canadian heritage behind. He would be called Jack; his parents had made a special request about that to Mr. Lataille who was himself French-Canadian. And his teachers respected his wishes. His last name, Bernard, was just ambiguous enough that his classmates might not guess at his true ancestry.

Within a few days one of Jack's classmates, Jeffrey O'Malley, spotted his full name, Jacques Honoré Bernard, on the teacher's attendance list and the whispering began. In the schoolyard during recess, Jeffrey and three of his friends approached Jack. Jeffrey was short, had a round, chubby face, and wore an annoying grin whenever he caught Jack's eye. Jack was bigger but the bully was emboldened by his two friends, Michael Shaughnessy and Dennis Donovan. Michael was tall and skinny with red-brown hair and freckles; his face bore a permanent, malevolent sneer. Dennis was short and stocky with black hair and a vacant expression in his eyes. Michael and Jeffrey, Jack had observed, were troublemakers, always on the lookout for mischief; Dennis was quiet and slow, clearly a follower.

"Look at the frog, *Jacques*, who tries to pretend his name is Jack. We know what you really are, *Jacques*, Frenchy, frog...Canuck," Jeffrey taunted.

Jack's blood was boiling as he approached his accuser and glared balefully at him. "Shut up, O'Malley, or else," said Jack forcefully.

"Yeh? Who's gonna make me?" replied Jeffrey. Just then another classmate who had been watching from a distance approached the boys. He was slightly taller than Jack with dark, wavy hair, and an air of confident self-assurance about him.

"What's going on, Jeffrey?" asked the tall boy. "Something wrong?"

"No, no," said Jeffrey, suddenly smiling. "We were just welcoming Jack here to Forestdale." Turning to Jack, he added, "You're gonna like it here, Jack...one big happy family we are." Jeffrey and his sidekicks quickly turned and disappeared among the children on the playground.

"Don't worry about those guys," the tall boy said to Jack. "They're not worth it."

"Thanks," replied Jack, "I wasn't worried." There was a momentary pause. Then Jack extended his hand. "I'm Jack Bernard."

"Tom Wellington. Glad to know you, Jack," offered Tom, shaking his hand vigorously and smiling.

From that day on, Jack Bernard and Tom Wellington were inseparable. They played catch on the playground every morning before the clanging bell that signaled the start of the school day. They chattered endlessly about baseball and football during recess and lunchtime. Some days after dismissal they walked together down Sargeant Street to High Street.

Holyoke was a thriving commercial and industrial city that teemed with life. Dozens of factories large and small - paper, textile, and specialty mills - stretched along three broad canals close to the river. The roar and clatter of the mills could be heard from miles away. Long freight trains rumbled through the city day and night bringing wood pulp, wool, and other raw materials to the mills, then departing loaded with paper, fabric, and other finished goods.

High Street was the center of Holyoke's shopping district and it was lined with businesses: grocers, butchers, bakers, tailors, clothiers, haberdashers, milliners, hairdressers, druggists, shoeshine shops, department stores, banks, restaurants, bars, theatres, and much more. Trolleys, motorcars, omnibuses, and horse-drawn carriages raced up and down the streets, bells clanging, horns trumpeting, operators shouting greetings, warnings, and curses at one another. There were no traffic lights and few crosswalks, so pedestrians ventured across the wide thoroughfare at their hazard.

The two friends spent much of their time downtown peering into store windows, browsing newspapers and magazines on the newsstands, or slurping colas at Liggett's Drug Store on Maple Street.

One afternoon the boys stood on the banks of the Connecticut River at Riverside Park. A week of heavy rain had swelled the river well above its normal level. Watching the waters roil and writhe, they pitched stones and pebbles into the swirling eddies.

"You wanna go fishing on Saturday?" Jack asked. "I know a great place at Hampton Ponds that's right on the trolley line. We could meet there."

"I don't know how to fish," admitted Tom. "And I don't have a pole or anything."

"Don't worry, I'll borrow my father's rod. And I'll dig us some worms for bait," added Jack.

They fished at Hampton Ponds that Saturday morning as planned, and thus began a weekly ritual. Jack boarded the trolley in Westfield, Tom boarded a car on the same line in Holyoke, and the two met beside the tracks at pond's edge. Since theirs was not a regular stop, each boy had to remember to ask the motorman to stop at Hampton Ponds. Should one of them forget to do so, he had to leap from the moving trolley, though that was strictly against the rules.

Often the boys caught small perch by the dozens, a few pickerel, and an occasional bass which Jack brought home for his mother to cook in the frying pan for supper. For Jack the best part of those fishing excursions was the endless banter between two good friends on all matters of interest to thirteen-year-old boys. Jack would recount stories he had read in *Boys' Life* or describe shocking photographs of naked African tribesmen he had seen in *National Geographic Magazine*. He often went on in great detail about the projects he and his father were working on together in the workshop behind the barn: building a chicken coop, repairing an old grandfather clock, installing a pump for the well. The family had a cow, a Guernsey named Angélique, and Tom listened wide-eyed as Jack described the birth of a calf.

Another favorite topic of conversation was sisters. Jack could prattle on and on about Marie and Claire, their silliness, and why girls were like that. But he ended each monologue with "...but they're okay, I guess. They look up to me, you know, 'cause I'm the oldest."

Tom had a sister, too, named Anne. She was a year younger than Tom and in grade seven at Forestdale, so Jack had seen her. Her hair was reddish, cut short in a boyish bob, her cheeks were rosy, her eyes bright green. She shared her brother's poise, cheery disposition, and air of self-possession. Sisters, Tom agreed, were hard to understand. But Jack saw how Tom watched out for Anne in the schoolyard at recess and he could see the genuine affection between the two. Other than that, Tom had little to say about his family life, at least until a Saturday in early October while the two boys were fishing.

"What does your dad do?" asked Jack.

"He works in a mill."

"So does mine, which mill?"

"Wellington Textiles...on Canal Street," replied Tom.

"Holy cow, that's where my dad works," said Jack. "Maybe your dad knows mine."

"I don't know, maybe," said Tom vaguely.

Suddenly Jack made the connection: "Wait a minute, your name's Wellington. Your dad...is he the owner of Wellington Textiles?"

"Well, he's <u>one</u> of the owners," replied Tom, trying to play down this revelation, "with my Uncle Richard and my grandfather. They run it together."

"Your family must be rich, I'll bet." Jack was remembering his father's uncomplimentary descriptions of the wealthy mill owners.

"Not really," replied Tom modestly. "It's not that big a company and business hasn't been too good the last few years."

This unexpected development occupied much of Jack's thoughts for days after their conversation. He liked Tom and admired him. But it surprised him that the son of the owner of Wellington Textiles wanted to be his friend. After all, Jack's family was of modest means and his father was just one of hundreds of men and women who labored at that very mill. For the first time Jack felt a little embarrassed about his family and his home when he was with Tom. So the subject was not discussed again for several months.

A few weeks later, Tom and Jack walked slowly down Sargeant Street after school carrying book bags. Both boys wore white, loose-fitting cotton shirts and brown woolen knickerbockers tucked into woolen stockings just below the knee and supported by suspenders, Jack's brown, Tom's bright red.

Several steps behind the boys walked Anne and her friend, Carolyn Ford, each wearing a colorful gingham pinafore over a white dress. Anne and Carolyn had been classmates at Forestdale Grammar School since grade one. Carolyn was tall with dark skin, black, lustrous hair, and large brown eyes. Her temperament was decidedly saturnine, and one would have thought the two girls an unlikely pair, but Anne's outlook seemed to bring out the lighter, gayer side of Carolyn. They shared many interests: needlepoint, for one thing, and reading, and music. Both took piano lessons with Miss Sheldon on Maple Street. When the four reached the trolley stop, Jack stopped and turned to Tom. "Well, I guess I'll see you tomorrow."

"Why don't you come with us, Jack? Anne and Carolyn are going to piano lessons and I have to wait around and walk them home afterwards. We can go to Whitman's while we're waiting."

Jack promptly agreed and he and Tom set out again, side-by-side, engrossed in talk of fishing, while the girls followed along quietly. In front of Miss Sheldon's house Anne spoke to her brother. "We'll be finished in an hour, Tommy. You be back here on time!" She turned and looked pleadingly at Jack: "Remind him, Jack...please?" Then a slight smile crossed her face, she wrinkled her nose, and whispered conspiratorially to Jack: "Sometimes he forgets."

Jack nodded. "Okay."

"We'll be here, Anne, don't worry about it," said Tom, abashed and a little irritated.

The two boys headed off. Finding their way to Whitman's Hardware at the corner of High and Suffolk, they snaked through a maze of narrow aisles to the fishing and hunting supplies. Tom was hoping to get his own fishing gear and Jack wanted to help him choose the very best. They browsed the rods and reels, from simple jig lines to the fanciest fly-fishing gear, trying out each, making feigned casts, reeling in imaginary fish, half shopping and half fantasizing about the next season's adventures. They pulled on waders and hip boots, laughing at themselves in the floor-length mirrors. They studied with fascination the selection of handmade fishing flies that beautifully mimicked the insects fish were attracted to.

"Tommy, we'd better go, it's getting late; Anne and Carolyn will be waiting for us," said Jack with urgency in his voice.

"Okay, okay, just one more minute," replied Tom vaguely as he examined a display of fancy reels.

Jack went off to find a clock, then returned. "It's already nearly quarter to five, Tommy, we should go."

It was almost dark and the boys ran the five blocks to Miss Sheldon's house and knocked on the front door. Miss Sheldon appeared; the girls had already left. They hurried up Hampshire Street, the route the girls would be most likely to follow toward the Wellingtons' home. Just then they heard screams from an alley across the street. They ran as fast as they could in the direction of the voices. As they entered the alley two younger boys came running out into the street; each was carrying something concealed under his jacket. Behind them emerged Anne and Carolyn, both very agitated. Carolyn was crying.

"They stole Carolyn's purse and my bookbag," cried Anne.

"Stay with the girls," Jack ordered Tom, and he sped off after the young ruffians, his legs little more than a blur under the gas streetlamp.

"Jack, be careful," called Anne as he turned into another alley where the two boys had just disappeared. Several minutes went by. Then Jack reappeared carrying Anne's book bag and Carolyn's purse.

"Wow, Jack, you got 'em," shouted Tom with admiration.

"It didn't take much," replied Jack. "As soon as I caught up with 'em they dropped the things and took off. I could've chased after them and given them the thrashin' they deserved, but I figured I'd better bring the girls their things."

Anne and Carolyn were shaken and they huddled together, consoling each other. "Did they hurt you?" inquired Jack.

"No, we're all right," responded Anne.

Jack and Tom carried the girls' book bags as well as their own several blocks up Hampshire Street. At the corner of Hampshire and Pine they stopped at an iron gate that appeared to be the entrance to the driveway, although large trees blocked the view of the house. "I better be going," said Jack.

"Thanks," replied Tom, looking a little sheepish.

"Thank you, Jack," added Anne. By now she had calmed down. "As usual Tommy let me down...but you saved the day!"

"It was my fault, too," replied Jack. "We were both thinking about fishing and just lost track of the time. I don't have a watch. Well, I gotta get going."

"See you in school, Jack," replied Tom.

CHAPTER 3

# The Gift

*December 1911*

The fishing season had ended and winter was approaching. Shorter days meant it was no longer possible for Jack and Tom to spend time together after school or go fishing on weekends. Weeks went by when their only contact outside of class was at recess or during lunch.

One December day amidst the clamor of the Forestdale Grammar School lunchroom, Jack and Tom talked about Christmas and how they hoped to spend their vacation time. Suddenly Tom had an idea: "Hey, Jack, why don't you come and stay at our house for a few days after Christmas? We could go skating and sledding...it would be so much fun. What do you say, Jack?"

Jack was uneasy about the prospect of being away from his family, but he enjoyed Tom's company and pleaded with his parents to permit him a two-day visit in Holyoke after Christmas. Tom's mother wrote a letter of invitation to Jack's mother, who quickly consented. "But you'll have to discuss this with your father," she added.

Jack's father by now knew all about Tom Wellington and the thought of his son spending time with the mill owner's family made him a little uncomfortable. But he also knew how much Jack liked his new friend and how important he had been in Jack's adjustment to his new school, so he agreed.

Christmas at the Bernard home was especially merry that year. For weeks the three children had been busying themselves making gifts for one another and their parents.

Marie secretly worked on knitting projects in her room, hand warmers for her mother, a woolen scarf for her father, a sweater for Claire, mittens for Jack. She helped Claire get started on potholders and an apron for her mother. Meanwhile Jack worked in his father's shop, building a bookshelf for Marie and a dollhouse for Claire. For his parents he had repaired an antique mantle clock and was painting it to match the furnishings in the parlor.

Evelyne and Charles saved all year long so that they could surprise each child with a store-bought gift, an easel for Claire, a dresser with mirror for Marie, steel ice skates for Jack. During the summer, Charles bought and refinished a handsome slant-topped writing table for Evelyne which he had secreted away under a blanket in the hay loft. For her husband Evelyne had purchased a new dress shirt and matching tie at Marshall's Clothiers in Westfield.

Christmas Day for the Bernards began with Mass at St. Agnes followed by the exchange of gifts at home, a feast at mid-day, and a long, leisurely afternoon of singing, games, and story-reading by the fire. But Jack's excitement at his impending visit with Tom was apparent and the family was happy for him.

The next day a horse-drawn carriage pulled up in front of the Bernards' farmhouse at precisely one o'clock and Jack was whisked away with a hearty wave to his family as they stood in the front doorway. A half-hour later the carriage turned from Cabot Street in Holyoke into an open iron gate. As Jack's eye followed the long curve of the driveway, he could not believe what he saw ahead. An imposing white mansion three floors tall loomed above a sweeping, snow-covered lawn. Huge copper beech trees stood at each corner of the house, their graceful, leafless silhouettes contrasting with the formal, rectilinear lines of what was surely one of the largest, finest homes in Holyoke.

As the carriage drew beneath the stately portico at one end of the house, a tall door opened and there stood Tom, smiling and waving. A maid took Jack's rucksack and Tom led him inside, chattering all the while. Down a broad hallway they walked, Jack's boots clicking on the marble floors that looked like a great checkerboard. Passing through a pair of heavy wooden doors decorated with elaborate carvings, they entered a long parlor with a grand fireplace.

Tom's mother was seated by the fire in an ornate chair with green velvet cushions. She rose to greet him: "Jack Bernard, hello and welcome. I am so happy to meet you," she said warmly, her eyes twinkling. She was a short, stocky woman with chestnut brown hair wrapped in a tight bun atop her head.

Jack found Mrs. Wellington's face and manner warm and reassuring, and he attempted a polite reply: "Thank you, Missus...Ma'am..." As he spoke he looked into her eyes. They seemed puffy, as though she had been crying but was trying very hard to conceal it.

At that moment Anne appeared and smiled demurely. "So good to see you, Jack," she offered, tipping her head coyly to one side. "Did you have a pleasant journey?"

"Eh, yeh, I guess so," Jack mumbled awkwardly in reply. The three children sat before the crackling fire sipping hot cocoa and sugar cookies served on an oval tray by the parlor maid, Margarita, who was dressed in a starched black and white uniform.

"Anne made those cookies especially for your visit, Jack," explained Mrs. Wellington.

"They're delicious," remarked Jack as he reached for a second. Tom and Jack exchanged stories from school and their fall fishing adventures. Mrs. Wellington listened with obvious pleasure, but Jack could see her eyes glistening in the fire's light.

As they talked, Jack looked around the large, elegantly furnished room. His gaze fell on the three Christmas stockings hung from the mantle above the fireplace. Each was hand-stitched and beautifully decorated with a different letter, "A,"

"T," and "M." This struck him as curious; there were, after all, only the two Wellington children, Tom and Anne, so far as he knew. When he realized that Tom had seen the perplexed look on his face, he quickly averted his eyes and changed the subject. "So, d'you think we could go skating?" asked Jack. "I brought my new skates that I got for Christmas."

"Let's go after supper this very night," Tom replied quickly. "Anne, Mother, you and me, we can all go to the pond at Highland Park. We'll bring oil lamps and blankets. May we, Mother, please?"

Skating at night was thrilling despite the cold air, and the three young people and Mrs. Wellington skated for over an hour. One of the servants waited on the shore with blankets should anyone get chilled. Eventually Mrs. Wellington tired, removed her skates, and stood watching, a blanket draped over her shoulders. The children played "crack the whip" with several other youngsters from the neighborhood to the amusement of all.

By the time they got home, the three children were exhausted and ready for bed. Tom and Jack shared a huge four-poster bed in a guest room on the second floor with a veritable mountain of quilts and comforters to keep them warm. One of the maids had placed a shiny brass bed warmer under the covers so the sheets were warm and inviting. A small fire crackled in the fireplace.

The two boys lay in bed staring up at the high ceiling, their cheeks still burning from the chill night air. "I'm sorry Father was not able to join us for supper or skating, he had to work late," explained Tom. "Perhaps he will have breakfast with us." There was a long pause.

"Tom," said Jack hesitantly. "I noticed the Christmas stockings over the fireplace, one for you and one for Anne. Who was the third one for? Who is 'M'?"

For the first time since he had known Tom, Jack sensed a crack in his friend's composure. The boy who was always so well-spoken and sure of himself was speechless and there was another very long pause. Finally Tom spoke: "'M' is for Matthew, my older brother." He hesitated again. "He...he died the summer before last. He and some friends were swimming in the quarry up on West Mountain and...he...had an accident."

Jack turned and looked at Tom's face, barely visible in the light of the fire. His eyes were wet and Jack thought he saw a single tear roll down his cheek. "I'm sorry," said Jack, "I shouldn't have asked. It's none of my business."

"No, Jack, don't apologize. I should have told you before. I didn't know how to say it," admitted Tom.

"Do you miss him?" asked Jack softly.

Tom nodded, his lower lip quivered, but no words came out. Soon both boys were fast asleep.

The next day was sunny and not too cold for December. The boys spent the morning sledding on a steep hillside at Lincoln Street Park. No more was said about their discussion of the previous evening. Anne and Carolyn rode a small toboggan down a much gentler slope nearby, shrieking with glee as they descended. They finally coaxed the boys to climb aboard, but the load was unstable and the ride ended abruptly as the toboggan tipped and one by one they fell into the snow, laughing hysterically despite their tumbles.

After lunch the carriage pulled up to the portico and Jack prepared to leave. "Thank you very much, Mrs. Wellington. I had a wonderful time," said Jack with words he had carefully prepared in advance.

"We enjoyed your visit so much, you'll never know," she replied. "Please come again."

Just then Anne appeared with a small package wrapped in silver paper and tied with a bright red bow. "Happy New Year, Jack," she said brightly with a sparkle in her eye that he could not miss.

"Eh, happy New Year, too...I mean...to you, too," said Jack.

"This is for you," said Anne. She paused, then added, "from all of us," as she handed him the gift. Jack stared at the beautiful bundle in his hand.

"Go ahead," said Tom, "open it. But read the card first."

Jack opened the crisp, beige envelope and removed a folded card with a gilded border. Anne had written in beautiful, studied script: "To our dear friend, Jack, with warmest regards, The Wellingtons".

Jack smiled, not knowing what to expect next. He pulled the ribbons apart and carefully removed the paper to reveal a small, felt-covered box with a hinged lid. He lifted the lid and gazed in disbelief at his gift. It was a silver watch with a glistening glass crystal. Beneath the glass were two small, elegantly curved black hands. The hours were inscribed in Roman numerals on the watch face. Attached to the watch was a handsome leather band, a fob, that allowed the watch to hang from a belt loop as was the fashion for well-dressed men. Jack was speechless.

"Look at the back," said Anne cheerily. On the reverse was a delicately engraved inscription. Jack read it aloud: "Jack Bernard, Christmas, 1911".

This was a gift beyond Jack's wildest dreams and he stood, staring at it, genuinely at a loss for words. He had never owned a watch. Even his father had only the watch his pépère had given him when he turned sixteen.

Finally Jack spoke. "Thank you, thank you very much…this is a handsome watch. I'll take good care of it, I promise." Still struggling to make sense of the gift, Jack said his final thank-yous and goodbyes.

"Please come again," said Anne sweetly.

Tom accompanied Jack on the carriage ride back to Westfield. Their conversation was about sledding and skating and ice fishing. When they drew up before the Bernards' farmhouse, Jack climbed out, thanked Tom briefly, and said he'd see him in school in a few days. He ran toward his front door as the carriage pulled away.

# CHAPTER 4

# Clara

*January 1912*

Helen Cooke was the eldest of four children. Her father was an accountant whose clients included the owners and executives of many of the largest mills in South Hadley Falls and Holyoke; her mother taught kindergarten before marrying and raising a family. They lived in a small home on a quiet side street in South Hadley, just across the river from Holyoke.

The birth of the Cookes' last child was difficult and Helen's mother's health was severely compromised. By age twelve Helen was managing much of the work of raising her three younger siblings including cooking, cleaning, and doing laundry. She left school for several years, only returning when the youngest of the family was of school age. Helen had an aptitude for the domestic arts and, rather than begrudge her lot, she embraced the opportunity to be of assistance to her family. Eventually she returned to school, received her high school diploma, and attended Worcester Normal School for two years, hoping to follow in her mother's footsteps and pursue a career as a teacher. Her career plans were never realized, however.

Helen met Thomas Wellington and married him in 1895. The Wellington family's mill was already well established and successful, and shortly after their marriage the couple moved into the imposing home on Cabot Street in Holyoke where they would raise their children, Matthew, Thomas the Third, and Anne. Helen's life changed dramatically as she was swept up in the social circle of Holyoke's most prominent families, but she never forgot her roots. She was determined not to become too intoxicated by the world of wealth and status in which she found herself.

Perhaps it was Helen's experience caring for her younger siblings that made her a particularly good mother. She never allowed the luxury of the family's life to come between her and her children. She exuded warmth and genuinely enjoyed the company of her three little ones. Her husband was also very fond of his children, but with the constant pressures of a large and successful business on his shoulders he seldom found much time to devote to them.

Just managing the Wellington household staff was a full-time job. Fortunately Helen had Hanna O'Toole, her head housekeeper, who oversaw the smooth operation of the house. Hanna had held that position for most of the Wellingtons' married life and so was regarded as a permanent fixture by the rest of the staff, all of whom deferred to her more or less willingly. She supervised the entire female staff including maids, waitresses, and laundresses. Mildred, the cook, supposedly reported directly to Mrs. Wellington, but Hanna did not hesitate to exercise her seniority over her from time to time, much to Mildred's dismay. As to the male staff, there was Mr. Bromley, the chauffeur, and Patrick O'Toole, Hanna's husband, the head gardener. Bromley worked for Mr. Wellington; officially Patrick reported to Mrs. Wellington, but Hanna managed to keep very close tabs on his comings and goings, and felt free to redirect his efforts whenever necessary.

One of the effects of the rapid growth of Holyoke was the influx of women from around the region and from Canada seeking employment in the mills. Some found success and happiness in the city, but others did not fare as well. Substandard housing, poor nutrition, inadequate health services, and few recreational opportunities made their lives very difficult, particularly for those of limited means. Recognizing these problems, a group of Holyoke's most prominent women, including Helen Wellington, opened a social center for young women on Maple Street in Holyoke in 1898. The Holyoke Women's Home provided temporary accommodations for women, meals, assistance in finding permanent lodging and work, as well as a variety of health and recreational services.

This project was a considerable challenge for the center's founders, and raising the funds for such an ambitious undertaking was not the greatest of those challenges. Some members of their social circle questioned whether the Women's Home was a necessary or appropriate endeavor for the city's most prominent women. Some felt these social problems were being exaggerated in a way that reflected poorly on Holyoke; others had doubts that these young women truly needed or deserved help. The project quickly gained momentum, however, thanks in part to the generosity of the founding members and their spouses, but also in large measure to the sheer determination of the founders.

Although Anne grew up in a home with a large staff to tend to her every need, she nevertheless developed many of the skills her mother had learned at a young age. She was a talented knitter and quilter, and she took considerable pleasure in cooking and baking, skills that she honed with the able instruction of Mildred, the Wellingtons' cook of many years.

By the time Anne was a young teenager, she too had been drawn into the work of the Women's Home. Anne knew that Carolyn's mother was director of the Women's Home, but beyond that she knew little about Carolyn's family life. She was surprised to learn that Carolyn's last name was different from her mother's. Once when she inquired about the apparent contradiction to her own mother, her question was tactfully fended off.

The Holyoke Women's Home was an austere brick structure on Maple Street in downtown Holyoke. Wide stone steps led up to the main entrance, a pair of heavy wooden doors that opened into a dark, sparsely furnished foyer. To the left was a small office cluttered with papers, forms, and the like. To the right an arched doorway opened into a large front room that stretched the width of the building and served as a communal living room for the residents. It was furnished with many mismatched upholstered couches and chairs. Shelves on either side of the tall front windows held books, playing cards, and board games like checkers and Parcheesi. Two swinging doors at the rear of the living room led to a large dining room. A narrow stairway off the foyer led to the upper floors where the residents lived. Rooms were small, each with a single bed, bureau, and desk. A few larger rooms were available for women with children. Every floor had two bathrooms, one at each end of the long, central hallway. No accommodations were provided for men.

Meals were prepared in a cramped kitchen at the rear of the first floor. The forty or so women who lived at the Home received breakfast and supper seven days a week prepared by a kitchen staff of five; the residents were required to take turns assisting with meal preparation and dishwashing several times each week.

On Saturday evenings the Home offered a community supper to any Holyoke resident needing a hot meal. These were popular; in winter the turnout sometimes approached two hundred guests. On these occasions additional tables and chairs were set up in the dining room and a dozen or more volunteers were recruited to assist.

Among the enthusiastic volunteers on this January evening were Anne, Carolyn, Tom, and Jack, who had been invited to stay the night at the Wellingtons' home. The four young people had been assigned to set places in the dining room. The boys pushed two wheeled carts of dishes and utensils up and down the rows of tables. At each place Carolyn carefully positioned one dinner plate, a soup bowl, and a small bread dish. Anne would set out the utensils, two spoons and a knife to the right of the plate, a fork to the left.

She would then place a linen napkin precisely in the center of the plate and the four would move along to the next position. It took them nearly an hour, but they completed setting all two hundred places with the same attention to detail. The boys then pushed the carts back into the kitchen where a member of the staff enlisted their assistance in loading additional utensils onto the carts for dessert and coffee.

"Follow me," whispered Carolyn. "I'll show you the upstairs." She led Anne up a flight of steep, narrow stairs at the back of the kitchen that led to the second floor. Stepping through an open door they found themselves at the end of a long, unadorned corridor lit by a single electric bulb that hung from a wire just above their heads. They walked slowly down the hallway, passing a dozen closed doors. Near the end, one door was slightly ajar, a thin shaft of light slicing across the hallway.

A small voice came from the room: "Ellen, is that you?" The girls stood frozen, not knowing what to do or say. "Ellen?" the voice repeated. Through the narrow opening they could just see the face of a girl of perhaps sixteen seated on the edge of a bed. Carolyn pushed the door open and the two peered into the tiny room. The girl's skin was pale, almost white, her features soft, a look of quiet sadness poised in her eyes. Her hair was tied tightly in a bun at the back of her head, making her neck appear very thin and long. She wore a plain muslin jumper that hung from her shoulders nearly to the floor, barely revealing a pair of gray house slippers.

"Oh, I'm sorry," she spoke softly, "I thought you were Ellen. She was gonna bring me some tea."

"No, I'm Carolyn. I just saw Ellen in the kitchen." Then she paused, looking at the thin wisp of a girl seated before her. "But I'll go down and see if I can bring up your tea, okay?" With a glance she hinted to Anne to stay with the girl, then disappeared down the dark hallway.

"Hello, I'm Anne. What's your name?"

"Clara."

"Are you coming downstairs for supper, Clara?" asked Anne brightly. "They are serving New England boiled dinner tonight; I'm sure it will be swell - corned beef, cabbage, carrots, and Indian pudding for dessert."

"I don't think I'd better," replied Clara, her eyes on the floor in front of her. "I ain't feeling too good this evening."

"Oh, I'm so sorry. Perhaps we could bring your supper up to your room? Even if you can only eat a little, you'll need to have something."

Clara shook her head and smiled briefly: "My appetite's not too good right now. But thank you jus' the same." There was an awkward pause, then she continued: "I ain't seen you girls before, did you just come to Holyoke?"

"No, we're just helping with supper tonight," explained Anne. "Carolyn's mother is Mrs. Calavetti, the Director. And my mother is on the board."

Clara nodded slowly, her eyes lifting only briefly to examine the pretty face that was beaming at her. Just then Carolyn appeared with a tray holding a cup of tea and a small glass. "I thought you might like some milk in your tea."

"I better not, but thank you anyway," answered Clara. Carolyn placed the tray on the bureau, then handed the cup to the girl. The two watched as Clara slowly sipped the tea.

"Thank you…I can't climb the stairs too good these days."

"Where did you live before you came to Holyoke?" asked Anne.

"North Brookfield. I came to Holyoke last year to work in the silk mill. But I lost my job and my parents won't let me move back with them. So here I am. I guess I'm lucky, though, you know, to have a place to stay."

"Don't worry," offered Anne enthusiastically. "There are plenty of jobs for girls in the mills these days. You'll find something soon."

"I don't think so; I'm gonna be pretty busy." As Clara spoke those words, her eyes dropped and one hand came to rest gently on her mid-section. She turned to place her teacup on the tray atop the bureau. In the half-light Anne could discern the bulging belly of the thin girl. Clara looked up into Anne's eyes: "I'm gonna have a baby."

Anne paused just a moment, taking in this new information, then spoke gently: "Your husband, does he have a job?"

Clara shook her head once. "I'm all alone," she replied, staring blankly at the wall.

Just then Mrs. Calavetti's voice could be heard from the back stairway. "Carolyn, where are you? You and Anne are needed in the kitchen this minute. Get down here now."

"We'd better go," Carolyn said hurriedly.

"We'll come and visit you again, Clara," added Anne.

Anne, Carolyn, Tom, and Jack were very busy for the next two hours. Guests streamed into the dining room and were quickly seated. Women circulated among them serving the boiled dinner. The girls were responsible for distributing hot beverages and they were on their feet constantly, one with a pot of tea, the other with a carafe of coffee, filling and refilling cups for the diners. The boys carried pitchers of water and milk. After supper all four helped with serving dessert and more beverages. As the guests stood up to leave, they carried their dishes and utensils to the back of the room and deposited them on a long counter. The four young volunteers stacked the dishes and carried them back into the kitchen for washing.

It was nearly nine o'clock before all the dishes were done. Mrs. Wellington spoke to Anne, Tom, and Jack. "We'd better get you home. You must be exhausted."

Anne whispered to Carolyn. "We have to do something for Clara. I'll talk to you in school on Monday."

The normally ebullient Anne was uncharacteristically sober on the short drive home. Her mother concluded that it was due to exhaustion. She entered her daughter's room a few minutes later to wish her a good night's sleep, but she could see that something was troubling her.

"Mother," began Anne as she lay in bed, "do you know Clara?"

"Clara? At the Home? No, dear, I don't think so. Is she one of the employees?"

"She lives there, Mother, she's a resident. Carolyn and I met her just before supper in her room on the second floor."

"What were you two doing up there, dear?"

"Just looking around, that's all. But she let us into her room and we talked to her for a while."

"Oh, I see," said Mrs. Wellington, sensing that there was more behind her daughter's question.

"Mother, she's just a girl, only a year or two older than Carolyn and me...maybe sixteen."

"There are some very young girls coming to Holyoke these days to work in the mills. It's not that unusual."

"But Mother..."

"What, Anne, what is it?"

Anne's voice was very soft and her words came slowly, almost as if she was trying to make sense of what she was saying even as she was saying it. "But she's...going to be a mother...and she's all alone."

"Oh, I see. Oh, dear, the poor thing. Well, that's why Holyoke needs a place like the Women's Home, don't you see?"

"But why is she alone, Mother? Shouldn't her husband be taking care of her?"

"Well, honey, she may not have a husband. You know, some men take advantage of young girls and then make themselves scarce. It's a terrible thing to do, but, honey, it happens all the time."

"But she's just a girl...like Carolyn and me. How could this happen?"

"Anne, dear, there are many reasons that girls get in a family way when they didn't mean to or want to. We've talked about this, remember?"

"Yes, Mother." Anne hesitated, then continued. "But why should she have to go through this alone? If she doesn't have a husband, what about her parents? She told us her parents don't want her back home. Why would her parents say that?"

"People can be heartless sometimes, dear. Her parents may feel Clara has brought shame to their family."

"It doesn't seem fair, Mother, that she is all alone. It seems so cruel. Doesn't it?"

Helen kissed her daughter. "Yes, dear, it does...it certainly does seem cruel. Now get some sleep, you've earned it."

The thought of Clara apparently abandoned and alone preoccupied Anne throughout the following day. When she and Carolyn met on the schoolyard on Monday morning, it was the first thing they discussed. "Somebody should do something for Clara," Anne asserted. "It's not right, Carolyn, no girl should face what she's facing alone."

Carolyn had obviously been troubled by the encounter as well. "I talked to my mother about her. She says the Women's Home does a lot for girls like her. They give them a place to stay and they help them to find work. She says Clara is lucky to be there."

Tom and Jack were nearby, but the girls chose not to discuss the subject with them. That evening Anne told her brother about Clara and he eventually told Jack, but the two boys quickly forgot about it. Anne and Carolyn did not.

For the next few weeks Carolyn and Anne spent every free hour after school, evenings, and on weekends, working on their new project. They knitted booties, bonnets, and a sweater, and with their mothers' assistance, they made a small coverlet with needlepoint, all gifts for Clara and her new baby. They were planning a party in her honor at the Women's

Home. They visited Clara once about two weeks after their initial encounter just to say hello, but gave no hint of what was to come.

One morning in the Forestdale schoolyard, Anne and Carolyn cornered Jack and Tom. They wanted to enlist Jack's help, knowing that he had some skills with hammer and nails.

"Oh, Jack," Anne began. "Tommy tells me that you and your dad have a workshop where you make things. We wondered if you could make us a cradle, you know, for a baby?" She didn't feel it was necessary to explain what baby she had in mind and was just as happy not to have to go into details.

"I don't know. I think that would be more than I could handle. I'm not that good at that kind of carpentry. My dad, maybe..." replied Jack. Then he had a thought. "I've got an idea, though. Let me talk to my dad tonight."

That evening as Jack was feeding the animals in the barn, his father came in to get some firewood. "Dad, up in the loft there's an old cradle. Maybe it was Claire's...or Thérèse's?"

"And yours and Marie's, too," added his father, nodding.

"We won't be needing it any more, right?"

"I guess not, Jack," replied his father, a smile creeping across his face.

"Could I fix it up, Dad, and give it to someone who needs it?"

Charles thought about that for a moment, then smiled again. "Something you need to tell us about, Son?"

Jack didn't catch his father's little joke. He explained that it was for a needy young mother-to-be at the Women's Home whom Anne and Carolyn wanted to help.

"It's okay by me, Son. You'd need to do some work on it, though. Maybe repair the rockers and put on a fresh coat of paint. Best ask your mother first. It likely has some sentimental value to her, you know, eh?"

Jack's mother was seated by the fireplace darning socks when Jack proposed his plan for the cradle to her. The thought of giving up the cradle was a little painful to Evelyne, Jack could tell. But when she heard about Anne and Carolyn's project, she quickly consented.

"Thanks, Mom," said Jack, and he turned to head out to the barn to get started. But there was something else on Evelyne's mind.

"Jackie, dear. Before you rush off, come sit down for a moment...please."

Jack sat, but she could tell he was anxious to be off to the workshop. "Tell me more about this mother-to-be, Jackie. How old is she?"

"Eh, sixteen, I think."

"And she's living at the Women's Home? Where is her husband?"

"I don't know. I don't think she's married. Can I go, Mom?" Jack was getting a little uncomfortable at the direction of the inquiry.

"You're going to be fourteen in a few months, Jackie, aren't you?"

"Yes, Mom."

"And of course you know all a young man needs to know, don't you? I mean, about babies...and things?"

"Yes, Mom. I helped you and Dad deliver Angélique's calf, remember?"

"Yes, I do, that was quite something, wasn't it?" she recalled with a smile and a twinkle in her eye.

Jack grinned, a little embarrassed as he remembered nearly fainting when the calf's head first appeared. But he had recovered just in time to assist by pulling on the rope wrapped around the calf's front hooves.

"But, Jackie, there's more for a young man to know than just where babies come from. Important things, like what it means to be a husband...and a father. And when..."

"Mom, I know all that stuff, really, I do. Can I go now?"

"Okay, Jackie. But I want you to promise me that you'll talk about these things with your father...and soon, eh? He's not likely to bring it up, so I'm depending on you to ask. Will you promise me that you will do that?"

"Yes, Mom, I promise." At that moment Jack would have said almost anything to get away from his mother.

CHAPTER 5

# Two Worlds
*February 1912*

F ishing was Jack's favorite pastime. He liked baseball and
he enjoyed reading, but fishing was more to him than just
a sport or a hobby. There was something about fishing that
drew him in and held him in its thrall. Standing on the banks
of Hampton Ponds, rod in hand, gazing across the still waters,
knowing that at any moment his bobber could spring to life
and his reel spin wildly, that was thrilling. At the same time,
the dark, unseen depths and the mysteries they held provided
rich nourishment for his young imagination.

Fishing through ice had its own special allure. Maybe it
was the sharp, smooth line between the known world of light,
sound, and sentient beings above and the dark, unknowable
depths below. Or maybe it was the way thick ice boomed like
thunder rolling across a lake. Jack's father assured him this
was due to expansion and contraction and nothing to worry
about, but the sound nevertheless stirred something deep
inside him no matter how many times he heard it.

On a blustery Saturday morning in February, Jack and his
father were preparing for a day of ice fishing at Hampton
Ponds. They hauled all their gear on a battered old toboggan:
tip-ups, bait, tackle, ax, shovel, pails, ladle, strainer, toolbox,
blankets, kindling, and lunch. On the pond's edge they built a
fire. As they tended the fire they could see Tom making his
way across the ice from the eastern shore where the trolley
had deposited him. Tom had become a capable fisherman
under Jack's tutelage the previous fall, but he would quickly

realize that there was much more to learn about fishing through ice.

After greetings and sips of hot cocoa prepared by Jack's mother and kept warm in an insulated thermos bottle, the trio set out across the ice to cut holes and set their tip-ups. First the boys cleared snow from a small patch of ice. Then Charles, carefully and skillfully wielding the ax, sculpted a neat hole in the ice until greenish water gushed up from below. In each hole the boys placed a tip-up, a reel of heavy line with a baited hook secured to the end of a foot-long vertical strap of wood. Two horizontal wooden supports lay on the ice, attached at right angles to the vertical strap. One end of a long metal spring was secured to the top of the tip-up, the other end to a wire loop below that was connected to the submerged reel. A small square flag of red cloth hung from the loop end of the spring so that a sharp pull on the line released the spring, causing the red flag to pop up when a fish had been hooked.

The three anglers cut a dozen or so holes, some in the deep center of the pond, some in the shallows on the west side where, according to Charles, the biggest fish lurked among submerged tree trunks and rocks. When all their tip-ups were in place, they retreated to the warmth of the fire, standing with eyes trained across the ice. The instant a flag popped up, the two boys were off like jackrabbits across the ice. They would lift up the tip-up, then reel in the line and, with luck, their catch.

Tending their tip-ups kept Jack and Tom busy for the next few hours. Most of their catch was small perch or pickerel. Jack would quickly remove the hook and drop the fish back into the water. But they also landed several larger bass and one foot-long pickerel. After lunch the pace slackened considerably and the two boys began to get restless.

"Come with me, Tom," said Jack at one point when there had been a long lull. And the two headed off across the ice toward the shallow western side of the pond. Jack led his friend into a small cove, then off the ice and into the forest.

Heavy rain in the fall had left pools of water in hollows among the trees. Jack fell to his knees and began pushing aside the snow, exposing an oval patch of ice no more than a foot in diameter. The two boys lay on their stomachs in the snow, peering through the thin, dark ice filled with air bubbles of many sizes suspended at different depths. Seen from above, the bubbles looked like stars in the night sky, each reflecting bluish and greenish light to the eye.

"Wow, Jack, I can't believe it, it's like a whole universe down there!" exclaimed Tom.

"Keep watching," added Jack, "there's more." Suddenly, the boys could see movement; a dark, undefined object was writhing in the water below the ice. It disappeared briefly, then reappeared closer to the ice and clearly visible. It was a tadpole or "polliwog" as Jack called it, and it was swimming in gentle arcs in the icy water. It was feeding on small submerged green plants, apparently perfectly content just inches from the bitter cold above.

"It's alive," cried Tom, "how can it be alive in that cold water? It doesn't seem natural. Jack, how did you ever find this?"

The two boys lay on the snow for a long while, peering down through the greenish-black ice. They eventually discerned two more polliwogs and lots of tiny, transparent creatures that were swimming around the polliwogs.

"It's like a secret world down there, Jack," exclaimed Tom over and over, "and only you and I know about it! It's like magic! I wonder if the polliwogs can see us…or hear us."

About then they heard Jack's father calling them. They carefully replaced the snow over the patch of ice, emerged from the woods, and crossed the pond. Snow and sleet had been falling all day. Charles had not seen a trolley pass in several hours and he knew what that meant. The Westfield to Holyoke car line was prone to disruptions during winter storms. Without the trolley Tom would have no way of getting back to Holyoke that day.

"I'm afraid the trolley line is shut down because of the snow, Tom. Why don't you come home with us and spend the night?" offered Charles. "We'll call your parents from the neighbors and tell them you're safe and sound."

That was more than agreeable to Tom and the three began to pack up their gear. Jack, however, was feeling a little uneasy. This would be Tom's first visit to the Bernard home and he was wondering what his friend would think when he stepped into the rustic farmhouse on Southampton Road. On the other hand, he had so many things he wanted to show his friend and talk about.

The two boys trudged through the snow, each with one hand on the toboggan rope. Charles followed a few steps behind the toboggan carrying the day's catch on a string. When he was certain his father was out of earshot, Jack spoke quietly to Tom. "Our house is pretty small, but it is keen in some ways, too. My mother will be very happy to meet you." Then he added as an afterthought, "I'm not sure how my sisters will behave. They can be kind of silly sometimes."

Tom was greeted warmly by Jack's mother. It filled her with pride to see these two fine boys getting along so well…"even if they are from different sides of the tracks," she thought to herself.

"It's very nice of you to allow me to stay tonight," offered Tom immediately.

"Well, you are most welcome, Tom. I understand you've been very kind to our boy."

"He is my best friend!" exclaimed Tom emphatically, snapping to attention and beaming as he wrapped one arm around Jack.

Marie, who was ten, and Claire, just turned seven, hid in the downstairs bedroom, peeking and giggling at Tom through the partially opened door. Eventually Claire emerged and was introduced, and she finally coaxed the more reserved Marie to come out.

Charles and Tom went next door to the Bousquets' to use the telephone. When they returned, Jack's mother was busy preparing supper in the kitchen. She suggested that Jack show Tom his bedroom, then take him out to the barn and tend to the animals. The boys were upstairs for a few minutes as Jack was eager to show off his rock collection that he kept in his bottom bureau drawer, much to his mother's dismay. He showed Tom his most prized possession, a small slab of red sandstone that he and his father had found along the river in Holyoke. Embedded in the rock was the unmistakable footprint of a small, three-toed animal. It looked like it had been made by a bird, but his father insisted it was a dinosaur track.

"There are some great dinosaur tracks along the river up near Smiths Ferry," Jack explained. "We should take the trolley up there sometime and search for them."

When they came downstairs, Jack showed Tom the parlor, the girls' bedroom, and the kitchen. As they passed the alcove Tom paused and looked at the neatly arranged objects on the table and the wall behind it. "This is our little chapel," explained Jack, our *'petit sanctuaire,'* my mother calls it. It's where we say our prayers and the rosary. We're Catholic, you know."

Tom knew this, of course, and took everything in, including the rosary beads laid out so carefully. The boys went to the barn where Jack introduced Tom to the cow, Angélique, the chickens, and, most important of all, his father's workshop. Then they sat on bales of hay watching the animals feed. "The rosary beads," said Tom in a low voice. "Does each of you have your own?"

"Yes, we say the rosary three times a week. It's a Catholic ritual," explained Jack.

"I noticed there were six. One must be for Baby Thérèse, right?" asked Tom. Jack had told him about the death of his sister almost six years earlier.

"Yup, we each take turns saying the rosary for Thérèse. She's still with us, you know, in spirit," explained Jack matter-of-factly.

Tom nodded thoughtfully, his eyes cast downward. Just then Jack's mother called the boys to a supper of fresh pickerel fried in butter with carrots and turnips.

It was tight quarters for the two boys in Jack's bedroom. Jack lay on a spare mattress placed on the floor beside the bed where Tom would sleep. They talked for a long while about the usual topics of interest to thirteen-year-old boys, but eventually it seemed they had run out of things to say. "I'm sorry everything's so cramped," said Jack after a while.

"It's not cramped," answered Tom, "It's cozy...and nice. Sometimes...," he paused, "sometimes our house feels empty...especially since...without Matthew."

A long silence followed. Finally, Jack began hesitantly: "Tom, have you ever tried to talk to Matthew? I mean, tried to tell him about things, about you, your family, school? It sounds crazy, but it might help. Tell him you miss him. He might be able to hear you, you never know." Jack paused again, not certain how his suggestion was being received. Tom showed no reaction, but Jack went on: "Maybe it's like that polliwog under the ice... maybe it's another world right close by if you know where to look for it."

Tom was looking down, apparently considering Jack's words. Then he looked up and into his friend's eyes and nodded: "Maybe you're right, Jack, maybe you're right." Tom paused, then smiled. "Thanks, Jack. Well, goodnight."

"Goodnight, Tom." And they both slept soundly through the night.

The next morning the Holyoke trolleys were running again. After breakfast, the two boys walked along Southampton Road to the nearest trolley stop.

"Here's something for you," said Jack reaching into his pocket. And he produced a string of rosary beads and placed them in Tom's hand. "You don't have to be Catholic to use it, just hold it and say a little prayer each day for Matthew. It helps you remember…"

Tom looked intently at the crimson beads linked in a silver chain and nodded. "Thanks, I will." Just then the trolley approached, Tom boarded and waved vigorously to Jack as the car clattered off down the tracks toward Holyoke.

A few weeks later, on a Saturday afternoon, Anne, Carolyn and their mothers sat with Clara in the living room of the Women's Home. Several of the Home's residents were also present. By this time Clara's belly bulged very large beneath her smock. She appeared uncomfortable and frequently had to change position on an upholstered couch, but she managed a weak smile as each of her guests presented gifts for the baby. Eventually all the packages had been opened and the young expectant mother blushed and thanked everyone again.

"There's one more gift, Clara," interrupted Carolyn as she nodded toward the front hallway. On that cue Jack and Tom entered carrying the wooden cradle. It had been rejuvenated with several repairs and a fresh coat of white paint and bore a large pink bow. The group broke into applause. Clara was speechless and thanked everyone, including the boys, tears now running down her cheeks.

After the group had broken up, Anne and Carolyn carried Clara's gifts up to her room. One of the other residents helped Clara up the steep stairway to the second floor. The two girls were about to leave when Clara spoke softly: "Thank you, Anne, Carolyn…" She shook her head as if trying to convince herself that this was all for real. "You been so kind."

"We're very happy for you," responded Anne. "We promise to visit more often…and we can't wait to meet the baby. That will be so exciting!" Clara smiled as each girl kissed her on the cheek, then departed.

# CHAPTER 6

# The Fairer Sex
## *April 1912*

S adie Magwood was a lady with a mission. She worked for many years at Besse Mills Clothing Store on Suffolk Street in Holyoke, catering to the fashion needs of many of the city's best-dressed, most distinguished women. But her true calling, as she often told her friends, was the proper training of youth in the social graces. While some disapproved, Miss Magwood believed that dancing was both a proper and healthful pastime for young people. Furthermore, she believed, the development of these skills would help to divert them from the evils of alcohol and other vices.

Miss Magwood's Dance School opened in 1904, offering classes for children ages twelve to sixteen on Friday evenings. Classes were held in a meeting room on the third floor of the YMCA on Maple Street. Chairs were placed against the walls leaving a large floor area for instruction. At one end of the room stood a long folding table on which was placed an Edison phonograph. An assistant, Miss Winthrop, stood behind the table, prepared to start and stop the recordings on cue from Miss Magwood.

Every Friday evening at seven-fifteen, several dozen of Holyoke's young people climbed the long stairways to the third floor of the YMCA. The girls wore frilly dresses and shining patent leather shoes. The boys were dressed in white shirts, bow ties, and dark trousers. Chewing gum, Miss Magwood decreed, was to be placed in the receptacle just outside the door before entering the "dance hall," as she termed it. The young people filed in quietly and took seats around the room, boys to one side, girls to the other. An uncharacteristic hush would linger in the room as everyone anticipated the beginning of each class.

Miss Magwood's entrance was always dramatic. She dressed impeccably for the occasion in a long, flowing skirt and a white blouse with a high collar that buttoned up tightly under the chin. She swooped into the room like a star from the silent movies. She possessed an unmistakable air of refinement that earned her the admiration of some of the children, occasional but discreet snickers from others. She spoke to her students as though they were adults, using formal English and a certain sing-song verbal style.

"Laaaadies and gentlemen," she would begin. "I am very pleased to see you aaall looking so well this evening. We have much to accomplish tonight, so I suggest we begin." Occasionally she found it necessary to pause and address one of her male students: "Mr. Jones, would you be so kind as to deposit your chewing gum in the receptacle in the hall? Thank you soooo very much."

Miss Magwood's skills in teaching etiquette and dancing were considerable, but her special gift was putting her young students at ease. The girls were invited to line up on one side of the room, the boys on the other. She and Miss Winthrop would then lead the two lines around the room in time to a spritely march, demonstrating as they did so proper posture and grace of movement. Eventually, the lines would come together, the music would stop, and each young man would find himself standing opposite a young lady, thus avoiding the awkwardness of choosing partners. There was bowing and curtseying, and the exchange of "how-do-you-dos" and "so-lovely-to-meet-yous."

A few minutes of these preliminary niceties were followed by the first dance. Hands were placed on one's partner's shoulders, the dual purposes of which were to avoid embarrassment over hand-holding and to maintain a proper distance between partners. Adequate separation was especially important as looking down at one's feet was a necessary part of the first lesson in each step.

Miss Magwood often chose one of the taller, more mature girls as her partner to demonstrate a step. The two would move around easily in the middle of the floor, then the young couples would begin to make their own efforts. The first class was devoted entirely to the fox trot. Each week another step was added to their repertoire, waltz, reel, square dance, polka, two-step, and so on.

Periodically the boys and girls would again be parted, formed into two lines, and marched about until a new configuration was achieved and new pairings formed. Thus everyone had the opportunity to dance with a number of partners in the course of the evening.

Toward the end of each session Miss Magwood would address the group, offering them generous praise for their accomplishments. She would also take the opportunity to remind them of how much enjoyment could be had by young people without resorting to alcoholic beverages and associated, though unnamed, evils.

In the last twenty minutes or so the dancers were allowed to choose their partners. One dance would be "men's choice," the next "ladies' choice." This would go on for a half dozen musical selections. At the end Miss Magwood would thank one and all for their hard work and praise them lavishly.

That spring Tom Wellington, using his considerable persuasive skills, managed to talk a number of the grade eight boys at the Forestdale Grammar School into enrolling in Miss Magwood's class. Jack was at first reluctant, but Tom assured him that it would be fun. Jack knew that his dancing skills were rudimentary and his mother was especially concerned that her son should have some instruction in anticipation of high school dances in the years to come.

Jack and Tom were both uneasy as they walked through the front entrance of the YMCA and climbed the stairs for the first class. At the start the pair sat bemused about the whole affair, exchanging smirks at their teacher's flamboyant dress and dramatic style of speech. But Miss Magwood's organizational skills worked like a charm; soon the two boys were entirely preoccupied with the minutia of posture, bowing, deportment, etc., and quite forgot their initial embarrassment and giddiness.

Jack's movements on the dance floor were rather awkward compared to Tom who had had some previous dancing experience as well as more instruction in good graces at home. But by the end of the fox trot instruction each was feeling rather proud of himself.

The two boys were surprised by the announcement of the first "men's choice." For a minute they stood awkwardly by, watching others pair up and dance. Tom's eye was on Jane Parker who was seated directly across the dance floor from him looking expectant. "Okay, Jack," volunteered Tom, steeling himself. "I guess this is it." And Tom made his way through the dancers toward Jane, leaving Jack alone and very uncomfortable. Soon Tom and Jane were moving tentatively across the floor. At first, thought Jack, Tom looked a little unsure of himself. He seemed to step on his partner's toes once or twice and her face turned bright red. But then she laughed, Tom laughed, and from then on they seemed to be having a good time.

Soon it was time for the "ladies' choice." Both boys were quickly snatched up by blushing young ladies and found themselves sashaying easily with their partners. After that they began to feel more at ease and the last few dances were all a blur of new tunes, new dances, and new partners.

On the walk back to the Wellingtons' home, the two boys compared notes, each talking excitedly about whom he had danced with and whom he had yet to dance with. Then each counted up the total number of dance partners he had had that evening; leave it to thirteen-year-old boys to turn a dance class into a competition!

"Jane kept stepping on my toes," grumbled Tom. "Pauline is too tall; I can't dance with a girl who's taller than me," complained Jack. Under a dim streetlamp Tom turned to Jack. "Hey, Jack, I got 'the hairy eyeball' from Margaret Thompson." Then he demonstrated, bending slightly, looking up at Jack, then fluttering his eyelashes as fast as he could. The pair thought this was hilarious and from that moment on "the hairy eyeball" became a standard part of their vocabulary.

For the next two months Miss Magwood's class was the social event of every week. Several of the grade eight boys could be seen in the Forestdale schoolyard on Fridays talking excitedly about that evening's program and who would be dancing with whom. Not far away a group of grade eight girls who were in the class could also be seen whispering conspiratorially among themselves with occasional, furtive glances toward the boys.

The culminating event of the season for Miss Magwood's class was the Spring Gala. It was held in the same room, although crepe paper was arranged sparingly to add a bit of festiveness. Light refreshments were arranged on the table next to the phonograph including ginger ale, apple juice, and plates of cookies and wafers. The dancers' attire was more formal this evening, girls in long dresses adorned with corsages, boys in dark suits, some with long ties.

At Miss Magwood's cue the music began with a march. The boys stood up as one and were led around the room by Miss Winthrop. The girls did the same led by a serious middle-aged man whom Miss Magwood introduced as Captain Turner, a distinguished veteran of the war against Spain. Eventually the lines were drawn together and pairings were formed. The music changed to another familiar march and the "grand promenade" began. The couples marched around the perimeter of the room, the boy on the right, the young lady on his left arm. After several circuits Miss Magwood and Captain Turner stepped up to the front of the room at which point each couple passed by. This was the opportunity for the young man to introduce his partner to the two adults.

"Miss Magwood, Captain Turner, may I introduce to you Miss Eleanor Simmons? Miss Simmons, Miss Magwood and Captain Turner. The young man would bow, the young lady would curtsey, everyone would smile, and the couple would move along. This was repeated until all the young ladies had been introduced.

By now Tom Wellington was clearly a favorite of the girls in Miss Magwood's dance class. He was dressed smartly in a dark blue suit, a white linen shirt emblazoned with his monogram, "TPW", on the pocket, and a red tie. His attentions were constantly in demand during "ladies' choice." Whatever reluctance he may have shown earlier, he was now completely at ease with the girls, teasing them, talking smartly with them, and showing them a good time. Jack's social skills were much less refined at this point; he still often preferred to stand aside and watch rather than approach a girl and ask her to dance. He wished he had Tom's confidence and he watched his friend with admiration.

Finally Miss Magwood announced the last dance, a slow waltz. It was "men's choice" and Tom was already dancing with a young lady, rather closely Jack thought, in the furthest, darkest corner of the room. Jack was standing alone by the refreshment table when Pauline Foley strolled by smiling.

"Hello, Jack," said Pauline. Jack smiled and nodded. She turned and stood next to him, looking out on the dance floor. "Last dance. Too bad, eh?" said Pauline, turning and smiling at him.

Jack was feeling very uncomfortable and wasn't sure what to do. "Would you like to dance?" he blurted out at last. Pauline accepted and the two were soon waltzing with the others. It was a long selection. But when finally it ended Jack looked into Pauline's eyes and smiled, a little embarrassed: "Thanks, Pauline."

It was a Friday afternoon in May and Jack and Tom were again walking along High Street, gazing in shop windows and talking idly about school, sports, and fishing. "Let's go to Liggett's," proposed Jack enthusiastically, "We can split a root beer soda with vanilla ice cream on top."

"I have a better idea, Jack. There's a new place over on Dwight Street. It's bigger than Liggett's and they've got colas, malteds, college ice...and a jukebox." Jack wasn't sure he knew what a malted was, nor college ice, nor a jukebox. But the two friends made their way down High Street to Dwight, whistles wetted by thoughts of cold drinks and ice cream.

Jerry's Soda Shop occupied a storefront at the corner of Hampden and High Streets and it was abuzz with activity on this Friday afternoon. A dozen or more young patrons sat on stools at a long counter sipping tall, cold drinks through straws, prattling excitedly over the sound of Victrola music. Behind the counter, three dashing young men in white uniforms and jaunty white hats scooped ice cream, poured drinks, and smiled widely at their customers. On the counter behind them were stacks of glassware and utensils, several electric mixers, and a long row of stainless steel freezer cabinets containing ice creams of at least a dozen flavors. On the wall behind hung a long mirror covered with signs advertising beverages, ice cream flavors, and specialties of the house. At one end of the counter was a large, ornate cash register that rang brightly with each sale.

Jerry, the proprietor, stood proudly behind the counter operating shiny nozzles of seltzer, scooping balls of ice cream, and applying mounds of whipped cream, all the while watching every movement of his customers and employees. The seltzer nozzle gave forth a harsh, fizzing sound every time he flipped the lever; two electric mixers ran almost constantly blending ice cream and milk concoctions. "Root beer soda for three...college ice with whipped cream for eleven...chocolate malted for five-b," barked Jerry in a loud staccato voice.

Jack nodded towards two vacant stools at the counter and started walking in that direction. "No, Jack, over here," insisted Tom. Opposite the counter stood a dozen small, round tables with glass tops, and matching chairs. Tom led Jack past several vacant tables to one near the rear of the shop.

"Why way back here?" asked Jack just as a tall, dark-haired waitress approached them.

"Hello, boys, what can I get you?"

"Hi, Julie, I'm Tom, Tom Wellington."

"Who?" she responded.

"Tom Wellington. I'm a friend of Bill Peterson."

"Oh, nice to meet you, Tom."

"You can call me Tommy. This is my friend, Jack Bernard. Jack, this is Julie."

She smiled briefly at Jack. "Very nice to meet you boys," she replied, allowing a little bit of a smile to break across her face. At that moment Jerry caught Julie's eye from across the room and her demeanor quickly changed. "What can I get you?"

"Jack would like a root beer soda with a scoop of vanilla ice cream on top. And I'll have a cherry phosphate, please."

"I'll see what I can do!" answered Julie with a wink. She turned and walked away. Tom gazed after her, grinning.

"Now I get it," Jack teased, "she's the reason you wanted to come here."

"Jack, you don't really think I'd bring you all the way down here just to see some girl? This place is neat. And the sodas are really swell. You'll see."

"…and what the heck is a cherry horseplate…or whatever you said?"

"Phosphate, Jack, phosphate. You'll see. It's the latest thing."

"How d'you know Julie?" Jack queried his friend. "I don't remember seeing her at Forestdale."

"Well, I don't exactly know her. She's a freshman at Holyoke High," explained Tom. "She's a friend of Bill

Peterson's sister, that's all. I just thought I'd say 'Hi.'" Just then their drinks arrived. Tom thanked Julie repeatedly and tried to get her to talk to him some more, but Jerry was watching. She tore a slip off her pad, slapped it down on the table, and abruptly spun away to wait on another table.

The boys sat sipping their drinks, gazing around at all the activity in the shop. It was mostly patronized by high school students and was obviously a popular spot. Near the windows a group stood around a large, chrome-faced cabinet with a Victrola mounted on top of it. That, Tom explained, was a juke box.

Jack quickly downed his root beer soda, then sat taking in the bustle of activity in the shop. Tom spent most of his time trying to catch Julie's eye. Finally, Jack spoke up. "You gonna drink your cherry whats-it, Tom, or just stare at that girl?"

"Okay, Jack, here's the story. Bill and his sister want me to invite Julie to a dance at the country club next Friday…I'm just not sure how to ask her."

"Well, don't look at me, Tom. I don't even know why you'd want to ask her…or any girl for that matter… to a dance."

"I have to, Jack. Bill will call me a chicken if I don't."

"I don't think this is a good time to be asking her, Tommy. She's pretty busy. Anyway, we gotta go. Unless you're gonna have another one of those cherry horsehairs." Tommy finished his drink, thinking over the situation. Suddenly he pulled a dollar bill out of his pocket and handed it to Jack.

"Take this up to the counter and pay the man, Jack."

"What? Why me?" Jack protested.

"Just do it, okay? For a friend?"

Jack stepped up to the counter and extended one hand with the dollar bill and the slip. Jerry took them and turned to the cash register to ring up the sale and make the change. In the few seconds that his back was turned, Jack caught a glimpse of Tom talking to Julie among the patrons near the jukebox. She was smiling at Tom and nodding.

Back on the sidewalk, the two friends walked along High Street together. "So, did you ask her?" Jack inquired.

"Easy as pie, Jack, easy as pie...Tommy's got a date!" replied Tom, an impish grin spreading across his face.

As the two boys waited for the trolley that would take Jack back to Westfield, he was still confused about what had happened in the soda shop. "I don't get it, Tommy. Why do you want to go to some dance with that girl? You hardly know her and she doesn't seem all that interested."

Tom shook his head and made a mock expression of brotherly concern. "Jack, Jack, Jack...you're gonna be fourteen this summer, am I right? And you're gonna be a freshman in high school next fall? Do I have that right?"

"Yeh, yeh," replied Jack, getting annoyed with his friend. "So what?"

"Jack, you are my best friend in the world. And only a best friend could tell you what I am about to tell you...Jack, it's time you were introduced to the fairer sex. There's so much you need to know, my boy, and, to be perfectly frank, time is running short!"

"I'm thirteen, Tommy," answered Jack with a note of irritation in his voice. "I don't think I have to worry about getting old too soon, if that's what you mean."

"You know, Jack, that's just what I used to think: 'some day when I'm older' – 'all things come to those who wait.' Well, forget it, Jack. You've got to wake up and take a stand, assert yourself, learn to be a man!"

"And I suppose you're the one who's gonna teach me, right?" replied Jack. "Now that you're an expert you're gonna tell me all about girls and...and be a model for me to follow. Wow, Tommy, I feel like the luckiest guy in the world...I don't know how to thank you!" exclaimed Jack in a sarcastic tone.

"No need, Jack, no need. It's just what a friend does for a friend...nothing more." Just then the Westfield car approached.

"I'll see you in school on Monday, Tommy; maybe we can start those lessons. Like you said, time's running short!" Jack hopped up the trolley steps, presented his pupil's pass to the motorman, then swung into a seat by the window facing Tom. The two friends smiled at one another through the glass and waved as the trolley pulled away.

Jack was shaking his head. "That Tom," he thought, chuckling to himself, "he's a crackerjack...a real crackerjack." But as the trolley left the city neighborhoods and entered the pastures and forests beyond, Jack gazed out the window, one thought running through his mind: "Maybe, just maybe, Tommy is right!"

CHAPTER 7

# Complications
*May 1912*

One afternoon in late May, Anne was in her room doing her homework when she heard a light tap on the door. "Annie, may I come in?" Her mother's face appeared around the partly open door. "I hope I'm not disturbing you, dear."

"No, just doing my algebra."

"Honey, I've just been at the Women's Home...for a Board Meeting...and...I have to tell you something."

"What is it, Mother? Tell me, please."

"It's about Clara."

"Oh, yes, Mother. How is she?" Then a look of excitement crossed her face. "Did she have her baby?"

Her mother's face brightened. "Yes, dear, she did. It's a little girl. The baby's doing fine."

"Oh, that's wonderful, Mother. How is Clara?" Her mother's smile vanished. "She, well, there were complications."

A look of confusion spread across Anne's face like a shadow. "Complications? What kinds of complications, Mother?"

Helen took her daughter's hand and sat beside her. "I'm afraid she passed, honey." Anne sat staring at her mother in disbelief. She took several deep breaths, shook her head, then looked into her mother's eyes.

"No, it can't be...she was just sixteen, Mother...it can't be."

Helen Wellington drew her daughter to her, held her, and cried with her.

# CHAPTER 8

# Changes
*Summer 1912*

Jack had been invited to stay with the Wellingtons for a month that summer. His parents agreed, but reminded him that he was almost fourteen and times were hard, so they would need him to work in Mr. Dunham's tobacco fields in August to help out the family. That seemed like a fair deal to Jack, and he departed for Holyoke on the first day after school ended in mid-June.

Looking back, that summer seemed like the most exciting, carefree time in Jack's young life. He and Tom spent every day together, doing whatever they wanted. They fished at Hampton Ponds, they swam in the river, they even went to watch the Holyoke Papermakers play baseball at the field on Beech Street.

Mountain Park on the north side of Holyoke was a popular summer destination for city residents young and old. You could ride the trolley from Holyoke to the park in just fifteen minutes. Among the attractions were rides, games, caged animals, playing fields, and a picnic grove. And there was a breathtaking cable car ride to the summit of Mount Tom overlooking the city.

One Saturday at the end of June, Mrs. Wellington offered to take Tom, Jack, Anne, and Carolyn on an outing to Mountain Park. They planned to take the trolley on Appleton Street. At the last minute Tom's father appeared at the portico and announced that he would be joining them.

It was a memorable day for Jack in several ways. First, Mr. Wellington proudly showed off his new Reo Touring Car to the boys and explained all of the advanced features of this latest model. They gaped in awe at the contoured, bright green body, the dazzling chrome grille and headlamps, and wide leather seats. This was also the first time that Jack got to know Tom's father, and he seemed a nice enough man and genuinely fond of his family. But above all, he was proud of his car! Everyone climbed in with blankets, picnic baskets, baseball bats and balls, and sped off.

At the park they laid out their blankets on the grass and Mr. and Mrs. Wellington sat in the sun while the young folks explored. The four quickly returned, pleading to ride the cable car to the Summit House. Permission was granted, but only on condition that they first sit and have lunch with the grownups. The excitement in the eyes of the youngsters was evident as they bolted their sandwiches, and finally Mr. Wellington said "All right, children, go for your ride. But be careful. Boys, don't stand too close to the edge up on the summit, do you hear me, and watch out for the girls."

The cable car, named the *Elizur Holyoke* in honor of one of the city's founders, was partially enclosed with two rows of seats on either side of a center aisle. Ignoring the girls, Jack and Tom climbed aboard and ran to the back of the car, taking the last seat at the rear on the left side so that they could look down on the park and the city as they ascended. Anne and Carolyn sat in the seat in front of the boys. As they waited for the ride to begin, Anne turned and smiled wide-eyed at Jack: "Isn't this exciting, Jack?"

"Uh-huh," was the only response Jack could muster, but while his words were few, his thoughts were many. Anne was looking intently into his eyes and he felt like he was seeing her for the first time, noticing things about her that he had not previously. Her auburn hair glistened in the mid-day sun, and with her green eyes and smooth, rosy complexion, hers was a face that was hard to ignore. She wore a pretty embroidered smock that hung loosely over her shoulders. Most of all it was her confidence, a Wellington trait, that impressed Jack, and set her apart in his mind from any other girl he knew. But Jack had one question on his mind, one single burning question: Why is Anne paying so much attention to me?

Meanwhile Carolyn was trying to strike up a conversation with Tom, but she was having difficulty. Tom tried to help her out, but his efforts were equally awkward. Jack was surprised to see his best friend, the one who was usually so cool and confident, apparently at a loss for words. Suddenly both boys were feeling trapped and uncomfortable. They wanted the ride to get going as soon as possible and, thankfully, it did. Everyone's attention was diverted to the stunning views as the cable car ascended to the area's highest peak.

At the top the four clambered quickly from the car. Tom and Jack immediately sprinted to the west-facing cliffs, precisely the place that Tom's father had warned them to stay away from. But they knew the girls would not follow and that was all that mattered. They looked out at the scenery, the city and broad river stretching to the south, the high rolling foothills of the Berkshires rising to the west. Jack pointed out the dim outline of Mount Greylock, the highest mountain in Massachusetts, far to the northwest, and Mount Monadnock in southern New Hampshire to the northeast. Tom recounted, as if he had been there in person, the day in 1899 when the President of the United States, William McKinley, and the First Lady rode the cable car to the Summit House and stood on this very spot, declaring it the most beautiful mountain scenery in the world.

In time the four climbed back into one of the cars and began their descent.

It was mid-July now and just a few days remained before Jack would return to his family in Westfield. He was surprised that he was not homesick in the least, but nevertheless he looked forward to seeing his family again. His return was timed so that he would be at home for his fourteenth birthday on July fourteenth.

Jack went to Mass on Sunday morning at Notre Dame, a large Roman Catholic church just a few blocks from the Wellington home, as he had every Sunday during his visit. The Wellingtons sometimes attended services at St. John's Episcopal Church on Maple Street, but this Sunday they stayed at home and Jack suspected something was up.

When he returned from church, the dining room had been decorated with streamers and a special meal was offered in his honor. It featured all his favorite foods, from roast beef and mashed potatoes to chocolate cake and ice cream. They played games like pin-the-tail-on-the-donkey and Jack was embarrassed by all the to-do on his behalf. There were several birthday presents for him including a baseball mitt and a tackle box for his fishing gear.

It was late afternoon before the party ended and Tom announced that there was yet one more surprise for Jack. The carnival was opening at the fairgrounds and wouldn't he like to go? Jack thought that sounded like a great idea, and he was ready to set out with Tom immediately when Tom added, somewhat as an afterthought, "But we'll have to wait until the girls are ready."

"The girls are going? Oh, yeh, sure, okay," said Jack, trying hard to hide some anxiety. An outing with just Tom and him, that could only be fun. But the addition of Anne and Carolyn changed everything. Soon the four were walking down Cabot Street, talking and laughing, the sound of the calliope floating up the hill from the fairgrounds below.

The carnival was a hurly-burly exposition of a side of life with which Jack was only vaguely acquainted. Muscular men, scantily clad ladies, racing pigs, a dance hall, and all manner of rides and events awaited them. Tom and Jack led the way, wandering aimlessly along the midway, not sure where to begin the evening's entertainment. They settled on a few games of skill like the baseball toss and Titan's Hammer. The girls complied politely, seeming to want the boys to have their way, at least for now. The boys gave wide berth to the Tunnel of Love, not wanting even the thought of that forbidden realm to enter the girls' heads.

Cotton candy and ice cream followed, and then there was the Freak Show. Tom and Jack laughed hysterically at the Bearded Lady and the man with two heads. They found the creature billed as "half-man, half-horse" at once too appalling to contemplate, yet too fascinating to ignore.

After watching the pig races in a long wooden building designed just for that curious event, the four emerged again onto the midway. Before them stood the Ferris wheel festooned with colored electric lights that twinkled brightly against the darkening sky. The calliope was playing loudly nearby.

Anne nudged Tom discreetly and he blurted out "Hey, let's ride the Ferris wheel...my treat!" The girls acted surprised and quickly consented. "Come on, Jack," said Tom, "let's get tickets." The two of them stood in line together, the girls several paces behind. Tom paid for the four tickets, handed them around, then he and Jack stepped up in line as the girls followed. There was a wait of a minute or so and Tom babbled idly about the workings of a Ferris wheel in an effort to distract Jack from what was about to happen.

Finally, Tom and Jack were at the head of the line, the ticket collector opened the door to the next chair, and Tom prodded Jack to go ahead. Jack clambered in, sat down, and turned. To his surprise, Anne was settled comfortably next to him.

"Where's Tom?" sputtered Jack, but his question was quickly answered when he looked back to see his friend taking Carolyn by the hand and politely and confidently assisting her into the next chair.

For a moment Jack felt trapped and a little bit aggrieved that the others had played a trick on him. Just then Anne spoke: "Don't worry about them," she whispered, leaning in close to Jack, smiling, and looking intently into his eyes. "They can take care of themselves." As the chair rose slowly skyward, Jack felt he was being lifted into a new and mysterious world. Then Anne's hand clasped his hand, her soft fingers interlocking with his, and in that moment Jack knew beyond a doubt that he was being catapulted into the unknown.

The Ferris wheel turned very slowly. Each time their chair approached the top of its arc, Anne commented on the city lights below them, the color of the night sky where the sun had just set, or the view of the Summit House on Mount Tom in the distance. Jack would look up, trying his best to be polite, but then his eyes would drop as if he had suddenly become very interested in his shoes.

Finally, Anne squeezed his hand: "Isn't the view pretty?"

Jack hesitated, then looked up, smiled shyly, and spoke very softly: "Yes, yes, it is…the prettiest I've seen." He was looking directly into Anne's eyes as he said those words, making it crystal clear what he was really talking about. Anne's expression softened, she smiled back at Jack, and gently laid her head against his shoulder. Suddenly Jack felt very proud of himself, and very happy.

The ride was soon over and Anne and Jack clambered out of the chair. Carolyn and Tom joined them and the foursome walked together up Cabot Street, joking and laughing, much as they had on the way down a few hours earlier. Many words were spoken, but no one was saying what they all knew in their hearts: that suddenly, that evening, everything had changed.

The next morning Jack headed home to Westfield on the trolley. His family was very excited at his return; preparations were already underway for a birthday party in the backyard that evening that included fresh watermelon from the garden, devil's food cake baked by Jack's mother with fourteen candles, homemade vanilla ice cream, and hand-made gifts from his sisters.

Later in the day Jack spoke to his mother about returning the favor and inviting Tom to come to Westfield for a few days before the end of the summer. "He could help us do some weeding and harvesting, and I want to show him around town," explained Jack. His parents quickly consented and a letter was sent to Tom with the invitation.

It was the second week of August, one of the hottest days of the summer, when Jack walked up Southampton Road to the trolley line to meet Tom. Jack stared impatiently down the track for several minutes, picking up pebbles and tossing them into the tall grass along the track. Just then he heard the clatter of the approaching trolley and watched it come into view. There was Tom, waving from the open-sided "breezer" car.

The two boys walked slowly along the dusty road toward the Bernards' house carrying Tom's bags, scuffing the gravel and talking non-stop. Jack brought Tom up to date on his work in the family garden, fishing excursions at Hampton Ponds, and his sisters' antics. Tom had been to the Connecticut shore with his family for a week and had stories to tell about swimming in the ocean, something Jack had never done. "By the way, I have a letter from Anne for you," added Tom, his voice modulating teasingly.

The two decided they should do the weeding that needed to be done in the garden before the day got too hot. Side-by-side they worked along the rows of tomatoes, potatoes, and lettuce, tossing weeds into a wooden bushel basket, all the while talking excitedly about their plans for the next two days. Marie and Claire sat in the shady backyard working on their needlepoint. Jack's mother was preparing a lunch for the children.

By noon the heat was oppressive and the four ate their lunch on a table in the yard, then Jack and Tom lay in the shade. They agreed that they should go for a swim at Jack's favorite spot on the Westfield River about a mile west of the house.

The walk to the swimming hole was hot and dusty, following a winding path between the north bank of the river and corn and tobacco fields. The swimming hole was at a sharp bend in the river. On the outside of the bend the rushing waters had cut into the high river bank and scooped out a deep pool, while on the inside a narrow, sandy beach had formed. A storm several winters earlier had undercut the bank and caused a tall cottonwood tree to slump out over the river. A thick rope had been suspended from the tree ending in a knot a few inches above the water. Despite the warm, moist summer air, a breeze and the deep shade cast by the tall trees above the river made the swimming hole cool and inviting.

"Watch this," said Jack as he kicked off his shoes and pulled his shirt over his head. Striding into the shallow water, he reached for the hanging rope, then carried it ashore. Up the steep river bank he climbed, slipping often in the soft sand. Finally he reached the top of the bank, fully ten feet above the water. He stood facing the river, rope in one hand, while Tom watched uneasily from below.

"You sure you want to do that, Jack?" asked Tom a little nervously.

"I've done it a thousand times," was Jack's self-assured reply. But he paused for several seconds, seeming to gather his courage. Suddenly he leaped up and out from the bank, grasping the rope as high as he could. He swung downward in a steep curve, his feet just touching the water's surface, then was carried upward over the middle of the river. Just as his forward momentum ceased, Jack let out an exhilarated whoop and let go of the rope. His long legs came together, his head and shoulders turned downward, and in a graceful curve he descended, entering the deepest part of the river with hardly a splash. He disappeared from view for a moment but soon emerged from the shallow waters right in front of Tom, smiling up at his friend.

"How did you do that, Jack? That was amazing," repeated Tom over and over, shaking his head in disbelief.

"Give it a try!" urged Jack, smiling up at his friend.

"I don't know, Jack, I don't think so."

"Go ahead, take it a little at a time. Just go up the bank about half way and take a swing. It's fun," said Jack, thrusting the knotted end of the rope toward Tom. Tom grabbed the rope and, with a half-smile, began to climb the sandy bank. Barely a third of the way up the bank, he turned and faced the river.

"You can do it, Tom, it's easy," assured Jack. "Just grab the rope as high as you can." Tom stood, rope in hand, shifting his weight from one foot to the other, looking out across the water, trying to marshal the necessary courage for his first swing.

After several minutes Jack climbed out of the water, scrambled up the bank, and taking the rope from Tom, again ascended to the top of the bank. This time he leapt, not nearly as high as before, but bending his knees, drew his feet up and rested them firmly on the knot as he was carried through the rope's arc. At the upward end of his swing, Jack pushed off from the knot and did an amazing leaping dive back toward the shore, again entering the water with barely a splash.

"How'd you ever learn to do that, Jack, it's perfect. I could never..."

"Sure you can, it just takes practice. Some days I come out here after work and swing on the rope for hours. Go ahead, just give it a try." Once again Jack handed the rope to Tom with a smile. Again Tom climbed less than half way up the steep embankment and turned toward the water. He held the rope, looking downward. The late day sun was golden in the sky but silver as it shone off the sparkling water. He held the rope in front of him, paused, then jumped and grasped it as he began to descend. But his grasp was not high enough and his legs hung low, dragging in the water and bringing his ride to a premature halt.

"That was good, Tom, you're getting' it," said Jack with genuine excitement. "You just have to jump a little higher. Try it again."

Without hesitating Tom climbed the sandy bank again, pausing only briefly, and in one smooth motion leapt well up on the rope, pulled his legs in beneath him, and rode the swing high out over the river where he released the rope and fell with a loud splash into the quiet water. He came up smiling and threw his hands over his head in celebration to Jack's cheers. "You did it, Tommy, you did it!"

The two friends spent the next hour riding the rope swing, trying every imaginable way to swing - standing, crouching, hanging upside down, spinning to the right, spinning to the left, diving with a flip, and back-diving. Each tried to outdo the other while still cheering his friend's successes and commiserating with his failures.

A distant rumble brought the rope swinging to an abrupt end. A thunderstorm was not unusual in late afternoon on a hot summer day like this one, and the boys quickly gathered up their towels and clothes and ran, barefoot and still in their swimsuits, back along the dusty road toward home. They were within sight of the barn when rain and hail began to pelt on them and they were dashing across the lawn and in the kitchen door as the first loud clap of thunder announced the arrival of the storm.

Safe inside, the two friends regaled the entire Bernard family with detailed descriptions of their exploits on the rope swing. "I never thought I could do that," admitted Tom to Evelyne when Jack had gone upstairs to change into dry clothes. "But Jack kept cheering me on…it was like he believed in me when even I didn't. That's what makes him such a great friend, Mrs. Bernard, do you know what I mean?"

Evelyne nodded and smiled.

The next morning Tom walked with Jack to the trolley stop and they waited together for the next car to Holyoke. "I wonder what it will be like in grade nine in September," said Jack. "Do you think we'll like it?"

Tom hesitated. "Jack, there's something I've been meaning to tell you…I won't be going to Holyoke High School in September. My parents are sending me to boarding school."

"What? Why? Where? How come?" stammered Jack.

"It's the school my father went to when he was a boy and he wants me to go there. It's like a family tradition," explained Tom.

"So that's it, you're going away? We're not gonna be friends anymore?" asked Jack, obviously stung by what he perceived to be a personal affront.

"No, not at all, Jack. It's the Dorchester School in Greenfield. It's only twenty miles away. I'll come home on weekends and during vacations and next summer, and you can come to Greenfield to see me. And we can write letters. It'll be okay, Jack, it'll be okay." Just then the trolley rolled up and shuddered to a stop.

Tom climbed on, paid the fare, and sat down in the breezer car just a few feet from where Jack was standing. Then Jack said, without expression, "Have fun at your new school." The car pulled out and Tom waved to his friend, but Jack had turned and started walking away without looking back.

CHAPTER 9

# Childhood's End
## *September 1912*

School began in September and Jack settled in easily at
Holyoke High School. He was reunited with many of his
friends from Forestdale Grammar School and made a number
of new friends from the other city elementary schools. He
found grade nine work challenging, especially algebra, and he
had to work hard.

Tom had written Jack a weekly letter, obviously hoping to
patch up their fractured friendship. Jack hadn't replied, and he
wasn't sure how he felt about seeing Tom again during a long
weekend in October when he would be home from boarding
school.

The first day of October, a Friday, proved to be a dark day
in the Bernard household. At noon Charles appeared in the
kitchen as Evelyne was taking a loaf of bread out of the oven.
The downcast expression on his face was all she had to see
and she knew the truth. Charles had been laid off from the
mill; he and dozens of other workers, without any warning,
were told to go home. No explanation was offered.

Jack's parents sat together in the parlor trying to
contemplate what this would mean for them. Jobs were very
scarce, and while Charles Bernard had many skills, it was
doubtful he'd be able to find enough work.

When Jack got home from school, his parents called him
into the parlor. He could tell from the expressions on their
faces that something very bad had happened. They told him
the truth. And although they reassured Jack that his father
would find other work soon, Jack suspected almost from the

start that it was a little white lie. When his sisters were told, Jack helped his parents to convince them that this was not something they should worry about.

For the next week Charles visited every mill and shop in Westfield looking for work. He took the trolley to West Springfield and downtown Springfield one day, then to Holyoke and Chicopee another day. It seemed no one was interested in his considerable skills and no one was hiring.

In his second week of searching for a job, Charles talked to Mr. Dunham, the tobacco farmer that Jack had worked for in August. They needed some workers now, especially since school had started. Charles reluctantly took the job. It didn't pay much, would only be for a few weeks at most, and it would be hard labor in the fields for a man of Charles' age, but at least it was work.

Jack was uneasy about the news of his father's new job. He was well acquainted with the rigors of that work and he feared that his father's back might not be up to it. But he kept his thoughts to himself.

The weekend of Tom's holiday soon arrived and Jack was leaving school at three-thirty on Friday, headed to the trolley stop. Standing before him on the sidewalk was Tom Wellington, smiling broadly. "Hi, Jack. Got time for an old friend?"

Jack was not expecting this sudden appearance by Tom and he was not prepared with a reply. At first his expression was sour, but Tom's good spirits were infectious and Jack allowed the slightest smile to creep across his face.

"You came back," said Jack. The two walked slowly up the street toward the trolley stop. Tom regaled Jack with stories of preparatory school, midnight raids on the girls' dormitory, and gay parties on Saturday nights.

"But it's not the same without my best friend," Tom said with feeling. "It's so good to see you, Jack. Tell me everything about your new class, your teacher, and what's this I hear about you going to the Harvest Dance at the country club with Anne?"

"Oh, that, I don't think I can go after all, I don't have any decent clothes," Jack explained.

"Come to my house, Jack, and I'll lend you one of my suits," offered Tom. "They're just hanging in the closet and they need the exercise!" Jack smiled. Tom was always generous, and always tactful, those were two good things about him.

"Okay, that's good. But I can't come today; I've got to get home. How about if I come by tomorrow afternoon? I have to be in Holyoke in the morning and I could be at your house by noon."

"Great, but what are you coming to Holyoke for on a Saturday morning?" asked Tom.

Jack hadn't intended to get into the matter now, but it seemed he had no choice. "My father is out of work, maybe you heard. So I'm quitting school and going to work. I have to do it, for my parents, I have to," said Jack, trying to convince himself as well as Tom.

Tom was shocked by this news and unprepared for how to react. But the old Wellington confidence came through: "You'll be back in school soon, I bet. There is still a lot to learn, you know," he exclaimed with a grin. "Come to my house at noon, tomorrow. Please come and we'll talk about it." The date was agreed to and Jack was off on the trolley to Westfield. But his heart was very heavy and he wasn't looking forward to the weekend.

"Mom, Dad, I have something to tell you," said Jack that evening after supper. "Please don't be cross with me, but I've made up my mind. I'm going into Holyoke tomorrow morning to look for a mill job. I've told Mr. Lataille that I'll be quitting school to work...for a while...until...well, for a while."

Charles and Evelyne were stunned and speechless. On the one hand they were devastated at the thought of their oldest child leaving school. Seeing their children through school was a matter of great pride to them. Neither had been able to complete school with their classmates in Québec and they wanted to do better by their own children. But at the same time their hearts swelled with pride that their boy was prepared to make such a sacrifice for his family. And although they talked long and seriously with him about the decision, in the end they consented. Jack's mother hugged his thin frame, tears welling in her eyes. His father shook his hand, told him how much he appreciated this, but abruptly turned and walked away. Jack could tell that he was feeling considerable pain at that moment over this decision.

Early Saturday morning Jack was walking the streets of Holyoke. The hiring offices at the mills were often open on Saturdays to attract young people like Jack. They could pay them much less than adults and work them even harder. Some critics accused the mill owners of intentionally laying off older workers to make room for younger men and women in order to save money.

Several of the paper mills had openings and would have hired Jack right away, but the best wage offered was twenty-five cents an hour, barely worth the trip from Westfield. The round trip trolley fare would cost him nearly an hour's pay now that he would no longer be eligible for a pupil's pass. And some of the jobs in the paper mills were dangerous as well.

By noon a very discouraged Jack Bernard was walking up Cabot Street to the Wellingtons' home, his head held low. Tom met him in the entry hall and quickly understood that Jack's job search had not gone well.

"I don't know, Tom, my parents are depending on me now and I can't seem to find anything that will pay enough. What am I gonna do?" he asked. Tom thought for a moment, choosing his words carefully: "Jack, they're fools if they would turn down a hard worker like you. They don't deserve to have you. But I've got an idea. Why don't we talk to my father? He can find something for you at the mill, I know he can."

Jack had thought of applying at Wellington Textiles and had decided against the idea. "I don't want to get a job that way, Tom. I can do this on my own. And my dad, he'd never allow it. He's still mad about losing his job, you know," explained Jack.

"Weeell," began Tom, his eyes rolling, "maybe your dad doesn't <u>need</u> to know. I bet Father can find you a job in the sorting room or someplace where no one knows your dad." Jack thought about this idea. Lying to his father didn't seem right, but this might have to be another one of those little white lies that were sometimes necessary in life. They decided that he would tell his parents he was working at the New England Mill, a woolen mill that had just opened not far from Wellington Textiles and with which he thought his father would be unfamiliar. Tom went inside to speak to his father who quickly agreed to the idea. Jack was to report to the hiring office at Wellington Textiles first thing Monday morning. The deception was complete. Jack's worries were, if not gone, at least assuaged for a while.

Just then Anne appeared, smiling brightly at Jack, then turned to her brother. "Tommy, I think Mother wants to see you in the parlor," and she rolled her eyes so obviously that even Jack detected the ruse.

Tom excused himself. Anne took Jack's arm and led him across the lawn and beneath the hanging branches of one of the copper beech trees. "How are <u>you</u> today, Jack?" Anne asked with a slight inflection at the word "you."

"I'm okay. Just okay. Anne, I have to tell you something," Jack began.

"I know, Tommy told me. You've quit school to go to work for a while. It's a wonderful thing you are doing for your family, Jack. I'm proud of you," said Anne with genuine feeling.

"I thought you'd be angry, or disappointed, that I quit school, I mean," explained Jack.

"But it's just for a while, right? Just until things work out for your father," she reassured Jack.

"And about that dance, I don't know if I can go after all."

"But Jack, why? Tom has a suit you can borrow. It will be such fun."

"But I won't know anyone, and I'll feel foolish."

At that Anne mustered up all of her considerable young feminine charms. She drew close to Jack, looked sweetly into his eyes, and said tenderly, "You'll know me, Jack, isn't that enough?" And she tugged teasingly at his shirtsleeve.

"But I'm not a very good dancer," Jack confessed with some embarrassment.

"I'll tell you a secret," whispered Anne, "neither am I. So we shall just have to teach each other." And with those words she turned so that she and Jack were facing one another, placed her right hand in his left, drew his right arm around her waist, and there, under the weeping copper beech, the young couple had their first dance.

CHAPTER 10

# The Mill
*December 1912*

The Wellington woolen mill represented the pinnacle in the development of the American textile industry for its time. A hundred years earlier, textile manufacture in the young nation took place entirely in the home. A farm family sheared their own sheep, then picked, carded, spun, and wove the wool to make their own clothing. In time small specialty mills appeared, each mechanizing just one step in the process. A family transported its fleeces to one mill for spinning, another for carding, a third for fulling, then carried home skeins of finished yarn for weaving into clothing, blankets, and rugs. The modern textile mill changed all that. It brought all the wool-making processes together almost literally under one roof: sorting, dyeing, carding, spinning, and weaving.

The brick edifice of Wellington Textiles stood five stories high and extended nearly three city blocks along Holyoke's second level canal. Long weaving rooms occupied the first two floors, their steam-powered looms clattering twelve hours a day. Spinning of yarn was accomplished on the third and fourth floors, carding on the top floor. Two sidings from the main line of the Boston and Maine Railroad ran close to the eastern side of the building. One track led to a large, wood-framed building, the sorting room, where raw wool fleeces arrived by rail from the central Atlantic and southern states. Another track led to the shipping house from which finished products, bolts of fabric, were dispatched.

Along the front of the building stood six brick towers that housed stairways for the workers and steam-powered elevators for wool and equipment. Atop one tower in the center of the mill, an enclosure with wooden shingles had been constructed and an enormous brass bell installed. Several times a day the bell tolled, warning workers of the start of another workday, signaling the beginning and end of lunch breaks, or announcing the end of the workday.

The vision for the American textile industry was of an ideal environment where owners employed skilled managers to oversee happy, hard-working, well-paid employees. The reality fell well short of that ideal. A woolen mill was a noisy, dirty place to work. The clatter of the looms was painfully loud. The air inside was full of wool fibers and dust. Huge vats of dye bubbled and boiled, acrid mists rising into the air and sticking to the workers' skin and clothing.

Charles Bernard's first job was as a doffer in the spinning room of a woolen mill in Sherbrooke, Québec. *"Grouille-toi!"* The command lashed the air like a whip as the shoeless ten-year-old raced to pull a full bobbin from a spinning rig, replace it, and deposit it in a wheeled hopper that would be transported by elevator to the weaving room downstairs. Charles' section included ten rigs and three hundred bobbins and his boss got very angry if a bobbin was not replaced within seconds of filling.

In his teens Charles worked in the weaving room of the same mill, refilling shuttles as they ran out of thread. His mechanical skills eventually won him an apprenticeship with a loom fixer in another mill with responsibility for several dozen looms including replacing warps, repairing broken harnesses, and freeing jammed shuttles.

It was as a loom fixer that Charles was first hired at the Wellington mill, but his mechanical aptitude quickly became apparent. Soon he was promoted to mechanic and was called upon constantly to repair one of nearly one thousand looms, spinning rigs, and other machines in the mill. His was a job with variety and challenges to his skills and creativity, unlike most of the mill jobs that involved monotonous repetition, back-breaking exertion, and dangerous maneuvers around heavy machinery.

Evelyne St. Onge was fourteen and had completed eighth grade when she began work at the same woolen mill as Charles. Her first position was as a loom tender, but her dexterity and sharp eyes eventually won her promotion to a position as a spinner where she worked for nearly ten years before marrying Charles Bernard in 1896.

"Trottière, Lacroix, Bernard...section five" shouted the sorting room chief that Monday morning over the roar of an arriving locomotive. Jack knew Jim Trottière from grade eight at Forestdale Grammar School. A tall, thin boy possessed of surprising strength and the ability to work for hours without a break, Jim was quiet, not easily provoked to anger or even to conversation. But Jack knew Jim was capable of a smile and wry laugh from time to time. Leo Lacroix had just arrived in Holyoke from Québec. Leo was a willing worker but his dour expression and limited English made engaging him a challenge.

Several times a day a train would arrive depositing hundreds of bundles of raw wool fleeces on flat wagons lining the loading platform. Smaller shipments of wool arrived almost constantly by truck from all over New England and New York. As recently as the 1890s teams of draft horses hauled the wagons through the tall doors of the sorting room, a process now accomplished with tractors that spewed acrid smoke as they pulled the heavy loads.

On the floor of the sorting room, a sorter tagged the bales according to quality. One of the teams of three boys struggled to attach a block and tackle to each bale, then guided it to its proper location on the sorting room floor where it was their task to break open the bales.

Section five was at the far right corner of the sorting room. Jack, Jim, and Leo stacked the newly arrived bales four or five high, trying their best to confine the stacks between lines painted on the concrete floor. Almost as quickly as new bales arrived in their section, fleeces would have to be removed and transported to the mill on low hand-pulled drays. Hard labor was not new to Jack. He had worked in the tobacco fields during harvest time the last few years. And he and his father did most of the work of preparing their gardens, planting, weeding, harvesting, and tending their crops themselves.

The air in the sorting room was warm and moist, laden with floating particles of dust, dirt, and wool fibers. Inhaling that air led to much coughing and wheezing for the young workers. Sickness was common, mostly chest colds and bronchitis, but more serious conditions such as brown lung disease were known to occur, even in the young workers. Deaths from anthrax, a deadly pathogen carried by sheep and cows, were not unheard of among mill workers.

The nearly constant noise in the sorting room made conversation impossible. But lulls in the activity did occur once in a while allowing brief exchanges.

"You done with school, Jack?" asked Jim.

"I hope to go back, maybe in a year or two. My dad was let go in October so I had to help out, that's all. We'll see." Jack paused. "What about you?"

Jim's voice dropped to a whisper. "I'd like to learn a trade, maybe smithin'. I like makin' things and I got the strength, I 'spose. But I need to find a smithy to apprentice with. In the meantime, I guess I'm lucky to have this," he said as his eyes scanned the canyon of fleeces around him.

"Bit of a death trap, eh?" observed Jack. Jim nodded.

At noon the three boys sat on the canal wall eating their lunches. "Tom Wellington, where's he at now?" asked Jim.

"The Dorchester School up in Greenfield...he's doing all right. His sister Anne is in grade eight at Forestdale."

"Nice kids," said Jim. "You'd never know their father was..." He paused, then gestured toward the mill: "You know."

Jack smiled and nodded. "Hey, remember that kid O'Malley, Jeffrey O'Malley? He still in school?"

"Naw, he's working at Falmouth Paper now. Never liked him," said Jim shaking his head. "Tried to push me around...called me a Canuck. Had to knock his lights out one time..." He paused and smiled as if enjoying the memory. "Put a stop to that!"

"Yeh," replied Jack, "too bad there's guys like him just lookin' to make life miserable for everyone else."

"Leo," said Jack, "how long you been in Holyoke?" Leo looked up but seemed not to understand the question.

"Holyoke...when did you come?" asked Jack speaking slowly and distinctly.

"Two weeks," replied Leo.

"With your mother and father?"

"*Oui*...," answered Leo. "Mother, father, two brother, two sister."

"Where'd you live in Québec?"

"Drummondville."

"Oh, yeh, Drummondville. That's near Sherbrooke, right?" Leo nodded.

"I was born in Sherbrooke," explained Jack, pointing to himself. Leo appeared to be thinking about that. There was a look of longing in his eyes.

"You'll like it in Holyoke...it's not bad," said Jack, peering into Leo's sad eyes and nodding. "You will." Jack thought he caught just a glimpse of a weak smile creeping across Leo's face.

CHAPTER 11

# Impertinence
## *December 1912*

C hristmas was celebrated as usual at the Bernard home
that December. Jack had only the one day off from the
mill so he was not able to assist with preparations as he had in
the past. His father had been working only sporadically since
October, filling in temporarily in a textile mill in Westfield for
a few weeks, delivering coal for another few weeks in
November and early December. So he was around the house
more than he would have liked to be, but it meant that he was
able to do more with his family than in the past.

On the Saturday after Christmas it was arranged that Tom
and Anne would visit with the Bernards for a day. They
arrived by horse-drawn sleigh, the roads already having been
buried by snow from several December storms. The entire
family greeted the two Wellingtons at the front door and Jack
did his best to properly introduce Anne to his parents and
sisters.

Almost at once Claire grasped Anne's hand and led her
into the parlor to show off a needlepoint project she had just
started. Marie followed and stood quietly by, watching her
younger sister who, she noted with amazement, was instantly
at ease with nearly everyone she met.

The boys promptly set out for a day of ice fishing at
Hampton Ponds. Anne had asked her brother several days
earlier if she could go along, but Tom had explained that ice
fishing was for boys only. When she protested, Tom began to
describe in gruesome detail how to bait a hook with a
squirming worm or a wriggling shiner and how to grasp a

catfish without getting stung by its deadly spines. Anne's interest in ice fishing quickly waned.

Evelyne had offered to teach the three girls tatting, making delicate lace by forming loops and knots with thread. She had learned to tat from her mémère when she was a child but it was nearly a forgotten craft now that manufactured lace had become readily available. She demonstrated the basic stitches for all three girls to see, then helped each to get started on her own project, a small round doily for Claire, a pair of cuffs for Marie, and a decorative collar for Anne. Claire required extra assistance from her mother while the two older girls, once started, were nearly self-sufficient.

Finally, Evelyne left the girls to work on their own and went to the kitchen to do some baking. As they worked, the girls talked casually about Christmas, school, and needlework. Anne could tell that Claire was studying her very intently. Finally, when there was a lull in the conversation, the eight-year-old spoke up: "What grade are you in, Anne?"

"Grade eight. What grade are you in, Claire?"

"I'm in grade two; Marie's in grade five. Aren't you, Marie?" Marie nodded. "Do you like Jack?" Claire queried. Marie shot her sister a look intended to discourage this line of questioning.

Anne smiled and nodded. "Yes, I do, Claire."

"Why?" was Claire's quick rejoinder.

"Sssh!" said Marie, turning deep red. "Don't be impertinent."

"Don't sssh me, Marie!" protested Claire. She paused briefly. "What's 'impertent' mean?"

"Claire, I think Mom needs some help with the bread. Why don't you go and see?"

But Claire couldn't be distracted that easily. "Is Jack your boyfriend?"

Anne laughed. "Well, we're very good friends. I hope you and Marie and I can be good friends, too."

"Okay," answered Claire, smiling. Anne thought that had put an end to the inquisition, but Claire had one more question for Anne. "Has Jack kissed you?" asked Claire, her face twisted into an expression of mock disgust.

Just then Evelyne appeared. "Claire, dear, won't you give me a hand with the kneading?" Reluctantly Claire rose, sighed dramatically, and followed her mother into the kitchen.

Anne was blushing a bit, but Marie was scarlet with embarrassment. Several moments of silence passed before Anne spoke again: "You're lucky to have a sister, Marie. Sometimes I wish I had a sister...you know, to talk to. Brothers are fine, of course, but they're not the same. Do you know what I mean?"

Marie gave out a little laugh and shook her head; she was looking down as she spoke. "I'm sorry about that sister of mine, she just doesn't know when to...well...keep her peace. What a thing to ask you..." Her voice trailed off, but there was an inquisitive look on her face as her eyes rose slowly to meet Anne's.

"Just between you and me," offered Anne with a wink, "the answer to Claire's last question is 'No'. But I have a feeling that's going to change soon."

The boys returned by mid-afternoon hauling the toboggan and all their gear, bursting with stories of booming ice and giant fish that got away. They had succeeded in landing two good-sized pickerel which Evelyne cleaned, wrapped in newspaper, and stored in the ice box.

Anne, Tom, and Jack sat by the fireplace in the parlor recounting their adventures. Then they exchanged gifts. Tom gave Jack a knife for fishing, recalling how Jack had lost his favorite fishing knife when it dropped out of sight through the ice last winter. Jack presented Tom with a handmade wooden box with a hinged lid and six divisions, each of which was filled with a supply of fishing necessities - sinkers, hooks, floats, lures, leaders - and one containing a pair of small pliers and clippers for making repairs to your tackle. Anne presented Jack with a handsome silk tie. Then Jack held out to Anne a long, narrow box with a pretty bow on it. It contained a set of delicately carved tortoiseshell combs for her hair. Anne blushed, smiled, and thanked him repeatedly.

"I helped Jack pick those out at the store," injected Claire.

Finally it was time for the Wellingtons to leave. As the family stood just inside the front door, Tom and Anne shook hands with Mr. and Mrs. Bernard and thanked them warmly. Anne spoke to Marie and Claire: "Perhaps we can have another needlework day sometime soon."

As the Wellingtons stepped out of the front door, Jack followed, closing the door behind him. Tom began to walk toward the waiting carriage, but Anne paused and turned to Jack.

"Thank you for my gift, it's perfect." She took his arm, leaned toward him, and whispered in his ear "Happy New Year, Jackie." Then she kissed him lightly on the cheek. As she did so, her eye fell on one of the parlor windows where Claire was gaping at what she had just witnessed. Just then her sister's hand could be seen grasping her by the arm and pulling her away from the glass.

# CHAPTER 12

# New Beginnings
## *Spring 1913*

The plight of millworkers was a subject of great interest and concern to the citizens of Holyoke and Westfield. Illness, injuries, and deaths were almost daily occurrences in the local mills. Beyond the mills, the social maladies associated with the rapid growth of Holyoke were apparent everywhere, from poverty to disease to labor unrest. Pressure had been mounting both regionally and nationally for years for Congress to enact laws protecting workers.

For some citizens the inauguration of a new president, Woodrow Wilson, in March of that year offered hope for the future. Well in advance of that event, the headlines of the *Holyoke Transcript* as well as much of the conversation among workers and families had to do with the President-Elect. Some were convinced that a new age was dawning for cities like Holyoke; others were not so sure.

Around the supper table one evening Marie Bernard raised the subject. "Daddy, it says in the newspaper that Mr. Wilson will be a friend of the working man. That will be good for us, won't it?"

Charles hesitated before replying. "Well, we'll have to wait and see. It's easy for a rich man to say something like that, but not so easy for him to do anything about it."

One event that did have direct benefit for the Bernard family that winter was electrification. Downtown Westfield had been wired some years earlier, but the outlying districts were slower to receive electrical service. It would have been a considerable expense to a family like the Bernards, but Charles and Jack were able to do some of the work themselves.

Electricity changed everyone's lives for the better. It meant that Jack's sisters could study much more easily, sitting anywhere in the house reading at any hour of the day. In time Charles was able to rig up an electric pump that carried well water right to the kitchen sink, a wonderful convenience for Evelyne and the whole family. Sewing would also be easier and faster once Evelyne had an electric sewing machine, the family's next purchase if all went well.

By March the rigors of winter had taken their toll and the entire Bernard family was looking forward to spring. Jack felt a special fondness for the last few weeks of winter, for this was the season of maple sugaring. In the eastern townships of Québec where his parents grew up, *le temps des sucres* provided income for farm families at an otherwise meager time of year. It required little investment in equipment but lots of labor by the whole family.

The Bernards' property consisted almost entirely of fields and orchards, but at the southwest corner stood a small sugarbush of several dozen old sugar maples. Their neighbors, the Bousquets, had many more trees on their property, and so the two families had a tradition of working together to produce enough maple sugar and syrup for their own needs while reserving some to sell.

For Jack the sugaring season had a certain magical appeal, part of which was watching fifteen-year-old Émile Bousquet and Thor work as a team. Thor was a Percheron, a breed of muscular workhorse introduced from France in the late nineteenth century. His coat was chestnut; he stood at least a foot taller than Émile and weighed better than a ton. His ears went up whenever the young man approached and his eyes turned glassy, then closed as Émile stroked his forelock. The bond between boy and horse was so intimate that it sometimes seemed that the two were of a single mind. Thor knew when to pull, when and which way to turn, when to slow and stop. The horse produced a rich repertoire of sounds and every nicker and neigh from that massive animal seemed directed at Émile.

Surprising, thought Jack, how well Émile and Thor communicated, considering that Émile Bousquet was deaf. He lost his hearing at the age of two when he suffered a severe case of German measles. His speech was limited to monosyllables and truncated phrases that only his parents and siblings could understand. But there were no barriers to communication between him and Thor. Émile often stood next to Thor, his hands on the massive animal's neck or flank. Jack wondered if he was "listening" to Thor's vocalizations with his hands. And when Émile spoke, other humans may have struggled to understand, but not Thor.

The Bousquets' sugarhouse was a rustic wooden shack in the middle of the sugarbush. Stacks of firewood had been placed along one side of the shack during the previous fall in preparation for the sugaring season. In late February Jack, Charles, and Pierre Bousquet rode the back end of a crude sled drawn by Thor, their snowshoes dangling. Every so often the three stepped off the sled carrying buckets, spiles, hammers, and bitstocks. A single tap was drilled in smaller trees, two or three in the oldest and largest. It was too cold yet for the sap to flow, but within two or three weeks it would begin and the gentle "poing" of sap striking the bottom of a bucket would be audible from some distance away.

Once the season began, the two families worked long days and sometimes well into the nights collecting the sap and carrying it to the sugarhouse where it was stored in two large staved barrels. The raw sap, looking very much like water, was drawn off by a wooden tap into an evaporator, a broad galvanized metal tray positioned on a stone fire pit in the center of the sugarhouse. Beneath the evaporator a roaring wood fire had to be stoked constantly. Gradually over many hours, the watery sap thickened to a golden brown, viscous liquid. A small spigot on the front end of the evaporator allowed it to be drawn off into one of several finishing pans. These were placed on a cast iron stove where the finished syrup was produced. Evelyne and Madeleine Bousquet oversaw the final steps, carefully sterilizing pint, quart, and gallon tins before they received the syrup.

Back in Québec, both climate and tradition dictated that sugaring begin after March 19, St. Joseph's Day, a Holy Day of Obligation that recognized the importance of this time for farm families. In New England the season often started earlier, but the Bernards, the Bousquets, and some of their neighbors still observed St. Joseph's Day with their own uniquely French-Canadian celebration.

A full moon rose over the mountains as families from the neighborhood gathered in the Bousquets' large kitchen, each making a contribution to the meal. Evelyne brought her *tourtière* (spiced meat pie), Madeleine her *paté chinois* (shepherd pie), another neighbor *paté au saumon* (salmon pie), as well as carrots, turnips, and onions. A selection of luscious desserts was arranged on the table after the main course including *tarte au sucre* (maple syrup pie) and freshly made maple ice cream.

A sleigh ride followed pulled by Thor and a neighbor's Clydesdale. Jack took the reins of the Clydesdale and he and Émile managed to get the two massive draft horses pulling their load more or less smoothly and in the same direction. As the sleigh emerged from the woods into a moonlit pasture, Jack looked back to see his sisters nestled snuggly against their parents in the hay, faces aglow with the moonlight and the magical spell of the evening. At fourteen he was not especially sentimental, but even Jack was warmed by the sense of comfort and well-being that the occasion evoked.

After the sleigh ride Pierre Bousquet raised his fiddle while another neighbor pumped on his concertina. Young and old alike stepped to the music as the flickering light of the bonfire illuminated their smiles and ruddy faces. No one paid heed to steps or style; they simply lost themselves in the spirit of the evening.

Charles and Evelyne danced slowly, smiling at one another as the music played. Despite his discomfort with dancing, Jack joined in this neighborhood tradition and allowed Madeleine Bousquet to coax him from the sidelines and swing him around for one number. Then Jack reached out and took the hand of eleven-year-old Marie. They danced two dances together and had just begun a third when Claire took Émile's hand and drew him out among the other dancers. Émile was inclined to be shy, but Claire's infectious smile and laughter helped him to relax and he appeared to be enjoying himself. At that moment Claire took Émile's hand and held it towards Marie's. In the same motion Claire grasped her brother's hand and pulled him away, leaving Émile and Marie together, still dancing though a bit dazed by what had just happened.

Jack and Claire finished the dance together. "That was quite a maneuver!" said Jack as his eight-year-old sister displayed an impish smile.

The evening's merriment ended with a familiar refrain that brought a tear to nearly every eye:

*Ô Canada! Terre de nos aïeux,*
*Ton front est ceint de fleurons glorieux!*
*Car ton bras sait porter l'épée,*
*Il sait porter la croix!*
*Ton histoire est une épopée*
*Des plus brillants exploits.*
*Et ta valeur, de foi trempée,*
*Protégera nos foyers et nos droits*
*Protégera nos foyers et nos droits.*

(O Canada! Our home and native land!
Thy brow is wreathed with a glorious garland of flowers.
As is thy arm ready to wield the sword

So also is it ready to carry the cross.
Thy history is an epic
Of the most brilliant exploits.
Thy valour steeped in faith
Will protect our homes and our rights,
Will protect our homes and our rights.)


That June a public gathering was held at the Holyoke Women's Home. The entire board of directors and many of the home's benefactors were on hand for an important announcement as were the mayor, members of the City Council, and several state legislators. Reporters from the *Transcript* as well as newspapers in Chicopee and Springfield had been invited to report on what they were told would be a new initiative for the organization.

The gathering marked the beginning of a campaign to raise monies for the purchase of a new residence especially for single mothers-to-be. It would include accommodations for a dozen young women and their babies and provision for baby-sitting so that the mothers could complete their education and receive job training. And it would be staffed by professionals providing medical, social, recreational, and other services to the residents.

That anyone was willing to acknowledge the problem of young unmarried girls bearing children was in itself a major breakthrough in Holyoke. Some members of the community were aghast, believing the problem represented a scandal or smirch on the city's reputation that did not deserve to be trumpeted. But the ladies of the Women's Home had faced that kind of opposition before.

The meeting began with comments from the President of the Home, Mrs. Ellen Steinberg, who then turned over the podium to the two driving forces behind the project, Nina Calavetti and Helen Wellington. Each woman spoke with feeling about the problem, the needs, and their hopes for this new facility. Carolyn Ford and Anne Wellington then rose, stepped up to the podium, and announced together the name for the new facility: "Clara's House."

The moment was especially poignant for Nina. Only a few of those present knew how very personal this project was for her, for just thirteen years earlier, she had been a lonely, frightened, sixteen-year-old girl in Holyoke, anxiously preparing for the birth of a child.

CHAPTER 13

# One Summer
## *Summer 1913*

Summer was once again on the horizon. Jack's father had been rehired at Wellington Textiles and his parents insisted that Jack give up his job and have some time to be a boy once again. They also wanted him to return to school in September.

Tom was already home from boarding school and the two friends were planning adventures together. Jack was also hoping to spend more time with Anne, but Tom and Carolyn had had a falling out. Anne seemed more disappointed than anyone at this turn of events. Tom had been completely engrossed in intramural sports at school and didn't seem to miss his old girlfriend back home in the least.

That spring Tom played on the school's tennis team and took readily to this sport. He loved tennis for itself, but he also enjoyed the attention he received from the girls at the Dorchester School. He did cut a very impressive figure on the court, his dark hair contrasting smartly with his white shirt and trousers. But there were few tennis courts in Holyoke, and for that matter no one that Tom knew even played tennis. One of Tom's friends, Bill Peterson, was a caddy at the golf course at the entrance to Mountain Park and Tom went to see him one day at the clubhouse. He got a tour of the course and played a few holes with his friend after his caddying duties were complete. Golf became Tom Wellington's new passion that summer.

Jack's last day working at the mill was a Friday in mid-June. Tom urged him to come directly to his house and stay a while, but Jack declined. He wanted to spend some time with his family first. But they agreed to a three-week stay beginning at the end of June.

Jack left the mill with no regrets that Friday afternoon. The work had been hard, the warehouse air stifling and filled with dust that irritated his lungs. Anne was waiting for him at the gate as she often did. School was out and she was footloose for the summer and anxious to make plans with Jack as well. The two walked up Essex Street, talking about the summer ahead and how they might spend their time. Jack couldn't stop looking at her face that only got prettier with time.

Jack spent ten days at home helping his parents around the house with much needed chores including weeding the vegetable garden and building a small pen for the merino sheep they planned to acquire. When the day of his departure for Holyoke arrived, Jack boarded the trolley with his old tattered rucksack and a new valise his parents had given him to carry the expanding wardrobe, toiletries, and other regalia of a modern young man.

For Jack and Tom the next few weeks would be a whirlwind of sheer fun. They both felt they were making up for lost time together, and each for his own reasons sensed that this might be the last summer he could afford just to be young and carefree. Anne and Carolyn might have other ideas in mind, but at least for the next few days the boys' plans didn't involve the girls. Jack and Tom stayed up until nearly midnight that night talking excitedly of their plans.

The next morning they were up early, stuffing rucksacks with all manner of gear, towels, swimsuits, jackknives, fishing poles, and provisions for a day of adventure. They boarded the trolley at Cabot Street and soon disembarked at Mountain Park. Tom's friend, Bill Peterson, and a fourth boy, Peter Buchanan, met them at the park. The four rode the switchback railway several times, played catch on the grass, then decided on a hike. Bill knew of a swimming hole in the woods beyond the park boundaries and led them on a rough trail for nearly half an hour before they emerged by a deep pool hidden in the forest.

They gathered wood for a small fire, had a lunch of bread and dried beef, then sat by the water's edge talking animatedly about their school day adventures of the past year. They donned swim trunks and took a bracing plunge in the cold water, then lay in the warm sun on the bank contemplating their next entertainment.

Bill led them further through the woods until they passed a large no trespassing sign and finally emerged close to a fairway of the golf course where he caddied. They watched unobserved from the woods as several groups of golfers teed off, driving their balls straight and long down a narrow fairway. Bill explained that these were the best of the area's golfers competing in a big tournament.

When no golfers were in sight, they dashed across the fairway and through the woods on the far side, emerging near a green on another hole. No one was around, but Bill warned them to stay hidden in the woods and wait quietly.

Suddenly a loud rush of air could be heard followed by a sharp "plop." A white ball had landed, apparently out of nowhere, on the edge of the green. "Shhhh," warned Bill. "Keep watching." Three more balls came rocketing out of the sky in the next minute or two. Each landed on the green or close to it. "These guys are really good," explained Bill. "This hole is what they call a dogleg. The tee is around that bend." He pointed up the fairway. "Most golfers take two or three shots just getting around the bend and onto the green, then two or three putts to finish the hole. But the real good ones can hit a ball from the tee, over the trees, straight to the green."

Soon the golfers appeared, walking down the fairway toward the green, followed by their caddies. One of them one-putted the green for what golfers call an "eagle," two below par. The others took two putts, but that was still an impressive "birdie" for this hole. Then the foursome moved along to the next hole and again the green was quiet. The boys were about to head back when they heard another ball land on the green with a hard "plop." Suddenly Peter bolted from his hiding place and ran out onto the green.

"Whatta you doin', Pete?" cried Bill in a loud whisper. "You're not allowed on the green." Peter picked up the shiny white ball. "You can't do that," Bill protested. "Put it back."

The three stood watching in astonishment. They thought Peter was about to steal the ball. But Peter's instincts were far more devious and clever. He strode over to the hole and dropped the ball in the cup. He paused nonchalantly for a moment in mock imitation of a figure from the silent movies, then dashed for cover just as a second ball landed with a loud "thwack" only inches away from him.

Tom looked at Bill and Jack with an expression of delight and devilry, stood up and darted toward the green. But Peter yelled: "No, no, they'll know it's a trick...just one." Tom understood immediately and rejoined his friends. "Okay, boys, now we just sit back and wait for the fun to begin!" said Peter with a crooked smile.

Soon the party of four golfers was approaching the green. They immediately found three of the balls, but the fourth ball seemed to be missing and the men began searching the tall grass around the margins of the green, then extended the search into the woods. "I thought I gave that ball a good ride," said one of the golfers, "but maybe I put a little too much spin on it and it bounced off the green and way into the woods."

Fortunately for the boys, the golfers were searching on the opposite side of the green from where they lay in hiding. The men looked for at least ten minutes, then gave up and returned to the green. "Guess I'll have to take a penalty and go back to the tee for another shot," said one of the golfers.

"Wait a minute, Wade," another member of the group said as he was pulling the flag out of the cup. "What kind of ball were you playing?"

"A Double Crown," answered Wade.

"Here it is," his friend replied in disbelief, "you got a hole-in-one!" The cheering and celebration went on for several minutes. Apparently there was a one hundred dollar prize being offered for anyone who got a hole-in-one during the tournament and Wade had just struck it rich!

When the boys heard that, Tom let out a loud laugh. Suddenly the golfers turned and looked in their direction. One of them started walking toward them and at that the four boys took off through the woods as fast as their legs could carry them, the golfers in hot pursuit. The boys managed to elude their pursuers and find their way back to the hidden pond where they had left their gear. Their hearts were pounding so hard, and they were laughing so uncontrollably, that it took them nearly half an hour to settle down.

They agreed that it was probably best not to show themselves anywhere near the golf course or the park for a while, and Bill led them by another route through the woods to the trolley tracks. They waved down the next car and rode back to Holyoke, still laughing at the prank they'd pulled off. "D'you think Wade'll try to collect his hundred dollars?" asked Pete. They all started laughing all over again.

That evening Tom and Jack recounted their adventure to Anne and she gave them a half-serious scolding. "You boys, you're going to get in trouble one of these days, I swear." But she promised not to breathe a word to her parents.

The first week of Jack's visit with the Wellingtons was devoted almost entirely to fishing. Jack was anxious for him and Tom to spend some time with the girls and he brought up the subject repeatedly, but Tom seemed reluctant. That evening Anne and Jack had a discussion on the lawn between croquet matches with Tom. They proposed inviting Carolyn to join them the next day for an afternoon of lemonade, croquet, and badminton. Tom consented but insisted that Anne discuss the matter with Carolyn.

Anne set out for Carolyn's house on Appleton Street, a few blocks away. Nearly an hour later she came back and reported to the boys, still playing croquet, that Carolyn would be delighted. But when Tom was out of earshot, Anne confessed to Jack that Carolyn's reaction was not exactly one of delight.

The next day was cloudy and rain threatened, but the gathering went ahead as planned. Carolyn arrived shortly after noon and she and Anne immediately drifted away from the boys for what appeared to be a heart-to-heart. Eventually they returned and Anne proposed a game of badminton. Carolyn's heart was obviously not in the game and Tom seemed confused about what he should do. Anne took him aside and spoke briefly to him; it seemed Tom was getting instructions.

Tom spoke quietly to Carolyn. She broke into tears and went running across the lawn. Tom looked at Anne with a mystified expression. He shrugged his shoulders and raised his hands, palms upward, as if to say, "What do I do now?"

Anne took Tom's arm, cocked her head emphatically, and spoke to him with stern, sisterly reproval in her voice: "Apologize to her, Tommy." As she said those words she must have dug her fingernails into her brother's arm, because Tom snapped it away with a loud, "Oww…okay, okay."

Jack had no idea what all this was about. "Gosh, I thought they were getting along just fine," he said to Anne. "What's wrong?"

"What's wrong," replied Anne with a note of annoyance in her voice, "is that my dear brother is a cad. He never wrote to Carolyn while he was away at school, and he never visited her when he was home. Now he wants to make amends and pick up where they left off last summer, but Carolyn is, well, you know, 'once bitten, twice shy.'"

Jack wasn't familiar with the maxim, but he got the idea. "Tommy will just have to try and patch things up with her," replied Jack. "He's good at that."

"I know," was Anne's only comment as she glared after her brother, "I know." Sure enough, after about fifteen minutes Carolyn and Tom returned to the badminton court. Carolyn's eyes were a little red, but Tom was on his best behavior and tried very hard to see that the rest of the afternoon went perfectly.

When Carolyn prepared to leave, Tom asked to escort her home. She agreed, smiled, and placed her hand on his arm. Just then a light mist began to fall, but Tom was prepared with a black umbrella that he opened and held over Carolyn's head as they strolled down the slate pathway toward the black, wrought iron gate. "Well, Tommy's done it again," commented Anne as she and Jack watched the couple in the distance. After a pause she continued: "Jackie, if I went away for a while, would you write to me every day?"

"Sure," was Jack's reply, "every day." And Jack thought no more of the matter. Anne turned away from Jack, as if still watching Carolyn and Tom, but the truth was that she didn't want Jack to see the look on her face at that moment. She carefully recomposed herself, then squeezed his hand gently, turned, and put on the sweetest smile possible as a heavier rain began to fall. She leaned toward Jack, closed her eyes, and kissed him softly on the lips. The rain dripped down their faces, but neither seemed to notice.

The next three weeks went by too quickly, and once again Jack and Tom had to count the days until their vacation was over. They went on several more fishing expeditions to the point that even Jack was trying to think of something new to do. One afternoon Bill Peterson appeared at the Wellington home and he and Tom talked excitedly about a possible overnight at the pond near Mountain Park. Jack thought it sounded great. But both boys knew it would be difficult to get permission from Tom's parents.

Again Tom came to the rescue with a subterfuge involving a supposed sleepover at Bill's house. He knew his mother was acquainted with Bill's mother from the Women's Club at church. He also suspected that she had the mistaken feeling that Tom would never be capable of lying to her and she would not feel it necessary to speak to Mrs. Peterson about this. He was right.

Once again Jack and Tom packed their gear, this time including bedrolls and extra provisions. They rode the trolley part way to Mountain Park, then leapt from the car. Bill and Pete were waiting for them and the four made their way through the dense woods to Bottomless Pond, as they had dubbed it.

The evening was spent baking potatoes in tin foil over the bright coals of the fire and telling stories of gruesome murders and the like. Pete's older sister had a secret stash of romantic novels and magazines that he had appropriated for the overnight, and the four exchanged insights and fantasies about the unspeakable things men and women did together, at least on those pages.

It was nearly eleven o'clock when Pete proposed an excursion. With nothing but a kerosene lantern the four set out and soon they were back on the golf course where their previous antics had ended hilariously. A full moon made walking around on the fairways easy, and Tom, Jack, and Bill were content to explore the eerie world of night, but Pete was always thinking a little bit ahead. As they crossed one of the greens, he pulled the flag out of the hole. It had the number 5 on it. "What are you doin', Pete, stealin' again?" asked Jack.

"Nope, just 'reorganizing,'" explained Pete. And at the next hole he removed that flag and substituted the one from the fifth hole. And so it went for nearly an hour, the four boys going to great lengths to be certain they had switched every one of the eighteen flags on the golf course that night. "See, boys, nobody's stealing nothing. Just rearranging," explained Pete as they planted the last flag back in the fifth hole where they had begun. With muffled laughter the four boys made their way back through the woods to Bottomless Pond.

The last night of Jack's stay with the Wellingtons was finally at hand. Mildred made a special feast in honor of the occasion including roast beef, fresh corn on the cob, and blueberry pie with homemade ice cream. After supper Tom and Jack stood on the wide veranda, looking out toward the setting sun. "I'm supposed to help Mother with something inside," said Tom, then added with false surprise, "Hey, look who's here!"

Anne was standing behind Jack, and she reached out with both hands and covered his eyes. "Guess who?" Tom disappeared as Jack turned, took Anne's hands in his, and gazed on that face that he couldn't ignore.

"I'm gonna have to be heading home tomorrow," he began. "This has been the greatest vacation ever. You and Tom are the bee's knees."

She tousled his sun-bleached hair. "You're going to need a haircut soon, young man." But as Jack looked into her emerald eyes, a single teardrop rolled down Anne's cheek.

"Don't cry, please don't cry. It'll only be a month and we'll be back in school and we'll see each other every day," said Jack, "Right?"

Anne hesitated and looked away toward the sunset. She grasped Jack's hand and squeezed it tightly. "Jack," she began softly, turning to face him. "There's something I've been meaning to tell you."

"What?" asked Jack, and then the expression on Anne's face made him wince. "Tell me, Anne, what is it?"

"I won't be going to Holyoke High in September. I'm going to Dorchester with Tommy." She paused. Jack turned away, as if watching the setting sun, but saying nothing.

Finally he turned back to Anne and smiled gamely. "That's wonderful, Anne. You deserve it. You'll do well, I'm sure. I'm really happy for you, and proud of you. I'll see you on holidays and vacations, and I'll write to you every day, like I promised."

"Yes," said Anne, a smiling reappearing, "you <u>did</u> promise, didn't you? And Tommy and I are already planning to have you visit us in Greenfield whenever you can come. It's only a half-hour train ride from Holyoke."

"Maybe we can get Carolyn to come, too," suggested Jack.

"I don't know about that," said Anne, "but we'll have a good time, with or without Carolyn, won't we?"

As the sun set, Tom reappeared from the house. Anne took them both in her arms, and together they watched the last rays of the setting sun fade over the distant hills. "My boys," said Anne, "You're my favorite boys."

In mid-August Anne and Tom surprised Jack with a letter asking if they could visit him in Westfield before they were off to boarding school. Jack had been working in the tobacco fields again but he responded promptly, writing that he would ask for a day off to spend with his friends. Jack's parents were excited; Marie and Claire were, of course, ecstatic.

On a steamy Sunday afternoon the two Wellingtons arrived in a horse-drawn carriage driven by Tom. They sat in the shade sipping lemonade with Jack, his parents, and his sisters. Marie and Claire brought Anne samples of the sewing and knitting projects they had been working on and Anne was genuinely impressed. As the afternoon drew on, Anne, Tom, and Jack walked slowly together through the Bernards' gardens and talked about plans for Jack to visit them in Greenfield in October. Tom started toward the house, leaving Anne and Jack alone. "I guess this is it, Jackie," said Anne. "We'd better be going."

"Okay," answered Jack, his eyes looking off into the fields.

"Remember your promise," Anne said with mock sternness.

"I'll write you, but you have to write first, okay?" said Jack.

"Okay," she replied softly, as she kissed him on the cheek and gave him that smile she knew he liked so much. And she added, "Don't forget, you and Tommy, you're my favorite boys, right?"

"Right," replied Jack.

In the Bernards' front yard thank-yous were exchanged all around. "Good luck in school," Evelyne and Charles said repeatedly to the Wellington children.

Tom and Jack shook hands. "See you in October, Tom," said Jack. "Thank you for coming, Anne. It's been lovely seeing you again," offered Jack with exaggerated politeness as his parents looked on. Anne knew that Jack wouldn't normally use a word like "lovely" and she smiled at the twinkle in his eye as he said it and shook her hand. They climbed into the carriage, Tom took the reins, and they were off down the dusty road.

CHAPTER 14

# Monique
*September 1913*

Jack had returned to Holyoke High School expecting to repeat grade nine and feeling a bit humiliated at the prospect. But the principal, Mr. Fairbanks, took him aside on the first day and surprised Jack with a proposition. Since he had left school the previous October, Jack had been doing schoolwork at home in evenings and on weekends. Every Friday after work he would stop at Mr. Fairbanks's house on Beech Street to pick up a folder of assignments his teachers had assembled for him. It was a matter of pride for Jack that he should keep up as well as possible with his classmates, even though it meant studying by a flickering candle or oil lamp - or lately by a single electric bulb - on many a late evening in his bedroom.

Mr. Fairbanks's proposition was that Jack enter grade ten. His one weakness was mathematics and it was suggested that he receive special after-school tutoring at the high school until he had caught up in math. This arrangement suited Jack just fine and his parents were very happy as well that his education was nearly on schedule in spite of his nine month's absence from grade eight.

During his second week at Holyoke High, Jack was called to the office after school to meet his math tutor. He was expecting a frumpy, matronly old woman and was surprised to find instead a student only one year older than he. Her name was Monique Fleury.

Miss Fleury, as Jack called her, seemed to take her assignment very seriously. She was soft-spoken, rather plain

Jack thought, but possessed of an intensity in her work that impressed him. From that first day she guided Jack ably through the confusing world of algebra. She made up problems for Jack to do, checked his work carefully, and corrected him frequently but politely. They worked at a desk just outside of the main office. As long as Mr. Fairbanks or his secretary, Miss Fulton, was close by, Miss Fleury remained serious and unsmiling and Jack thought of her as just another teacher. After their third or fourth session, Jack perceived just the slightest smile and twinkle in her eye when no adult was looking.

Anne kept her part of their promise and wrote Jack a long letter that arrived just a few days after her departure for the Dorchester School. She sounded happy and Jack sensed that she had quickly adjusted to her new school. She brought him up to date on Tom's busy academic, athletic, and social life. She asked him many questions about his new school year, his family, and how he was spending his spare time. Jack laughed at the expression "spare time"; when did he ever have spare time, he thought? She signed the letter, "Yours always, Anne."

Jack sat down that evening by the light of a kerosene lamp and wrote a long letter to Anne in reply. He told her about his advancement to grade ten. He decided not to mention Miss Fleury as he did not wish for Anne to know about his difficulty with algebra. He also described the excitement surrounding electrification of his and his neighbors' homes and how it would make his family's life so much easier. He signed the letter, "Sincerely, Jack."

In their letters of the next few weeks Anne and Jack made plans for his trip to Greenfield and his visit to the Dorchester School. Finally, on a Friday afternoon in mid-October, Jack boarded the train in Holyoke with his rucksack and valise. The ride to Greenfield was only about 30 minutes and as he stepped off the train onto the platform in Greenfield he heard Tom's voice.

"Jack, Jack," Tom called enthusiastically from the far end of the platform. The two best friends approached each other smiling broadly and shook hands vigorously. "Oh, Jack, it's so good to see you," said Tom with feeling. "Let me take your things. Follow me." Tom carried both of Jack's bags and led him down a flight of stone steps to the street. A taxi was waiting and they both clambered in and were quickly off to the Dorchester School.

The campus of the Dorchester School included a dozen red brick buildings on High Street at the base of Poet's Seat, a steep rocky ridge that bordered the east end of Greenfield. The broad lawn surrounding the buildings was covered with a carpet of brilliant autumn leaves. Tom led Jack to his room in Phillips Hall. Jack would be staying in Tom's room and sleeping in the bed of Tom's roommate, Digsy, who had gone home for the weekend. The two boys lay on their beds for quite a while, bringing one another up to date on their lives of the past month. Jack told Tom about school and admitted that he had to do some catching up in math.

"But I have a tutor, Miss Fleury, who I see three afternoons a week. She's really smart and helps me out a lot," explained Jack. "She's going to Mount Holyoke when she graduates."

Tom thought about that for a moment. "This Miss Fleury," asked Tom, "she's a girl...a student?"

"Yeh," answered Jack, "she's in grade eleven. She's really swell," he repeated.

"Sounds like someone's a little sweet on the teacher," teased Tom.

Jack blushed and started to protest, but just then one of Tom's friends appeared. "Come on, Wellington, the game is starting out on the quad. We need you." Tom and Jack sprinted down three flights of stairs and across the broad lawn to where two teams of boys were just organizing themselves for a game of touch football. Jack was urged to join them but declined. He stood watching the game from the sidelines, but by the way his eyes scanned the surrounding lawn and buildings, anyone could tell that his interest wasn't with the game.

In a few minutes Jack felt a gentle tap on his right shoulder. He turned and beheld Anne looking sweetly into his eyes. "There's my favorite boy," she exclaimed with a lilt in her voice.

Jack blushed. "Hello, Anne, it's so nice to see you," was his rehearsed reply. He had been nervous in anticipation of their reunion and had practiced what he'd say again and again. But now that the time had come, he'd forgotten all his other well-rehearsed lines and had to ad lib. And he knew he wasn't too adept at that. But he also knew Anne, and he expected she'd do most of the talking.

"It's so good to see you. I've missed you," said Anne, and she kissed him on the cheek and hugged him. Soon they were chatting comfortably over the boisterous calls and cheers from the touch football players and their audience. At one point three girls approached Anne and she turned to talk with them quietly. Each was sneaking glimpses of Jack as they talked with Anne.

Finally Anne pulled on Jack's arm. "Jackie, I'd like you to meet my friends, Ellen, Emma, and Maude."

"Eh, how d'you do?" said Jack with a slight smile.

"Aw," said Ellen, "he's shy."

Jack turned beet red. "Not really," he added, trying to correct the first impression. The girls giggled and wandered off. Just then silence fell on the football field. All the players were gathered around someone who was lying on the grass. "Tommy," cried Anne. They rushed across the grass to where Tom lay on his back, eyes closed. As they approached a dark-haired girl bolted in front of them, fell to her knees, and hugged Tom.

"Oh, Tommy, what have they done to you?" cried the girl melodramatically.

Tom was lying flat on his back and he slowly opened his eyes. Looking up at Anne and Jack, he rolled his eyes, smiled wryly, then stroked the girl's hair. "I'll be okay, Liz. It's just a slight concussion. Can you help me up?" He got to his knees, wrapped one arm around Liz and the other around Anne, and was lifted to his feet. "Thanks, girls. Liz, can you help me to the sidelines?" he asked. Tom sat out the rest of the game, talking to Liz and not paying attention to his team's fate in the least.

Anne and Jack stood a short distance away. "I'm sure glad Tom's okay, that was a close call," said Jack seriously.

"Yes, he's just fine, just fine," said Anne with a note of irritation in her voice. She was watching Tom talking animatedly to Liz, apparently fully recovered from his "concussion."

That evening Jack and Tom sat on either side of Anne in the dining room of Phillips Hall. Jack gazed around at the high, vaulted ceiling with carved chestnut beams supporting many ornate brass chandeliers. On the walls were brightly colored banners for Harvard, Yale, Brown, Princeton, Smith, and Mount Holyoke.

As they ate their meal, Tom brought Anne up-to-date on some of Jack's news. Jack was a little annoyed that Tom felt free to provide all these details to her while he, Jack, just sat there. But that was Tom. "Did Jack tell you about his algebra tutor?" Tom asked Anne. Jack's eyes narrowed and his jaw clenched as he looked at Tom. "Her name is Monique and he says she's really cute. She's going to Mount Holyoke next year."

Anne turned slowly to Jack, "How cute is she, Jack? Do tell us!"

"Tommy's exaggerating," said Jack. "I didn't say she was cute. She isn't particularly good looking. She's just a girl that is tutoring me, that's all."

Anne was silent for a moment. Then, cocking her head, she spoke curtly: "I see." And that was the end of the discussion about Monique Fleury, thought Jack, at least for now.

The next morning the Dorchester girls' field hockey team had a match against a team from another school and Anne was on the team. Many of the boys turned out for the event, not because of any great upswing of interest in field hockey, per se, but to watch the girls running about. Their uniforms consisted of white, loose-fitting blouses buttoned up the front and sporty plaid skirts. The hemlines of the skirts fell well below the knee, but revealed a tantalizing bit of ankle and leg in the heat of a match, things upon which young men were seldom allowed to gaze. Jack and Tom watched with great interest and cheered Anne on at every turn. She was new to the sport and not as aggressive as some of the girls, but she carried herself well nonetheless.

After the game the boys ran up to Anne and congratulated her on her team's win. She was excited but didn't have much to say except a few self-deprecating remarks about always being in the wrong place at the wrong time. That afternoon Jack watched Tom play in a tennis match. Anne declined to join them, choosing instead to do some studying in her room. Jack had a definite impression that she was upset about something and he was pretty sure he knew what.

When they returned to Tom's room in late afternoon, Digsy was already back from his weekend at home. His parents had apparently made plans of their own and wouldn't be around, but as a consolation they had given him the use of one of their motorcars, a shiny red Packard. "Hey, fellas, let's go up to Poet's Seat after supper tonight and climb the tower," proposed Digsy. "It's really beautiful up there. I'll drive."

"Can my sister go along?" asked Tom.

"Sure," replied Digsy. "It'll be a hoot."

Darkness had already fallen when the red car pulled up to the entrance to Phillips Hall. Digsy had a date, Gloria, seated beside him. Anne and Jack crawled into the small back seat. Tom and Liz were happily relegated to the rumble seat. The car took off with a roar. Digsy drove fast and a little erratically, and Anne looked concerned.

Thankfully, Poet's Seat was only a five minute drive. All six clambered out and mounted the stairs to the tower. At the top they looked out on the lights of Greenfield. Digsy drew a silver flask from his vest pocket and took several deep swigs, then offered it to Gloria who took a small sip. "Eee-oo," she squawked, "that's awful," and she offered it to Liz who declined. Jack was surprised at what was happening and wondered how Anne was feeling about this turn of events. Just then Tom produced a flask of his own and shared it with Liz. The four were already laughing uncontrollably.

Anne stood close to her brother and spoke in a low voice: "Tommy, you shouldn't be...we shouldn't be...we're underage, you know."

"Annie," said Tom loudly, "Annie, Annie, Annie, relax. Here, have a sip. It'll be good for you. Jack, loosen up a little." They declined and, being nervous about what was going on and annoyed at Tom, Anne and Jack started down the narrow tower stairs. Back on the ground, they stood looking at the view.

"Anne," Jack began. "You got the wrong impression about Miss Fleury. It's not like that, really, I swear. She's just one of my teachers, that's all, nothing more." Anne stood stiffly in the darkness. "It's Tom, you know, he just likes to talk sometimes. Besides, there's just one girl for me."

Anne relaxed a bit and allowed Jack to sidle up behind her. "And who would that be?" she asked coyly. Jack put his arms around her waist and kissed her hair, intoxicated by the fragrance of the perfume she had used sparingly but very effectively.

"You," he answered softly. Anne turned to him and hugged him. Just then they heard shouts from above. Looking up through the darkness they could just see Tom's silhouette against the evening sky. He was standing on the stone parapet atop the tower, his arms waving erratically back and forth.

"Tommy, Tommy, get down, please, get down," shouted Anne.

"Hi Annie," called Tom from above, "Jack. Come back up, the view is great." At that Tom's outline dropped abruptly from sight.

"Tommy, oh my god, Tommy," cried Anne. She ran around the base of the tower with Jack close behind her, fully expecting to find Tom's body lying crumpled on the stonework. At that moment Tom appeared from around the corner, walking unevenly but at least with both feet on the ground.

"I fooled you guys, huh? Ha-ha-ha," said Tom in a maniacal tone.

"Digsy, get the others," ordered Anne. "We're going back to school right now." Anne, Jack, and Tom were deposited summarily in front of Phillips Hall, then the car roared away.

"Go to your room," commanded Anne to her brother, "and stay there until you are sober. I've had it with this, do you hear me, I've had it." She turned to Jack: "I'm sorry about this, I really am. I'll see you tomorrow. And Jack," she added, "don't let him out of your sight!" Jack took Tom up to his room, deposited him on his bed, pulled his shoes off, and the lanky fifteen-year-old was quickly fast asleep in his clothes.

Tom was still asleep, snoring loudly, when Jack headed downstairs for breakfast. He checked on his still sleeping friend again after eating, then went off in search of Anne. He had to wait in a small foyer while the housemistress of the girls' dormitory, casting suspicious glances toward him, called upstairs for Anne. In a few minutes she appeared. "How's Tommy?" she asked.

"Still sleeping," said Jack. "I made sure he didn't go anywhere last night."

"Thank you, Jack," said Anne, "Let's go for a walk." And they strolled across the campus. A light frost glistened on the grass.

"Anne," Jack began delicately. "Last night, when you told Tommy 'I've had it with you,' what did you mean? Has he done other things like this?"

At first Anne spoke firmly and confidently, as she usually did. "It's just a lark, that's all. Sometimes Tommy is 'overly enthusiastic.'"

"Anne, what's really going on? Tom's my best friend, I want to know…I need to know," said Jack. He was feeling that there was something more here than met the eye and Anne was holding back on him.

She started to cry. "I can't take it, Jack, I can't. All he does here is flirt with the girls and make jokes with the other boys. And every weekend he's out late and drinking." Jack was feeling very badly for Anne, and increasingly angry with Tom.

"Jack, you're his best friend, talk to him, please. I'm afraid he'll do something stupid some day and get hurt…" sobbed Anne.

"But I don't understand, he isn't like this at home. It's gotta be this place," said Jack. "I hate the way these kids…"

"Jack," Anne began. "It's not just this place, it's more."

"What do you mean, Anne, what more?" pleaded Jack. He was genuinely confused. Anne paused for what seemed like an eternity. Jack could see that she was trying to regain her composure. Finally she spoke.

"It's Matthew. Ever since we lost Matthew, Tom's been different. It's like he's sad and he misses him, and he can't get over it. It's like the albatross in *Moby Dick*. It just won't go away." Jack wasn't familiar with the literary reference, but he was beginning to understand. He'd seen the tears in Mrs. Wellington's eyes at Christmastime. He knew firsthand how deeply Tom was hurt by the loss of his brother and how distant his father often seemed to be. And he recalled Tom's silence when Jack told him how his family coped with the death of Baby Thérèse.

"Jack, dear Jack, you're Tom's best friend in the world. What you say means everything to him. Would you talk to him before you leave, please, for me?" pleaded Anne, the tears cascading down her cheek.

"Shouldn't you and your parents talk to him about this?" he asked after giving it some thought. "This is kind of a family matter."

Anne looked intensely into Jack's eyes and the tears seemed to stop momentarily. "You're like family, Jack, and we need you..." She paused and then continued, "I need you." Jack hugged Anne and reassured her, although he had deep misgivings about whether he could do anything.

It was practically noon when Tom finally woke, bleary-eyed and looking "like the deuce" as Jack's father would say. They went to lunch together and exchanged small talk. After lunch Jack gathered his belongings and prepared to leave. Tom was about to go down to the dormitory office to call for a taxicab when Jack stopped him.

"Tom," Jack began. "Before you call a cab, I want to ask you something." He felt as though he was skating on very thin ice. "When we're back home, you're like the 'All-American Boy.' We have such fun and we're so alike. And I don't ever want that to change; we'll always be best friends."

"What's your point?" said Tom hostilely, and Jack was suddenly very uneasy, but he continued.

"My point is that the Tom I see here isn't my old pal, Tom, it's somebody different. It scares me, Tom, it really does. And I don't know what to do about it."

"There's nothing for you to do," said Tom sharply. "Just mind your own business." Tom had never spoken like that to Jack before and the words stung.

"Anne," began Jack, "she's as worried as I am and..."

Tom interrupted Jack. "Anne? You've been talking to Anne about me? What right have you? What right does she have? This is lousy, Jack, that's what I have to say, it's lousy....and I thought we were friends."

Jack knew then that his effort had failed. More importantly, he feared that there was now a wide gulf between him and his best friend. "Go ahead, call the cab. I have to get to the station," Jack said with resignation. Soon the cab came, Jack said goodbye to Tom without shaking his hand, climbed into the cab, and was off. Looking back he could see Tom standing on the dormitory steps alone and stone-faced.

CHAPTER 15

# Hurting
## *November 1913*

Jack had wanted to see Anne again before he left the Dorchester School, but there was no time. He boarded the train at the Greenfield station with a heavy heart. The ride back to Holyoke was just a blur as he tried to make sense of that disastrous weekend.

Immediately upon arriving at home, Jack sat down at his desk and wrote a long letter to Anne recounting his argument with Tom and apologizing to her again and again for being unable to get through to him. He hesitated to bring up the subject to his parents as he suspected what their reaction would be, that he was meddling in the affairs of others.

Soon Thanksgiving approached and Jack realized that he hadn't received a letter from Anne for at least two weeks. Jack continued to write to her thinking that perhaps the mails had been disrupted by bad weather.

Thanksgiving was not widely celebrated in Québec, so that uniquely home-centered holiday was something new to the Bernard family when they moved to Massachusetts, but the family embraced the celebration enthusiastically. Their table was covered with all manner of delectable dishes from the bounty of their own vegetable garden, stewed beets, mashed potatoes, late-season Brussels sprouts, onions in cream sauce, and sweet turnips, all surrounding a huge turkey that Jack had fattened up just for the occasion.

As they sat enjoying the feast, Evelyne observed a certain reserve in Jack's mood. He had raised and slaughtered the turkey with pride, he had helped with the cooking, and he usually had a robust appetite on this of all days. But he ate very little and seemed distracted. She knew her son was discreet about his personal life and she hesitated to intrude, but she was worried about him.

After supper, as the rest of the family sat by the fire digesting the immense feast, Jack retreated to his room and lay sprawled on his bed. In a few minutes he heard a gentle tap on the door and his mother entered.

"Jack," she said softly, "What's wrong? Something's wrong, I can tell." Jack lay face down on his bed, unwilling to bare his soul. His mother sat down beside him and stroked his hair. "Remember how we used to talk, Jackie? About everything that was on your mind? We still can, you know, even though you're almost a man, we can still talk, can't we?" she asked quietly. And then she waited. That's what Evelyne Bernard did best, waiting. She had the gift of knowing when to speak and when to be silent, and this was a time for silence. She could hear Jack breathing heavily and she knew there was emotion pent up inside that had to be given time to reveal itself.

Finally Jack rolled over and looked up. "Mom, I've done something terrible and I'm so ashamed." Evelyne had no idea what her son was referring to, but she waited patiently. Suddenly, Jack broke into tears and she gathered him in her arms and let him cry. These were not the tears of a little boy who had scraped his knee or fallen off his bike. These were the tears of a young man whose heart was breaking, she was sure of it. But she waited.

"It's Tom," Jack admitted at last, "he hates me."

"But you and Tom have been best friends for some time now. What happened?"

Jack recounted the story of the weekend in Greenfield. He had kept all this from his parents until now and his mother was aghast to hear of Tom's behavior.

"I don't see that you have anything to be ashamed of, Jack. What about Anne, what does she think about this?" she probed further.

"Anne's not even speaking to me now, Mom. I haven't received a letter from her in two weeks. She hates me, too, I'm sure of it," he blurted out, his adolescent voice cracking.

"I'm sure that's not true, Jack. Maybe you need to talk to her; you know, a little heart-to-heart? Maybe she can help you make things right with Tom," she added. She paused for several minutes. Finally, she spoke. "Why don't you go to Holyoke and call on the Wellingtons? The children will surely be at home for Thanksgiving. I bet they'd love to see you, all of them," she added.

"But I wouldn't feel right just showing up at their door uninvited."

"You're right. But you could call them. I'm sure the Bousquets would let you make a call." Jack thought about this while his mother went downstairs. She felt she had intruded quite enough in her son's personal life for now.

Soon Jack climbed down the stairs and spoke to his mother in the kitchen. "I'm going over to the Bousquets for a few minutes. I have a book I borrowed from Émile that I want to return," he explained with a twinkle in his eye.

"*Grouille-toi,*" said Evelyne, and she slapped him firmly on his backside, sending him on his way with a smile. Jack made the call from the Bousquets and spoke to Mrs. Wellington. She seemed genuinely pleased to hear from Jack and urged him to come as soon as possible.

"We've been missing you, young man," she added.

Jack boarded the trolley the next morning bound for Holyoke, not sure what kind of welcome he would receive from the Wellington children. But when he rang the bell at the Wellingtons' home, the door opened quickly. Before him stood Anne smiling sweetly. "There's my favorite boy," she said. "Come in." And she hugged him tightly but briefly.

Just then Mrs. Wellington appeared and repeated her comment of the previous day: "We've missed you, young man, you'll never know." She ushered the two into the parlor by the fire. Hot cocoa was served and everyone talked gaily. "Excuse me, Jack. I have some business to attend to. You two get caught up. And please, won't you stay for supper?" asked Mrs. Wellington.

"Thank you, Ma'am, I'd like very much to stay for supper," said Jack. And then he added "That's very kind of you, Ma'am," just for good measure.

When the two were alone Anne pulled her chair up close to Jack's. "It's so good to see you, Jackie, I've missed you," she confessed.

"I was afraid you were cross with me," said Jack. "Your letters, they just stopped."

"Jack," she hesitated, "Tom has been furious with me ever since that weekend." Jack winced at the thought. "And he got even angrier when I told him you'd said to say 'Hi' in one of your letters. He told me not to write to you anymore, that's why my letters stopped. He was so angry and I didn't want to disobey him and have him find out. I didn't know what he would do. But I still wrote letters to you, I just didn't mail them...I needed to talk to you, I guess."

"Can I see him? I want to apologize to him," said Jack.

"You have nothing to be sorry for, Jack. You did what I asked you to do and it's only Tom's pride that is responsible for all this. He doesn't want to admit that you were right, that he has a...that things cannot go on like this," she explained with a pained expression on her face.

"But maybe he and I can talk it over...please tell him I'm here," said Jack.

Anne paused. "Jack, Tom's not here. He didn't come home for Thanksgiving. He called Mother and Father Wednesday afternoon and said he was staying at Dorchester. Something about Digsy being at school all alone and wanting to keep him company."

Jack look concerned. "How'd your parents take that?" he asked.

"Mother was upset. She couldn't understand why he would do this. She offered to send Bromley to Greenfield and bring both of them back here for Thanksgiving but Tom refused...and Father, well, he just stood there when Mother told him, just like a statue, cold and silent."

"I know that look, Anne. That was the look on Tom's face after we had that fight. I don't like that look," Jack confessed.

Just then a telephone rang somewhere in the house. They could hear Mrs. Wellington's voice on the phone and she was shouting: "My Tommy, my Tommy, when...where...?" Anne and Jack rushed to the library in time to hear her say, "We'll be there shortly. Tell him we're coming to him." Mrs. Wellington turned to Anne and Jack, her face white as a sheet. "Tommy's been in a motorcar accident, on the Deerfield Road, with his roommate. They're taking him by ambulance to the hospital in Northampton. We've got to go to him."

In minutes the three of them were packed in the Reo with Mr. Wellington at the wheel. It was a trip neither Anne nor Jack ever expected to be making together. They didn't hold hands, but Anne pressed against Jack, seeking some support, and Jack could feel her entire body shaking.

"The doctor will be out in just a moment," said a nurse in a heavily starched uniform and a peaked white cap. The family had been seated in the waiting room for nearly half an hour and the tension was visible on their faces. Another ten minutes went by before a doctor finally emerged with a stern expression on his face.

"Mr. and Mrs. Wellington, I'm Dr. Stoddard. Thomas is going to be all right. He has a fracture of the right femur that's not too bad, and he has abrasions on his head and chest where he struck the windscreen. But those will heal. You can go in and see him for a few moments, but just the two of you for now, please. He needs to get some rest."

The Wellingtons looked much relieved when they returned to the waiting room. They explained that Tom was medicated and very groggy and that they should all go home and return during visiting hours the next day.

At ten o'clock sharp the next morning the four were back at the hospital. Jack had stayed overnight in Tom's bed wearing a pair of Tom's pajamas. He sent a message to his parents via the Bousquets reporting on his whereabouts and Tom's accident. Again Mr. and Mrs. Wellington went in to see their son, leaving Anne and Jack in the waiting room. In a few minutes they returned and showed the two teenagers into Tom's room. Jack had no idea what to expect or what kind of reception he would receive. Before them lay Tom, the always confident, always laughing Tom, swaddled in bandages around his head and chest and with one leg, covered in a plaster cast, suspended in traction.

"Hello, Tommy," said Anne softly. Tom looked at her with a dazed expression on his face. "I want to kiss you but I don't know where. I don't want to hurt you," said Anne.

Tom didn't speak but just looked into his sister's eyes, smiled weakly, and wiggled the fingers of his right hand until she took them in her hand, leaned down, and kissed them gently.

"Look who's here, Tommy, it's Jack." Jack had been standing near the door, still unsure whether he should be there at all. He stepped forward tentatively.

"Hi, Tom...long time, no see," was all Jack could muster for the occasion. Tom looked intently into Jack's face. He seemed to be struggling to reconstruct the events that had led to this moment.

"Jack," said Tom at last. There was a long pause and Anne was about to make some small talk when Tom continued: "I hate..." Jack steeled himself for what he feared was to come.

"I hate for you to see me this way, Jack. I'm a mess," Tom added. He chuckled a bit, but the pain was too much and he winced.

"Forget it, Tom, forget it. Just as long as you're all right, that's all that matters," Jack said. Tom seemed to be thinking about that for a moment. Then he looked steadily into Jack's eyes.

"Best friends?" asked Tom hopefully.

"The best," replied Jack. And he took Tom's hand and pretended to shake it, but held it gently for a moment. Anne was beside herself with emotion but she kept it under control until she and Jack were back in the waiting room again. She would have flung her arms around Jack and cried, but her parents were right there and the four of them stood beaming at one another, silently sharing the relief they were finally able to feel.

"But what about Digsy?" asked Anne at last. Just then a loud clatter could be heard in the hallway and Digsy appeared pushing himself through the swinging doors in a wheelchair. When he spied Anne and Jack he smiled impishly and spun the wheelchair around. A burly nurse appeared through the doors in hot pursuit.

"Master Digsworth, you are going back to your room and you are to stay there until further notice... doctor's orders," said the nurse sternly. Then she produced a large syringe with a long needle from her pocket and Digsy quietly reversed directions and disappeared through the swinging doors.

"I guess that answers my question," said Anne.

"Digsworth, what kind of a name is that?" asked Jack. "I thought his real name was Digsy."

"If your name was Master Chester Arthur Digsworth the Third, you'd probably prefer to be called 'Digsy,' too," said Anne. And with that Jack and the three Wellingtons laughed long and hard.

The next day was Sunday. A family friend had delivered some clothing from Jack's parents so that he would have some of his own things to wear. Jack went to early Mass at Notre Dame in Holyoke, then he and Anne were transported to

Northampton in a car driven by Bromley. The two sat by Tom's bedside for a long time, laughing and exchanging stories. Finally, Tom got serious. "I guess I'm gonna be in here for a few weeks, then home for a while. But I bet I'll get back to Dorchester in time for the spring term," he boasted.

"Maybe you can do some studying at home like Jack did last year," offered Anne. "I could help you during vacations."

"Yeah, maybe," said Tom. He paused, then spoke as he looked innocently off into space: "Hey, Jack, maybe I could have your Miss what's-her-name, Miss <u>Flowery</u>, visit me a few days a week to help me with my math. What'ya think?"

Jack blushed, then through clenched teeth said, "Cut it out, Tom. She's not <u>my</u> Miss Fleury...and I bet she's too busy for you."

Then Anne spoke up in an uncharacteristically wry tone: "Stop arguing, you two, I'm sure there's plenty of Miss Fleury to go around."

Just then there came a knock at the door to Tom's room. Anne opened it and brightened with surprise as the rest of the Bernard family, Evelyne, Charles, Marie, and Claire, entered. Claire carried a small vase of pretty flowers to adorn Tom's room. The parents hugged their son and Anne warmly, then talked quietly to Tom who was clearly touched by this unexpected visit. He knew that the Bernard family seldom traveled far from home and he seemed both pleased and honored by their appearance.

Then Mr. and Mrs. Wellington entered. After brief introductions and greetings, the Bernards said their goodbyes and left, wanting the Wellingtons to have some time alone with their son. As they walked down the drab hallway, Mrs. Wellington caught up with them and shook hands with Jack's parents, then hugged each of his sisters warmly. Her eyes glistened as she spoke to Charles and Evelyne: "This boy, I should say this young man," taking Jack's hand, "has done so much for our family...you'll never know how much he means to us."

The Bernards walked out of the hospital into the cool autumn air. They boarded a trolley right in front of the hospital and made their way home to Westfield, proud of their son and thankful that his best friend - and friendship - were on the mend.

CHAPTER 16

# Healing
*Winter 1914*

Throughout the several months of Tom's recuperation at home, Jack visited his friend after school and on weekends. He told vivid stories of ice fishing on Hampton Ponds with his father, of skating and sledding with his sisters, and of doing projects in his father's workshop. He read aloud stories from *Boys' Life*, *St. Nicholas Magazine,* and *The Youth's Companion*, and he brought Tom treats from the candy shop on Linden Street. The two boys talked endlessly about plans for adventures to come that summer.

Anne came home from Dorchester nearly every weekend during Tom's recovery, doting on her brother and reading to him. His literature class was studying *The Merchant of Venice* and his teacher had suggested that Tom keep up with the reading at home. Anne was only too happy to assist in this. She even coaxed the two boys to take parts in the reading of several scenes. "Tommy, you can be Antonio...Jack, you can be Antonio's best friend, Bassanio...and I shall be fair Portia, wealthy heiress and beloved of Bassanio. Won't this be fun?" enthused Anne as Tom and Jack exchanged dubious glances.

During Holyoke High School's winter vacation in February it happened that St. Agnes School was also closed because of Saint Valentine's Day, a Holy Day of Obligation. After attending Mass, Jack and his sisters rode the trolley to Holyoke, then walked up Beech Street to the Wellington home. By this time Tom was able to get about the house on crutches and was seated in the library when the three Bernard children arrived. Marie and Claire stood wide-eyed in the foyer, gazing at the grand home around them.

"Tommy?" whispered Jack, peeking into the library. Tom looked up and grinned at the sight of his best friend. "I brought some special guests to see you...I hope it's all right." Jack turned and gestured to Marie and Claire who were still gawking in the hall. Silently the girls entered the library. They stood close together, Claire clinging to her older sister's hand. "You remember Tommy? Tom, this is Marie and Claire," said Jack.

Tom smiled. "Well, look who's here. I haven't had two such pretty young ladies come to see me in a long while."

"They have some gifts for you, Tommy," said Jack. "Go ahead," he whispered to the girls. There was an awkward pause. Then Marie produced a prettily wrapped package and handed it to Tom. It contained a box of fine artist's paper.

"Thank you, Marie, that is very thoughtful of you," said Tom sincerely.

Claire immediately stepped forward holding out another package. "This is from me, Tommy," she said brightly. "Open it." It was a set of artist's pencils of many colors.

"Oh, Claire, these are swell. Thank you so much."

"Do you see? They go together. You can use the pencils to draw on the paper!" replied Claire, beaming at Tom.

"Why, I see what you mean, Claire. And that's just what I'll do. Thank you so much."

Just then Mrs. Wellington appeared, greeted Jack and Marie, and began talking with them in whispers. Meanwhile Claire had climbed onto the couch next to Tom and begun giving him instruction in the proper use of the colored pencils and paper. "Won't that be pretty?" she was asking Tom as she showed him how to blend red and brown. "You could draw a horse with a red mane, just like the Bousquets' horse, Thor. Do you know Thor? He's beautiful." Tom smiled. "Here, I'll start it for you and then you can finish it, okay?"

Jack, Marie, and Mrs. Wellington watched Claire's antics with amusement. "I dare say Tommy's in good hands now," said Mrs. Wellington with a grin. "I do believe Claire could teach him a thing or two!"

As Claire drew a mighty roan stallion, Tom looked up at Jack and Marie and smiled. "The doctor thinks I'll be able to go back to Dorchester in another month. I can't wait."

Soon it was time for the Bernards to be leaving. But Claire was still engrossed in her drawing. "I'll finish that, Claire," said Tom. "Thank you for starting it for me, though. You've been a great help."

"Well, Tommy, I'll try to come by again on Friday afternoon," promised Jack.

"Okay, Jack, thanks. Thank you, Marie, for visiting and for the paper. That was very kind of you."

"We are very glad you are feeling better," replied Marie softly with a shy smile.

"Say goodbye, Claire, we have to go," added Jack.

Claire climbed down from the couch, paused, then looked up at Tom. "You should be more careful driving your motorcar, Tommy. Don't do anything foolish, please." She turned, crossed the room, and took her sister's hand.

"I'll remember that, Claire, thank you."

Tom's return to the Dorchester School, he soon learned, would be with an unexpected wrinkle. At the insistence of his parents, he would be a "five-day boarder." On weeknights he would report to a proctored study hall. Bromley would pick him up every Friday afternoon and return him on Sunday evening. His mother would be his very attentive personal tutor at home. Tom's social life would suffer, but it was hoped that his academic progress would benefit a good deal from this new arrangement.

During her two week school break in March, Anne worked nearly every day as a volunteer at the Holyoke Women's Home. She served as receptionist at the front desk, greeting visitors, answering the telephone, and doing filing and organizing of the office for Mrs. Calavetti. Carolyn was in school throughout the two weeks, but most days after dismissal she walked the six or seven blocks to the Women's Home. For an hour or more each afternoon she and Anne amused some of the residents by playing Parcheesi and doing needlework projects with them in the Home's living room.

As the two girls walked up Essex Street on the last day of Anne's school break, Anne was thinking about the future. "What your mother does at the Home, Carolyn, it is wonderful. It must be very rewarding to help all those young girls who are trying to get themselves settled in Holyoke. I wish I could have a job like that someday." Carolyn nodded, smiling. The two girls stood on Cabot Street at the iron gate in front of the Wellingtons' home.

"And Clara's House...Mother tells me that would never have gotten off the ground without your mother's drive and determination. How does she do it, Carolyn, I mean...all the work she does...and all the energy she has...plus being a mom?"

Anne detected a hint of unease in her friend's face. "Carolyn, what's the matter? Did I say something wrong?"

"No, Anne...there's just something I should tell you about Mother... about me...something we don't talk about much. In fact I've never told anyone..."

"Dear Carolyn, what is it? You can confide in me. I would never betray your confidence."

Carolyn looked down at the sidewalk, then up at the sky, biting her lip. Finally she spoke. "It's about...my...my father."

While Anne had always wondered about Carolyn's father, she had never felt right about raising the subject. "Yes, Carolyn, what about him?"

"He was...well...he worked in one of the paper mills in Willimansett. My mother was working in the silk mill at the time...she was just sixteen. She met him through a mutual friend and was smitten with him. They courted for just a while when Mother learned that she was going to have a baby..." Carolyn paused, looked up at Anne and smiled. "Me." Then she turned and looked out across the city, her eyes glistening with tears.

"When she told him, he seemed very happy. They talked about getting married. But Mother had an uneasy feeling when he bid her goodbye that day. She feared he wasn't as happy as he claimed to be." Carolyn looked again into Anne's eyes, then her gaze dropped.

"What happened, Carolyn?" asked Anne softly.

Carolyn wiped a tear from her cheek; her voice was thin and tremulous. "He just vanished. Several months later Mother's friend told her he had moved to Lowell to work in the mills there. She never saw him again and never heard from him...neither have I."

Anne put her arm around her friend. "I can't imagine what that must be like, dear Carolyn, to wonder where your father is, what he is like, why he...I am so sorry." Carolyn took several deep breaths and seemed to recover her composure.

Anne spoke: "I have always admired your mother and the work she does. But I realize now that I am only beginning to appreciate what she has done for herself...and for you...and now for so many young girls in Holyoke. You must be very proud, Carolyn...very proud." Carolyn nodded and smiled briefly. Then her eyes fell to her feet once again. "How long have you known?" asked Anne softly.

"It was when Clara passed that mother decided she should tell me. It's taken me that long to get up the courage to tell you. I wanted you to know, I just didn't know how to tell you."

"Carolyn," said Anne, not sure she should say what was on her mind. There was a long silence before Carolyn lifted her eyes and looked into Anne's face. Anne was whispering: "Have you ever thought you might want to meet him?"

A look of doubt crossed Carolyn's face like a cloud before the sun. "I have thought of it, Anne, I have. But I'm not sure I want to...or should. I just don't know how Mother would feel. Do you see what I mean?" Anne nodded, took Carolyn's hands in hers, and kissed her on the forehead. The two girls who had been friends for nearly ten years were now joined by a bond tighter than ever before.

Jack visited the Wellingtons' home that Saturday, the day before both Anne and Tom would be returning to school. He and Anne walked through the glasshouse among the palms, palmettos, a mango, even a coffee tree. She told Jack about her work at the Women's Home.

"The girls who live there, the residents, so many of them have had such difficulties in their young lives. I guess it was Clara that convinced me of how wonderful that place is. And Mrs. Calavetti...she is truly a saint!" There was conviction in her voice. She paused, fingering a shining monstera leaf. Then she looked up into Jack's eyes. "I've been thinking maybe that's where I belong, after I finish school, I mean. Working at the Women's Home...or someplace like that."

"It sounds like a very good situation for you, Anne. They'd be lucky to have you," said Jack.

"I don't know, Jackie. Somehow I think I'd be the lucky one."

CHAPTER 17

# The Oxbow Incident
*July 1914*

The summer of 1914 found both Jack and Tom hard at work in the sorting room of Wellington Textiles. This was familiar territory for Jack as he had worked there for nearly eight months during the previous school year. He also had the advantage of several years working in the tobacco fields and on his family's farm and he had the strength and stamina to show for it. It was Tom's first introduction to hard work and it required a bit of an adjustment. He was still favoring his right leg and so was unable to do too much heavy lifting.

On a warm, sunny Friday afternoon in late July, as the two friends were walking home from work, they decided it was time for one more fishing expedition before the summer ended. But they had exhausted the fish in most of the nearby ponds, or so it seemed, and Tom had another idea, an outing to a place just a few miles up the valley from Holyoke known as the Oxbow.

The term "oxbow" aptly described a long, slender pond shaped like the curved brace around an oxen's neck. It was a former channel of the Connecticut River that had been partially cut off from the main flow during one of the great floods of the previous century. Across the narrow outlet where the south end of the Oxbow joined the river, a bridge had been constructed to carry the trolley tracks from Holyoke to Northampton.

By all accounts the Oxbow had some of the best fishing in the area. Besides the usual perch, pickerel, and pout found in most of the area's smaller ponds, the Oxbow occasionally yielded more interesting species like shad, salmon, and striped bass, denizens of the great river that happened to stray through the connecting channel. The prospect of catching one of these large, unusual creatures added considerable allure to a day of fishing on the Oxbow.

Tom and Jack set out early the next morning, boarding the trolley marked "Northampton" at Cabot Street. At the Highlands station their old friends Bill Peterson and Pete Buchanan climbed aboard, ensuring that fishing would most certainly not be the only entertainment on this day.

The foursome disembarked just before the Oxbow trestle. With rods and tackle boxes in hand and rucksacks on their backs, they descended by a well-worn path through the dense vegetation to a point just upstream from the bridge where they could gain easy access to the water. The channel was deep at that point, the water the color of well-steeped tea. Tall cottonwoods and silver maples grew along the sandy banks of the Oxbow. Small trees and shrubs grew below, in some places bending out toward the water from both sides of the narrow channel creating a tunnel-like effect.

The four friends angled all morning, landing the usual warm water fishes. But just as they were beginning to think that there was not much excitement to be had at the Oxbow on this day, Jack's line gave a hard pull and was drawn rapidly downstream toward the trolley trestle. Jack pulled hard on his pole, then began furiously reeling in his catch. What emerged from the water on the end of his line startled him and his fellow anglers. It was a fish nearly two feet long with a flattened body, a tapered snout, and a series of horny plates running down its back. It was a sturgeon, Bill explained, an ancient, primitive creature that lives part of its life at sea and comes up river to spawn each spring. The boys looked at it with awe as it lay on the sand, gasping for air. They examined it carefully, but as it didn't appear edible, they decided to return it to the water while there was still a chance that it could survive.

That event sparked more intense fishing by the foursome, but by early afternoon they, and the Oxbow itself, seemed pretty much fished out. The mid-day sun was intense, the August air heavy and humid. Sweat poured down the boys' faces as they sat in the sand eating their lunches.

"Hey, let's have a swim," suggested Tom. "Jack and I brought trunks; we can change in the woods." But Bill and Pete had not brought trunks and the four sat silently in the sand, gazing into the cool water.

"Well, boys," said Pete at last. "I don't know about you, but I gotta cool off." And with that he kicked off his shoes, pulled his jersey over his head, and stepped out of his trousers. Wearing only his underwear, he plunged into the dark waters and disappeared. After several seconds, his head popped out of the water in the middle of the channel.

"Come on, you cowards," he taunted the three boys sitting stunned on the beach, "the water's fine!" Bill rose, stripped down to his underpants, and dove in. Tom and Jack looked at one another sheepishly, then followed suit. Soon all four were in the water, shouting and splashing each other unmercifully. This went on for quite some time before they grew tired and climbed out onto the sandy shore, beads of water cascading down their backs and legs as they emerged. They stood in the sun for a few minutes drying off. While none of them was accustomed to being out-of-doors in the near-altogether, the dense forest and shoreline vegetation lent a feeling of privacy to this setting that allowed them to relax their Victorian standards of modesty.

Jack had just stepped into his trousers and begun to pull them up when Pete, who was sitting looking out on the water with a bit of mischief in his eye, suddenly stood up. "Wait, boys, before we go...we have to do the white swan dive," he said with urgency in his voice. And he stepped out of his underwear, turned, and disappeared up the path to the trolley tracks. In a moment he reappeared, some twenty feet above, standing entirely naked at the middle of the trestle, looking down at the deep waters of the Oxbow beneath him.

"This is an old Indian ritual, boys. Once you have dived like the swan, you are truly a man. So, who wants to be a man?" challenged Pete. And he dove from the trolley bridge into the deep water, an arc of bare flesh curving gracefully through the air, much like a swan that had lost its feathers! The others hooted and jeered, but each was weighing his own feelings about decency, modesty, and pride. Suddenly, as if of one mind, the three pulled off their underpants and dashed up the trail to the bridge. Pete, not wanting to miss a trick, was quickly out of the water and climbing the trail after them.

For one moment they stood, the four of them, proclaiming to one another and to the world that they were men, that they were brave, and that they were not bound by the prudish conventions of their times. Each hesitated, waiting for someone else to take the first swan dive.

Just then, from out of the tangle of vines and trees overhanging the narrow channel below, emerged a slender canoe. A mustached man dressed in a black suit and a bowler hat was seated stiffly in the stern, paddling. In front of him, in a long, flowing white dress, a woman sat on cushions that lined the bottom of the vessel. In front of her were two teen-aged girls wearing pretty lace dresses of peach and lime, each holding over her head a delicate parasol of matching color.

When the man looked up and saw the four naked figures on the trestle above, he began back-paddling furiously, apparently in an effort to turn the craft around. But the current was faster where the waters passed under the narrow bridge, and his efforts were in vain. The canoe slid inexorably toward the trestle and the four boys. Meanwhile the woman could be heard shouting: "Arthur, Arthur, do something, do something..."

The two girls at first were unaware of what was happening, their parasols blocking the scene above them. But as the canoe veered in response to their father's diversionary tactics, the view became all too clear, and each screamed and averted her eyes. The boys were equally mortified, and would have run for cover, but at that very moment a trolley came clacking up the tracks from the direction of Holyoke. To run off the bridge to the north would have separated them from their clothing, but the trolley was now blocking their only other earthbound route of escape.

Then, in perfect unison and without saying a word, the four boys leaped from the trestle into the water downstream from the bridge. The canoe sailed past them just as their heads popped out of the water, and they were suddenly face-to-face with the canoeists, their nakedness now thankfully well concealed by the dark waters. As the canoe slipped by, the man and woman pretended to be looking in the opposite direction as did one of the girls. But the girl in the bow had pivoted, discreetly placing her parasol between herself and her parents, apparently in an attempt to catch a furtive glance of the diving white swans.

Jack was closest to the canoe and looked upward at the very moment that the girl looked downward, and there was a brief moment of recognition. The naughty peeper was none other than Monique Fleury! She said nothing, and Jack, never one for quick repartee, was also silent. But he thought he detected the slightest little glint in her eye as they floated past. The canoe quickly entered the river beyond and was out of sight.

At supper that evening Mrs. Wellington asked the boys about the fishing expedition. "It was swell," said Jack. "I caught a sturgeon that was nearly two feet long!"

Then Tom added, "And there were four white swans in the Oxbow!"

"Ooh, how lovely," answered his mother. Jack shot Tom a warning look and quickly changed the subject. But Anne, seated across the table from the two boys, detected a mixture of devilishness and embarrassment that suggested there was an interesting story behind the white swans. After supper, she tried to probe the two for more information, but the boys had made an unspoken pact that neither Anne nor her parents should ever learn what really took place at the Oxbow that day.

# CHAPTER 18

# A Proposal
*August 1914*

Despite the hard work the boys did in the Wellington Textiles warehouse that summer, the weeks flew by. Tom, Jack, and Anne spent many evenings and weekends together, each dreading the inevitable separation that would come at the start of school.

On a Thursday evening in late August Mrs. Wellington called the Bernards' home where the installation of a telephone had only recently been accomplished. Jack's mother was surprised to hear the ring and even more surprised to find herself talking with Tom's mother. Mrs. Wellington asked if she could visit and Mrs. Bernard quickly agreed, though she was a bit unnerved by the prospect of serving tea to one of Holyoke's most prominent ladies. Jack was staying at the Wellingtons' that week and Mrs. Wellington informed neither him nor her children of her destination when she drove off in the family's touring car the next morning.

Mrs. Bernard greeted Mrs. Wellington warmly on the front lawn and invited her in. They sat in the parlor which had been specially primped for the occasion. Marie and Claire were visiting with the Bousquets next door.

"This is so very kind of you, Mrs. Bernard," began Mrs. Wellington, "you have a lovely home."

"Please, call me Evelyne," said Mrs. Bernard.

"Thank you, Evelyne, and please do call me Helen," replied Mrs. Wellington. "Our children are such fast friends, why should we not be as cordial?"

"I quite agree," responded Evelyne. After some polite conversation about the weather, the subject came back to the children. Helen took that as her opening.

"Your Jack is such a fine young man, Evelyne. You must be very proud of him. We feel very close to him, my husband and I, as do Tom and Anne. That is why I would like to ask you, or suggest to you and Mr. Bernard, that Jack attend the Dorchester School with Tom and Anne this year." She continued, "It would mean a lot to Tom if Jack would be his roommate. And I know your boy would find many opportunities at Dorchester that would not be...well many opportunities that he could take advantage of." She paused. "I know this probably comes as a complete surprise and a bit of a shock. That is why I wanted to sit down with you, mother to mother, and talk about it. If Jack were my son I would certainly not make a decision like this lightly."

Evelyne was astonished at the idea of a Bernard attending a prestigious school like Dorchester. "But," she began, "the expense..."

"Mr. Wellington and I would be fully prepared - actually delighted is a better word - to cover all of your son's expenses for tuition, room, board, travel, everything. It would be our pleasure," she explained.

"Mrs. Wellington - I mean Helen - I am overwhelmed by your kindness and honored that you think so highly of Jack. But naturally I would need to discuss this with my husband...and with Jack. I hope you will understand," she added.

"Of course, Evelyne, of course, there's time to think it over with Charles and with Jack, naturally," she agreed. The conversation lapsed momentarily.

Evelyne had one more thing she wished to say to Helen. She had been waiting for the right moment, and that moment seemed now to be upon her. "Helen, I want you to know how very, very sorry I was to learn from Jack about the loss of your oldest." Helen turned and looked out the window as Evelyne continued. "I understand he was a fine boy and much loved. It must cause you great pain."

Helen's lips were pursed tightly; she nodded. "To lose a child is...sometimes my grief is still..." began Helen, shaking her head. But she was unable to continue.

"Yes, yes, I know. Little Thérèse ...to watch her waste away was..."

Helen seemed to be thinking about this. Then she spoke softly: "I am sure you miss her dearly."

Evelyne nodded, then placed her hand on her chest. "Yes, I do, Helen, I do. It's been nearly eight years but I do miss her still..."

A long silence followed, neither woman able to speak. Finally Helen Wellington looked up at Evelyne, took a deep breath, and smiled. "Well, I must be on my way. Thank you so much for your hospitality."

Evelyne Bernard washed dishes in her kitchen, but she found herself greatly distracted as she thought over the unexpected proposal. Jack and Charles came home together on the trolley that evening as they often did on Fridays. The family ate supper together, then sat in the back yard watching as the August sun set in a blaze of glory. Soon Jack and the girls went off to bed and Charles and Evelyne were alone. Jack was fast asleep when his parents finally went to bed, their decision having been made.

The next morning Jack arose early and went outside to tend to the animals. A few minutes later both parents were standing in the barn door. "Jack," said his mother. "May we talk with you, dear?"

Jack was as stunned as had been his mother to hear of the Wellingtons' offer. It was so much to absorb, a new school, a new home, being with Tom, being with Anne, all the time, and being away from his family. His parents could see that he was having difficulty grasping all the implications. "But Mom, Dad, how could we ever afford for me to attend the Dorchester School? We're not rich like the Wellingtons." When they told him that the Wellingtons wanted to pay all his expenses, he gasped. He could find no words to speak at that moment and he stood there, looking off across the fields, smiling and shaking his head in disbelief. Finally, he looked his mother in the eye, then his father. "What do <u>you</u> think?" he asked.

Again there was a long pause before his mother said, carefully, "Jack, the question is, what do <u>you</u> think? We trust you to make this decision, dear, you and only you. If you say yes, we say yes, if you say no, then that's all we need to know."

He couldn't believe that his parents were willing to place this decision in his hands. It made him feel proud, on the one hand, and frightened on the other. It would have been easier if they had simply made the decision for him. "Think it over, Son," said Jack's father. "Take your time."

Jack looked at his parents, took a deep breath, then spoke: "I better get to the garden." And he headed off pushing a wheelbarrow with a rake and hoe. His parents stood side-by-side, arms around each other's waist, watching Jack walk away, trying to keep their pride and their emotions in check.

At lunchtime Jack came in from the fields. He and his sisters ate a luncheon their mother had prepared for them, then the girls went outside, leaving Jack and his mother alone in the kitchen. As they washed the dishes, Jack spoke. "Mom," he began, "Do you think Tom is 'broken'?"

Evelyne considered the question carefully. "Well, dear, I don't know him nearly as well as you do. What do you think?"

"I'm afraid...I'm afraid that Mr. and Mrs. Wellington...well, that they expect me to 'fix' Tom...to make him better, I mean." He paused, thinking. "I'm worried about that, d'you know what I mean?"

"Yes, dear, I do. No one knows Tom better than you, but to 'fix' him, that's a tall order for a sixteen-year-old boy...for anyone."

Tom thought about that, then nodded. "I just remember how he spoke to me last fall in the dormitory, after the Poet's Seat business. I don't want to ever feel like that again, ever. Maybe that's selfish of me," he added. Mother and son stood at the sink, wiping dishes, thinking about Jack's last words. "I really want to go to Dorchester, Mother, I really do. But I just don't know if I should," said Jack.

After another long pause Evelyne reached out, stroked her son's hair, and looked into his soft eyes. "How did you get so wise? You're my son, and I've known you since the day you were born, but I cannot for the life of me figure out how you got so wise."

Later that afternoon Jack lay in the grass beside the house in the shade, his lanky arms and legs sticking out at odd angles. He was reading a book on American history. His father sat down beside him, anxious to know what his son was thinking about the Wellingtons' proposal. "Have you made up your mind, Son?" asked Charles, who lacked his wife's infinite patience.

"I want to go to Dorchester, Dad, I really do. I could learn so much, and do so many things there. They have a stable and horses and there's an observatory where you can look at the stars. It would be swell," said Jack.

"So you've made up your mind, then," said Charles.

Jack went on, as if not hearing: "I just don't know if I would fit in there, Dad. It's so different, and the other students, not Tom and Anne but the others, they're different. Do you think I'd fit in?" he asked.

"That's a good question, Jack. But you know the place better than your mother and me..." He left it there and walked away.

Two more questions were still agitating Jack's mind, questions that he chose not to discuss with his parents. They had to do with Anne. He liked Anne a lot. He loved her company and her attention. There were times when he could think of nothing else. But how, he wondered, would he feel about being with her, or around her, all the time? And how would she feel about having him around so much? These were not matters that he cared to discuss with anyone else.

Just then Marie and Claire came around the corner of the house with the garden hose and sprinkled him liberally with cold water. He got up and chased them across the lawn, pretending to be angry. He lifted ten-year-old Claire over his head and spun her around to her screams of delight. At thirteen Marie was a little too old to be similarly manhandled.

"And as for you, young lady, I will have to consider an appropriate punishment," he said with a troll-like growl and leer. And he chased her several times around the yard until they both collapsed on the lawn in gales of laughter. Jack sat watching the two girls play with the hose and in that moment his decision was finalized. When he told his parents, they approved whole-heartedly. It was, after all, his decision to make.

Late Sunday afternoon Jack boarded the trolley for the ride back to Holyoke. He would be staying with the Wellingtons just one more week, but this evening his first task was speaking to Mrs. Wellington. When he arrived at their home, Tom greeted him and they sat on the lawn talking for a few minutes. Soon Tom's mother appeared with lemonade for the two boys and sat with them as they sipped it. When they were finished, she asked Tom to return the tray to the kitchen. That was Jack's cue.

"Mrs. Wellington," he began, "I'm very sorry, but I must decline your generous offer...about attending the Dorchester School, I mean. It is such a kind thing for you to do and I hope you won't be disappointed. It's my family, they need me, you know."

Mrs. Wellington understood too well how families needed one another and she was gracious in accepting his decision. Neither Mrs. Wellington nor Jack could imagine at that moment just how much Jack's family would need him in the coming months.

On the final evening of Jack's last week in Holyoke the Wellingtons held a special supper for him. He, Tom, and Anne celebrated the occasion by going to a silent movie at the Bijou Theatre on Main Street. Afterwards they walked up Hampshire Street together, Anne in the middle, one hand on Jack's right arm, the other on Tom's left arm. Since nothing had been said, Jack felt certain that neither had been in on the discussion about his attending the Dorchester School and he was not interested in bringing up the subject. "This is going to be a good school year," Jack said with genuine enthusiasm. "Grade eleven, Tom, imagine that, grade eleven!"

"Yeh," replied Tom, "Look out Dorchester School, here comes Tommy!" Both Tom and Anne would be full-time boarders again this year, so the times would be fewer when the three would be together, but all agreed that those times would be very, very jolly.

As they approached the house, Tom felt a little squeeze on his arm and suddenly remembered that he had some business to attend to inside. Anne and Jack lingered on the lawn, the lights of the city twinkling below.

"I really hoped you'd be joining us at Dorchester, Jack. It would be so nice to have my two favorite boys around all the time." Anne paused to give Jack a chance to adjust to this revelation.

"Does Tom...?" Jack started to ask, but Anne interrupted him by placing one finger to his lips, then shaking her head. "Good, I was afraid being at Dorchester might hurt our friendship," he added.

"Who knows what it might have done to the way two people feel about one another?" Anne replied. There was a long pause, then Anne added "Write every day?"

Jack nodded. "You first?" Anne nodded, took Jack's hand, and they stood on the grass, gazing up at the stars together.

Late that summer Charles and Jack began work on a one-story addition to the Bernard farmhouse that would include a guest bedroom and a bathroom. They dug the cellar hole adjacent to the original fieldstone foundation at the back of the house and fabricated forms using old boards pulled from a neighbor's dilapidated shed. They poured the concrete themselves using a portable mixer owned by one of Charles' co-workers. Then they began framing the new room and applying the sheathing and siding. The roof was completed by early October. Another family friend assisted with the plumbing and electrical wiring. In the old basement a coal-fired furnace was professionally installed, connected by a system of pipes to carry steam to radiators in every room in the house.

CHAPTER 19

# Reckoning
*October 1914*

That fall Jack joined the high school track team. The idea wasn't Jack's; it came from several classmates who thought he had the makings of a good long distance runner. The track coach was Mr. Donahue who was also Jack's chemistry teacher, and he was the one who actually approached Jack and urged him to join the team.

Jack tried out for several events before deciding that the mile run was his choice. Shorter runs were more like sprints that made few demands on the runner except to pour on everything he had from the starting gun. But the mile run, Jack concluded, was as much about strategy as sheer speed, and he liked that. Practices were after school on Mondays, Wednesdays, and Thursdays. Fridays were reserved for meets, the first of which would be held on the last Friday of September. Jack worked hard at practice and, per Coach Donahue's orders, he also ran at home on the weekends. By the day of the first meet, which would take place at Cathedral High School in Springfield, Jack felt he was ready. He didn't do very well, finishing dead last, and he was glad that no one from Holyoke was there to watch his disappointing performance.

The second meet was the following Friday in Holyoke and Jack was determined to do better. He had a special session with Coach Donahue, worked out intensively, and doubled up on his practice. At least, he told himself, he had to come in better than dead last before a home crowd. Jack surprised himself when he ran his fastest mile yet, finishing third, only a few seconds behind the second place finisher. Many of his classmates were cheering him on and he found that made a big difference in his energy level.

After the race Jack was resting on the sidelines watching some of the other events when a voice from behind took him by surprise: "Hello, Jack." He turned and found himself face-to-face with Monique Fleury. She appeared a bit different from the way he remembered her and she was smiling impishly as she spoke: "Nice to <u>see</u> you again. Great race - you've got good form!" Then she winked and walked away with a self-satisfied smile and a little swing in her step.

"She makes me uncomfortable," thought Jack.

The next meet was scheduled for the weekend that Tom and Anne would be home for the autumn holiday observed by the Dorchester School. Tom tried to interest Jack in visiting them in Greenfield again, but Jack was not comfortable with the idea and neither was Anne. They arranged that Jack would visit with the Wellingtons on Saturday and stay overnight, giving the three time to have some fun together.

Holyoke was the home team again for that Friday's track meet against the South Hadley High School team. Again Jack trained hard and it paid off. This time he finished second. The cheers from the bleachers showed him he had lots of friends in the crowd, but he had no idea exactly who was watching until moments after the end of the race. He was walking off a cramp, still dripping with sweat and panting deeply, when Monique was once again in front of him.

"Another great race, Jack. I never get tired of watching you run," she gushed, and again she stood a little too close for his comfort, resting one hand on his left arm.

"Hey, Jack," came a familiar voice from his right. It was Tom with Anne at his side.

"Oooh, hiiii," said Jack, momentarily confused, his eyes swinging from the Wellingtons on the right to Monique on the left, then back to the Wellingtons.

Still clinging to Jack's arm, Monique smiled at the two Wellingtons, and said, "Introduce me to your friends, Jackie."

Jack's face turned several shades of red as he struggled with the introductions: "Ohh, uh, well, Tom, I'd like...I mean Tom and Anne...I mean Anne, Tom, this is Monique, Monique Fleury."

"Pleased to meetchya," said Monique sassily. "Isn't Jackie something?"

Anne's voice was flat, her stare cold and expressionless: "Oh, he certainly is <u>something</u>."

To put the icing on the cake, Monique planted a kiss on Jack's cheek, added, "Keep up the good work, Jackie, I'll be seeing you!" and waltzed away. Anne stormed off and Jack started after her, saying that it was all a big misunderstanding. But his pleas went unheeded and he did not feel he could follow her off the field in his track uniform without drawing still more unneeded attention. He stopped and hung his head.

"Don't worry, Jack, I'll straighten everything out with Anne," Tom offered in a sincere tone. But the smirk on his face told Jack that Tom was enjoying this a little too much.

"No, Tom, I'll deal with this myself, tomorrow at your house...that is if I'm still welcome in your house," said Jack as he watched Anne stalk away.

Jack approached the front door of the Wellingtons' home the next morning with trepidation. He believed in his heart that he was totally innocent and merely a victim of circumstances, but he was not at all certain that he could convince Anne to see it that way. Tom answered the door, set Jack's rucksack inside, then ushered him out onto the front lawn.

"I've taken the liberty, Jack..." Tom began, at which words Jack's mood deteriorated still further and he glared at Tom. "Now Jack, hear me out, please. I'm on your side in this. I told her everything, everything, that's what had to be done...be totally honest. She was mad at first, but I think she's coming around. She said she would be willing to listen to what you had to say. So that's good, right?" Jack was not sure, not sure at all that Tom's efforts on his behalf were helpful.

At that moment Mrs. Wellington appeared and told the boys that luncheon was served. Tom and Jack entered the front door, walked the long, wide hallway together without a word, and entered the dining room. Anne was already seated and sipping her soup. She did not look up as Tom and Jack took their seats on either side of her. Barely a word was spoken through the meal. Mrs. Wellington could sense the tension in the air and she tried in vain to get some conversation going. After the meal was over, she spoke to her daughter: "Anne, dear, won't you play a piece for us? Wouldn't that be lovely, boys?"

Tom and Jack agreed and Anne rose without a word, went into the library, and took a seat at the piano. She played Beethoven's "Für Elise" with only a few small mistakes. When she had finished, the boys and Mrs. Wellington clapped enthusiastically. Anne rose, turned, and ran from the room in tears.

"Jack," said Mrs. Wellington, "Could you have a word with Anne for me? She seems to be upset and neither Tommy nor I have been of any help at all." Jack agreed and sat quietly in the library while Mrs. Wellington retrieved her daughter. Tom wisely made himself scarce. Soon Anne returned alone and stood by the long windows, looking out on the front lawn. Jack had rehearsed his words carefully in bed the previous evening and on the trolley ride that morning.

"Anne, I know why you are upset, and I owe you an apology. I should have told that girl to stop bothering me once and for all. She just keeps hanging around and talking to me. I never gave her the slightest encouragement, you have to believe me. Won't you forgive me? There's only one girl for me."

There was a pause, Anne whimpered, then said, "Seems I've heard that line before."

"It's not a line, Anne, it's the truth...so help me God." Anne's sniffling stopped and she turned slightly as if she was finally willing to hear Jack's apology. But Jack sensed she needed a little more convincing. If only he had shown some of his mother's patience at this point, things might have turned out differently. "And that business at the Oxbow, that was nothing, just an embarrassing coincidence," added Jack.

Anne looked up at him, her face the very picture of innocence. "And what exactly did happen at the Oxbow?" asked Anne. Tom had mentioned nothing about the Oxbow and Anne sensed an opportunity to be let in on the events of that day.

"It was just a fluke," said Jack. "We were...fishing...and Monique and her family came paddling by in a canoe. That's all. But she made it into some big thing and now she acts like we're old friends because of it."

"I see," said Anne. "So that's everything, Jack, the whole truth and nothing but the truth?" Jack could tell that Anne was probing him for more information, but he had no idea how much of the humiliation at the Oxbow Tom had blurted out to his sister. He was pretty certain that Tom would not have told Anne about the "diving white swans." He couldn't imagine telling his sister about something like that.

"Yes, Anne, I swear it," said Jack. "Why, did Tom try to tell you a lot of ridiculous things? That boy has too much imagination for his own good," said Jack, trying to think of all the possible angles and with each moment getting himself in deeper and deeper.

Anne thought for a moment, then spoke. "Well, Jack, I'm inclined to accept your word and forgive you." Jack relaxed and smiled adoringly at Anne, but she was not finished. "Before I do, however, I am going to ask that you remain here while I have a few words with my brother in the other room."

This whole conversation, Jack began to realize, was going very badly. Anne was much too clever for the two of them and she would most certainly now get Tom to reveal the whole truth about the events at the Oxbow, leading him to think that Jack had confessed and she was only trying to get Tom to admit to lying. And who could tell how Tom might react under those circumstances and what further damage might be done?

With his pain exceeded only by unbearable mortification, Jack recounted to Anne in detail the events at the Oxbow, "diving white swans" and all. Anne sat patiently and listened to Jack's confession. As he spoke her expression changed from anger to surprise, then horror and embarrassment. But finally she began to laugh uncontrollably. Jack relaxed and began laughing, too.

Suddenly, Anne ceased laughing and wagged her finger at Jack. "You are going to pay for this, young man, believe me," she warned with wrinkled brow. She feigned throttling Jack with both hands, then hugged him. "What are we going to do with the two of you?"

CHAPTER 20

# Waiting
*February 1915*

The winter of 1915 was exceptionally long and cold in New England. Snowstorms were frequent and roads often impassable for days at a time. With Jack at school and Charles back at Wellington Textiles full-time, many of the household chores fell on Evelyne's shoulders. The Bernards still did not own an automobile and she had to walk nearly half a mile to the nearest grocery store or take the trolley into downtown Westfield to shop. The trolley line was often delayed due to snow and ice on the tracks and waiting exposed to the elements on Southampton Road was very difficult for her, especially with bags of groceries in her arms.

Both Jack and Charles tried their best to keep up with the chores in the barn, rising before dawn or working late into the evening. And the new heating system made the house more comfortable. Nevertheless, the rigors of the winter began to take their toll on Evelyne's health. In mid-January she had a hacking, persistent cough. Dr. Gibson prescribed a patent medicine that seemed to be of little benefit. Evelyne's skin looked wan, her face drawn with fatigue. She would rise to make breakfast, barely able to keep herself upright at the stove, then retreat to her bed after Charles and the children had left. Madeleine Bousquet checked in on her daily and helped with some errands, but her health was none too good that winter either.

One February night Evelyne's condition suddenly deteriorated. She developed a fever and was sweating profusely. She felt weak and was repeatedly nauseated.

Charles stayed home from work the next morning awaiting the doctor's arrival. Jack wanted to stay and help as needed but his father assured him that all would be well and sent him off to school.

That afternoon Jack returned to find Charles waiting for him in the parlor. Evelyne had been taken by ambulance to Noble Hospital. They had diagnosed her condition as influenza and this was very, very bad news. As Jack knew, there was no treatment for the disease; all that could be done was treat the symptoms, wait, and hope the patient survived until the infection passed.

Jack was stunned by the gravity of his mother's condition. He had heard of the dangers of influenza but had no idea that it could strike so suddenly and become so serious so quickly. He pleaded with his father to allow him to visit his mother in the hospital, but Charles insisted that Jack remain at home with his sisters, make supper for them, do the evening chores, and see them to bed. Jack agreed.

Jack knew well how to read his father's moods. Charles was not one to speak about his feelings. But Jack could tell by his father's actions when he was upset. This man who was normally a hard worker would have difficulty completing even simple tasks and would wander from one chore to another. On this day Jack's father's actions spoke more clearly than words: his mother might not survive the influenza.

Jack tried gamely to keep his sisters from worrying, assuring them that their mother's illness was nothing more than a bad cold, that she would likely be coming home in the next day or two, and that she would soon be good as new. But after they were asleep, he sat in the parlor by the telephone, his eyes pivoting regularly from his history book, to the clock on the mantle, then back to his book. His head, neck, arms, and legs ached from the worry and fear in his heart as he witnessed his mother's fight for her life.

Late in the evening Charles returned. He reported that Evelyne's condition had stabilized and the doctor felt she had passed the worst. Jack listened carefully to his father's words, but more importantly watched his actions. His father was more relaxed and Jack took that as confirmation of the improved prognosis.

As Jack prepared for bed the enormity of what had happened swept over him and he began to shake uncontrollably, the fears and anxieties of the last day finally manifesting themselves. He donned a coat, boots, and hat and went to the barn, ostensibly to check the animals, but it was really an effort to regain his composure. Watching Angélique and the sheep placidly chewing hay and hearing the chickens clucking contentedly gave him a feeling of normalcy and well-being that his tired body and aching heart needed badly.

Evelyne did return home two days later looking thin and frail but smiling. Her daughters hugged her almost too vigorously. Jack took her hand and kissed her lightly on the cheek. "Welcome home, Mom," he spoke softly. "We missed you."

His wife's illness took its toll on Charles as well. His back injury of the previous year had slowed him down. He often walked with a cane, slightly stooped. But Jack could see a decline in his father's vigor after Evelyne's ordeal and it worried him.

In his frequent letters Jack kept Anne informed about his mother's illness. He tried not to worry her but Anne was worried, nevertheless, and called him from school almost daily when her condition became serious. Jack called Anne the day that his mother came home from the hospital, anxious to reassure her. At that time he mentioned to Anne his concerns about his father's health.

Several days later Mrs. Wellington phoned the Bernard household and spoke to Evelyne. "We are all so concerned for you, Evelyne, and wish there was something we could do to help. Anne will be coming home for a two-week school vacation on Friday. She would like very much to be able to assist you in any way she can. How would you feel about having her come and stay with your family for a few days, just to help while you are recuperating? She's willing to do cooking, cleaning, shopping, tending to your daughters, whatever you would like. Please say yes, it would mean a great deal to Anne and to our entire family if she could help you."

Evelyne was touched by this generous offer and she would have agreed right then and there but for one reservation. "You are so kind to offer Anne's services. I certainly could use some help around here. But may I call you back tomorrow?"

The source of Evelyne's concern was Charles. She simply was not sure how he would feel about having Anne around and, more to the point, of accepting this sort of charity from the Wellingtons. Her concerns were well-founded. "I don't know, dear. Anne is a lovely girl and I know that Jack is fond of her, but she's just a girl. Will she be of much help? I'm not sure. Besides, we're not in such a bad way; we have Marie and of course Madeleine Bousquet is always willing to help in any way she can. Maybe we should say no."

Evelyne was about to call Helen Wellington and decline Anne's offer when the telephone rang. Pierre Bousquet, their next door neighbor, was calling to say that Madeleine was not feeling well and would be unable to help Evelyne for at least a few days. Evelyne was concerned about how she was going to get her housework done without Madeleine's help, and also feeling a bit guilty that they had relied too much on Madeleine's good heart of late. She was lying in bed that evening when Charles came in from the barn.

"Pierre called, Charles. Madeleine is ill and won't be able to help us for a while." She paused and for the first time admitted to Charles, and perhaps to herself, that the situation was serious. "Perhaps we could take up Anne Wellington on her offer, just for a few days."

Two days later, on a Friday evening, one of the Wellingtons' motorcars turned into the Bernards' driveway. Bromley escorted Anne to the front door carrying a small valise. Jack greeted them at the door with a broad smile and carried her valise into the guest bedroom. Charles thanked her for offering to help out and asked her to sit by the fire in the parlor while he made her some tea. Anne thanked him but declined.

"Mr. Bernard, I'm not here to make extra work for you. You just sit there and let me make tea for you, how about that?" Charles refused several times, but Anne insisted politely, and he finally agreed. Her kind ministrations already seemed to be having an effect as Charles sat quietly sipping his tea by the fire while Anne busied herself in the kitchen. With Jack's help she planned breakfast, then drew water for a hot water bottle for Evelyne. Finally she visited with Marie and Claire in their bedroom and much laughter could be heard as Jack and his father sat by the fire. It pleased Jack to watch his father fall asleep in the chair by the fire for the first time in a long time.

Anne was the first one awake and about in the Bernard household the next morning. She made coffee, gathered eggs in the henhouse, baked a loaf of bread, set the breakfast table, and cleaned the hearth in the parlor, all before anyone else had stirred. For a young lady who had grown up in one of the largest homes in Holyoke staffed with all manner of household servants, she was surprisingly well versed in the domestic arts and more than willing to practice them for this family.

Charles and Jack were amazed when they came downstairs to see all that Anne had done already. They had a hearty breakfast of buckwheat cakes and sausage before heading to the barn to tend to the animals. Sometime after seven Anne tapped lightly on Evelyne's bedroom door, then entered carrying a tray with hot oatmeal, fresh bread and jam as recommended by Jack. Evelyne was surprised but very pleased by Anne's attentiveness and a little embarrassed as well. But Anne made it clear from the start that she wanted to help in every way possible. And she also wisely and diplomatically asked Evelyne to tell her if she overstayed her welcome or stepped on anyone's toes.

Even if Evelyne had wanted to decline any of Anne's kindnesses, she was too weak and frail to do so and readily permitted Anne to fill her shoes. She accepted Anne's help getting dressed. "Thank you, Anne, you've been a great help and I want you to know how grateful I am."

Anne smiled, nodded, and started to leave the room. "Jack thinks the world of you, I hope you know. He's very fond of you."

"He's a wonderful boy, Mrs. Bernard."

"He is, isn't he? Sometimes I just don't know how he turned out so well! His father and I are very proud of him, very proud indeed," her eyes reddening as she spoke. Minutes later Anne was back in the kitchen preparing to serve Marie and Claire their breakfasts.

CHAPTER 21

# Parting
*March 1915*

B y late March spring was beginning to break through in Westfield. During his week-long school vacation, Jack borrowed a neighbor's tractor and manure spreader and dressed the gardens that had just been released from nearly five months of snow cover. He and Charles began plans for planting that included starting tomatoes, lettuce, and peas in cold frames on the south side of the barn.

Evelyne's condition had improved somewhat. She could do most of the cooking, cleaning, and mending. She had to enlist the assistance of Charles, Jack, Marie, and Claire when it came to laundry and heavier cleaning chores. But the rigors of the winter had clearly left their marks on her face, Jack noticed. Her usually china-smooth skin was rough, dry, and splotchy, and there were deep, dark wrinkles around her eyes.

On the evening before Jack was to return to school, he heard a loud crash in the kitchen. His mother had collapsed, dropping a piece of crockery as she fell. Jack picked her up and carried her to the couch where she lay, still unconscious. He ran to the barn for his father. She soon revived, but her color was gone and she was confused. She felt hot and was dripping with perspiration. Jack went next door to get Pierre Bousquet. They carried Evelyne to Pierre's car and Charles held her in his arms as they drove off to the hospital at breakneck speed.

The diagnosis was pneumonia, likely due to a relapse of influenza, and the chances of recovery were not good. The doctor gently instructed Charles to prepare for the worst.

Charles called Jack and reassured him that his mother's condition was stable, but Jack was worried.

The next afternoon the ambulance pulled into the driveway. Two attendants wheeled Evelyne on a gurney through the front door and up the narrow stairway, then deposited her in her bed. Again Charles tried to reassure his son that things were not dire. He did not reveal to him that Father Lévesque had visited Evelyne in the hospital and administered extreme unction, the last rites of the Catholic Church. But Jack could tell by his father's actions that his mother was dying.

Charles sat alone at his wife's bedside for nearly an hour while Jack waited downstairs. When the waiting became unbearable, he went to the barn and gave the animals an unnecessary extra feeding. At last Charles appeared at the barn door. Every last glimmer of hope was gone from his face and his voice as he spoke to his son: "Mother would like to see you, Son."

Jack climbed the stairs, tapped lightly on the bedroom door, then entered. His mother lay on her back, the covers up under her chin. All that was visible was her head, her skin white as milk, eyes sunken and dim. Her lips trembled and she spoke in a barely audible whisper:

"Jackie, *mon petit*." She smiled and her eyes lit up briefly. "What a fine young man you have become. You've made your father and me very proud. You know that, eh? Very proud. Your schoolwork, are you keeping up with your schoolwork, honey?"

"Yes, Mom, don't worry. I'm studying all the time."

"Good, I know, you're a good boy, you're always working, always studying. A good boy. You've made us so proud. And you're running, you're still running?"

"Not too much in the winter, Mom, but we begin again in just a few weeks."

"Good, that's good for you. How is Anne? Is she well?"

"Yes, Mom, she's very well. She'll be home next weekend and she, Tom, and I are planning to spend some time together."

"She's such a fine young lady, Jack. You like her, don't you?"

"Yes, Mom, I do," whispered Jack, barely keeping his emotions under control. "I like her because she is so much like you."

"Be sure to tell her how you feel, dear, promise me? Love is too precious…and life is too short…to put it off." Evelyne closed her eyes. Her breathing was barely audible and Jack was suddenly worried. But then she opened her eyes, looked directly into Jack's eyes, and spoke softly. "On the dresser…there's a little box…" Jack reached for the box and held it in his hand.

"Open it, Jackie." Jack lifted the top and gazed upon a delicate gold ring with a sparkling green stone. "It's an emerald. It was my mémère's. I want you to have it, honey. It will remind you of me…maybe someday you'll give it to…someone special…"

Jack looked intently at the intricate ring with a small, luminous green stone that glittered in the lamplight. "Thank you, Mom, it's beautiful."

Evelyne managed a weak smile, looked into Jack's eyes, then said. "You'd better get some sleep now, dear."

"Okay, Mom, good night." He kissed her gently on the forehead. When he stood up and looked down on her again her eyes were closed and she seemed to be asleep. He gazed up at the needlepoint sampler on the wall above her bed:

*L'œuvre d'Evelyne Marie St. Onge,*
*née à Sherbrooke, Québec,*
*dans l'année de notre Seigneur 1868.*

All that night Jack sat by the fireplace in the parlor, sleeping fitfully for a few minutes at a time. Periodically he climbed the stairs and looked in on his father who was seated at Evelyne's bedside. He brought him a cup of tea around one o'clock. The first glimmers of dawn were just appearing in the eastern sky when Jack rose and went to the kitchen. He made some oatmeal and was just preparing coffee for his father when Charles appeared in the kitchen.

"I'm sorry, Son. Your mother...has passed." He approached Jack, took his hand, and led him up the stairs to the bedroom. They looked down at Evelyne's face. What little color she had had the previous evening was gone and her pale skin appeared stiffened and gray. Her arms lay on top of the covers, rosary beads in her right hand. Both Bernards knelt by the bed in silent prayer. "Why don't you take a few minutes to say goodbye, Son?" suggested his father.

Jack remained kneeling, motionless until his father was gone. He raised his head and looked on his mother's face. He held her cold hand, kissed it gently, then sniffled. Finally, he stood. "Goodbye, Mom," he whispered. And he turned and left the room. Charles had awakened Marie and told her of Evelyne's passing. The two waited for Claire to awake, then spoke to her.

Jack came down the stairs, went straight to the barn, and again tended to the animals. "The Peaceable Kingdom," he thought, remembering a familiar Bible verse and the famous painting of the same name introduced to him by Anne. He needed more bedding for the sheep and he climbed into the loft where the bales of hay were stacked. He tried to open the hatch in the floor that would allow him to drop hay directly into the sheep stall. The hatch wouldn't budge and he pulled harder and harder, feeling frustrated and exhausted by lack of sleep. Suddenly the crude wooden handle broke off in his hand. Jack held it in his hand, looking at it with annoyance, then threw it with all his strength against the floor. He stood staring at the broken handle, then fell to his knees in the hay and began to sob quietly.

Just then he heard Marie's frail voice from below: "Jackie, Daddy wants to talk to us in the house." Jack quickly composed himself, wiped his eyes, and tossed several hay bales ahead of him before climbing down the ladder.

Father Lévesque arrived at mid-morning and spoke at length with Charles in the parlor. Soon after the priest left, the funeral home attendants arrived and removed Evelyne on a gurney, her body covered with a long white sheet. A wake would be held the next day at the funeral home; the funeral Mass would be said the day after at St. Agnes Church. Charles explained all of this to Jack and Marie in a matter-of-fact tone.

Charles also informed his children that their Aunt Yvette, Evelyne's sister, would be arriving soon and would be helping them all for a few days. Yvette Brousseau was several years older than her sister. She had married Raoul Brousseau in Sherbrooke, Québec, in 1895, and the newlyweds had emigrated to Southbridge, about forty miles east of Westfield, where Raoul was employed in a large factory. Early in their marriage he proved himself unreliable. Divorce was not a consideration in those days and the two simply parted, still married. When Jack asked his mother about his Uncle Raoul, Evelyne would talk vaguely about his work and how he was transferred. Once she used the term "unfaithful" in his regard and Jack wasn't sure until years later what that might suggest.

Yvette was short with graying hair and many wrinkles for her age. She was clearly an unhappy woman who seldom found anything in life to smile about. She showed little pleasure in visiting her sister, even in good times, and the children endured her visits quietly, trying to stay out of her way. But she wanted to be of some assistance and Charles needed help, so she took the train to Springfield, then the trolley to Westfield where Charles met her in the family's newly-acquired but dilapidated Model-T Ford. He carried two large valises into the guest bedroom and Yvette got settled.

She spoke curtly to each of the children before busying herself in the kitchen preparing the evening meal.

After Charles said grace, the family and Yvette sat silently eating their supper. In the evening she instructed Charles and the children to lay out their best clothes on their beds for her to inspect. She shook her head in disapproval at the condition of some of their garments, slurred *mon Dieu* under her breath, then sputtered about having to do some laundry and ironing early the next morning. Almost immediately neighbors and friends began delivering food to the Bernards' front door. Yvette accepted the gifts on behalf of the family but gave no encouragement to anyone to come in and offer their condolences.

Shortly after nine o'clock the next morning a shiny black limousine pulled into the driveway. The Bernards and Yvette were escorted to the vehicle by four men in black suits. At the funeral home the five were led into a long room. Rows of chairs faced a varnished, wooden coffin, the lid open. Many large, elaborate floral arrangements had been placed on either side of the coffin, each with a carefully printed card.

Charles took his daughters in hand and led them before the open coffin; Jack and Yvette followed. They all knelt, crossed themselves, and prayed silently. Jack prayed briefly, then raised his head and looked on his mother's face which by now was gray and waxen, her hair uncharacteristically stiff and shiny.

The guests had not yet begun to arrive. Jack stood up slowly, his hands folded in front of him, and walked from one bouquet to another, reading the cards and looking at the flowers. One arrangement, not the largest, was particularly beautiful, a bouquet of pink and white carnations, his mother's favorite flower and colors. The card read, "With love, Helen, Thomas, Tom, and Anne Wellington."

Jack stood looking at the card for several minutes. He recognized Anne's meticulous handwriting. For a moment he was transported to the Wellingtons' home, Tom waving to him from the front door as he arrived for his first visit, Mrs. Wellington seated by a crackling fire and smiling at him, Anne presenting him with the silver watch.

"Jack," a familiar voice from close behind him said softly. He turned and looked up and into Anne's face, the face he could not ignore. He smiled and she hugged him for a long time. Jack couldn't speak, but simply nodded as she spoke: "I'm so sorry, Jackie, so sorry. I came home from school as soon as I heard. I would have called but I wanted to see you, to hold you."

She paused a long time, not sure whether Jack was trying to speak. Finally she went on. "Your mother was such a wonderful lady, Jack. She was so patient. That's what I remember most was how she listened to you, and to me, and to everyone. And she was so proud of you. She told me, you know."

Many guests were now arriving. "We'll all be at the church tomorrow, Jack. I'll see you then, okay?" Jack nodded, looked briefly into her eyes as if to say, "Thank you," but turned without speaking and stepped into line next to his father. Anne spoke briefly to Jack's sisters and father before leaving.

After four hours of heartfelt condolences and kind words, the Bernard family returned home physically and emotionally drained. They spent the remainder of that day in prayer or deep in thought. Yvette served a good meal that evening, much of which went untouched. She reminded them that they needed to keep up their strength for the funeral the following day.

The Funeral Mass began at eleven o'clock the next morning. As the pipe organ played mournfully, the Bernard family walked up the center aisle surrounded by friends. Jack held Marie's hand, his eyes trained on the carpet ahead of him. The Wellington family sat in a pew on the right side of the church, Anne closest to the aisle, then Mrs. Wellington, Mr. Wellington, and Tom. As Jack approached their pew, Anne stared intently at him and he must have sensed it. He looked up briefly, their eyes met for just a fleeting moment, then his gaze dropped again to the carpet.

After the Mass, the family left the church first. They walked to the cemetery next to the church, the congregation following, until they were all gathered in a large semicircle around the open grave. The Wellingtons stood together at one end of the circle. Anne could see Mr. Bernard and his daughters but she could not see Jack. Her eye scanned the congregation intensely for several minutes. Finally she looked past the mourners to the street beyond and saw Jack walking away, apparently headed back to the Bernards' house about a half-mile away.

Jack arrived home several minutes before the rest of the family to find an unfamiliar automobile parked in front of the house. In the kitchen he was astonished to meet Bromley and Marguerita, the Wellingtons' maid. They had carried in baskets and bundles of food, enough to feed a sizable crowd, and were arranging things carefully in the tiny kitchen. Jack thanked them, then exited by the kitchen door into the back yard. The lawn was wet and muddy in places, but he waded through in his best shoes, unaware.

He stood on the edge of the vegetable garden, looking out at the freshly turned earth, smelling the sweet fragrance of manure that he had spread just a week earlier. He remained there, motionless, for many minutes.

"Jack," called Anne from the corner of the barn. He looked up but did not respond as she walked slowly toward him, his face an expressionless mask. "Jack," she repeated when she was a few steps away. She took his hand, stroked his arm, and waited.

After several minutes, Jack spoke in a low, steady tone: "Anne, please don't take this the wrong way. But I think I have to do this myself right now. You understand, don't you?"

"Of course," replied Anne. But she stood fast and maintained her composure. "Jack, I'll go along, but before I go, may I just say one thing?" Jack stood motionless, his head down, then nodded slightly.

"I know how you're feeling right now. Your heart is breaking. You're a young man with lots of new responsibilities suddenly thrust upon you. You have to be strong, for your father, your sisters, for yourself. I understand that." Her voice became thin and tremulous as she continued. "But, Jackie, I have two men in my family who felt like you do when Matthew died. They had to be strong, they had to carry on, they wanted to be rocks for Mother and me...but they turned to stone, Jackie, to <u>stone</u>."

Anne's voice quavered, she paused, then continued. "Father got himself all wrapped up in his work, started leaving the house earlier and earlier in the morning, coming home later and later in the evening. And Tommy... you know Tommy." Jack nodded. "You know what he does, how he acts all the time. That's exactly what it is, an <u>act</u>, because he can't tell anyone, not even himself, how he really feels. Tommy and Father are paying a terrible price for refusing to admit that they're not always the strong ones. And we're all suffering because of it, the whole family."

Anne paused again, then held Jack's hand in hers and looked up into his eyes. "Don't try to pretend, Jack, don't fight it. For your family's sake, for the sake of everyone who knows you...and loves you..." She paused, then said very softly: "For me, Jackie, I'm begging you, you don't have to be strong...."

With those words Anne turned to walk away, but she felt Jack's hand on her arm. She turned back and looked up at him, not sure how he would react to her outburst. For the first time since his mother's death, Jack looked squarely into Anne's eyes. Then his face contorted, his breathing became labored, tears streamed down his face, and he started to cry. He clung to Anne, his chest heaving. His legs were weak and he put his weight on Anne's slight form, but she was determined to support him.

After several minutes Jack regained his composure, stood up, and looked again at the fields on both sides. Just then his father appeared around the corner of the barn. Jack tried to turn away to hide his tears. Seeing Anne with Jack, Charles turned and walked back toward the farmhouse. "Don't stop, Jack, just keep it up as long as you have to," said Anne.

With that Jack began to talk through his tears. "When I was a kid and fell off my bike or scraped my knee, Dad would tell me not to cry. But Mom..." his voice cracked, "she would just let me cry as long as I needed to. So I always went to her when I was hurting." He paused briefly. "That time when Tommy was so mad at me, I told Mom about it and she hugged me while I cried. I felt foolish, a fourteen year old boy crying on his mother's shoulder, but I was afraid I'd lost my best friend...and I was afraid I'd lost you." He cried softly, then continued. "I wanted to say goodbye today, at the cemetery, but I couldn't, not in front of all those people. I'm sorry, Anne, I should have stayed, but I couldn't."

Anne thought for a few moments, then spoke. "How about if you and I go back to the cemetery so you can say goodbye in private, how about that?" Jack nodded and Anne walked him toward the house, her arm around his waist. When they reached the side yard, she asked him to wait a moment. She entered by the kitchen door, but shortly reappeared with two carnations, one pink and one white, from one of the arrangements in the parlor.

They climbed into the Wellington motorcar and Bromley drove them slowly back to the cemetery. They stepped out of the vehicle and walked together toward the freshly covered grave. A short distance away Anne handed the pink carnation to Jack. "You go ahead, I'll wait here." Jack shook his head and gently led her, at his side, to the grave. He stooped and placed the pink carnation on the grass in front of the grave, then Anne did the same with the white flower. They stood side by side as Jack crossed himself, said the Our Father, then spoke softly to his mother.

"Mom, I'm sorry I didn't come with the others, I didn't have the strength." He paused. "But Anne gave me the strength to come back and say goodbye. You always listened, Mom, and never pushed me, and never stopped showing me how much you loved me. That's a lesson I will never forget. Goodbye, Mom, I love you." The two stood in silence before the grave for a long time, then turned and walked slowly back to the waiting motorcar.

Back at the house Yvette was coming out of the front door just as Anne and Jack arrived. Charles followed carrying her two large valises. Each of the children stood and thanked her, kissed her on the cheek, and said their goodbyes as she climbed into Pierre Bousquet's automobile for the ride to the train station.

Marie and Claire were playing hopscotch in the driveway. After watching them for a few minutes, Anne joined the game, much to the delight of the sisters. Charles stood on the porch watching Anne and his daughters, then turned and spoke to Jack for several minutes. Finally, Anne returned to Jack's side. "Well, Bromley's waiting and I should be going along. If there's anything I can do…"

Jack interrupted her. "Dad asked me to ask you…if it's all right with you…and your parents…would you please stay, just for tonight and tomorrow? For Marie and Claire…and for me, too," he added with a slight smile. "You could stay in Aunt Yvette's…I mean the guest room. And you could borrow one of Marie's nightgowns," he added with a blush.

Anne stepped to the curb, opened the trunk of the waiting automobile, and lifted out a small traveling suitcase. "That won't be necessary," she replied with a smile, "I brought my own." The two stood on the front lawn watching Bromley and Marguerita drive away, then entered the house. Charles greeted Anne with his first smile in two days.

As it turned out Anne stayed with the Bernards for three days, helping with meals, doing some housework, and providing whatever assistance and cheer she could to the household. On Friday she accompanied Marie and Claire as they went back to St. Agnes School for the first time, hugging them both and waving to them as they joined their schoolmates on the playground before the bell rang.

Jack accompanied Anne on the trolley back to Holyoke later that morning and carried her valise as they walked the several blocks from the trolley stop to the Wellingtons' home. Anne invited him in but Jack declined. Standing on the front step, he thanked her again and again for taking time away from school to be with his family. "It meant a lot to all of us, Anne, I hope you know," he added.

"There isn't any place I would have preferred to be, Jackie. Don't mention it." Then she paused, looking into his eyes. She saw a tear form on his cheek that he quickly wiped away. She took his arm and stroked it gently. "It takes time, Jackie, lots of time. Don't try to rush it, okay?" Jack nodded.

CHAPTER 22

# Celebration
*June 1915*

It was the first week of June and the Wellington household
bustled with preparations for Thomas and Helen's twenty-
fifth wedding anniversary. In anticipation of the event the wall
between the formal parlor and the hallway had been removed
and replaced with six marble pillars. Graceful wood-paneled
arches spanned the intervals between the pillars. The result
was a long, magnificent space that but for the pillars
approached the scale of a small ballroom. Potted palms and
large ferns were placed along the long side of the room. Two
enormous brass chandeliers hung above the largest space, the
formal parlor; four smaller chandeliers illuminated the other
side of the room that was formerly the hallway. Adjoining one
end of the new room was an expanded glasshouse where Mrs.
Wellington and the gardeners had developed and exquisitely
displayed a colorful collection of orchids, bromeliads, and
other exotic tropical plants. The glasshouse opened by tall
doors onto the front lawn. The overall effect of this grand new
space was a clever combination of spaciousness and intimacy.

A temporary platform at one end of the grand parlor had
been constructed to accommodate a small orchestra. Long
tables along the inside wall would hold a sumptuous
collection of canapés arranged around decorative centerpieces
of cornucopias and elaborate pyramids of fruits interspersed
with orchids in glorious bloom.

Every family member had a busy schedule that week.
Mrs. Wellington and Anne traveled downtown on Tuesday
afternoon for coiffures at the city's finest salon. On

Wednesday morning they met at home with Helen's seamstress for final adjustments to their dresses. Mrs. Wellington had chosen a deep burgundy dress of fine silk that hung straight from the shoulders to just above the shoes. Across the front were rows of horizontal pleats of the same fabric. An overjacket of a lighter burgundy silk was closed at the waist with a drawstring. It was decorated with deep burgundy brocade in a vine pattern on each side of the front and along the tapered hem. A large, wide-brimmed hat of matching color was accentuated with a long, white plume.

Anne's dress of pale green velvet hung from her shoulders to her ankles. It was gathered at the waist by a wide, darker green velvet band. The neckline was a matter of extended discussion between Anne, her mother, and the seamstress. The result was a compromise, higher in the front than Anne wished but dropping a bit over her shoulders. She wore a small hat of the darker green velvet decorated with a single short plume. It sat high on her head revealing her auburn hair pulled back in an intricate French braid.

The Wellington men also had haircuts on High Street on Tuesday followed by final alterations at the tailor's just a few doors away. Mr. Wellington would wear a black evening jacket over a pleated white shirt, black trousers with a sharp crease, and black patent leather shoes. Tom's outfit included a black cotton suit, white shirt, black tie, and bright red cummerbund.

The following day Tom was asked to assist the staff with some interior decorations and arrangement of tables and chairs. Mrs. Wellington oversaw all the activity with the aid of Hanna O'Toole.

On Wednesday, three days before the anniversary party, Jack appeared in the grand parlor after school. Tom was busy setting up chairs along the walls. "I can't believe this," said Jack to Tom as he pivoted around, taking in everything he saw with astonishment, "this party is going to be out of this world."

Tom rolled his eyes: "If we survive it," he replied sarcastically. "Mother is beside herself these days. Without Hanna ordering the troops around, I don't know how she would make it through." Half-listening, Jack wandered around the room, then out into the glasshouse. As he stood gazing at the colorful flowers, Anne came through the doors from the grand parlor.

"Tom told me I would find you here." She kissed his cheek, then stood next to him. She took extra pains these days to treat Jack tenderly. Her instincts told her that she was caring for a patient who was still recovering from trauma. She didn't gush, or smother him, but simply held his arm with one hand and stroked it gently with the other. She tried not to talk too much, and she always waited patiently for Jack to speak, a talent she had learned in part from her own mother, but even more from Jack's mother.

Anne had just returned from the salon. That spring she had let her hair grow longer than it had been since she was a toddler, and she insisted on the absolute minimum trimming and styling that her mother, in consultation with the hairdresser, would accede to. She wanted her hair to flow down onto her shoulders where the subtle shades of amber and gold would complement her dress. Her mother wanted her daughter's hair to be up in a tight bun secured with a tortoiseshell comb, the fashion of mature women and of young ladies trying to look grown up. They compromised, leaving it long but thinned just enough to permit it to be formed into a French braid at the back of the neck.

Jack was subdued. He was new to the grieving process and was not sure how he felt about or how others would interpret outbursts of gaiety or mirth. He managed a brief smile at Anne, then noticed her hair. "You look pretty today," he offered, his eyes following her hair down to where it just touched the shoulders of her dress.

Anne smiled sweetly, then looked into his eyes. "How are you? You look a little tired." Again she stroked his arm gently.

"I haven't been sleeping too well lately," Jack confessed. Anne detected a momentary twitch around his eyes and she drew close to him, then gazed around the glasshouse.

"It takes time, Jackie, lots of time," she added finally.

After another pause Jack suddenly brightened: "This house is...," he shook his head, "just amazing. This is going to be a celebration like Holyoke has never seen!"

Again there was a long pause. Anne was reading behind Jack's words, trying hard to perceive not just the handsome young man before her but the fragile soul within. "Jack, please don't feel that you must be here for the party. Maybe it would be too much for you too soon. I'll understand, Mother and Father and Tommy will understand, if you do not feel up to it," she explained gently.

Again Jack's face twitched slightly and he nodded. "I want to be here, I really do. You, Tom, your parents, well...you know." Anne nodded, then Jack continued, "I'm just not sure I can, that's all."

"Listen to your heart, Jackie. Do what you can. No one asks any more of you than that," said Anne.

Jack paused again. "Maybe I'll just see how I feel on Saturday...if that's okay?"

"That would be fine," replied Anne, still stroking his arm.

Again Jack brightened. "I really want to see you in your new dress, that's for sure."

"Well, if that's what you want, Jack, we can always arrange a private showing...just for you." And she poked him playfully in the ribs.

"By the way, who's Tom bringing?" asked Jack. "He's been very secretive."

"I haven't heard a word," responded Anne.

By six o'clock on Saturday evening the pace at the Wellingtons' household had reached a fever-pitch. The orchestra was setting up, the staff was bustling about the food tables, arranging dozens of champagne glasses in precise patterns, linen napkins in overlapping curves, china plates and sterling ware in geometric precision at every table.

The guests began to arrive at seven o'clock and by seven-thirty the grand parlor was packed with dozens of Holyoke's most prominent couples, their older children, and a few unattached men and women. The orchestra played quietly and waiters and waitresses in starched uniforms circulated briskly with trays of drinks, glasses of wine, and all manner of elegantly-prepared canapés.

Anne and Tom got the cue from Hanna to stand at the doorway at the far end of the room. The staff immediately stopped serving and stood silently facing the doors. The orchestra played *Let Me Call You Sweetheart* as the doors swung open. Arm-in-arm, Thomas A. Wellington the Second, and his wife, Helen P. Wellington, strolled into the grand parlor, beaming, looking first to their left, then to their right, then back to their left, and so on, meeting every smiling face with a smile, and greeting each by first name.

Anne was watching the procession and as she turned she saw Jack standing at the other end of the room. He was beaming at the couple as they strolled by. On seeing him, Mrs. Wellington stepped out of the procession momentarily and kissed him on the cheek, then stepped back into lock-step with her husband.

At the end of the room Thomas and Helen mounted the platform in front of the orchestra to boisterous applause. Thomas spoke, welcoming all and thanking them for sharing this important occasion with them. He then turned to his wife, raised a glass of champagne, and offered a toast to Helen and their twenty-five years together.

"Here-here, here-here!" resounded through the room. The orchestra struck up a Strauss waltz, and the couple began to dance. The guests stepped aside, allowing the Wellingtons to have the floor alone for one minute. Then, at Hanna's nod, couples stepped out in twos and joined the Wellingtons in the waltz.

At that point Anne made her way through the onlookers, trying to relocate Jack. She couldn't see him anywhere in the grand parlor, and eventually she walked out into the glasshouse. There he was, about where she had found him a few days earlier. "Jack," said Anne from some distance away. He looked up at once and brightened when he saw Anne. As she approached, his expression suddenly changed from pleasantly surprised to awestruck. He looked her up and down, then spoke:

"You are a sight," he started, "I mean a good sight, I mean...that dress is...you are...beautiful." He spoke the word "beautiful" in a whisper and it hung in the air.

Anne was taken aback by the depth of feeling in Jack's voice and face. She stood beaming at him for some time before she regained her composure and responded: "Look at you. That suit is perfect, Jack, and your tie, and new matching shoes. Oh, Jack, what a handsome young man you are." She had just violated her own rule about gushing, but it came from her heart and somehow she felt she needed to say it, and Jack to hear it, at that moment.

After several minutes of small talk Anne could tell that Jack was looking with special interest at her hairdo. "Is something amiss, Jack?"

"No, not at all. It's just...your hair. What's that?" he finally asked, pointing to the braid.

"It's called a French braid," answered Anne. "Mother is not too happy with it, but I like it just fine. What do you think?"

"It's pretty," answered Jack. The music had stopped for a moment, but just then the orchestra struck up *You Made Me Love You* and Jack and Anne watched many of the guests get up to dance to the popular tune.

"Miss Wellington," said Jack, his face feigning a serious expression, "May I have this dance?" Anne was not expecting this. She suspected Jack might feel uncomfortable dancing before all these people. He might even have doubts about whether it was proper for one still in mourning to be seen enjoying himself in this way. Her instincts told her to decline politely, but her heart sent a different message.

"With pleasure, Mr. Bernard," she replied. Jack confidently took Anne in his arms, fixed his eyes on hers, and the two began to sway very slowly and very easily to the music, in perfect harmony. They were still in the glasshouse and it was quite dark amidst the greenery. The mingled scents of wisteria and jasmine combined with the sweet music lent an air of magic to the moment.

Finally, Anne's curiosity got the best of her, and she broke the spell. "So there's something about my hair that you don't approve of, hmm?" she teased. Jack gave out a little laugh, but then he stopped laughing. He wasn't certain he should speak his mind, and he hesitated.

Anne sensed Jack's serious reaction to her taunt. She paused, then she spoke softly: "Go ahead, Jack, tell me." There was no rancor in her voice, she simply wanted to know what was on his mind.

There was a long pause, then Jack began: "I like it better when it hangs down...on your...," he swallowed, "...shoulders."

Anne thought about this, paused, and looked softly into his eyes. "Like this?" And she reached up, removed her hat, and pulled gently on the braid. Her hair fell in cascades of glistening amber onto her partially exposed shoulders.

Jack looked down at her hair against the green velvet dress and smiled a half-smile. "Yes," he replied softly, "just like that." Then he reached up and stroked her hair with one hand, then her shoulder. Anne was looking intently at his eyes looking at her hair, then their eyes met. Jack leaned forward and kissed her. It was a long, tender kiss, and it ended with just the slightest parting of their lips, their foreheads almost touching. The music echoed from the other room, but the two were unaware of anything but what was happening between them. They kissed again, just as long but with more intensity.

Then they embraced in the darkness, each feeling the other's heart beating.

The loud voice of the bandleader in the other room broke the spell and they separated. They stood gazing at each other, the heavy air of the glasshouse mixing with the emotional heat of the moment. Then Anne reached out, took Jack's hand in hers, turned, and led him through the glass doors onto the lawn. They walked across the gently sloping grass beneath one of the massive copper beeches, then into a dark, secluded corner between the tree and the surrounding privet hedge.

Anne turned to Jack, took both his hands in hers, and kissed him again on the lips softly but firmly. Jack placed his hands around Anne's thin waist and they kissed again. But this time Anne wrapped her arms around Jack's neck, pulling herself to him in a tight embrace. Jack kissed her firmly on the lips, then lowered his head and caressed her bare neck very lightly with his lips.

Anne was breathing very heavily now as was Jack, and she caressed his hair, neck, and shoulders with her hands. Suddenly she pulled him downward, his knees bent, and the couple fell to the ground. Anne lay lightly on Jack's chest, kissing him softly on the lips. After several minutes Jack turned toward Anne and she rolled onto her back, looking up intensely into his eyes. "Anne," said Jack in a whisper, "your dress…you'll stain your dress."

"It's all right," she replied softly, "it's green!"

They both giggled softly and sat up. After a long pause Jack said innocently: "Anne, would you be my girl-friend?"

"Jack Bernard," replied Anne without hesitation, "I thought I'd been your girl-friend for the last two years! But, all right, if you ask, I must answer. Yes, Jack, I will be your girl-friend."

"Good, now that's over with," added Jack.

"Oh, no, Jack, I don't think so," replied Anne. "For us, it's only beginning." Just then they heard a rustle from the beech tree and Tom's head appeared through the hanging branches.

Next to him was a young lady barely visible among the dense foliage.

"Hi, folks. How are you two doing?" he asked, then added, "Pretty well, I see." But before Jack or Anne could answer, he and his companion had disappeared into the darkness. Anne and Jack walked nonchalantly back into the grand parlor, danced a few more dances, and smiled at Anne's parents and friends as if nothing had happened. But inside each knew – the earth had truly moved that evening.

Anne and Jack had not seen Tom since their brief encounter on the lawn. Anne was standing on her toes trying to spot her brother on the dance floor when she blurted "There's Tommy. Who's that he's dancing with?" Just then Tom spotted Anne and Jack and made his way through the crowd toward them, his partner in tow.

"Hi, Anne. Hi, Jack," said Tom, a smear of lipstick showing conspicuously on his cheek. "You know Monique, Monique Fleury. Monique, you remember Anne and Jack?"

It was nearly midnight when the crowd began to thin out. Anne and Jack were exhausted and bleary-eyed despite the evening's excitement. Jack had been invited to stay the night, so he eventually admitted to being tired and started upstairs to Tom's bedroom. Anne kissed her parents goodnight, then ascended to her room.

Jack settled into the extra bed in Tom's room and was almost asleep when he heard Tom enter. "Jack, Jack, are you awake?" asked Tom in a stage whisper.

"Now I am," replied Jack sardonically.

"Did you and Anne have a good time?" asked Tom.

"Yup, fine," said Jack. He was about to ask about Tom's evening, but he decided against it. "The less I know about that," thought Jack, "the better."

"Good night, Tom," added Jack.

"Sleep well, Jack," was Tom's reply.

The two boys were the first to enter the dining room for breakfast the next morning, still showing some signs of fatigue from the late night before. The waitress served their breakfast of oatmeal, poached eggs, and ham, but hearing Mrs. Wellington talking to Mildred in the kitchen, the boys waited politely for her to join them before beginning their meal.

Anne entered a few minutes later, greeted her mother, Tom, and Jack brightly, and was seated next to her mother and across from the two boys. She smiled sweetly at her brother, then gave the slightest wink in Jack's direction at an angle that avoided her mother's detection.

"Well," began Mrs. Wellington, "what did you young folks think of last evening's festivities?"

"It was grand," offered Tom. "Everyone in Holyoke was there, everyone!"

"You looked lovely, Mother," added Anne, "absolutely lovely."

"Jack, I was delighted to see you standing there, smiling so," commented Mrs. Wellington enthusiastically. "Thank you very much for coming." Jack smiled, trying to formulate an appropriate reply that wouldn't repeat what Tom and Anne had said. "I didn't see much of any of you once the dancing began," Mrs. Wellington continued. "I was hoping you would join in. Do you not like dancing?"

"Oh, we danced, Mother," answered Anne. "We danced a good deal, actually, all three of us. We were out in the glasshouse most of the time; that is why you did not see us."

"Hmm, I went out to the glasshouse once but didn't see any of you," said Mrs. Wellington with mild surprise.

"Well, it was pretty dark out there, Mother," responded Anne.

"Yes, it was," replied her mother, "and a bit cramped as well. I wish you could have joined us in the grand parlor so I could enjoy watching you dance. And Thomas, you never introduced us to your young lady friend."

"I apologize, Mother. That was very rude of me. She had to leave early," explained Tom. Tom was feeling that he had covered himself pretty well with that little white lie, and perhaps he had. Unfortunately, he fell prey to a frequent weakness of his, the inability to quit while he was ahead. "We were out on the lawn with Anne and Jack for a while looking at the stars. They were so beautiful, Mother. That must have been when you came looking for us in the glasshouse."

"You are probably right, Tom," replied Mrs. Wellington with a smile and a relieved look. But then she seemed to be confused and added "I thought it was cloudy all last evening; several of the guests mentioned fog." She glanced from Tom to Jack to Anne, all of whom appeared preoccupied with their meals.

Jack was feeling particularly uncomfortable at that moment and he was praying for some miracle to deliver him from the situation. He wasn't sure whether Mrs. Wellington was simply curious or was intentionally making him and her children suffer. If it was the latter, she was doing it very effectively. Jack recognized a striking similarity between her style of interrogation and Anne's equally skillful skewering of him and Tom the previous autumn in the matter of the diving white swans in the Oxbow. Thankfully the inquisition ended there. Perhaps Mrs. Wellington was satisfied with the explanations provided; it was difficult to tell.

# CHAPTER 23

## Surveillance
### *July 1915*

Anne began her summer job at the silk mill in Holyoke the following day. A silk mill was quite a different place from a cotton or woolen mill. Silk threads were imported from China, so the mill mostly employed workers to oversee the machines that wound the delicate silk onto spools and wove them into fine fabric. The lighting was indirect lest it damage the threads. They employed women almost exclusively and held their female workers to very strict standards of dress and deportment. Silk was an elegant, refined product, reasoned the mill owners; so should be the employees who worked with the silk.

The ladies of the silk mill took their lunch breaks at different times each day, so it wasn't until Wednesday that Anne and Jack managed a mid-day liaison. They ate lunch together at a picnic table in the shade outside of the mill office, then walked a short distance along the second level canal. Where there was a narrow alley between two mill buildings, the pair wandered to a somewhat sheltered location. They linked hands, then arms, and stood side-by-side looking across the canal. Jack was once more mesmerized by Anne's proximity and gave her a furtive kiss on the neck. She could feel herself melting, but she resisted. "Jack, my mother knows about...Saturday night...about us...on the lawn."

"How did she find out? I'll bet it was Tom. Was it Tom?"

"No, Jack, it wasn't Tom. It was Hanna," said Anne through clenched teeth.

Jack was bewildered. "Hanna? You told Hanna?"

"No, no, silly. It was the grass stains on my dress. I forgot all about them. One of the chambermaids was putting my clothes away and discovered the stains. She told Hanna and Hanna…told Mother."

"What did your mother say?" Jack asked with a note of panic in his voice. "Was she angry?"

"She wasn't angry, she just gave me a lecture."

"A lecture? What do you mean?" Jack pressed.

"You know, dancing in the glasshouse, looking at the stars…it didn't add up. And the stains on the dress, that was the icing on the cake, I guess," said Anne.

"So what did she say?"

"She told me to remember that I am almost a woman now, and boys will be boys, and that I have my…reputation to consider…and that she trusts me. But it made me think that maybe she doesn't trust me anymore."

"But…we didn't…do anything wrong, did we?" asked Jack. "We didn't…" Jack's voice trailed off, his face almost scarlet.

"Jack, we just have to be more, um, discreet, that's all, for my parents' sake. From now on, when they are around, we're just friends, agreed?"

"And when they're not around?" asked Jack with an impish smile. Anne leaned in and kissed him firmly on the lips. Jack got the message, loud and clear! They walked casually back toward the silk mill with no contact and only the smallest of small talk.

"Jack, one more thing," said Anne as they were about to part. "You know what we agreed on regarding my parents? The same goes for…"

"Hi, Tommy," interrupted Jack as his friend suddenly appeared.

"What's going on?" asked Tom.

"Nothing!" replied Anne and Jack in perfect unison.

That summer Anne and Jack put on a public show of being nothing more than good friends. On a Saturday or Sunday afternoon they often could be found playing croquet, badminton, or quoits with Tom on the Wellingtons' lawn, the light-hearted laughter of the three a clear sign of friendship and nothing more. Friday and Saturday evenings the trio would plan an innocent outing, sometimes to Mountain Park, sometimes in downtown Holyoke, often involving friends of Tom's or of Anne's. What Mrs. Wellington was told about these plans was always of light, trivial, teenage merriment. What actually went on once they were out of sight of her parents was not always what Mrs. Wellington was led to believe.

Tom was fond of the silent movies and could often be found in a balcony seat next to Monique at the newly opened Bijou Theatre on Main Street. After the movie the two would relax in one of several downtown establishments. They drank sarsaparilla while in the front room and visible from the street, but occasionally quaffed certain other beverages while in the back room out of view, although their consumption was generally in moderation. Tom knew that his parents, his mother most especially, would be monitoring his comings and goings, as well as the contents of his pockets, with the assistance of Hanna, the chambermaids, even the laundresses. Other evenings Tom occasionally slipped away via the trolley to South Hadley Falls where he had yet another "friend" in need of his attentions.

Anne and Jack began many an evening walking down Cabot Street with Tom, but their destination was often Mountain Park. They would ride the rides, look at the scenery, then drift away in the gardens or by the pond to share a few moments alone. The heat of their attraction was not diminished in the slightest. If anything it was enhanced by the days of separation and feigned cool casualness that they endured between these encounters.

While their strategy of discretion seemed to be going well, each had reason to suspect that Mrs. Wellington's "eyes" were everywhere. Some of this may have been imagined, a certain paranoia lurking in the minds of the young couple, but some was very real. One evening at Mountain Park, as the two were playing mini-golf, Anne caught sight of Marguerita, the maid, in the company of a young man, watching from the picnic area close by. Probably a coincidence, thought Anne, though she had never before seen Marguerita with that young man anywhere. Mr. and Mrs. Wellington appeared quite by surprise walking along Appleton Street one evening as Anne, Jack, and Tom were coming home. And Anne was aware that her mother had talked with Bill Peterson's mother before a casual gathering Bill had organized for a few friends in the family's garden house one July evening and had later inquired of Mrs. Peterson as to the time Anne and Jack had left the get-together.

One weekend in early August Mrs. Wellington asked Anne to walk with her in the gardens. From his bedroom window Tom watched them strolling, at one point arm-in-arm, then apart. Then after what appeared to be heated words, Anne could be observed, her back to her mother, shaking her head. For days after Anne was uncharacteristically sullen. She was polite but curt with her family. She showed a certain reserve when with Jack, an unwillingness to look him in the eye. The usual wit in her conversation was lacking and Jack was uneasy.

A week later, the couple planned an evening at Mountain Park. Jack was pleased to see Anne's mood more upbeat; there was a youthful skip in her step as she hopped off the trolley with him in front of the Dance Pavilion. "Let's take the cable car to the top," said Jack, apparently on a whim, "and watch the sunset." Anne at first was reluctant, but Jack persisted and they bought their tickets and took the ride to the Summit House. This was the first time the two had made that trip since the picnic excursion in the Reo three summers before. The view was breathtaking and the couple stood facing the brilliant, setting sun on the same spot where Jack and Tom had once tried to avoid Anne and Carolyn when they were "just kids."

"Remember that?" asked Jack. "I was terrified of you! Girls were so mysterious back then. Even Tom was befuddled."

"When did that change, Jack?" asked Anne thinly.

"It started to change that very day," admitted Jack. "The look in your eyes as we sat waiting for the cable car to start...I couldn't figure out why you were even talking to me. And your hair, and your skin...," he paused, blushing..."it just got to me, I guess." Jack looked at Anne, but she was looking away at the sunset, hearing Jack's words but holding herself in control, her lips tightly closed. Jack knew that this beautiful creature who was always so composed, so single-minded and sure of herself, was about to break his heart. But he had to speak.

"Anne," he whispered in her ear, "ever since that day, I've been loving you. Every hour, every day, my heart has been yours."

This confession transformed Anne's steeliness to mush. She turned to him, looked into his eyes, and whispered "I do love you, Jack." And she wrapped her arms around him and held him tightly for several minutes.

"But, Jack, I have to go away," said Anne, a tear rolling down her cheek.

"I know," answered Jack. "Argentina...for a year...right?"

"How did you...Tommy...He promised not to, I told him to button up, that I had to tell you this myself."

Anne looked at Jack and the setting sun and seemed confused. "You mean, you brought me up here knowing I would be telling you this? Why?"

Jack pointed to the distant horizon just as the last orange slice of the sun slipped behind the Berkshire Hills. "See how beautiful the sun is as it drops out of sight? But it comes back, it always comes back, just as beautiful, just as bright, just as warm, with the next sunrise."

"I will come back, Jack, and we will be together again, I promise."

"And I'll still be here, I promise," replied Jack. Then he paused, inserted one hand into his vest pocket, and produced the emerald ring. "This was my mother's. She gave it to me that...last night. I want you to have it, Anne. Maybe it will remind you of someone who loves you."

Jack put the ring on Anne's finger. She smiled and kissed him.

# CHAPTER 24

# "David"

## *August 1915*

A nne's departure was only a few days away. She was very much occupied with preparations for the train ride to New York where she and her father would set sail on a transoceanic steamer with her Aunt Sarah the last day of the month. Since the evening on Mount Tom, Anne and Jack had loosened their rule on discretion just a bit. Partly they were allowing themselves some extra time together to build up their strength and courage for the long separation that was looming. But they also had the feeling that Anne's parents would slacken the reins somewhat.

The two avoided talk about the painful topic of the impending separation until their final day together. The Wellingtons had planned a small going away party for Anne in the grand parlor. Only a few dozen of the family's best friends and Anne's schoolmates were invited. After supper Victrola music played and the young people paired off and danced. Anne was being the gracious hostess, wandering among the adults, thanking them for their gifts and accepting their wishes of good luck and "Bon voyage."

Jack and Tom stood watching the dancing and laughter, but Jack was following Anne's movements closely. She turned from a conversation with one couple, looked across the room, and their eyes met. Jack walked toward Anne, eyes fixed on hers, smiling. He extended his right hand. "May I have this dance, Miss Wellington?" he asked with a twinkle in his eye.

"Why, Mr. Bernard, I feared you would never ask," replied Anne with a smile. Just then the music changed to a sprightly ragtime tune. Neither could figure out how to dance to the syncopated rhythm and they stood laughing at themselves for a moment.

Jack stepped in close to Anne, looked soulfully into her eyes, then took her hand and led her off the dance floor, through the glass doors into the glasshouse. Among the dangling vines and stately tree ferns he led her, then stopped and turned. "We can dance to our own tune here," he explained. Jack put his hands around Anne's waist, Anne put both hands around Jack's neck and clasped them. Pressed tightly together, the couple began to move in perfect harmony. Soon a sultry waltz could be heard from the next room and it fit perfectly with the mood of the two dancers. They moved slowly, gently, savoring their last evening together.

Finally Jack spoke. "Let's go outside and look at the stars," he joked. They both laughed, and Anne clung to Jack as they stepped out into the moist, windless night air. They walked beneath the copper beech and beyond to their private corner by the privet. "Anne, I still don't understand why," began Jack. "Why are you going away?"

"It's partly family tradition. My aunt studied for a year in Paris when she was my age and my parents want me to have the same experience. But Europe is at war now. Father wants to go to South America to find new sources of wool for the mill...or so he says." Anne paused, choosing her words carefully. "Mother has a different explanation. She says that this...separation...will be good for her and Father. She says they need some time apart." Tears glistened in her eyes. "I'm worried about them, Jack. Since Matthew died, there's been a wall between them. That anniversary party...it was a wonderful event, but it was just a show. Underneath, things haven't been so perfect."

"Anne, I had no idea," began Jack. "This is awful. I mean, it's awful what your parents are going through and it seems a terrible time for your family to be apart. Are you sure it's the right thing for them, for the whole family?"

Anne shook her head. Jack had never seen her so dejected, so unhappy. And yet he felt helpless. "And I'm worried about Tom," she went on. "Mother says she'll keep a close eye on him, but I know...you know...what really goes on at school."

"Does Tom know...about your parents, I mean?"

"No, Mother says they're afraid to tell him, afraid of how he might react. So they've decided to keep it from him. You mustn't tell him, Jack, please."

"What about us, Anne? Do they think this separation is the best thing for us?"

"Lots of young couples are separated for a time. Boys, men, go off to war and their girlfriends or wives stay home and pray for them. We've got it good compared to them, you know." She lowered her voice and looked intently into Jack's eyes. "Besides, we've got something that a few months apart cannot erase. I feel that, Jack, I really do. Do you?" Jack nodded and they embraced. "I'm going to miss you so much, my dear Jack."

"And I you, Anne. Every minute of every day. And nighttime, too," he added, looking around in the darkness.

"But Jack," Anne began slowly. "I don't want you to sit at home pining for me for the next year. I would hate that. It would be like sentencing you to prison for a year. It would cause me pain, Jack, and it wouldn't be fair to you."

Jack wasn't sure what Anne was trying to say, but he didn't share her concern. "I won't mind. I've got so much to do...my senior year, work, my father and my sisters to take care of...it will go by fast, I'm sure it will."

"But you need to have some good times, too, and I want you to have them. I want you to socialize, darling...dance, laugh, go to parties, your class's Fall Gala, and the Senior Formal. You need that, Jack, you've earned that!"

"Anne, what are you asking me to do, to be unfaithful to you? I could never...we promised, remember?"

"Jack, I want to release you from your promise, just until I return." With that she took the ring from her finger, Evelyne's beautiful emerald ring, and placed it in his hand, gently closing his fingers around it.

Jack was stunned and momentarily speechless. "But what about you, Anne? Are you asking me to release you from your promise?"

"Jack," Anne began. She had rehearsed this over and over again lest the emotions she was feeling should impede her words. "How do you feel when we're together? Is there any doubt in your mind about your feelings for me when I'm standing before you or wrapped in your arms?"

"None."

"Nor for me," Anne went on. "But that's not the greatest test of love. The greatest test of love is whether two people, separated by distance and time, meeting and enjoying the company of others, will in time reunite, willingly. Don't you see, this will be good for us both, it will prove what we feel in our hearts is real and can endure."

"But I could never...love another girl, Anne, I don't want to, ever."

"You say that, Jack, but you won't know if you don't try. The thought of you with another girl," she said, her voice cracking, "is hard to bear. But it can only make our love stronger. I truly believe that."

"Will we write?" asked Jack.

"Of course, Jack, we'll write, but not every day. How about one long, newsy letter a month?"

"Anne, the way I feel about you, sometimes I just need you close to me, very close. How am I going to..."

"When you feel those feelings, Jack, go out and run a mile, run ten miles. It will make you feel better, and it will make you a better runner, too. Consider it...training!"

"And what about you, Anne, do you ever have those kinds of feelings for me?"

"Jack Bernard," Anne scolded in mock offense. "I'm a sweet, innocent girl, and sweet innocent girls don't have those kinds of feelings." Then she kissed him firmly on the lips.

"So you'll be training for your own track team?" asked Jack with a grin.

"No," replied Anne, "but every time I feel the need to be close to you, I'll look at the lithograph of Michelangelo's *David* in my art history book. I'll be looking at David, but I'll be seeing my Jack."

Jack didn't know about Michelangelo's famous sculpture. During the first week of the new school year he went to the library and found a book of engravings of great works of sculpture. When his eye fell on the statue of David, his face turned scarlet. He slammed the book shut and headed out to the track. He ran five miles that day.

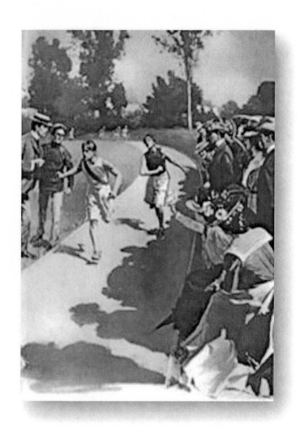

CHAPTER 25

# Socializing
*October 1915*

From the day of Anne's departure, Jack's training became intense. He ran every day after school, at home on weekends, and some evenings as well. He found the double pain of loss that he had endured in the last six months easier to bear when his energies were focused on running, stride, pace, breathing, strategy. That, he believed, was what made the mile run the perfect event for him. He finished first or second in each of his first three meets and was written up with superlatives in the *Transcript*. On several occasions friends of the Bernards commented to Charles after reading mention of Jack's accomplishments in the Westfield newspaper.

In mid-October the track team traveled by trolley to South Hadley for a meet with the town's high school team, regarded as the strongest in the valley. Jack ran his best race yet and won, beating his nearest competitor by several strides.

As he sat on the bleachers watching the other events, he heard an all-too-familiar voice from behind: "Hi there, stranger...good race."

Jack was surprised to see Monique standing before him. "Thank you," began Jack. "I've been training hard this term. I guess it's just paid off."

"The way you ran that race," Monique observed, "It was as though you had a strategy, and it worked; very impressive. A good competitor is always thinking, don't you agree?"

"Yeh, uh, sure," stammered Jack. "That's very true."

"That's been my experience in competition."

"Oh, you're a runner?" asked Jack.

"No. Tennis is my sport. Singles. Do you play?"

"Tennis? No, not really. A little badminton, that's all."

"I'm on the Mount Holyoke tennis team now," Monique replied. "Maybe you could come and root for me sometime."

"Yeh, sure, maybe," Jack replied vaguely. He looked away, studying the horizon.

"We have a match with Smith tomorrow. Why don't you come over? I could use the moral support."

"I'm...ehhh...pretty busy this weekend, maybe another time," responded Jack.

"Okay, Jack, anytime. It's always nice to see you," she added with a wink, then walked away.

The following weekend Jack finished his chores early, then took the trolley to Holyoke. On High Street he transferred to a South Hadley car and in twenty minutes was stepping off at the gates of Mount Holyoke College. He had been to South Hadley before, but never onto the Mount Holyoke campus, and he gazed with amazement at the imposing buildings of red sandstone surrounding a broad green quadrangle. When he spotted an athletic field in the distance he began walking in that direction. He found the clay tennis courts and could see girls in long white skirts huddled together in two groups at courtside. He had read in the *Transcript* that Mount Holyoke had a match against Wellesley at home scheduled for that morning. He took a seat on the bleachers with the warm October sun on his back.

Jack was interested in tennis and curious to learn more. The idea that young women could enjoy athletic competition was new to him and it intrigued him. But he was also somewhat ill-at-ease. He had told no one of his true destination and only hoped that nobody he knew would be at this match. In some way he felt guilty that his attendance might be interpreted by others as an indication of interest in Monique; he was particularly conflicted as to whether Monique herself might get that impression. Finally, he had to admit, there was a tiny flicker of curiosity about that beguiling girl of seemingly contradictory personas.

He first knew Monique as a tutor. "Miss Fleury," he thought, with a chuckle. She seemed dour, plain, and single-minded as a teacher. Then there were the somewhat secretive associations with Tom when she appeared to play at being mindless and slightly naughty. There were her repeated appearances at his meets, the discussion about strategy and competition, and the flirtatious winks. Finally, there was the thoroughly mortifying encounter with her at the Oxbow which Jack was trying very hard to put out of his head.

"Hi, Jack," came a shout from across the tennis courts. Monique was coming his way, smiling, her racket in one hand. "Come to cheer for me?"

"Yeh," Jack returned enthusiastically. "Good luck!"

Monique's face was only inches from Jack's when she replied. "I didn't expect to see you today. I thought maybe you weren't interested…in tennis."

"It's great," Jack replied. "I don't really know that much, but I want to learn."

"We're playing Wellesley," said Monique as she rolled her large, brown eyes. "They look awfully strong; I'm not sure how we'll do. But if I know you're here it'll give me a little extra courage! Well, I'd better get warmed up," she offered as she touched his shirtsleeve. "Wait for me after the match and you can tell me how I looked."

Jack sat back, prepared to enjoy the match. He was surprised and shocked, frankly, when the members of both teams removed their long dresses, revealing loose fitting white blouses and short white pants. But the other on-lookers seemed to take it in stride. Monique showed admirable control of her shots, placing them well and forcing her opponent to move from side to side, using both her forehand and backhand. But she was slower and had more limited range, and she often failed to return her opponent's volleys. The

Mount Holyoke team was badly mismatched; Wellesley won every set.

Jack stood by the field house after the match, waiting for Monique to emerge. He wasn't sure what would happen next and whether he wanted to stay and find out, but he had nodded at Monique's request and felt obliged. When she finally appeared from the field house, she was again wearing the long white dress and cradling her racket under one arm.

"Well, that was a fiasco," she conceded. "I'm sorry you had to see that. You must think our team is absolutely horrid!"

"No, not at all," offered Jack reassuringly. "I could see how you were working at that Wellesley girl's weaknesses and making her run hard for every point."

"You're very kind, Jack, but be honest, it was a disaster," Monique gushed melodramatically. "But thank you for trying...you're very sweet." She paused. "Come and have some tea, won't you? Or lemonade? Stay for lunch if you like."

Jack was feeling conflicted about his own motives and began looking for a way out. "Thank you, I'd like to, but I really have to get home," he uttered with a note of urgency in his voice.

"Oh, all right," replied Monique with disappointment in her voice and in her eyes, then she paused. "Jack, there's a social in two weeks at my dormitory. Would you like to come as my guest?"

"I don't think I can," answered Jack quickly, then hesitated. "I'm pretty busy with, you know, school and track and my family."

"Is it Anne, Jack? I guess I thought you two had, well, agreed, I mean decided..."

"No, no," Jack replied quickly, shaking his head. "It's not like that."

"Jack, just for your information, Tom and I are not seeing each other anymore. We've separated, not that we were ever an item, you know what I mean...Tom's just not...well, you know."

"Yeh," nodded Jack, "I know."

"Soooo," Monique paused, "What do you say…about the social?"

Jack looked into her almond-shaped eyes, her brows raised in an expression of innocence and sweetness. "I guess I could," he replied. Almost immediately he was having second thoughts. But if there was anything he tried to avoid at his age it was appearing to be indecisive. "The die has been cast," he thought to himself.

Two weeks later, on a Friday evening, Jack found himself once again riding the South Hadley trolley, almost in spite of his own instincts, and getting off at the gates of Mount Holyoke. He had just received his first letter from Anne reporting on her trip and her first few weeks in Buenos Aires. The city was fascinating, she exclaimed, but also overwhelming. Her school was small and very welcoming. Her studies were beginning well, especially her French literature and art history classes. She asked about him, his family, school, and track. In the last line she added that she missed her family "and my favorite boy." She signed it, "Always, Anne."

The last line and the closing sent pangs of guilt and self-recrimination throughout his body. Just then Monique spotted him as he entered Roosevelt Hall.

"Hello, Jack. Aren't you looking handsome tonight?" She took his arm. "Come into the lounge and let me introduce you to some of my friends."

The evening was sheer torture for Jack from the beginning. He knew no one other than Monique, had no idea how to act among college students, and felt utterly lost. Early on he ran out of things to say to Monique and stood pretending to be interested in the dancing, loud conversation, and boisterous laughter on all sides.

Finally, Monique asked him to dance. He knew what to do and held Monique lightly as they moved to the strains of

*By the Light of the Silvery Moon,* but he couldn't bring himself to look into her eyes for more than a fleeting instant at a time.

"Relax, Jack," Monique urged, "I won't bite."

Jack felt almost ill and it must have been apparent. "You look like you need some fresh air. Come with me." She led him onto a patio lit by one dim electric light over the door. They walked to the far end and stood next to a curved, wrought iron railing. Revived by the cool air but still uneasy, Jack was wishing he'd never agreed to come and was trying to think of a tactful way to extricate himself. Monique was looking up at him and batting her long eyelashes coyly.

"Jack," she spoke softly, "do you like me?"

Jack nodded, his eyes focusing briefly on hers, then down at the stone patio. Monique was leaning against him, pressing him lightly against the railing, and then she kissed him. It was a moist, warm kiss and it startled him. It felt good, but it immediately reminded him of the only other girl he'd ever kissed in that way and he froze. Monique pressed against him again, a little more assertively, but Jack twisted away.

"I really can't stay," said Jack, feeling both relieved and remorseful that he was not able to respond as Monique obviously hoped he would. With that he walked back into the building, found his jacket, and headed for the door. Monique followed, trying to get him to talk, apologizing for being so forward, reminding him that there were refreshments inside. Out on the lawn he turned to Monique and confessed: "I can't, I'm sorry, you're very nice, but I..." He shook his head. "I can't." And he disappeared into the darkness.

Jack was up early the next morning and doing his chores in the barn. He fed the animals, mucked out Angélique's stall, and began gathering eggs, all while deep in thought. Soon Marie was at his side offering to take over for him.

"You look like you need to go back to bed, Jackie. Let me finish up here," she offered.

After their mother died, already nearly six months in the past, Jack observed a distinct change in his fourteen-year-old sister. Her sense of loss was real, but she had inherited her mother's steady disposition and urge to nurture her little sister, father, and big brother. Jack was touched by her concern and a little surprised. He had expected to be the one who took on the main responsibility for caring for the family. It was comforting to know that Marie could be his partner in those responsibilities.

"You got home late last night; I hope you were having fun," queried Marie gently.

"Fun," replied Jack with a sardonic smile and slow shake of his head, "is not what I would call it." But he immediately wished he hadn't said even that much.

Marie looked into his eyes and tried to probe a little more: "Everything okay, Jack?"

"Oh, yeh," replied Jack with a studied air of confidence. He left Marie collecting eggs in the hen house and went inside and up to his room. He removed a stack of writing paper from his desk, filled his pen with ink, and began his letter to Anne.

Jack took pains to keep the tone of the letter light. News of the family, school, and the track team filled several pages. A few paragraphs were devoted to Holyoke news, rising worker discontent, and upcoming city elections. Before ending he recounted what little he had heard from Tom since summer's end. He was playing tennis for Dorchester and doing well, he understood. Jack added that he had watched a few tennis matches himself and thought he'd like to give it a try.

Following Anne's pattern, he wished her well, thanked her for her letter, and added, simply, "I miss you," then closed with "Affectionately" and "Jack" below. After some thought he added "yours" following "affectionately."

CHAPTER 26

# Revolting
### *November 1915*

S ince Charles Bernard's abrupt firing four years earlier, he
had harbored resentment toward the Wellington mill and
its owners. He did his best to hide those feelings from Jack out
of respect for his son's association with the Wellington family,
and he genuinely felt for them on the occasion of Tom's
accident. But his sudden dismissal after nearly eleven years of
devoted service to the company had created resentment that
neither time nor his eventual rehiring could assuage.

Unions as such were non-existent at that time in Holyoke.
Low wages and exploitative labor practices of all kinds were at
least partially responsible for the rapid growth of the textile
and paper industries in Holyoke and other western
Massachusetts manufacturing cities. But labor activity was on
the rise and the mill owners were clearly worried about the
potentially harmful effect on their profits.

The mill workers of Holyoke were just beginning to
organize in the fall of 1915. Distrust and enmity among the
various immigrant groups in the city at that time made joint
action impossible, so each group acted independently. The
French-Canadian textile workers were among the most active.
Meetings took place under strict secrecy at a number of
locations around the city. Rumors circulated that some kind of
mass action - picket lines, a work slowdown, possibly even a
strike - was being planned for the following spring.

Jack knew about the labor unrest in Holyoke. He heard
rumors every day in school and he read the *Transcript*. He
understood as well as anyone how difficult and dangerous

work in the mills could be. He felt very personally the humiliation of his own father's summary dismissal and the effect it had had on the Bernard family. So when talking with his classmates about the labor situation in Holyoke, Jack saw it in simple terms: conditions were bad and the workers should act. But he soon learned that it was more complicated than that.

One afternoon Jack and a neighborhood friend stood in the side yard talking loudly about the possibility of a strike. His father overheard their conversation and spoke to him after supper. "Jack, times are very hard, I know you know that. But I'm not sure you realize how difficult my position is at the Wellington mill. I need that job. The last time I was laid off, you had to leave school, and I didn't get back into the mill for over half a year. Well, things are even worse now. If I were to lose my job again, I don't know what we would do. We don't have any savings to speak of. I hate to think about what we would do."

"But Dad, maybe a strike would make Mr. Wellington realize, maybe it would change things. Maybe it would improve conditions for all the workers in Holyoke in the end."

"Maybe so, maybe so. But I have to confess that I'm scared. And a lot of the men I work with are as well. We're afraid that we'll be accused of labor activity and fired. It's happening every day, and it's got us all worried." Charles hesitated for several seconds, then continued. "Some of the younger workers who don't have families, they're the ones behind this. They don't have as much to lose as the rest of us. Son, if someone overheard you talking about a strike and passed that along to someone at the mill, I could be out of work that very day. Do you understand what I'm saying? It's very worrisome, very, very worrisome."

This was the first time Jack really understood what was at stake for his father, for the whole Bernard family, and for all the mill workers. He felt very badly for the way he had been talking earlier. "My friends and I talk a lot about this at school and around town like we know what's best. But I can see we're pretty foolish to think that all you have to do is go on strike and everything will be solved. You have my word, I won't say a thing from now on."

The two Bernard men sat together for a moment, each absorbed with his own thoughts. Finally Jack spoke: "Even if the worst happened, I could drop out of school again and find some work, if it came to that."

Jack's words had an immediate effect on his father. A pained expression spread over his face and he shook his head slowly. "No, Jackie, I want you to get that diploma. I don't want anything to stand in the way of you and the girls finishing high school. It's important to me, Son, and it was a promise I made to your mother when...when she was so ill. That's a promise I intend to keep."

Then Charles brought up something the two had never before discussed. "And Jack, I want you to go to college. Do you hear me? So that you don't have to work like a slave in that mill the rest of your life. That's my dream for you."

Jack was astonished. He was, after all, a high school senior and some of his classmates had already started talking about attending two-year or four-year colleges the next fall. But he hadn't allowed himself the luxury of dreaming those dreams. "Dad," said Jack incredulously, "how could we ever afford college for me?"

"Somehow, we'll find a way, Son. Maybe if you keep up your grades, you could get one of those scholarships. If you want it badly enough, Jack, you can have it. I know my boy."

Master Jack H. Bernard

Rural Route N° 5

Westfield, Massachusetts

USA

CHAPTER 27

# Fracturing
*December 1915*

Jack had written several letters to Tom that fall, but had received no reply. He had called the Wellington home on Thanksgiving weekend when he thought Tom would be at home, but learned that Tom had already returned to school. He was worried about his best friend, yet he felt helpless to do anything more. Maybe Tom didn't want to be in touch with his old friend, Jack feared.

A week before Christmas the Bernard household was busy preparing for the holidays. Jack and Claire had cut a tall spruce sapling on the back of their property. Jack put it up in the parlor, and Charles and the three children spent that Saturday afternoon decorating the tree with cranberries, popcorn, and handmade ornaments. In the evening candles were affixed to the tree and lit one by one to the delight of all.

Among the Christmas cards that arrived by mail that day was a letter from Anne. It had been nearly two months since her last letter and Jack was anxious to read it, but he waited until he was alone in his room at bedtime to open the envelope. He was surprised to find it was just two pages long. Anne reported that school was going well and that Buenos Aires was a fascinating city. She missed the comfortable environs of Holyoke, she said, and her friends and family. In the middle of the second page, Jack's world began to crumble.

> I have met a young man at my school who
> has been kind and very attentive. His name
> is Theron and he is from Scotland. His

father works in the British embassy in Buenos Aires. I must tell you, Jack, that I have given my heart to Theron. He is serious, industrious, and very good-hearted. I am sorry if this causes you pain, but life takes us ever in new directions. I wish you and your family all the best.

    Yours truly,
    Anne

Tears seared Jack's eyes as he read and reread that paragraph, certain that he must have misread it or misunderstood Anne's meaning. He was stunned by the letter, not just by the shocking message, but the tone. It was so unlike Anne, so cold, so abrupt, so unsparing of his feelings. "I am sorry," thought Jack. "That's all she has to say to me?" How could Anne, his Anne, write such a letter, say such things, to the one she professed to love so deeply a mere three months earlier? It didn't make sense, he thought, to profess such deep feelings, then turn so suddenly and write with such cruelty.

Jack was in a daze. He did his chores, he finished his schoolwork, he celebrated Christmas with his family, but anyone who knew him knew his heart wasn't in it. This young man who had always approached life with vigor and earnestness was clearly foundering. It was Marie who detected this change on Christmas Day. She had seen the letter from Anne among the Christmas cards and it didn't take too much divining to conclude that something had happened between the two young lovers.

A few days later while they were washing dishes together, Marie decided the time was right. "Jackie," she began. "Is everything all right between you and Anne? You've been so down since her last letter."

"Everything's fine," said Jack sharply, knowing his curt reply would only add fuel to Marie's suspicions. Just then

Claire entered the room and Marie decided to let the matter lie for the time.

That evening Marie rapped on Jack's bedroom door. She heard his muffled voice: "Come in." As she slowly pushed the door ajar she could see her brother lying on his side on the bed, his back to her. She entered and sat on the edge of the bed.

"If Mom were here, you'd talk to her, I know you would. You always talked to her, so did I. And she always listened. I miss her, Jackie, I know you do, too."

Jack lay motionless except for a slight nod of his head. Marie waited. Finally Jack rolled over onto his back, looking up at the ceiling. Marie took that as an opening. "If Mom were here, Jackie, what would you say to her?"

Jack thought for a long while, then spoke coldly: "Don't ever fall in love is what I'd say. It's not worth it. It's just not worth it."

Marie waited again, then spoke. "Anne?"

Jack nodded. There were no tears; he couldn't allow himself to cry in front of his sister. But his jaw was set as he spoke. "She told me she gave her heart to another boy. Just like that. No explanation, barely an apology. How could she do that?"

"Maybe she's lonely in South America. Maybe she misses you so much and he's just a temporary substitute, until she gets home. Have you thought of that?"

"Why even tell me about him, then? I don't understand. I know we were supposed to be free to 'socialize' while she's away, that was our agreement. But to write me and tell me that she's in...in love with someone else, just like that, it doesn't make sense."

Marie thought about this for a while. "Maybe you should write to her and ask her for an explanation. Tell her how you feel. It couldn't hurt. Maybe she's doing this to somehow protect herself."

Jack shook his head. "I'm finished with Anne, finished with girls...finished."

"Don't give up, Jack. Think about it, give it time." Then she paused. "What about Tom, have you talked to him about this?"

At that Jack's eyes filled with tears, but he did his best to keep his composure. He shook his head, but could say no more.

"Mom would tell you to listen to your heart, Jackie, I know she would. If your heart tells you it's really over, then you must listen to it. But if your heart tells you otherwise, pay close attention. Your heart won't lie."

Jack decided not to write to Anne, not to pursue her or plead with her. He had his pride and she had treated him poorly. He owed her nothing. He decided simply to put Anne Wellington out of his mind, and heart, forever. "The die is cast," thought Jack.

CHAPTER 28

# Being Earnest
*February 1916*

The pressures of school completely consumed Jack for the next five months. He was in the last half of his senior year and taking a challenging college preparatory course that included world history, English literature, trigonometry, chemistry, and Latin. He had little time to think about the past or to allow thoughts of what might have been to intrude.

"AUDITIONS TODAY" read a sign on the bulletin board in front of the principal's office as Jack entered school one January morning. Dramatics was not something that interested Jack and he would not have thought any more of the matter on that day, but just then he heard a familiar voice calling his name.

"Jack Bernard, may I have a word with you?" It was Miss Edwards, Jack's English teacher. She was the director of the senior class play, *The Importance of Being Earnest*, and was busy recruiting in the hallway and in her classes. She was one of the younger members of the faculty. Short and stout, she had a round, pink face and bright, determined eyes. Everything Miss Edwards did she did with passion and emotion, making her classes stimulating, even for those who were not particularly literary.

"Jack, I was hoping I could entice you to audition for the senior play. We have a role that would be perfect for you. Won't you come to the auditions today right after school?"

"Uh, thank you, Miss Edwards, that sounds very nice, but I can't. I have practice today."

"How about after practice? We could extend the auditions so you could come by a little later."

"I...I don't think so. I have to get home right after practice. I'm sorry, Miss Edwards, I really am. But thank you for asking. I have to get to class."

Miss Edwards watched with disappointment as Jack walked briskly down the long hallway.

Later that day, Pauline Foley spoke to Jack in Latin class. She was tall with chestnut hair and light skin. Jack had known her since grade eight at Forestdale Grammar School. They had become friends during ninth grade when they sat together in English class.

Pauline was a serious student and on the quiet side, he thought. "Jack," she whispered, "I heard you might audition for the senior class play. Is it true?"

"No, I can't. Miss Edwards asked me, but I'm too busy. Anyway, I'd be a lousy actor."

"I bet you're wrong there, Jack. You'd be superb for the part of Algernon. He's smart and funny...and very popular with the ladies...or so he thinks. It's the best part in the play. Please say you'll try out, please!"

"I can't, Pauline, it's impossible. I've got track, and the farm, and everything. Are you gonna audition?"

"Miss Edwards has asked me to be Assistant Director; it'll be fun."

"That's great," Jack enthused. "You'll be swell."

Just then Latin class began and the conversation ended, but Pauline's efforts had not.

Rehearsals for *The Importance of Being Earnest* began the next week. Now that the track season was over, Jack's schedule was a little more relaxed, and one day that week he appeared at the auditorium door, curious to see how the play was coming. Pauline spotted him and came running up the aisle toward him.

"Oh, Jack, do we need you! Our Algernon had to drop out of school and go to work. We're desperate, Jack, won't you reconsider, please?" She took his arm as if to draw him to the stage. Jack resisted, but as he turned to fend off her efforts, she looked him squarely in the eyes and spoke softly: "Please?"

Just then Miss Edwards approached the two. "Oh, Jack, you would be perfect."

Jack stood silently, unable to mount any further defense against these two determined thespians. Then he nodded his head. "Okay, when do we start?"

Pauline handed him a script. "Act Two, page sixty-two. Let's go over our lines right now."

Jack was confused. "<u>Our</u> lines? But I thought you were the Assistant Director. Why do you have lines?"

"Miss Edwards has asked me to take the part of Cecily."

"Oh, eh, great. Who's Cecily?" asked Jack.

"Algernon's sweetheart," answered Pauline innocently. "Isn't it funny how things work out sometimes?"

"You are my little cousin Cecily, I'm sure," said Jack, reading from the script.

"You are under some strange mistake. I am not little. In fact, I believe I am more than usually tall for my age," read Pauline, then she paused, blushing, and looked at Jack. "I guess it's no secret why Miss Edwards cast me as Cecily," she confessed. "Well, maybe being tall does have some advantages for a girl." She smiled at Jack.

Jack shook his head. "I'm not sure I can do this, Pauline. I'm no good at acting."

"You're doing just fine, Jack. You have natural talent and you'll make the perfect Algernon. You'll be great…and it will be fun. Please believe me, it will."

They continued to rehearse their lines.

"You are like a pink rose, Cousin Cecily," read Jack.

"I don't think it can be right for you to talk to me like that. Miss Prism never says such things to me," read Pauline.

Jack began the next line: "Then Miss Prism is a short-sighted old lady. You are…"

Jack paused, his eyes fixed on the line, "You are the prettiest girl I ever saw."

"I can't do this, Pauline, it's…it's just not for me," Jack protested. "I'm sorry." He got up, handed the script to Pauline, turned and started up the aisle toward the exit.

"Jack, please…wait…," pleaded Pauline, following behind him. She reached out and touched his arm. He stopped and turned to face her.

"Jack, it's just a play. And it's a good play, a funny play…you'll love it and you'll be great. Please, give it more time."

Jack stood expressionless, his eyes cast downward at the carpet.

Suddenly Pauline's demeanor changed. Her voice cracked as she spoke. "It's me, isn't it? You don't want to have anything to do with me. I guess I should have realized…I tricked you into this and I pushed you, and it embarrasses you to say that I'm the prettiest girl you ever saw…" She turned away from Jack, looking at the stage, then continued: "…when I'm not pretty at all."

Jack suddenly felt ashamed at how he had been behaving.

"No, Pauline, that's not it. You're very pretty, everyone thinks so…and you're smart…and talented. Play-acting…it's just not for me, that's all, I can't act."

"Is this because of Anne? Is that what's holding you back? Maybe you're still secretly pining for her…and this feels in a way like a betrayal of her?"

Jack stood quietly, thinking. Several awkward seconds went by. Then he looked up and smiled at Pauline.

"Okay, I'll give it another try."

From then on rehearsals went well and Jack warmed a good deal to his role. The other lead role was played by a classmate, George Bradley. George was a natural actor, thought Jack, and he admired how George addressed the empty auditorium as if it was full of people. He delivered his lines confidently and his timing and gestures were perfect. So perfect, in fact, that Jack and the other members of the cast couldn't help responding to him as if they were his audience. In short, George's talent made everyone in the cast a better actor.

"How's the play going, Jack?" inquired Marie as she and Jack washed dishes one evening.

"It's pretty funny," said Jack. "Even though I don't get half the jokes, you can't help but laugh. That George Bradley, he's a corker. I just watch him and try to act like him."

"And Pauline, how's she?"

"She's fine, too, I guess. She's helped me a lot. We rehearse our lines together practically every day, before school, during lunch, after school. She's a big help."

"And the scene where you two kiss, how's that going?"

Jack blushed, then shook his head. "We haven't rehearsed that scene too much yet."

"I was looking at your script and there was something I couldn't understand...about Bunbury...who's Bunbury?"

"He's a made-up friend that Algernon pretends to go off to visit on weekends in the country. When he says he's 'Bunburying' it means he's sneaking away to visit one of his other girlfriends."

"Well, that's not very nice of him, Jack. It's deceitful and unkind." She paused. "Speaking of Bunbury, have you heard from Tommy Wellington lately? What's he up to these days?"

Jack shot his sister a surprised look and they held each other's gaze for a moment. Then he smiled and shook his head. "I haven't heard a thing...not a thing."

The pace of worker unrest was on the rise in Holyoke that winter. Rumors swirled around in the mills, on the streets, and in the city's neighborhoods about clandestine meetings, visits by labor leaders from Boston and New York, and plans for various kinds of action.

On a snowy night in February a group of mill workers who had been fired for union activity gathered in the home of one of their group in Willimansett, a section of Chicopee just across the Connecticut River from Holyoke. A neighbor reported a suspicious assembly next door and several dozen police soon arrived from Chicopee and Holyoke. A heated confrontation took place in the street; some of the leaders of the union group were arrested on charges of disorderly conduct.

A few weeks later some of the same men formed a picket line in front of Wellington Textiles with signs proclaiming unfair labor practices. Particularly at issue was the mill's practice of firing older workers, then hiring underage workers for the same jobs at a fraction of the pay. A representative of the mill came out and attempted to address the picketers but was greeted with catcalls and boos. Soon the Holyoke Police Department descended on the scene in large numbers. Picketers were warned to disperse and most did. The few that remained were arrested, handcuffed, and taken away in paddy wagons. One of the men arrested had to be transported to the hospital and rumors circulated that he had suffered a severe skull fracture after being arrested and handcuffed.

No one could have anticipated the intensity of public fury that resulted from the still unsubstantiated reports of the injured worker. A large crowd of mill workers and their families gathered the following Saturday afternoon in front of City Hall and the mayor addressed them, promising an investigation and punishment of any wrongdoing by the police.

No investigation was ever made.

Three performances of *The Importance of Being Earnest* were scheduled for a weekend in early February. The dress rehearsal had been difficult; between missed cues and technical problems it seemed to go on forever. But the Friday night performance went much better and the audience seemed to be enjoying themselves. By the Saturday matinee the confidence of the cast had improved a good deal and things went even better.

Just an hour before the final performance on Saturday evening, one of the cast members became ill and had to be replaced. It was a minor part, one of the servants, and a stage hand volunteered to fill in at the last minute. But the change unnerved Miss Edwards and the cast was uneasy as they awaited the rise of the curtain on the last performance.

The new cast member was slow and hesitant with his lines but George Bradley saved the day by feeding him cues and covering them adeptly. Once this had happened several times, everyone relaxed and enjoyed the rest of the performance. Jack was especially aware that his father and sisters were in the audience. By the end of the third act the crowd was on their feet, applause cascaded through the auditorium, and the cast was called back for two curtain calls.

After the curtain dropped for the last time, the atmosphere backstage was electric. The members of the cast and crew congratulated one another. Miss Edwards thanked them all and commended them for a job well done. Then Pauline stepped up next to Miss Edwards and, on behalf of the entire cast and crew, thanked her heartily and presented her with a bouquet of beautiful red roses. In tears, the director told them they were the best group of students with which she had ever had the privilege of working. Then she urged them to adjourn to the lobby where their families and friends waited to greet them.

Pauline and Jack stood watching the others stream out the stage door. When at last the backstage was quiet, Jack spoke.

"Well, thanks," he said.

"For what?" teased Pauline. "For annoying you…for pushing you…for twisting your arm?"

"Yeh," said Jack, smiling shyly. "I needed that. You would have been justified in telling me to get lost when I kept backing out. But you didn't."

"That's because I believed in you, Jack. I knew you could do it and do it well."

"Well, I didn't deserve all that, Pauline. So thank you. I don't know what I can do to repay the favor. But thank you."

Pauline smiled, took him by the arm, and lightly kissed his cheek.

"'Tis I, sweet Cecily, who should thank <u>you</u>, dear Algernon," said Pauline. They both laughed and headed to the lobby together.

# CHAPTER 29

# Remembering
## *March 1916*

The first anniversary of Evelyne's death happened to occur on a Saturday in March. Arrangements were made with Father Lévesque for a special memorial Mass just for the four family members to be held in the chapel at St. Agnes Church. The family was up early that morning. Breakfast and chores were tended to first, then they donned their best Sunday clothes.

Jack was cleaning out the Model T and he looked up just as his sisters and father stepped out of the front door of the farmhouse. He was struck by how much his sisters had grown in the last year. Marie, now fifteen, was tall and thin, and in her Sunday dress looked very much like her mother. She wore her brunette hair in a bun, fastened with a comb, a black veil covering her pretty face for this solemn occasion. Claire, at twelve, was stocky with light brown hair that she preferred to keep short; she wore a black dress like her sister. Charles was wearing his best black suit and a black top hat. He walked with a slight stoop and limp but was able to do quite well without his cane most of the time. As he watched the three walking toward him across the lawn, Jack wondered what his mother would think if she could see the family today.

After Mass the four stepped out of the chapel of St. Agnes and walked slowly along the flagstone walkway that led through a wrought iron gate to the cemetery next door. Jack held Claire's hand, Marie held her father's, as they stepped up to Evelyne's grave.

*Ici repose*
Evelyne St. Onge Bernard
1868 - 1915


To the left of the stone had been placed a large, lovely bouquet of white and pink carnations. Jack knew it had not been there when they entered the chapel an hour earlier and he turned and looked toward the street. Another car was parked there.

The family stood by Evelyne's grave and recited the Our Father together. Then each read a Bible verse in honor of Evelyne:

I know that my Vindicator lives,
and that he will at last stand forth upon the dust;
And from my flesh I shall see God.


… the winter is past,
the rains are over and gone.
The flowers appear on the earth,
the time of pruning the vines has come,
and the song of the dove is heard in our land.
The fig tree puts forth its figs,
and the vines, in bloom, give forth fragrance.
Arise, my beloved, my beautiful one,
and come!


We know that all things work for good for those who love God, who are called according to his purpose.

The LORD is my shepherd; I shall not want.
In verdant pastures he gives me repose;
Beside restful waters he leads me;
he refreshes my soul.

After a few minutes the family turned together and retraced their steps along the stone walkway to the church yard, then down the walk toward the parked car. At that moment Mrs. Wellington stepped out of the other car and came toward the four, greeting each with a smile and an embrace.

"Thank you for the beautiful flowers, those were Mom's favorite. That was very thoughtful of you," said Jack.

"The flowers were Anne's idea," Mrs. Wellington explained to Jack. "She's been reminding me in every letter since January to have them delivered to you today. I thought I'd bring them in person and had Bromley take me to your house first. Your neighbors told us where to find you. I know if it were possible Anne would be here today. She cares so much for you and your family, and she loved your mother dearly."

Jack nodded and thanked her again. But he could tell that Mrs. Wellington had something else on her mind. The two stood together looking out across the cemetery. Then she took his arm: "Jack, there's someone else who wants to see you." She gestured to the car. "But he's not sure you want to see him."

Only then did Jack realize that there was another passenger in the rear seat of the Wellington car behind Bromley. He was stunned by this unexpected visit and walked slowly toward the car as Tom stepped out onto the wet pavement. He was dressed in a dark suit, a black hat, and well shined leather shoes. But he looked thin and tired and his eyes were set deep into his head.

"Tom," Jack began, extending his hand. "I...I really didn't...I'm so glad to see you, Tom." Tom stood still, unsmiling, then grasped Jack's hand and shook it. "How are you?" asked Jack.

"I'm okay, Jack. I'm sorry to come unannounced like this. I should have called or written to ask if it was all right. But I wasn't sure what you'd say. If you don't want to see me I'll understand..."

"Tom, why wouldn't I want to see you? You're my best fr...."

Tom interrupted him. "Don't say it, Jack, please, don't say it. I don't deserve it." His eyes glistened.

"Tom, we're still friends, we have to be, we go way back. A few differences or disagreements can't change that."

"I wish that was true, Jack, I really do. But I can't be your friend, ever again, I don't deserve to be. I didn't want to come today and make things worse for you, I just wanted to show you I care about you and your family, that I'm not entirely self-centered."

Jack couldn't understand what Tom was saying, why he was so adamant about not deserving his friendship. But he didn't feel he could pursue it, not here, anyway.

Tom brightened a bit as he continued. "It looks like you are doing okay. God, I swear you've grown six inches since last fall. And I hear you're doing great in school...beating everyone in track. I don't know how you do it, I mean, carry around your sorrow. You must miss her so much...your mom, I mean."

"How's school going? You're graduating in June?" asked Jack.

"Well, I'm not too sure. I've missed some time and fallen behind, but I'm getting back on track. We'll see, I guess."

There was a long pause as the two young men stood looking across the churchyard toward the cemetery. Finally Jack spoke. "You know what I wish, Tom? What would really make me happy? I wish we could go fishing, just the two of us, up at Hampton Ponds. You know, the way we used to? Couldn't we do that sometime, please?"

Tom was looking at the ground, shaking his head slowly. He looked up and into Jack's eyes, but then quickly looked away. "We'd better be going now."

Jack looked at Tom in disbelief. He wanted to press Tom on this, to understand what had happened between them. But all he could say was, "Thanks for coming, Tom, it really was good of you and your mother."

Jack and Tom shook hands again. Mrs. Wellington, who had been talking with the others, rejoined her son. They climbed into the back seat of the car and Bromley drove them away.

CHAPTER 30

# Perils
*May 1916*

It was early May and Jack was busy with practice and meets four afternoons each week. His workload at school was mounting as the end of the year approached. And the activity in the family garden consumed nearly every minute when he was home.

Marie was now a freshman at Holyoke High School. She was reserved and somewhat shy, and it took her several months to make friends and feel comfortable in this new school; seeing her brother once or twice a day in the corridors or the lunchroom was a source of comfort for her. Once a week, usually on Tuesdays, Marie and Jack rode the trolley home together. It afforded them a few minutes to talk, brother to sister, something they found little time for otherwise.

"Jackie, have you asked anyone to the Senior Formal? It's only a few weeks away, you know."

"I'm not going, I'm too busy. Besides, it's not my kind of thing, getting all dressed up…I hate it."

"You're probably smart. Some of the freshman girls are just completely consumed with it…it's all they ever talk about. It's kind of silly."

Jack laughed and nodded. There was a pause of a few seconds. Then Marie continued: "But if you <u>were</u> going, just suppose you were, who would you want to go with? Anyone special?"

"I told you, I'm not interested. So just drop it, okay?" snapped Jack, a note of annoyance in his voice.

Marie was taken aback by Jack's tone and sat quietly for the rest of the trip to Westfield. The two stepped off the car onto Southampton Road together but Marie strode several steps ahead of her brother. Jack could tell she was upset and hurried to catch up with her.

"I'm sorry, Marie, okay? I just don't have the time, you know?"

Marie relaxed and looked up into her brother's eyes. "I understand. I won't bother you about it again."

On the front lawn of the Bernard farmhouse Marie stopped and turned to Jack. "I only mention it because it's the last big social event of your high school years, and I'm afraid that you'll miss out...that someday you'll look back and wish you'd made the time. That's all. But I'll stop bothering you, I promise."

Jack looked his sister in the eyes and smiled: "Promise?"

"Promise," repeated Marie with a twinkle in her eye.

Several days later Jack and his sisters were tending the animals in the barn. When they had finished, Claire asked her sister to play hopscotch with her in the driveway.

"You go ahead and make the squares. I'll be there in a minute," answered Marie. Then she and Jack stood, leaning against the fence, watching Angélique chew on some fresh hay.

"Pauline Foley is in my civics class, you know," Marie started. "I never noticed before how pretty she is. You know what I mean? She has very agreeable features, not flashy, but very agreeable, don't you think so?"

"I guess so," replied Jack.

"I heard her telling someone she wasn't going to the Senior Formal. I don't understand why not, she's pretty, she's well-liked, and respected. Any idea why she's not going?"

"Nope."

"It's surprising...if I were a boy I'd ask her. I mean, she's nice, she's smart, and she's pretty...she's very pretty."

Jack looked at Marie: "I thought you promised!"

"I'm just saying it's surprising...I wonder if maybe she's waiting for someone... someone in particular... to ask her...Oh, well, I better go play hopscotch with Claire."

Jack watched his sisters at play, a little cross with Marie, but also thinking about Pauline.

The track team had a shorter schedule in the spring than in the fall, only four meets in six weeks. In a way it made it more difficult for Jack. It always took several meets in the fall before he really started to feel like he was running his best. In spring that meant he was at his peak about when the season was winding up. So he practiced especially hard for the first meet and it was nearly five o'clock one Monday afternoon in May before he finished his workout on the athletic field. He pulled a pair of loose trousers over his running shorts, picked up his gym bag and books and started walking toward the gate. Just then he noticed a single figure rising from a seat in the bleachers.

"Long day, eh?" It was Pauline, smiling and walking toward him. "You must be getting prepared for a big win over Northampton on Friday."

"I don't know,' said Jack shaking his head. "I'm just having a hard time concentrating...too many distractions." They walked together through the gates onto Hampshire Street, then stopped. He knew Pauline lived in the Highlands and would be turning left; he was headed to the trolley stop on Sargeant, down the hill to the right.

"So, how's your mom doing? Is she any better?" Jack had heard that Mrs. Foley was fighting influenza.

"She's a little better," replied Pauline, her voice straining. "But she's still weak. You know how that is."

Jack looked down and nodded. There was an uncomfortable silence.

"Well, I better get home. If I don't see you again before Friday, good luck," said Pauline brightly. And she turned and started walking up Hampshire Street.

"Hey, Pauline..." began Jack. She stopped and turned around, facing him from several feet away. "Yes, Jack?"

Jack looked around, then took several steps toward Pauline.

"Are you going to the Formal? I mean, has someone already asked you?"

Pauline looked away and didn't respond.

"I mean...would you like to go with me?"

Now she was looking straight into his eyes and Jack hoped she would say "yes" or "no" quickly and get it over with. But she hesitated long enough to make Jack feel nervous.

"Jack," she finally said, slowly shaking her head.

"If you don't want to, that's okay," replied Jack, trying to save face.

"Oh, no, Jack, it's not that."

"Or you already have a date?"

She shook her head again, then bit her lip. Jack was feeling confused and very uncomfortable. Pauline was not making this easy.

"Jack, are you asking me because you feel sorry for me? You know...my mom?"

"No, no, not at all."

"Is it because you feel you owe it to me for getting you into the play? You said you wanted to repay me somehow. That's probably it, right?"

"No, it's not that either, Pauline. I just want you to go with me to the Formal. You're the only one I want to go with."

"But why?"

"Why do you have to ask a question like that?" replied Jack sharply. As soon as he did he wished he hadn't; he was sounding like he was annoyed with her. He lowered his voice: "I like you, Pauline...and we always have fun together. That's all, okay?"

Finally, Pauline's defensiveness attenuated. She looked into his soft eyes and smiled.

"Okay….I mean, <u>yes</u>, Jack, <u>yes</u> I would like to go with you. Thank you. That would be wonderful." And she hugged him and kissed him on the cheek.


Pauline stood before Jack in the parlor of her parent's home, smiling. Her floor-length dress of aqua chiffon had lace at the neck and at the wrists. Her rich, dark hair hung to her shoulders.

"You look real nice, Pauline," said Jack with a shy smile. He presented her with a corsage of white orchids which, with her mother's help, was pinned to her dress.

Pauline's parents stood looking proudly at their daughter and Jack.

"Have a wonderful time, you two," offered Mrs. Foley. "Don't be too late now."

The Formal was very formal, indeed. Nearly all of Jack and Pauline's classmates were there and acting uncharacteristically serious and mature. A small orchestra composed of several faculty members and parents played slow, sedate tunes as the young couples danced.

Jack was feeling awkward and uncomfortable at first, but Pauline had a way of making him relax.

"Remember Miss Magwood's dance classes?" asked Jack with a smile.

Pauline nodded and rolled her eyes. "It seems like a thousand years ago, doesn't it?"

"I remember how nervous I was about asking girls to dance. And how at the Spring Gala you stood right next to me before the last dance and practically <u>made</u> me ask you…"

"I did not," disputed Pauline. "I just…well…tried to help you."

Jack looked down, then nodded and chuckled. "And I needed help, didn't I?"

"Yes, you did!" replied Pauline, and they both laughed at the memory.

As the orchestra struck up *All I Do is Dream of You*, Pauline drew closer to Jack.

"I received some good news, today, Jack. I've been accepted at Wellesley College."

"Wellesley? Wow, that's great, Pauline. Congratulations. You'll do swell, I'm sure of it."

"I'm already feeling the jitters about it. All those smart girls from around the country... I'm not sure I'm equal to that!"

"Of course you are, Pauline. You're salutatorian of our class, right? That means the second best student out of a class of sixty. You're smarter than you give yourself credit for; you'll do great."

"Thanks, Jack. I wish you could be there to give me courage."

"I don't think I'd fit in at Wellesley!" replied Jack with a twinkle in his eye. "But I'll write you and see you when you come home for holidays and vacations. You'll probably have some Harvard boy on your arm by then, but maybe you'll still speak to me."

"Jack, don't say that. Of course I'll speak to you. We'll always be friends, I promise."

Jack was uneasy with promises these days. "We'll see, we'll see. But you're gonna be in a different world at Wellesley."

Jack slept late the next morning. By the time he appeared bleary-eyed in the kitchen Marie was already preparing a soup for lunch.

"How was the Formal, Jackie? Did you have a good time? You got in pretty late."

"It was okay," replied Jack.

"Just okay?"

"All right, it was good...it was fun."

"And Pauline…did she enjoy herself?"

"I guess so…"

Marie seemed to be waiting for something more from her brother and she looked at him expectantly.

"Okay, okay…thank you, Marie…"

"For…," said Marie.

"For annoying me and plaguing me and just generally being a nuisance about the Formal and Pauline…" Then he turned and looked squarely into his sister's eyes. "You were right. It was fun and I'm glad I went and I'm glad I went with Pauline…and yes, she is pretty…so thank you, okay?" Jack smiled at Marie and she smiled back.

"By the way, I was talking to Eleanor Simmons yesterday," said Marie. "She heard that Anne Wellington and her father have returned from Argentina. Mr. Wellington was taken ill; it sounds serious, his heart I guess."

CHAPTER 31

# Commencing
*June 1916*

Holyoke High School's commencement ceremony was scheduled for the first Friday evening in June in the school auditorium. The graduating seniors were dressed in long, black robes. The boys wore white shirts with stiff white collars, the girls wore white, collarless blouses. They all had black mortar boards with black tassels decorated with purple and white, the school colors. Families and friends of the graduates, seated toward the rear, stood in unison as the school band played the processional march. The graduates filed in two-by-two, stern faced, taking seats in the front rows with their backs to the audience. Jack knew his father and sisters would be present but did not spot them as he marched in.

The ceremony went on for nearly an hour, highlighted by a long-winded congratulatory message from the mayor. Sixty diplomas were conferred, applause broke out, and the graduates recessed wearing broad smiles. As it was a sunny June evening, a reception was held on the school's front lawn on Hampshire Street. His family hugged and congratulated Jack and admired his two awards, silver medals for Outstanding Student in Chemistry and Outstanding Student in History. Many friends commented to Jack on the unusual combination of interests.

Several neighbors and friends from Westfield were also in attendance and they shook Jack's hand, then congratulated the rest of the family. Jack felt truly exhilarated, especially at the two unexpected awards. He and Pauline congratulated one another, shaking hands; then she kissed him quickly on the cheek. They were smiling and laughing together when Jack raised his eyes and saw Anne. She was standing with her mother, some distance away, looking his way. Jack froze, not knowing what to do. The two Wellington women approached him.

Jack had not laid eyes on Anne in nearly eight months and her face was, as always, difficult to ignore. Her hair sparkled in the mid-day sun, her skin touched with a rosy flush. But she was clearly uneasy and struggling to maintain her composure. Her green eyes were uncharacteristically dull.

Mrs. Wellington looked gray and tired, but she strode up to Jack first and spoke with warmth and enthusiasm: "Jack Bernard, my dear boy. It is so good to see you again; we've missed you so…you'll never know." She hugged him, then looked him squarely in the eye. "Congratulations, young man, you have certainly distinguished yourself. We always knew you would go far, didn't we Anne?" She turned to her daughter who was smiling at Jack.

"Yes, Jack, always. Congratulations." Anne shook Jack's hand briefly.

There were a few awkward moments, then Jack's father, who was watching the encounter from a respectful distance, stepped in. "Tell them about your plans, Jack…for college."

Jack flushed and rolled his eyes. "I'm hoping to go to college to study engineering, but not for another year."

"And…," prompted his father.

"And I've been invited to apply to Worcester Polytechnic Institute. They say I might qualify for a scholarship."

At that news Anne beamed and lost some of her restraint. "Oh, Jack, that is such good news. I am…we are so happy for you and your family."

"Thank you," was all Jack could say at the moment. He wanted to say much more, to ask about Tom and her father, to ask her to explain that terrible letter and the way she had treated him, and what had happened to their promise, and more and more. But all he could find the words to say was, "Thank you."

Anne was holding a delicate bouquet of pink and white carnations. She handed them to Jack as she whispered "These are for you. Your mother would be so proud of you!" Her eyes glistened with tears. Then she touched Jack's hand: "Be sure to read the note."

With that Anne and Mrs. Wellington departed. The well-wishes of friends continued for quite some time and there were refreshments served. Jack was thoroughly enjoying this moment in the spotlight; it felt good to feel good for once, he thought.

When the Bernard family got home, Jack put the bouquet in a vase with some water and set it on the mantle in the parlor. He opened the note, expecting a simple card of congratulations. Instead it was a request from Anne for Jack to visit her at his earliest convenience. It ended with

> I have so much to tell you, so much to explain
> to you, so much for which I must beg your
> forgiveness. Please come to see me soon.
>     Always, Anne

Jack stared at the note for a long time. Finally he inserted it carefully back into the small envelope and placed it in his pocket.

Jack worked only part-time at the Wellington mill that summer. After graduation in early June he and his father had discussed the matter at length and agreed that the gardens and orchard required more time than either could devote to them while working full-time at the mill.

The Bernard gardens now exceeded fifty acres, roughly twenty on their own land and another thirty on land belonging to the Bousquets which they agreed to cultivate in return for sharing some of their produce with their neighbors.

Marie and Claire did much of the weeding, staking, and harvesting. They also set up and tended a small stand on the road in front of the farmhouse. Jack had modified an old farm cart for them, building a sloped counter and shelves on which they could display fruits and vegetables from the gardens for sale to passersby.

Jack's co-workers in the sorting room were all Jack's age or younger. Several were classmates of his from Holyoke High School. The work was hard and there was little time for conversation outside of lunch breaks that were usually spent on the grassy strip between the mill and the canal. Common topics of discussion included the school year that had just ended, the prospects for that year's Papermakers baseball team, and plans for the coming weekend. Most of these young workers had fathers and older brothers who worked in the mill so some discussion of union activity frequently arose. Jack was careful to avoid those discussions, never knowing who could be trusted.

One morning in early July Jack noticed a small group of men huddled in an out-of-the-way corner of the warehouse among bales of wool. He sensed that something was up and wanted to find out more, but he waited until his lunch break. He sat on the canal wall next to Jim Trottière. Jim's father worked in the mill.

"Any good fishing these days, Jim?" asked Jack casually.

"We've been getting some bass and shad up river the last couple weeks," replied Jim, "nothing too unusual. How about you?"

"Haven't had much time this summer; working here and on the farm keeps me pretty busy," explained Jack, then he paused. "I saw some men in the back room this morning hangin' around, talking. Any idea what they're up to?"

Jim seemed to hesitate, turned and looked toward the mill, then back to the water. "Somethin's up, I s'spect...not sure."

Those few words from Jim told Jack all he needed to know. The conversation returned to fishing.

That evening Jack and his father sat in the back yard as the sun set. Jack had sensed a particular unease in his father over the last few weeks and wondered if it had to do with things at work.

"Everything okay at the mill these days, Dad?" asked Jack.

"Yeah, pretty much, why do you ask, Son?"

"No reason, really. The guys in the sorting room are, you know, just kids like me. But some of the men from the mill seem to be on edge the last week or so. I just wondered."

"Well, everyone's on edge, Jack, that's for sure. They're just worried about their jobs, no doubt, just like all of us. I wish it weren't like that, but it is."

Marie and Claire were giggling as they played with Rufus on the grass.

"That's why I want you to go to college, Son, so that you don't end up working your whole life in that place, getting old and sick and tired. You know what I mean?"

"Yeh, Dad, I know," answered Jack. This was a frequent topic of his father's lately, and Jack sometimes tired of it. But he also understood the depth of his father's feelings about the matter. Watching his sisters playing only emphasized the point – don't give in to a life of drudgery, there's more to life than that.

The two Bernard men sat quietly, Charles smoking his pipe, Jack watching his sisters.

"Jack, I been meaning to ask you, will you be able to watch the girls for a while on Saturday? I've got some errands I need to do in town. I'll be home by three or so."

"Yeh, sure, Dad, I'll be here. Pauline and I are going up to Mountain Park Saturday night for a while. I won't be late."

"Sure, Son, that'll be fine."

Jack was up early Saturday morning. He spent several hours working in the gardens, watering, weeding, then harvesting the first tomatoes. By mid-morning he walked back to the house. He made himself a cup of tea and sat in the backyard drinking it, gazing out across the gardens toward Mount Tekoa in the distance. He was looking forward to seeing Pauline that evening and feeling truly at peace with himself for the first time in a while.

At that moment he heard the telephone ringing in the house, then he heard Claire's voice. She was talking gaily as if to an old friend she hadn't heard from in a while. Finally there was silence and Claire was stepping out of the kitchen door, walking toward him, looking intently at her brother.

"Jackie, there's a telephone call for you...it's Anne Wellington."

Suddenly his demeanor changed, his heart raced, his face reddened. Even Claire could see the change.

"Jackie, did you hear me? It's Anne."

Jack stood, walked slowly to the door, and entered. The telephone was on the wall in the parlor, just around the corner from the kitchen. Claire had left the receiver dangling. He picked it up, held it to his ear, then leaned against the wall as if for support as he spoke into the mouthpiece.

"Hello?"

"Hello, Jack. This is Anne."

"Hello, Anne."

"It's good to hear your voice, Jack."

"Yes, Anne, it's good to hear yours."

"How are you, Jack?"

"I'm doing very well, thank you. Very well. How are you?"

"I'm fine, Jack." Even over the scratchy phone line he thought her voice sounded weak and forced, as if she was struggling to keep herself under control.

"Good, that's good."

"It was so nice to speak with Claire, Jack. I only saw her from a distance at your graduation. I'm sorry I didn't get to speak to her then. And I'm sorry I couldn't spend more time with you that day, too. It didn't seem...well, Mother and I couldn't stay."

"I understand."

"Jack...did you get my note? It was tucked into the bouquet."

"Yes, yes, I got it." There was an awkward pause.

"Jack...Jackie, I was hoping you would come to see me... that we could talk. I have so many things I need to say to you. Please give me a chance...to make amends."

"Anne...I...there's no need. Life has many twists and turns that we can't predict, I know that. Like you wrote in your letter..."

"But Jackie, you don't understand. That letter, it was all a terrible misunderstanding."

"It seemed pretty clear to me, Anne." He paused, choosing his words carefully. "Let's just let it lie...I think that would be best." He was leaning against the door jamb, looking down at the floor as he spoke. Then he looked up and into the kitchen. Claire was standing in the kitchen doorway, not wanting to appear to be listening, but trying to catch his eye. She turned and walked away as he looked at her.

"Jackie? Are you still there?"

"Yes, Anne, I'm still here."

"Can't we just talk about this, the two of us, face to face. Please?"

There was a long pause.

"Jackie?"

"Anne, I really don't know what to say. I just don't know. I'm trying hard to get my life back together. I'm just not sure I know what to say right now."

"Will you promise me you'll think about it? Please? Just promise me you'll think about it."

"Okay, I promise. Thank you for calling, Anne."

"Okay," she replied, her voice cracking.

"Goodbye, Anne."

Jack stepped out of the kitchen door into the side yard looking for his little sister. He wasn't really angry with her for eavesdropping, but he felt the need to talk to her, to console her. He'd never talked to her about Anne, even though he knew that Claire was very fond of her.

Jack found Claire behind the barn, watching the chickens. She looked away as he approached and spoke with her back to him. "I didn't mean to listen in on you and Anne. I'm sorry. It was rude."

"I'm not angry with you, okay?" He touched her on the shoulder. She turned, buried her head in his chest, and started to cry.

Jack stroked her hair but let her cry for a minute. She stopped crying, but he just waited, like his mother always did with him. Finally she spoke.

"I miss her, Jackie…she was my friend, too, you know."

Jack stroked her hair. "I know."

CHAPTER 32

# Recreating
*June 1916*

That evening Jack and Pauline took the trolley from the Highlands station to Mountain Park, a ten minute ride. They walked the midway with no particular destination in mind. The calliope music drew them to the merry-go-round and they mounted two horses, side-by-side, and rode around and around, laughing at themselves, young adults surrounded by children half their age.

They spent the longest time playing mini-golf, although the golfing itself took a back seat to animated conversation and much laughter. It was perfect, thought Jack, he and Pauline playing mini-golf. Just like being with Pauline, mini-golf was easy: no pressure, no expectations, just fun.

When it was time to leave, the couple walked toward the trolley stand. They passed the Ferris wheel and although neither was inclined to take that ride, they watched for several minutes as children, young adults, and older couples boarded the chairs and were lifted skyward. Jack's eye was drawn to one boy and girl a few years younger than they. The girl was smiling as she took her seat, but the boy was looking a little ill at ease. As the chair began its ascent, their eyes were filled with excitement. In an instant Jack was transported back to a time four years earlier and he felt again, just for a moment, the thrill of rising into the unknown, a little scared but at the same time exhilarated. That feeling was nothing short of electric. His eyes glistened at the memory.

Pauline's voice intruded: "The trolley's coming, we have to hurry." And the two broke into a run down the midway toward the trolley stop. When they got off the trolley at the Highlands, Jack walked Pauline the two blocks to her home on Nonotuck Street. She thanked him for a wonderful afternoon and kissed him lightly on the cheek. They were well practiced at this. During rehearsals of *The Importance of Being Earnest,* when Algernon was to kiss Cecily, Jack would always brush her lightly and briefly on the cheek. Only after Miss Edwards spoke to him during dress rehearsal did Jack finally kiss Pauline squarely on the lips, but even then it was the lightest and briefest of contacts. Now that the play was behind them, they went back to the old habit of light brushes on the cheek. Both seemed to be content to leave things that way, very light, very casual.

The following Friday evening the couple once again found themselves at Mountain Park playing mini-golf. But this evening had an air of melancholy for them both. The next day Pauline was leaving to spend a month on the coast of Maine with her aunt and uncle. When she returned, there would be only a few days remaining before she left for Wellesley. This, each knew, was likely to be their last outing to Mountain Park for a long while.

They played two rounds of golf, laughing and teasing one another as they always did. Then they walked up the midway, just content to be together, enjoying the sights and sounds of the evening at the park. Just as Jack was feeling very comfortable, he spotted a familiar figure striding through the crowd in their direction. He was trying to think of what to say, or what to do, but there was no time.

"Jack! Hey, Jack! Hi, there. What a surprise!" It was Tom, smiling and extending his hand. As they shook hands, Jack's eye turned to the young lady by Tom's side.

"Hello, Jack, long time no see." It was Monique Fleury.

As often happened at times like these, Jack became flustered. "Hi, Tom…Monique…well, hi…I'm…er…oh, Monique, Tom, this is…" For one anxious moment the name eluded him and he dragged out the "this is" until finally he blurted out "...Pauline. This is Pauline Foley...Pauline, this is Tom...I mean Monique and Tom. They're old friends."

Just then a figure came out of the crowd. It was Monique's brother, Armand. He pulled Monique aside and whispered to her, a worried look on his face. Monique turned to Tom. "Tommy, we have to go, it's my father. Hurry."

Abruptly Tom and Monique departed with only very brief apologies and no explanations. Shortly afterward, Jack and Pauline boarded the trolley to return to Holyoke.

They stood on her front porch, not wanting to say their final goodbyes. Jack was going on about his family and the farm. He was obviously trying a little too hard to make conversation. Finally Pauline interrupted him.

"It's been a wonderful senior year and a very pleasant summer and I have you to thank for that. I'm going to miss you, dear Algernon, really, I am."

"It <u>has</u> been nice, Pauline...I mean sweet Cecily..." Jack began, then his voice trailed off and there was an awkward pause.

"I'm glad that I finally got to meet Tom and Monique, but I'm sorry it was so brief. I hope everything is okay with Monique's father. Has he been ill?"

"I don't know, I really don't know."

Just then the city fire alarm sounded in the distance, the strident notes echoing off the rocky face of Mount Tom. False alarms were fairly common, especially in summer, and neither Jack nor Pauline thought much of it.

Pauline looked into Jack's eyes. He could tell there was something on her mind that she wasn't sure she should say. She hesitated, then spoke softly.

"Jack...you and Anne, maybe you can patch things up. I know she still means a lot to you."

"It's not like that, Pauline, really. It's over. I put that behind me months ago, honest."

Pauline smiled, then shook her head. "I know you pretty well, Jack, and I'm no Beatrice Fairfax, but here's my advice: don't give up on her...on the two of you...just don't give up."

She kissed him gently on the cheek and whispered "Goodnight, Jack." Then she turned, opened the front door, and was gone. Jack stood facing the closed door. His lips were saying "Goodnight, Pauline," but no sound came out.

Jack turned and walked down the brick sidewalk, then walked the three blocks to the Pleasant Street trolley stop where he waited. More sirens were sounding in the distance and he began to think there really was a fire. He boarded the trolley and rode to Beech Street, then disembarked and walked four blocks to Sargeant Street where he hoped he would be in time for the last car to Westfield. Now the sky to the east was glowing and he knew there was a fire, a big fire, somewhere down by the canals. But he had to catch the last trolley.

As the Westfield car plunged into the dark woods and pasturelands west of town, Jack was deep in thought. It really hurt, saying goodbye to Pauline. And he was embarrassed that she thought he was still mooning over Anne.

"How could she think that?" he asked himself. "Did I ever give her any reason to suspect such a thing? I thought I was doing a pretty good job of hiding all that... not good enough, I guess."

# CHAPTER 33

# Burning
## *July 1916*

E arly the next morning Jack was awakened by the murmur of low voices that carried up from the yard through his open window. He rose and looked out. His father and Pierre Bousquet were standing in the side yard talking. Both men looked very serious. Sensing something was amiss, Jack dressed quickly, climbed down the stairs and stepped out into the front yard just as his neighbor was leaving.

Charles was standing alone, his head down, in the driveway. "There was a fire in Holyoke last night, Jack. A bad one. Pierre got a call from a friend early this morning."

"Yeh, I could see the smoke from the Highlands as I was coming home...lots of sirens, too. Where was it?"

"An empty warehouse on Lyman Street, I guess."

"Probably some kids, eh?" replied Jack.

But his father shook his head.

"No, Son, I don't think so. There was a secret workers' meeting going on there. Then the fire broke out. The police and fire trucks all came, but by that time the fire was out of control. It burned the place to the ground."

"Anyone hurt, Dad?"

His father nodded. "One of the workers. He died."

"Who was it, Dad, do they know?"

"No one I've heard of, but I guess he was from the New England Mill."

Jack could see his father was shaken. Not only was there the shock of knowing that a millworker had died, but a sense that the labor situation in Holyoke had taken a very serious turn. The situation was now even more tense, more unsettling, than it already had been.

"This is bad, Jack, this is very bad," said his father grimly. He stood looking across the lawn and out toward the fields.

# CHAPTER 34

# Never Forgetting
*October 1916*

Jack was able to return to a nearly full-time schedule in the sorting room that fall. Weekends were taken up almost entirely with work in the gardens and the barn. One thing that he had missed all summer long was fishing and on a Saturday in October he decided he needed to spend a day at Hampton Ponds. It felt like a pilgrimage, a return to a sacred place whose meaning for him went considerably beyond catching fish. Claire asked if she could go along and he would normally have said yes, but this time he politely declined.

"I just want to go alone today, Claire...another time, okay?"

It was a calm autumn day and the leaves of maple, oak, and ash shone with exceptional brilliance, scarlet, gold, and subtler shades of mauve, tan and brown, their colors further magnified by reflections off the still pond waters. Jack stood on the steep bank not far from where he, Tom, and his father had built their fire and sipped cocoa four years ago. He cast his line first in the shallower waters close to shore, then out into the deeper water. He was seeing little fish activity but it didn't seem to matter.

Jack was thinking about memories, how some are clear, crisp, unmistakable... and some are vague and unsubstantial. His mother's face, thought Jack, for a while after she died he could still see her face just as clearly as though she were there before him. But lately he felt he was losing her all over again, losing the memory of her soft features, adoring eyes, gentle smile. He wanted that memory back more than anything, he didn't want to lose it. Once was enough, he thought. Once was painful enough.

A slight breeze had come up and the glassy surface of the pond broke into small patches, each reflecting the sunlight a bit differently. The result was an intricate patchwork of light and dark that was mesmerizing. At one moment it looked like a radiant sunset. Then the breeze shifted slightly and the sunset disappeared. Then it looked like the water was covered with sparkling jewels - diamonds, emeralds, rubies. Again the breeze slackened and the jewels faded.

Then he saw it, clear, distinct, unmistakable…his mother's face, looking up at him and smiling, her lips parting and moving. The leaves of a small aspen over his head rustled and then he was sure he heard his mother's voice.

"Jackie…you like her, Anne, don't you? Tell her, honey, tell her…love…it's too precious…life is too short…don't put it off."

The breeze slackened again, the image gradually faded, and the rustling leaves were silenced.

Jack stood on that spot for a long time, willing the waters to produce his mother's face once again and the leaves to conjure again the sound of her voice, her words. Finally he lay his rod down on the embankment, crouched down, grasped his knees under his chin, and sat immobile. Eyes closed, he concentrated with all his abilities, and yes, he could remember her again, his mother's face was clearer to him now than it had been in a year and a half. He could even remember her voice as if it was she who was speaking.

CHAPTER 35

# Reunion
*November 1916*

T he Boston-bound train was moving at last, but very slowly. Once it left Springfield Jack could see little from the window save for an occasional electric street lamp shining dimly through the driving snow, a perfect backdrop for his reveries. He was getting hungry and he snacked on a pear and two vanilla wafers that he dug from his rucksack.

The train was delayed over two hours in Palmer waiting for another train from Vermont that was scheduled to join his. He was awakened by a jolt when the two at last were linked. He lay along the full length of the seat, eyes open, still submerged in the past. There was another delay of nearly an hour in Worcester. Jack used the lavatory in the next car, then returned to his seat and stretched out once more.

It was nearly dawn when his train finally arrived in Boston and Jack was exhausted and hungry. As soon as he had disembarked he plunged one hand into his rucksack and extracted another small snack from his meager provisions. He followed the crowds through the doors at the end of the platform and was suddenly in the heart of Boston's South Station.

This was Jack's first trip to Boston. In fact, it was his first visit to any city other than Holyoke or Springfield, and he was not prepared for the scene that lay before him as he emerged from the train station. Narrow streets radiated in all directions, towered over by tall gray buildings of brick and stone. Motorcars were everywhere and driving very fast in what seemed to Jack to be totally random, unpredictable patterns.

He didn't dare attempt to cross a street until he found a crosswalk with a traffic light, and when he did he sprinted across lest the light should turn green and he would be run down.

The storm that had deposited so much snow inland had left only an inch or two of slush on the streets of New England's largest city, and a light rain was now falling. Jack walked in whatever direction required the fewest street crossings until, by chance, he came to a sign for Charles Street. He turned left and walked several blocks until Charles Street appeared to end at a large intersection. He turned and walked in the opposite direction. In a few minutes he was looking across the broad expanse of the Charles River. How different it was from the Connecticut and Westfield Rivers that were so familiar to him.

Another ten minute walk brought Jack to the entrance to the Charles Street Jail, a five-story stone structure that looked as much like a forbidding castle as a prison. He shuddered at the sight of the barred windows and the heavy iron gate at the main entrance. A small sign indicated a side entrance for visitors and Jack followed it around the corner to a window with a sign, "Visitors inquire here." This, he realized, was the end of one long, difficult journey, and likely the beginning of another, possibly even more difficult one.

"I would like to see Tom Wellington, please," he said meekly through the narrow opening in the window.

"No visitors until ten a.m.," was the curt reply. "Come back in two hours."

"Thank you, sir," said Jack, and he turned and walked away, somewhat relieved that he had time to think.

Jack crossed the street and strode across a broad swath of grass to the banks of the Charles River. The rain had stopped and the temperature was surprisingly mild. He sat on a bench facing the river and pulled the last remnants of a snack from his rucksack. The scene before him was dreary, a perfect mirror of the state of his heart at that moment. As he ate he thought about the events that led up to his hasty departure from home for Boston.

He had been working in the warehouse just two days before when a mail clerk from the mill office came looking for him.

"Jack Bernard? A letter came addressed to you today care of the Mill." The clerk presented it, turned, and left. Jack stood motionless, looking at the hand-written letter postmarked Cambridge, Massachusetts, one week earlier. He immediately thought of Tom, but the handwriting wasn't Tom's, he was certain of that.

The note was very short:

Mr. Bernard,
Your friend Tom Wellington needs your help. He is in the Charles St. Jail in Boston.
Yours,
H. Sampson, Harvard College, October the 28th, 1916

Jack stared at the note, refusing to believe what he had read. Apart from the brief encounter at Mountain Park in July, he had not had any contact with Tom in nearly six months. But the thought of his former friend sitting in a jail in Boston was more than Jack could bear. He wondered if this was the result of a college prank like the ones Tom had been fond of at the Dorchester School. Maybe it was all a misunderstanding that would be resolved in a few days, perhaps it already had been resolved.

After his shift he hurried to the trolley stand on High Street. Throughout the ride home he was consumed with questions about Tom and what he could do. That evening he told his father about his plan. He must travel to Boston and try to see Tom. He wasn't sure what he could do for his old friend, but he had to try.

"I don't know what young Tom has done to deserve this, but you know your own heart, my boy," said the senior Bernard to his departing son the next afternoon.

Jack returned to the visitors' entrance at the Charles Street Jail at ten o'clock and asked again to see Tom Wellington. After he signed the register, he was frisked, then told to be seated in a drafty hallway. After a wait of nearly fifteen minutes he was ushered through a series of locked doors by a guard swinging a massive ring of keys. He showed him into a long, dreary room with a wooden counter along one side.

"Window five," said the guard brusquely.

Jack walked slowly the length of the room, then turned at the numeral five on the wall and looked through the bars. A head of black, matted hair was bowed on the other side of the bars.

"Tom? Tom Wellington?" Jack spoke softly.

At first there was no reaction, then very slowly the head was raised and two dark eyes peered through the hair. It was Tom, all right, but his face was barely recognizable. He had a rough beard, his eyes were dull and lifeless, set deeply in his head, his skin a sickly gray color.

"Tom, it's Jack, Jack Bernard," he said speaking louder and leaning in closer to Tom.

There was a long silence and Jack wondered if Tom was hearing him.

Finally Tom spoke. "What are you doing here? Who told you I was here?"

"I got a letter from one of your Harvard friends," explained Jack. "Tom, what's this all about?"

"None of your business, Bernard. Go away...just go away," said Tom angrily.

"I wanna help, Tom. Maybe I can get you out of here. Please, Tom, let me help," Jack pleaded.

"Why do you want to help me? You don't owe me anything," said Tom defiantly. There was a long pause, then he added, "I don't deserve anything from anyone, least of all from you. Go away."

Jack couldn't believe what he was hearing. He stood up straight and turned away from the barred window, his eyes focused on the distant wall of the long room. He was close to giving up and leaving. He turned and looked back toward Tom whose head now was buried in his arms.

Jack leaned forward once again and spoke slowly. "Tom, why do you keep saying you don't deserve to be my friend anymore? I don't understand. What did you do that was so bad that I should hate you forever?"

"Come on, Jack, don't you know by now? I'm the reason Anne broke it off with you. Isn't that cause enough to hate me? It's enough for _me_ to hate me." Tom buried his face in his arms on the counter.

Jack was dumbfounded. There was a long pause as he tried to make sense of what Tom had said. Nearly a minute went by without a word. Slowly Tom raised his head and looked at Jack through black, bleary eyes.

"Anne explained it all to you, didn't she? She promised me she would when I finally told her...after she returned from South America. You know all about that, Jack, right?"

Jack stood stone-faced, disbelieving. He shook his head slowly. There was another long pause, then Tom continued.

"Monique...last November...she told me you and she were carrying on behind my back. She made it sound like the two of you were quite an item and that everyone knew it except me. I got mad...at her...at you...I just lost my mind, Jack, I can't explain it any other way. I had a lot to drink that night and I wasn't thinking straight. I wrote a letter to Anne...I don't know why, I guess I just wanted to get even. I told her what Monique had told me about you two...and I made up some things to make it sound even worse. They were lies, I know that now...I just wanted to get revenge. A couple of months later Monique told me she'd been lying...I was so ashamed at what I'd done to Anne and to you, I just couldn't bring myself to admit it."

Jack had turned his back to Tom. He couldn't look him in the face and he wasn't sure he wanted to listen to his words at this point.

"You see? You should hate me, Jack. I betrayed you, I turned on you. I never bothered to ask any questions, or talk to you, or even accuse you to your face. I just wanted to hurt you...and I used my own sister...I broke her heart, Jack." For the first time, Tom's voice cracked and he began to cry.

"She hates me, you hate me, my parents hate me. So whatever happens to me, I deserve."

There was another long pause. Jack was still standing with his back to Tom.

"Go home, Jack. Forget about me. I'm not worth your time."

Still Jack did not respond.

"Are you listening to me?" Tom was shouting now. "Can you hear what I'm saying? Isn't that reason enough to hate me? Huh?"

Then Tom's voice became hushed.

"If you really want to do something for me, Jack, there's just one thing I want. I want you to go back to Holyoke and set things right with Anne. 'Cause the worst thing of all for me right now is thinking about what I did to her...to the two of you. She's probably too ashamed to tell you what her own brother did. She should be ashamed of me; I'm ashamed, too."

"All right, Tom. I'll go. And I'll talk to Anne. But before I go, tell me why you're here. What's this all about? What are you charged with?"

After a long pause, Tom spoke softly: "Arson. And murder. The warehouse fire...in Holyoke...in July. They say I started it...and I was responsible for the death of that guy..."

The weight of those words hit Jack like a roundhouse punch to the jaw. He was not expecting this. He was expecting to hear about some foolish college boy's mishap, drunken disorderliness, mayhem, perhaps, but not arson, not murder. He remembered his father's advice in times like these, took several deep breaths, and tried to focus his thoughts on the next step.

"But you were at Mountain Park that evening, remember? I saw you there. That was the last time I saw you. You couldn't...you would never..."

"That's not what the prosecutor is saying," countered Tom. "He says there's a witness who will testify that I was at the warehouse just before the fire broke out."

"They're lying," cried Jack, "I know they're lying."

Tom's head dropped.

"You know they're lying, they can't get away with this, it's a frame-up. Maybe they're mad at the mill and they're taking it out on you," said Jack. Tom's head was shaking and Jack was confused: "You weren't anywhere near there, Tom, we can prove it!"

Tom shook his bowed head again, then looked up slowly until his eyes met Jack's. His lips were trembling.

"What, Tom, what are you trying to say?" pleaded Jack.

"They're not lying, Jack. Monique's brother, Armand, he came to tell me that his father was in that meeting and that there might be trouble. He didn't know where the meeting was being held, but he thought I would know. And he wanted me to go there and warn his father. So we went back to town, I dropped the others off at Monique's house, and I drove home. I left the house by the back door and ran straight to the warehouse to look for Mr. Fleury. I was there," he exclaimed loudly. "I _was_ there," he repeated, this time softly, his voice shaking with emotion.

Again, Jack could not believe what he was hearing.

"You were at the warehouse...just before the fire broke out?" said Jack in disbelief. And as he stood shaking his head, his mind contemplated the impossible. He began "Tom, you didn't. You couldn't..."

"No, Jack, I didn't set the fire, I swear it. But when I saw the police had already arrived I ran out the back...and I tripped over a can of gasoline. It spilled all over the floor and splashed on my trousers. I kept running, so I don't know for sure, but I could have caused the fire. Don't you see? I was there, and the fire happened, and it's just my word against all theirs," replied Tom in desperation.

"How did you know where they were meeting?" asked Jack.

"Father had gotten word that there was going to be trouble. The police had been called and they were preparing to raid the meeting. They said they planned to 'crack some labor skulls.' Father tried to stop it, he really didn't want this, I swear."

"The Holyoke police...did they question you about this after the fire?" asked Jack.

"No," replied Tom. "The first I knew of any of this was when the State Police came to my dorm room." He buried his head in his arms and was breathing roughly.

"Tom, it's gonna be okay, I'm gonna help you, I swear," promised Jack.

"But Father, you can't tell him. It will kill him, I'm certain of it," protested Tom.

"Okay, I'll do my best. I have to get going, Tom. I've got to get home to my father and sisters right away. But trust me, I won't let you down."

"You've never let me down, Jack, never. I'm the one who let you down...but somehow you are willing to forgive the unforgiveable," said Tom.

"You're still my friend, and friends stick together," said Jack. "Godspeed."

Tom nodded, his eyes welled with tears, and Jack turned and left.

# CHAPTER 36

# Setting Things Right
### *November 1916*

T he return trip from Boston to Springfield was shorter and easier than Jack's eastward trip of the previous night. By now the snow had ended across the state and the tracks had been cleared, yet the train ride still took nearly five hours including the switching time in Palmer. As Jack gazed out on the snow-covered New England countryside, he found himself reviewing again and again the events of the months before the warehouse fire.

It was nearly nine o'clock in the evening when Jack stepped off the trolley in Westfield and walked up Southampton Road to his home. A single travel lane had been plowed and he was able to trudge along, stepping into the piled snow on the road's edge when an occasional automobile or horse-drawn carriage approached.

Charles had fallen asleep by the fire. He was startled by the sudden rattle of the front door latch but greatly relieved when his son appeared from out of the wintry darkness. They sat talking for nearly an hour. Charles was as shocked as his son to learn of the reason for Tom's arrest.

"But at least you and Anne, maybe you can work things out, eh?"

"Maybe, I don't know," replied Jack. "I've put her off so many times and refused to talk with her. I wouldn't blame her for not wanting to have anything to do with me."

"But let her be the one to make that decision, Son. Speak from your heart...that's what your mother would tell you to do."

"Yes, Dad, I know."

It was Sunday morning. The Bernard family attended nine o'clock Mass at St. Agnes. As they stood to leave, Mr. Bowen's round, smiling face greeted Jack from the next pew. "Did you ever get to Boston, son? I was worried awfully about you that night. "

"Yes, Mr. Bowen, I made it all right."

"It's good to see you, son." He turned to Charles, smiled warmly, and spoke softly. "That's quite a boy you got there, Charles, quite a boy." Charles nodded.

When they returned home, Jack made a telephone call. Quickly he changed his clothes and soon was walking down Southampton Road to the trolley stop. A half hour later he was in Holyoke and making his way up Beech Street to the Wellington home.

A maid answered the door and ushered Jack into the library. He stood uneasily by the window, looking out at the silhouette of one of the copper beeches against the snow. Several minutes went by, then he heard soft footsteps in the hallway. He turned as the door opened and there was Anne.

Five months had elapsed since he had seen her last. She was lovelier than ever, stood a bit taller and looked a little shapelier than he remembered. She was smiling, but it seemed to him a smile that required all her effort.

"Hello, Anne," he began, standing rigidly.

"Jack, it's so good to see you," she replied quickly, but she must have detected the look of concern in his demeanor. "Something is wrong, Jack," she said. "What is it?"

"Anne, I...I..." He was stammering, but he knew he had to be strong and he brought his emotions under control. "Tommy's in trouble."

"I know, Jack, I know." Her composure crumbled. She hung her head and cried. Instinctively Jack stepped toward her, took her in his arms, and held her. She clung to him, inconsolable.

"Come, sit down," said Jack softly. He took her hand and led her to an upholstered couch. She sat, then he sat next to her. He handed her the letter, she opened it and read it in silence.

"Harold Sampson...he's Tommy's roommate at Harvard. He must have heard Tommy speak of you. Oh, Jack, I feel so helpless. What are we going to do?"

"How long have you known?"

"About a week," replied Anne. "We received a telegram from someone at Harvard telling us that Tommy had been arrested. But we didn't know any of the details. Mother called Mr. Earles, the attorney at the mill, and he made some telephone calls to Boston. One of his attorney friends in Boston visited Tommy last Friday, but we haven't heard any more. We were waiting for him to tell us what to do next."

"Did they tell you what he is charged with, Anne?"

"We still don't know, Jack. We don't have any idea."

"Anne, I was in Boston...yesterday."

"Oh, Jack, in the middle of the blizzard? How could you possibly...?"

"I left Friday afternoon before the storm had gotten too bad. It took all night, but I made it." Jack paused. "I went to the Charles Street Jail...I saw Tom...I talked to him."

Anne brightened briefly and looked hopefully into Jack's eyes. "How is he, Jack? Is he all right?"

"He didn't seem too bad, Anne," said Jack, trying to offer her some bit of good news first. He knew he had to tell her about the charges, but he had already given a lot of thought to how he would break the terrible news.

"At first he just refused to let me help him. He kept saying I should hate him and if I knew the truth I wouldn't want to help him. I had no idea what he was talking about."

A pained expression spread across Anne's face. She bowed her head, speaking softly. "Jack, I..."

Jack interrupted her, trying to spare her an explanation. "Anne, Tommy told me everything... about Monique... about the lies she told him about me... and about his letter to you."

"Jack, I'm sorry you had to hear it from him. I wanted to tell you myself..."

"But I wouldn't listen, Anne. I was just so cross with you that I wouldn't even let you explain. I'm the one who should be apologizing. I knew in my heart that I should talk to you, listen to you, try to set things right. Marie told me, Dad told me, Pauline told me, but I wouldn't listen. Even Claire tried to tell me..."

At the thought of Claire's plea that day by the chicken run, a tear ran down Jack's cheek. Quickly he turned away from Anne and stared out the window at the snowy landscape, so fresh, so white, like a clean slate to be written on anew.

"But it was my mother's words that really got to me...at Hampton Ponds, just a few weeks ago. I went out there to do some fishing for the first time in I don't know how long. I was trying to concentrate on the fishing...but I was seeing her face reflected in the water and hearing her voice." He paused, then looked up and into Anne's eyes. "It was my heart speaking, Anne, I swear, and it was so loud and clear."

The color began to return to Anne's face as she looked hopefully into Jack's eyes. "What did it say, Jackie? What did your heart say?"

"That I should stop being a fool and try to make amends." He paused. "Anne, it told me that I still loved you. And it was right, I do, I still do."

At that Anne took his hands in hers. "We promised each other, Jack. Remember? And I believe we both kept those promises."

"What about Theron?" asked Jack uneasily.

"Jack, he was never anything but a friend. I wrote you that letter because I was hurt and angry and I wanted to get even. I was so foolish. I was like Elizabeth in *Pride and*

*Prejudice* who wouldn't listen and refused to open her heart to Mr. Darcy because of false rumors she had heard about him."

Jack was confused and it must have shown in his expression. Anne slid over next to him and held his hand tightly in hers. "Remember the carnival...the ride on the Ferris wheel?" she asked. Jack nodded. "Can we pretend we're at the top of the Ferris wheel again? Can we start all over?" Jack nodded again.

"I remember how beautiful the view was," said Jack, looking deep into Anne's eyes, "and, you know, it's still the most beautiful I've ever seen." He kissed her, then held her. It seemed like minutes went by before either spoke.

Finally Anne broke the silence. "Jack, it feels as though one enormous weight has been lifted from my heart. I just couldn't bear being apart from you. But Tommy...what are we going to do?"

"Anne, Tom did finally explain to me what his arrest is all about." Jack hated to have to bring up the subject. The look on his face must have telegraphed the depth of his feeling.

"What is it, Jack? Please tell me." Anne's expression changed from curiosity to fear.

"He's been charged with arson, Anne. The warehouse fire in July? They say he started it."

"But that's absurd. He was at Mountain Park with some friends that evening, I remember."

"I know, I saw him there. But while I was talking to him someone came to find him, something about the mill, and they left in a hurry. Anne, Tommy told me he was at the warehouse just before the fire started. You know that worker who died in the fire? They've also charged Tommy with murder."

At that Anne broke down and wept uncontrollably. Jack held her and stroked her hair. Many minutes went by before she was able to bring her emotions under control.

Finally Jack put his hand under Anne's quivering chin, lifted it, and looked into her eyes. He marshaled all the conviction he could find and spoke firmly. "Anne, listen to me. We're going to help him. We can, I believe we can."

"We have to talk to Mother about this," replied Anne. And she left to find her mother. She was gone some time. Jack guessed that she was trying to explain to her mother what he had told her. Eventually Anne returned with Mrs. Wellington behind her.

"Oh, Jack, it is so good to see you. How we've missed you, you'll never know." She kissed Jack on the cheek, then hugged him vigorously. Jack's usual reserve around Mrs. Wellington began to melt and he hugged her back.

"Jack," she began, smiling. Then she paused, seized with emotion. "After what Tommy did to you and Anne, no one would blame you for wanting nothing to do with him...or this family...ever again."

"Mrs. Wellington, I want to do whatever I can to help Tommy. I'm not sure what that might be, but I can't let my best friend suffer without trying to do something."

"Bless you, son, bless you." And again she hugged him tightly.

She explained that the company lawyer, a Mr. Earles, would be coming to see her the next day. She had arranged for Mr. Wellington's brother, Anne's Uncle Richard, to be present. She promised to give Anne and Jack a full report after that meeting.

Then Mrs. Wellington left the room. "What about your father, Anne? I heard he was sick and that was why you came back from Argentina ahead of schedule. Is he better?"

Anne shook her head glumly. "He has a very serious heart condition, Jack. He can't work and his doctors insist that he remain in bed. He has a nurse who watches over him night and day. Mother doesn't want him to know anything about Tommy."

Jack held Anne and tried to reassure her. Then he took his leave promising to see her right after work the next day.

CHAPTER 37

# Clothes Make the Man
### *November 1916*

I t wasn't until well after five o'clock the next day that Jack arrived at the Wellington home. Both Anne and her mother seemed tired but hopeful as they tried to explain to Jack what they had learned from Mr. Earles.

"There is a witness, Jack," began Anne, "who claims he saw Tommy outside the warehouse acting suspiciously just moments before the fire broke out. So far as Mr. Earles knows right now, it was that identification that led to Tommy's arrest."

"What about the charges?" asked Jack. "Did he find out exactly what the charges against Tommy are?" He was hoping that Tom had been mistaken.

Mrs. Wellington shook her head. "I'm afraid what Tommy told you is correct: arson and murder. They claim he set the fire that led to the death of the worker." She paused, then continued. "Mr. Earles says that to bring such serious charges the prosecutor will have to show evidence that Tommy had a motive and intended to do bodily harm. That's ridiculous. Anyone who knows Tommy knows he would never do such a thing."

"Jack," said Anne. "He said that part of Tommy's defense will be testimony of his family and friends about his state of mind. We can help him, we can...we have to...you, me, Mother, Father, Monique...we can all help him...if he will let us."

"Did Tommy tell them about the can of gasoline he tripped over?" asked Jack.

"Yes, Jack. That's the problem; he seems convinced that he did cause the fire," explained Anne.

Mrs. Wellington continued: "Mr. Earles also said that the prosecution will have to show physical evidence linking Tommy to the fire. Right now he's not sure they have anything like that, but he's trying to find out." She hesitated. "Oh, he also told us that the state fire marshal's office has completed an investigation of the fire and filed a report with the Holyoke Police Department. He plans to review that report today or tomorrow."

"But the biggest problem for Tommy right now is Tommy," explained Anne. "The attorney who visited him in Boston told Mr. Earles that Tommy was suspicious of him and uncooperative. We have to get through to him, Jack. If he isn't willing to fight this it will hurt him badly, especially if this goes to trial."

"That jail is such an awful place," said Jack shaking his head. "What about bail? Can they get Tommy out on bail?"

Mrs. Wellington nodded slowly. "In time, maybe. Mr. Earles says that in cases like this a decision on bail is usually made after entering a plea. He recommends that we file a motion right away for what he calls a change of venue…to transfer Tommy to the Hampden County Jail in Springfield and try him in the Hampden District Court. That way we can visit him and try to convince him to cooperate in his own defense. It's also possible that the case might be assigned to a judge that Mr. Earles or one of his colleagues knows. We agreed that the petition to move Tom to Springfield should be requested as soon as possible."

"And Mr. Earles knows an experienced criminal lawyer he recommends to handle Tommy's defense, a Mr. Marcus Wentworth of Springfield," added Anne hopefully.

Who was the eyewitness, asked Jack, the one that claimed he had seen Tom at the warehouse that evening? Neither Anne nor her mother had thought to ask. But Mrs. Wellington promised to find out. Jack declined an invitation to stay for dinner. He needed to get home to his family. But after Mrs. Wellington excused herself, Jack and Anne sat talking for some time in the library. The petition for a change of venue would probably not be ruled on until the next scheduled court date for Tom's case which was still a week away. That would give them time to do something, but neither had any idea what.

"I think you'd better leave this to the lawyers, Son," was Jack's father's comment at home that evening. "They'll know what to do and how to do it. It's admirable that you want to help Tom, but really, I can't imagine what you could do. If you can just give Anne and her family moral support, I'm sure they will appreciate it. This must be a terrible ordeal for all of them."

Although Jack was exhausted, sleep did not come easily to him that night. He kept turning over and over in his head the few things that he had learned about the case against Tom. Finally he slept, but early the next morning he was wide awake and thinking about his friend, the Charles Street Jail, and the prospect of spending the rest of one's life in such a place.

"We've got to convince Tommy to fight this," thought Jack. "Somehow, we've got to."

As he worked in the warehouse that day, Jack kept thinking about the eyewitness who claimed to have seen Tom leaving the mill. He wished he knew more about this mysterious individual. Jim Trottière was working in the sorting room that day and Jack sought him out during lunchtime.

"Planning on doing any ice fishing this winter, Jim?" queried Jack casually.

"Oh, yeh," replied the laconic young man. "My dad and I usually go up to the Oxbow. We have a shanty we haul out there. You never know what you'll get."

The two exchanged stories of fishing at the Oxbow. Jack described the sturgeon he had pulled in on that fateful day three summers ago. After several minutes of fish stories, Jack gently plied Jim for information.

"Guess you heard about Tom Wellington, eh Jim?"

Jim nodded his head: "Pity, real pity."

"Know anything about that guy who says he saw Tom at the warehouse the night of the fire? I'm just curious."

"Heard he's a cop. Other than that, not a thing," replied Jim.

After work Jack went directly to the Wellingtons' home. Anne was working on a quilt by the fire in the parlor when he was shown in. She brightened at the sight of him, stood and hugged him. She smiled, but her smile quickly vanished.

"Have you seen this?" She showed him the evening edition of the *Transcript* that had just arrived. The headline read "Mill owner's son arrested in warehouse fire." It stated the charges and mentioned an eyewitness, then recounted the events of the night of the fire and the death of the worker. Mr. Earles had warned them that the story would surely appear in the local newspapers very soon. That morning Mrs. Wellington had made several telephone calls to friends around Holyoke telling them about Tom's arrest. It was a painful task, but she wanted them to hear it from her before reading about it in the newspapers. She also had spoken with Hanna and asked her to prepare the household staff.

"Mr. Earles came and talked to Mother, Jack. He found out the name of the witness. His name is Donovan; he's a Holyoke policeman. The name doesn't mean anything to me. Does it to you?"

Jack thought for a moment, then shook his head.

Anne continued. "Mr. Earles saw the fire marshal's report. He says the fire was caused by some kind of homemade bomb, a liquor bottle filled with gasoline. Have you ever heard of such a thing, Jack?"

Jack nodded. "Yeh, I think they've been used in the war in Europe. It has a wick. You light the wick, toss it, and run. It explodes and sends burning gasoline flying in all directions."

A look of deep despair crept across Anne's face. "He says it looks pretty bad for Tommy." She paused, staring into the fire.

Jack held Anne to him as she cried softly. "It's gonna be okay, Annie, it's gonna be okay. So far it's just the eyewitness's word against Tommy's. We'll figure it out, I promise." But in his heart he really wasn't sure that was a promise he could keep.

Jack worked a long shift the next day. It gave him lots of time to brood on Tom's case and brood he did. Even Jim Trottière noticed that Jack seemed distracted and mentioned it as they stood waiting for a bale of fleeces to be lowered from a railroad car. But Jack kept his thoughts to himself.

One thing that puzzled him was the nearly three month delay between the fire and Tom's arrest in Cambridge. If a policeman saw Tom at the scene and thought he was acting suspiciously, wouldn't Tom have been brought in for questioning immediately? Tom had told him that his arrest in Cambridge in October was the first he had heard from the police.

Jack wanted to discuss this question with Anne but it was too late when he left work. It would have to wait for the following day. When he got home Marie relayed a telephone message from Anne who had called earlier in the evening.

"She wants to see you tomorrow. She said it's important. She'll be waiting for you at noon outside the mill. Jackie, she sounded really worried...and scared."

As soon as the noon bell rang Jack hurried out the sorting room door. It was a cold November day and Anne was waiting on the sidewalk by the canal, clutching her wool coat around her as a biting Northwest wind raised whitecaps on the water.

"Oh, Jackie, I'm so glad to see you. I have to talk to you." They walked along the canal, the same route they had followed many times during the summer when Anne worked in the silk mill. So much had happened in a year and a half, thought Jack, so much had changed. But at least the two of them were together again, he reassured himself, though facing a terrible calamity.

"You look cold, Anne, let's get out of the wind," said Jack. They sought refuge in an alley between two mill buildings, just as they had done so often that summer.

"Mr. Earles talked to Mother by telephone yesterday. He had some new information. The police have a shirt... it was found in a garbage can in the alley behind the warehouse a couple of days after the fire. Jack, they say it's one of Tommy's shirts, one of his monogrammed shirts. It was soaked with gasoline." Anne was shaking. Jack held her and stroked her hair.

Jack went directly to the Wellingtons' home after work on Friday. Anne was waiting for him in the library.

"Mr. Earles took Mother to police headquarters today and showed her the shirt. It's one of Tommy's, all right. It's his size and it has his monogram and the label of Forbes and Wallace where Hanna buys his and Father's clothes. He says it looks really bad...but he said Mr. Wentworth is thinking maybe they could get the charges reduced to manslaughter."

"How could they do that, Anne?"

"The state would have to agree to drop the charges of arson and murder if Tommy agreed to plead guilty to involuntary manslaughter. He says he would be admitting that he started the fire but not on purpose...accidentally. Tommy thought all along that he started the fire when he tripped over that can of gasoline; maybe he's right."

Jack wasn't sure he understood the meaning of all this and was about to ask another question.

"Mr. Earles also showed her the letter from the state fire marshal."

"Did she have anything to say about that, Anne?"

"No, nothing beyond what we had already been told. But Jackie, there's one thing Mother said that's got me confused."

"What, Anne? What is it?"

"It's about that shirt. Mother didn't see Tommy before he left the house that night, but she wonders why he would have worn a long-sleeved dress shirt to Mountain Park ...on a warm summer's night."

"Anne, there's a lot of things we need to think about. Maybe that fire marshal's report would provide some answers. How about if we go to police headquarters together and ask to see it?"

Jack was scheduled to get out of work early on Monday and they agreed to meet at City Hall at three o'clock.

It was the weekend and Jack had promised to help his father in the orchard. The apple trees needed pruning and Charles could not climb ladders or handle a pruning saw; the best he could do was hold the ladder for Jack and stack the pruned limbs. The two worked nearly all day and Jack was glad to have his mind off of Tom's situation, at least for a time.

That evening Jack remembered that his mother had a friend, Irene, at St. Agnes Church who worked as a clerk at the Holyoke Police Department, but he couldn't remember her last name or where she lived. His father would know, but Jack was sure he would not approve of his inquiries. Just then he saw Madeleine Bousquet taking sheets off the clothesline in her back yard. She was a good friend of the family and active in the church. Jack strolled across the lawn and struck up a conversation with her. Eventually he got around to the real reason for his visit. Madeleine knew exactly whom Jack was thinking of, Irene Gamache. She lived on Elm Street in

Westfield; Jack recalled the house as he had visited Irene with his mother on a few occasions when he was younger.

The next morning Jack spotted Mrs. Gamache in church. After Mass he looked for her but she had already left. As his father and sisters climbed into the Model T, he explained that he wanted to walk home. When the car was out of sight, he turned down a side street, walked the three blocks to Mrs. Gamache's house, and rang the doorbell.

"My goodness, Jackie, what a nice surprise." She smiled briefly, then her expression darkened. "Is everything all right, Jackie? Your father, your sisters?"

"Oh, yeh, everything's fine. I just...well, I wondered if you could help me out."

"Well come in, Jackie, come in. Can I fix you some tea...or coffee...or milk?"

"No, thank you, ma'am."

Jack explained to Irene about Tom's arrest. She had read about it in the newspaper and knew that Jack and Tom had been friends.

"But what can I do, Jackie?"

"I want to look at the fire marshal's report, Mrs. Gamache. Tom's lawyer has seen it and told Mrs. Wellington about it, but I want to see it myself."

"Well, unless it's been secured by a court order, anyone can look at it, Jackie, just by coming to the station."

"I was hoping I could see it without anyone else around..." said Jack.

"Why don't you come by some day next week when I'm there and I'll get it out for you? Ask for me downstairs."

Jack thanked her again and again.

"Your mother was one of my dearest friends. We knew each other in Sherbrooke, long, long ago. Such a lovely woman...I miss her; I know you do, too, sweetie." Jack nodded.

"Jackie, I'd do anything I could for you and your family, please don't hesitate to ask." A tear glistened in her eye, she kissed Jack on the cheek, and he left.

Anne had invited Jack to Sunday dinner with the Wellingtons. Marie and Claire had a surprise for him as he prepared to leave. They had been up early cutting apples and baking and they presented him with a beautiful apple pie, fresh out of the oven, to bring to the Wellingtons.

Tom's court appearance in Boston was only twenty-four hours away and it was very much on Jack's mind that Monday morning as he and his father rode the trolley to Holyoke. The eastern sky over the river was just beginning to brighten to a rosy hue as the two Bernard men disembarked on High Street. Jack had tried to pretend that all was well, but Charles could tell that his son was carrying a heavy burden of care for his friend and the Wellington family and he wished there were something he could do to lighten his load. This young man had borne too many burdens in his short life, Charles was thinking as they parted ways in front of the sorting room.

Jack left work at three o'clock and rushed up Dwight Street. Anne was waiting on the broad front steps of City Hall and the two walked together to police headquarters next door. He asked for Irene and was directed to an office on the second floor. As soon as they entered Jack saw Irene and she saw him. She gestured for them to enter a private office and soon appeared through another door.

"This is my friend, Anne Wellington."

"Hello, Anne. Irene Gamache. I'm so sorry for what you and your family are going through." She smiled sweetly at Anne. "Have a seat, please." She left the room, then reappeared, placing a plain folder on the table in front of them. It contained a document of three pages entitled "Report of the State Fire Marshall." Anne had with her a pencil and a sheet of paper and she proceeded to copy everything she saw:

the letterhead, the title, the names of the investigator and the state chief fire marshal, the date of the report, the details of the fire, and the conclusions of the investigator. The single paragraph under "Conclusion" on the third page was short but clear. Jack read it in a whisper.

*Fire caused by ignition of gasoline. Accelerant delivered in two glass bottles thrown simultaneously at opposite ends of the warehouse.*

"Jack," said Anne in a whisper. "It sounds like those bottles could not have been thrown by one person; there had to have been two people involved."

"You're right, Anne...of course. And did you notice the date on the report?" Jack turned to the front page. "Not the date that it was sent, but the date it was received here." Jack pointed to a stamp that had been applied to the front of the report.

RECEIVED
*Holyoke Police Department*
*Holyoke, Massachusetts*
*October 25, 1916*

"That was the day before Tommy was arrested in Cambridge," Anne observed. They thanked Irene and left police headquarters without a word, then walked up Suffolk Street together, trying to make sense of what they had just learned.

"One thing that's been bothering me all along is why they waited so long to arrest Tommy. It looks like they waited until they received the fire marshal's report before issuing the arrest warrant for Tommy," explained Jack. "That makes me wonder if they really didn't trust the eyewitness. "

"And the shirt, Jack, could it be that they had doubts about the shirt, too?"

The next day seemed very long to Jack as he worked in the sorting room. All he could think of was the proceedings taking place in a courtroom seventy miles away that were out of their control, out of anyone's control. It seemed Tom's fate hung in the balance, to be determined by people who didn't know him or care about him. As soon as he left work he ran up Dwight Street toward the Wellingtons' home. One of the maids let him in. Anne appeared in the hallway and ran to him smiling.

"Jackie, Mother just received a telephone call from Mr. Earles. The petition to move the case to Hampden District Court was granted. He says Tommy should be transported to the Springfield jail by the end of the week."

"Oh, Anne, that's wonderful," Jack replied.

"I hope so," said Anne with some hesitation in her voice.

"What do you mean, Anne? Isn't that what you wanted?"

"Yes, Jack, it is. But Tommy's case has been assigned to a Judge Dirlham. The lawyer says he has a reputation for being tough. And they've already scheduled a date for Tommy to appear; it's next Tuesday. They've told Mr. Wentworth to be ready to enter a plea." Anne hesitated, her voice suddenly thin and weak. "It's all moving too fast, Jackie. I'm so afraid..."

# CHAPTER 38

# Change of Scenery
*November 1916*

T he next day at noon Anne was again waiting for Jack outside the sorting room. "Jack, Mr. Earles just called Mother. Tommy was moved to Springfield this morning; he's at the Hampden County jail. Mother and I and Uncle Richard are going to Springfield tomorrow morning to see him. I want so much to see him, to talk to him. I hope he'll want to see us."

"Anne, of course he will." He held her tightly and reassured her, only hoping that he was right.

It was Thursday and Jack was scheduled to work a short day. A few minutes after three o'clock he appeared at the Wellingtons' door. One of the maids let him in and showed him to the library. She explained that Mrs. Wellington and Anne were expected back from Springfield at any time.

Jack stood looking out the window at the bare trees in the yard. Soon he heard activity in the foyer and the library door opened. It was Anne. She looked tired, thought Jack, very tired.

"Anne, did you see Tommy?"

"Yes, Jack, we did."

"How is he doing? Did he talk to you?"

"Oh, Jack, it was awful...seeing him like that. Mother was beside herself with despair. On the way home she kept saying 'What has happened to my son? I hardly knew him.' We were fortunate that Uncle Richard was there. Tommy always liked him and he actually spoke to him for a few minutes. But I'm so discouraged, Jack, I fear for my brother if even he cannot speak up in his own behalf."

Anne paused, then continued. "Jack, I want to go back and see Tommy alone. I just feel maybe I can get him to talk more. Maybe, just maybe I can make him see that he has to help himself. I couldn't today, not with Mother there, Tommy was...he just couldn't be reached, that's all. Would you take me, please?"

"Of course, Anne, of course."

"Tomorrow, Jackie?"

Jack agreed. He'd be out of work at noon.

"But Jackie, let's not tell Mother, okay? She probably wouldn't permit me to go; and it might upset her to know that I wanted to see Tommy without her."

"So what do you think you can do, Anne?"

"I want to try to get Tommy to think more about this, to have some courage." She paused. "And I want to ask him a few questions...in private, okay?"

"Okay, I'll come by as soon as I get out of work and we can take the trolley."


Jack could tell that Anne was upset as she left the visitors' room at the Hampden County Jail the next day. He held her hand and the two stepped out into the daylight. All he could think of was how long it might be before Tommy could do the same. A few minutes later they were on the return trip to Holyoke.

"How did it go? Did he talk to you, Anne, more than yesterday?"

Anne looked into his eyes. It was an expression of utter despair.

"I'm so afraid, Jackie. I can't sleep, I can't read, I can't study. About the only thing I've been able to do these last few days is my knitting. I'm getting pretty good at my needlework," she boasted with a wry smile. Then she shook her head. "Jack, I'm sorry you have to be involved in all of this. My family, we're in a shambles. I'm ashamed of what we've become."

"Anne, don't blame yourself or your family. This is not your fault, or Tommy's fault. And we're going to figure it out, I swear we will."

Anne looked into his eyes. "I don't know what I'd do without you, darling. You're my rock, you really are. But Jackie..." Anne looked away as she spoke. "...I have to tell you something, something dreadful."

"What, Anne, please, whatever it is, tell me."

"The night of the fire..." She hesitated, her gaze cast downward.

"Yes," replied Jack, unable to imagine what he was about to hear.

"That night I saw Tommy come home shortly after the fire broke out. It was late, maybe ten o'clock, and I was already in bed. I heard him come up the stairs and I got out of bed and peeked out into the hallway. I was going to ask him if he'd heard anything about the fire. I saw him just as he entered his room."

"Yes, Anne."

"Something looked unusual; he was wearing overalls...like the ones Bromley wears when he's working on one of the motorcars. You know, with suspenders and a bib. He didn't know I saw him, but I did. That's why I wanted to talk to him alone. I wanted to find out why he was wearing those overalls. He'd told me he was headed to Mountain Park with some friends, so there's no reason he would have worn that outfit."

"Did you ask him, Anne?" She nodded, biting her lip.

"And what did he say?"

"He said that when he ran out of the warehouse he tripped over a can of gasoline next to the loading dock. The cap came off and gas spilled on his trousers. So he ran home, snuck into the garage, removed the trousers, and put on a pair of Bromley's overalls that were hanging there."

"Anne, did he say what he did with the trousers?"

Anne looked down and nodded her head once. "He stuffed them in a cracker tin with a tight-fitting lid so the odor of gasoline wouldn't be noticeable. And he hid the can behind a rock in the wall behind the garage. He thought he accidently caused the fire; that's why he hid them. Don't you see, Jackie, if the police have any doubts about the shirt, this will convince them for sure. And the fact that he hid them, well, it just makes it look all the worse. They can't force him to testify to it, I don't imagine. But now that I know, what if they ask me? If I tell the truth, that could be just enough to convince the judge or a jury...but if I lie, then I will have committed perjury. I wish he hadn't told me. What am I going to do, Jackie? This just gets worse and worse."

"I don't know, Anne, I don't know. Let me think about this. I have to think about it."

When they returned to Anne's house, the couple sat alone talking quietly in the library. Over and over again Jack tried to reassure her that they would find a way out of this mess.

The next day was Saturday and Jack worked most of the day chopping and splitting firewood in the barn. In late afternoon he spoke to his father in the parlor, explaining that he would be visiting the Wellingtons. It was not really a lie, thought Jack. He was planning to visit the Wellingtons, although with luck they would not be aware of his visit. He had already checked the *Old Farmer's Almanac* and determined that the moon would not be rising until nearly midnight. He needed the cover of darkness for what he was about to do. He had prepared a rucksack that he left in the barn containing a dark hat, gloves, a garden trowel, a candle, and some matches.

He entered the Wellington property by the rear gate. He knew the nearest streetlamp was some distance away and a row of evergreens would block any light. As he approached the garage he disappeared into the shadows on the back side of the single-story building. He lit the candle only long enough to locate the stone wall, then extinguished it. There were only a few dozen stones in the wall and he was hoping he could find what he was looking for by groping over the stones with his gloved hands in the dark. Most of the stones were too big to be moved easily. Midway along the wall there were several smaller stones that were easily moveable. He lifted one and felt under it. Finding nothing, he lifted the next, and there he found a cracker tin. He pried off the lid and it fell onto the grass. Immediately he smelled a familiar odor, vapors of a volatile liquid that had been trapped in the sealed container. He removed the contents, a pair of trousers that looked very much like the style and size Tom would have been wearing that evening. He stuffed them back into the tin and reattached the lid. Then he replaced the tin in the stone wall, repositioned the rock, and made his way in the darkness back down the driveway to the gate on Cabot Street.

What Tom had told Anne was true. There, right in their own backyard, was physical evidence that Tom had been at the warehouse that night, had fled, and had kicked over a gasoline can as he told Jack he had. If the prosecutor found out, it would make his prospects of acquittal very dim indeed. It might even make it more difficult for his lawyer to negotiate a reduction in the charges. The fewer people that knew about the cache, Jack thought, the better.

Jack was home by eight o'clock and went straight to the barn to tend to the animals. His father was in his workshop. He seemed to be curious about his son's whereabouts and asked several questions about Anne, Mrs. Wellington, and about Tom's case.

"You're not getting mixed up in that are you, Son? That's really a matter for the lawyers."

Jack responded: "I know, Dad." But he quickly looked away from his father, furthering Charles' suspicions. Jack walked past his father and headed toward the barn door.

"Hmm, been using kerosene, Jack?"

"No, Dad, why?"

"Thought I smelled kerosene, that's all."

"No, Dad, not on me," said Jack. But then he added hastily: "I used some out here the other day to clean some tools. Maybe that's what you smell." Jack went out the door quickly and headed for the house. He was removing the items from his rucksack in his room when he handled the gloves he had been wearing earlier. Then he noticed what his father had noticed: the smell of kerosene. It was easily detectable on his gloves and on his hands.

Suddenly it struck him. "That's it," he thought, "Tommy's trousers weren't soaked with gasoline, they were soaked with kerosene. Could it be," he wondered, "that the can Tommy tipped over was a can of kerosene, not gasoline? If that's true, then the fire could not have been caused by Tommy. The fire marshal's report said it was gasoline that was used to start the fire."

Jack lay in bed thinking about this. How could he prove that Tommy had knocked over a can of kerosene rather than gasoline? He could present the trousers with Tom's monogram; anyone who knew the smell of kerosene would recognize it. But the prosecutor might try to suggest that Jack had planted the kerosene-soaked trousers in an effort to protect his friend. But late that night, Jack realized how important those trousers might be.

After Mass Jack rushed home to make two telephone calls before his father and sister returned. In half an hour he was in Holyoke and walking along Northampton Street. He turned into the walk in front of a large house, climbed the stairs, and struck the knocker. The door opened quickly.

"Jack, how nice to see you. How are you doing, son? Is everything okay?"

"Mr. Donahue, I need your help."

"Come in, Jack, and sit down."

Jack didn't want to reveal all the details of the situation. Fortunately, Mr. Donahue knew Jack as a serious student who wouldn't be asking a favor if there weren't good reason.

"Mr. Donahue, I have a friend who's in trouble. I can't explain everything but I was hoping you could give me some advice."

"What kind of advice, Jack? I'll do whatever I can."

"What I need to know is if there's a way to determine whether a volatile liquid is gasoline or kerosene. "

"Well, sure, Jack. The simplest way would be to do an ignition test. Kerosene has a much higher flash point than gasoline. You can also do a miscibility test with a petroleum solvent. But the smell, Jack, that's pretty hard to mistake, you know."

"Could you help me, tonight, say, after seven? If I brought a sample to the chemistry lab, could we do both tests?"

"Well, sure, Jack. But could it wait until tomorrow? I'll be in school all day."

"No, it can't. Believe me, it's a matter of life and death."

Jack must have looked desperate. Mr. Donahue looked at him, then nodded. "Okay, Jack, tonight it is. I'll meet you at the front door at seven o'clock. We'll see what we can do. You have a sample?"

"I'll get one," responded Jack.

Jack walked along Northampton Street, then Lincoln, then Nonotuck. He turned in at a familiar brick sidewalk, climbed three familiar steps, took a deep breath, and knocked. In a moment the door swung open. Before him stood Pauline Foley, a wide smile illuminating her face.

"Oh, Jack, it is good to see you. I was so excited when you called. It's been so long." She took his hand and kissed him on the cheek.

"You look swell, Pauline. Wellesley must be agreeing with you!"

"I guess it is, Jack, I guess it is." She was still beaming at the sight of him. "You look good, too, Jack...maybe a little tired...but good."

Jack nodded and tried to smile.

"I heard about Tom. Jack, I'm awfully sorry. I can't believe it, really. We saw him that night, up at Mountain Park. Remember? Come in and sit down."

"Please, tell me all about Wellesley." At that Pauline described the campus, her classes, and roommate, all with enthusiasm and good humor.

Finally Jack spoke again. "And how is your family? How's your mother doing?"

"She's doing fine, Jack, just fine. It was pretty serious, but she has made a complete recovery."

"That's good to hear," replied Jack.

"So, Jack, tell me all about yourself...and your family...and the Wellingtons."

Jack brought Pauline up to date on his family's activities. "I went to Boston, Pauline, just two weeks ago today. I would have visited you but there was a terrible snowstorm and I couldn't stay. I went to see Tom...in jail in Boston."

Pauline nodded. "How did that go, Jack?"

Jack was looking down, not sure how to proceed. Then he raised his head and looked into Pauline's eyes. "You were right, Pauline. I don't know how you knew, but you were right. I was still pining over Anne. Tom told me the truth...it was all his doing...he lied about me to Anne...it was shocking to hear...but it made me realize that I had pushed her away and refused to give her a chance to explain."

"And you and Anne have set things right?" she asked softly, looking squarely in his eyes.

"Yes," replied Jack, watching for Pauline's reaction. He thought he detected a moment's hesitation, the slightest shadow across her face, but it quickly turned to a smile.

"I'm very happy for you, Jackie. Really, I am."

"And you? I'll bet you've got a couple of Harvard boys on the string!"

"Not really. They're notorious, you know...sort of, well, Bunburyists."

They both laughed.

"But I am seeing a young man from Boston College. His name is Michael. He's a lot like you, Jack, sweet, serious..." She paused. "You could call him _earnest!_"

Again the two friends laughed together. It felt good, thought Jack, good to laugh...something he hadn't done very much lately. "I'm very happy for you, Pauline. I knew you'd take to Wellesley. I knew it." He paused. "Well, I'd better get going."

"Jack, before you go, tell me about Tom. Is it bad?"

Jack told Pauline as much as he felt he could about the case against Tom including the witness, the fire marshal's report, and the shirt. His pain must have been apparent; Pauline seemed genuinely concerned for him, for Anne, for the Wellington family. She listened without interrupting. When Jack had finished his monologue he paused.

"Well, I'd better be off. It was so good seeing you, Pauline. I hope you and your family have a wonderful Thanksgiving."

As he looked at Pauline's face he thought he detected some slight confusion, a shadow of doubt, in her expression.

"Is something wrong, Pauline?"

"That night at Mountain Park, the night of the fire, when we ran into Tom and that friend of his...I'm just trying to remember...it all happened so quickly..."

"Uh-huh," replied Jack, not sure what Pauline was getting at.

Pauline looked momentarily perplexed. Then she shook her head quickly as if her confusion was gone. "Nothing...I'm sorry, Jack, I don't know what I was thinking."

"Well, I'd better be going. Thank you again for seeing me on such short notice. I thought you'd be home and wanted to say hello. Please give my best to your mother and father."

Jack walked from the Highlands to Cabot Street. It was nearly four o'clock when he arrived at the Wellingtons' home. He told Anne about his visit with Pauline. He was careful to remind her that Pauline had urged him not to give up on Anne, even back in the summer when he was refusing to listen. And he told her all about Michael at B.C.

It was dark when Jack left Anne's house. He told her he was headed home, but failed to tell her that he had two important tasks still ahead of him. He walked several blocks to a diner and had a cup of soup. When it was fully dark he made his way back up Cabot Street, keeping to the unlit side of the street. At the Wellingtons' iron gate he disappeared into the shadows, then stole across the lawn toward the garage. Again he briefly lit a small candle to locate the loose stone, removed it, found the tin, and pulled out the trousers. With his fishing knife he cut off one of the pant legs, wrapped it tightly, then replaced the rest of the trousers in the tin and the tin in the wall. In just two minutes he was on the steps of Holyoke High School just a block away; Mr. Donahue was waiting for him at the door and let him in.

Jack's head was spinning as he rode the trolley back to Westfield. It would be too late to call Anne when he got home. He would try to reach her early the next morning. He would be late for work, but this was too important. In fact, he might just have to miss work entirely tomorrow, he thought.

# CHAPTER 39

## Volatility
### *November 1916*

Jack did not choose to share his thoughts or his plans with his father who left early on Monday morning. He saw his sisters off to school, explaining that he was working a later shift that day. At eight o'clock he telephoned the Wellingtons' home and asked to speak to Anne. There was a delay of several minutes before he heard Anne's voice. He told her about all he had learned from Mr. Donahue.

"Jack, we have to go to see Tommy right away," said Anne.

"I can be there in an hour."

It was eleven o'clock when Anne and Jack arrived at the Hampden County Jail.

Anne spoke softly to her brother, seated at a long table with his head down. "Tommy, it's Anne." Tom raised his head, a look of confusion in his dark, deep-set eyes. "Jack is here, too, Tommy. We want to talk with you."

"Hi, Tommy. It's Jack. How are you doing, buddy?"

Tom looked up into Jack's eyes, but he seemed to be looking right through Jack, almost not seeing him.

"What are you doing here?" asked Tom. He seemed perplexed.

"We've got some good news, Tommy," replied Anne. "We're going to try to help you, okay?"

Tom shook his head. "Good news...I could use some good news about now."

Anne continued. "Tommy, I told Jack about your trousers. Don't be angry...I thought he could help. And he did, he really did."

"Tommy," interjected Jack. "I found your trousers...in the cracker tin...in the wall...Tommy, they aren't soaked with gasoline as you thought...it's kerosene...kerosene, not gasoline..."

"So?" replied Tom. "What does it matter? So the kerosene caught fire. What's the difference?"

"Tommy, the fire marshal's report says the fire was caused by gasoline. They said there were two gasoline bombs thrown through the windows of the warehouse at the same time...from opposite ends..."

"See, Tommy?" said Jack. "You didn't start the fire after all. It was somebody else...and they're just trying to frame you. But we have proof that the can you knocked over was kerosene."

Tom looked more alert now. He seemed to be taking in the information and trying to make sense of it.

"Tommy," said Anne. "Mr. Earles told us you are thinking of pleading guilty to involuntary manslaughter. That would mean you admitted to starting the fire by accident. But you didn't...don't you see? You didn't."

"But..." Tom began. Then he seemed confused. "But if I plead not guilty there will be a trial, and a jury, and if they convict me of arson and..."

"Tommy, dear Tommy," said Anne, tears filling her eyes. "You have to fight it, please. Don't give in. We're going to help you. You're innocent, you know that!"

There was a long pause, then Tom replied. "I am innocent...but that doesn't seem to matter...I'm going to jail no matter what I do. The best I can hope for is a lighter sentence. I have to plead guilty to manslaughter, if they'll let me."

Both Anne and Jack knew there was no point in pursuing the matter right now. They needed something more, something that would give Tom the confidence to plead not guilty.

They were about to leave when Tom spoke directly to Jack. "You two, you've set things right?"

"Yes, Tommy, we have," replied Jack, his arm around Anne. Tom nodded and smiled weakly. There was a long pause as Jack looked at Tom. "What about us, Tommy...you and me? I want my best friend back, too...please? All is forgiven."

Tom sat looking at Jack. Then he slowly extended his right hand. Jack grasped Tom's hand, shook it, and smiled.

"If you want him, you've got him," replied Tom.

Neither Anne nor Jack could think of much to say on the ride back to Holyoke. Both knew that there was precious little time remaining to try to change Tom's mind about pleading guilty to manslaughter. And neither could really blame Tom for fearing the consequences of pleading not guilty to arson and murder and facing possible conviction for both.

Jack left the Wellington home at two o'clock and headed to the mill to complete his shift. When he got home his father was sitting in the parlor by the fire. "Pauline Foley called just a few minutes ago. She wanted to speak with you, Son. She said it was urgent and asked that you call her back right away."

Jack went to the telephone and gave the operator Pauline's number. She answered on the first ring.

"Pauline?"

"Jack, I was thinking... about Mountain Park...that night when we saw Tom? It was kind of dark and we only talked with him for a short time, but somehow I couldn't picture him in a dress shirt. It was a warm evening and the place was crowded."

Jack thought about that. He knew he wasn't too observant when it came to peoples' clothing. "Uh-huh."

"I don't know why but it suddenly came to me when we were joking about Harvard boys and Bunburying...it just came to me."

"What, Pauline?"

"Harvard, Jack, Harvard. That was it," said Pauline excitedly. "I remembered what Tom was wearing that evening. He had on a collarless jersey with short sleeves and an "H" for Harvard."

"Pauline, I think you're right." His father was within earshot so he didn't want to say anything more. "Thanks...yup...goodbye, Pauline."

The next morning while Anne was having breakfast alone, Mildred entered and stood quietly by the kitchen door.

"Good morning, Mildred. How are you today?" asked Anne brightly.

"Fine, thank you, Miss Anne. May I speak with you?"

"Of course, Mildred, what is it? Is something wrong?"

"Perhaps I should be talking to Mrs. Wellington, but she is so overwrought with Mr. Wellington and Master Thomas...well, I thought perhaps I might speak to you. It's about Etta, the laundress. She's in a very bad way, Miss, and I am worried so about her."

"In a bad way? How do you mean? Is she ill, Mildred?"

"Not exactly, Miss, but she is terribly distressed and has been for some time now. She has submitted her notice just today and I...well, I probably should discuss the matter with Mrs. Wellington but, as I said, I hate to add to her burdens."

"Has Etta given a reason, Mildred, for giving her notice? Why does she wish to leave?"

"That's just it, Miss, she refuses to say. But she seems so distressed...almost hysterical. It troubles me and, well, I thought perhaps you could talk with her. She thinks so much of you, Miss."

"Of course, I will. Why don't you ask her to see me after I've finished my breakfast?"

"Well, Miss, she's in her room and she refuses to come out or let me in."

"Take me to her now, Mildred, please."

"Oh, thank you, Miss."

Anne followed the cook up to the third floor and through the narrow doorway leading to the female servants' rooms. They walked down a dark hallway to the last door. Mildred tapped lightly on the door several times.

"Etta…Etta…"

There was no response.

"Etta, Miss Anne is with me…she'd like to speak with you."

Some movement could be heard within. Then the door opened slowly and Etta stood in the darkened room. Her face was red; she appeared to have been crying. Anne spoke softly.

"Hello, Etta. May I come in?"

The young woman nodded and stepped back as Anne entered.

"I am sorry, Miss, that you have been bothered about me. You shouldn't have…it's very kind of you, but you shouldn't be bothered with me."

"Sit down," replied Anne. And she guided the girl to the bed, then sat beside her.

"Mildred tells me you've given notice."

Etta nodded.

"I am very sorry to hear that…and I know my mother will be very sorry as well. May I ask why you wish to leave?"

Etta sat, eyes cast downward. She made no reply.

"Etta," said Anne, leaning down and looking up into her eyes. "If something is wrong…something troubling you… please tell me. Perhaps I can help."

The girl sat silently and Anne waited, sensing there was something she wanted…or needed…to say. Finally she spoke. "I been disloyal to Mrs. Wellington - to the household - and I must leave. I'm sorry."

"Disloyal? Dear Etta, you've been a good worker for some years now and we value your service." The girl shook her head. "What have you done that is so bad, Etta? Please, tell me...I promise I won't be angry with you. And you'll feel better when it's off your chest."

Again there was a long pause. Finally the girl spoke. "I...I'm guilty of theft, Miss. And I cannot be trusted. I must leave at once."

"Well, Etta, if that is so, you could simply return the item and I'm sure that all would be forgiven. What was it, dear...money? A piece of jewelry?"

There was another long pause. Then Etta looked up and into Anne's eyes. "Master Thomas, Miss...one of his shirts. I stole one of his lovely shirts and I can't return it. That's why I must go."

Anne was suddenly very curious about Etta and eager to know more. But she knew enough to proceed with caution. "When did this take place, Etta. Can you tell me?"

"It was some time ago, Miss, in the summer."

"I see. And what kind of a shirt was it?"

"One of his linen dress shirts...with the pleats."

"Did it have Tom's monogram...his initials...sewn on the pocket, Etta? Was it one of those shirts?"

"Yes, Miss."

"Etta, I'm sure this idea was not yours. I know you and you are much too serious and conscientious a young woman. May I ask...Etta, did someone put you up to this?" The girl did not respond and she gazed downward. Anne looked up at Mildred who shrugged and shook her head. "Etta," said Anne very quietly. "Whose idea was it that you should...obtain one of Tom's shirts?"

"I can't say, Miss. I'm sorry."

Anne felt she had probed enough for the moment. "I understand," she replied. "Well, you are a brave girl with a strong sense of loyalty, I can tell that. So I shall not trouble you any longer. As to the shirt, Etta, I know my brother would forgive you. Perhaps you could pay a little out of your wages over several months to compensate for the cost of the shirt. Wouldn't that be acceptable? Since you've owned up to your transgression I'm sure that would be a satisfactory resolution."

The girl's tears were finally abating and she wiped her eyes with her handkerchief.

"Now, can we forget about your notice?"

Etta smiled weakly and nodded. "Thank you, Miss. You've been very kind."

"I want you to take the rest of the day off, get some sleep, take a walk in the fresh air, and be back to work tomorrow morning. Will you do that, Etta?"

She nodded and Anne stood, about to take her leave. "Etta, if ever there is anything on your mind that you would like to discuss with me, please feel free to come to me. All right?"

Anne and Mildred walked down the two long flights of stairs to the first floor, then stood talking in whispers in the hallway. Anne had known Mildred for many years. The cook had always been generous with her time and had taught Anne much about cooking and baking.

"Thank you so much for bringing this to my attention, Mildred. I hope Etta will feel better now that this matter is settled." Anne paused, trying to phrase her next sentence carefully. "But it would be useful to know who was behind this."

"I can't imagine who, Miss. I'm sure if you insisted on it Etta would tell you."

"I don't know; she seems very frightened. I didn't want to upset her more."

"Etta doesn't have many friends that I know of, Miss. In fact she often spends her days off upstairs in her room. Her family is in Vermont and she seems to have little contact with them." Mildred paused, thinking. "Oh, dear, Miss. I hesitate to even mention it, but do you suppose it could be another member of the staff that prevailed upon her?"

Anne headed to the dining room to finish her breakfast. But within a minute Mildred caught up with her. "Miss, something just occurred to me...about Etta. One of the waitresses spoke sharply to her a while back and the poor thing just came apart. I remember thinking at the time that there must be something behind their little dust-up. It seemed as though Etta was inordinately afraid of the girl even though she's barely sixteen."

"Which girl is that?" inquired Anne.

"Bridget, Miss... Bridget Feeney."

"Maybe I should have a talk with Bridget," suggested Anne.

"But Miss, Bridget left service two weeks ago. She's to be married."

"Hmm, have you any idea how we might locate her?"

"I believe she has already moved in with her young man's family, Miss."

"Do you know his name, Mildred?"

"Jeffrey, Miss, Jeffrey O'Malley. He's a patrolman with the police department." Anne was suddenly very interested but decided she had best keep her thoughts to herself for the moment.

"Would you like me to make an inquiry and try to contact Bridget?"

"No, thank you, Mildred, that won't be necessary. Thank you, you've been a great help."

Just then the telephone rang. One of the maids entered the dining room. "Miss Anne, there's a telephone call for you."

Before Anne could say a word Jack began. "Anne, I think I've stumbled onto something important. When I got home last night there was a message from Pauline. She remembered something...about Tommy that night at Mountain Park. One thing about Pauline, she's really observant...she notices things that other people don't. And when I told her about the shirt with the gasoline she felt something wasn't right. But it wasn't until later that it came to her. She remembers that Tommy was wearing a jersey with short sleeves that evening up at the Park. And she's sure it had an 'H' on it, 'H' for Harvard. It hadn't occurred to me, but once she said it, I remembered, too. I remembered noticing the 'H' as Tommy was talking and wondering if maybe he'd been accepted to Harvard. I didn't know, but the thought crossed my mind. Then I got distracted by Monique's brother and then there was the fire and, well, I forgot all about it. But Pauline remembers. She's sure of it."

"Well, Jack, that's interesting because..." began Anne, but Jack interrupted.

"Don't you see, Anne? Somebody must have gotten hold of one of Tommy's shirts, soaked it with gasoline, then planted it in the garbage can on purpose to make it appear that Tommy had thrown one of those bombs. Anne, someone's trying to frame Tommy..."

"Yes, Jack, and I think I know who," replied Anne. "Etta, Etta the laundress. She has confessed to stealing one of Tommy's shirts."

"Why would she..." began Jack.

"Someone put her up to it, I'm sure of it. And I have an idea who it is." She recounted Mildred's words about Bridget Feeney. "And, Jack, Bridget is engaged to be married...to a Holyoke police officer...named Jeffrey O'Malley."

"O'Malley, a cop?" Jack thought for a moment, then a look of disbelief spread across his face.

"Jack," said Anne. "You don't suppose he threw one of those gasoline bombs? Why would he do something like that?"

"Because he hates French people...he always has." Jack paused. "And that Donovan that claims he saw Tommy, I wonder if that could be Dennis Donovan, one of O'Malley's cronies? Maybe he threw the other one!"

"Jack, we have to talk to Mother...and to Mr. Earles...right away."

Jack, Anne, and Mrs. Wellington sat in the library waiting for Mr. Earles to arrive. When he finally appeared, first Anne, then Jack recounted their discoveries about the shirt.

"I'll call right away," responded the lawyer. "Thomas's appearance is scheduled for three o'clock this afternoon and we have to give Mr. Wentworth time to consider this development. At the very least this might help convince Thomas to plead not guilty. Mr. Wentworth may also want to bring these developments to the attention of the prosecutor." Mr. Earles hesitated, then continued. "We might hope that there would now be sufficient grounds for dropping the charges against Thomas altogether, but I don't want to give you false hopes. There's one complication I must tell you about."

"Complication?" replied Mrs. Wellington.

"I hate to even suggest this, but the district attorney's office isn't exactly impartial when it comes to the police. The DA may be very reluctant to see this crime pinned on the Holyoke Police Department."

"You don't mean that they would allow an innocent man to take the blame for such a crime?"

"I would hope not, ma'am, I would hope not. Well, I'll go right to my office and place a call to Mr. Wentworth."

"I have to talk to Father," whispered Anne to Jack.

"Officer, officer, please, come quickly. My...my wife...she needs help. Please hurry!" shouted Jack to a patrolman on his beat on Main Street the next morning.

He led the policeman into the alley and through a narrow opening in the iron fence. Anne was sitting on a barrel, her back to the officer.

"Ma'am...what's the trouble?"

Anne turned and smiled. "Hello, Dennis. How are you?"

Patrolman Donovan was confused. He looked at Anne, then at Jack, then back to Anne. "Your husband here tells me there's a problem?"

"Yes, Dennis, you could say that," replied Anne.

"It's about the fire...the warehouse fire..." Jack began. "We need to talk to you about it."

The officer's expression suddenly turned sour. "I don't know what this is all about, but I'm on duty...I've got to get back to my beat." He walked toward the opening in the fence.

Jack stepped in his way. "Not until you come clean, Donovan."

Anne rose from where she sat and approached the patrolman, her demeanor changing. She spoke sweetly. "Dennis, we've known each other a long time, right? I know you're not a bad person. But your friend, Jeffrey, well, he's been saying some things about you that I find hard to believe."

"Like what?"

"That the whole idea was yours...that you talked him into it...that you threw the bottles of gasoline, not him. It just doesn't sound like you, Dennis. I just have the feeling he's trying to pin it all on you. But you're too smart for that."

Donovan looked confused.

"I wasn't anywhere near the warehouse the night of the fire. I was at home. It's all a lie."

"Well, you told the chief you were there, Dennis. But I'm betting you weren't the one responsible for that fire. Maybe you let Jeffrey talk you into going along...and maybe he got you to toss one of those bottles thinking it would just scare the men in the meeting. You didn't mean to hurt anyone. But the way Jeffrey's talking, it was all your idea. Maybe you should go up to headquarters and set the record straight."

"All right, I was there, but it was O'Malley's idea and I just went along. He tossed one bottle and we heard a crash and a lot of shouting inside. I dropped the other one in the alley, then I ran..."

At that moment Chief Hanrahan and two other officers came around the corner. Donovan saw them.

"O'Malley's lying," Donovan blurted to the Chief. "It wasn't my idea, it was his idea. I just went along...I didn't realize those bottles would explode...I thought they would just light up like flares and scare the workers...that's all."

The chief nodded to the officers who disarmed Donovan and led him away.

"How did you know, Chief?"

"Your father, Miss. He called me and told me what you had told him. We have to get to Springfield right away. Your brother's appearance is still scheduled for three o'clock."

CHAPTER 40

# Pleading

*November 1916*

"**A**ll rise," called the bailiff. A stout, stern-faced man in a black robe entered the courtroom and took his seat without looking up. "The Honorable William T. Dirlham, justice of the Hampden County District Court, presiding. Be seated."

The judge spoke in a monotone: "In the case of the Commonwealth of Massachusetts versus Thomas P. Wellington III... Mr. Wentworth, on the charges of arson and murder, is your client prepared to enter a plea?"

"Your honor, the prosecution and the defense have reached an agreement."

"Go ahead."

"Your honor," said Mr. Randal, the prosecutor, "the Commonwealth has agreed to reduce the charges against the defendant to involuntary manslaughter in exchange for a plea of guilty."

"Mr. Wentworth, do you concur?"

"Yes, your honor."

"Mr. Wellington," said the judge in a loud voice, "stand up."

Tom was sitting with his head down. Mr. Wentworth took his arm, shook it gently, then coaxed him to stand up.

"Mr. Wellington, do you understand the terms of this agreement? The charges of arson and murder against you would be dropped. In exchange you would plead guilty to involuntary manslaughter. In so doing you would waive your right to a trial. A sentence would be handed down by this court within seven days."

Tom didn't respond.

"Mr. Wellington? Do you understand?"

Tom raised his head and looked at the judge. After several seconds he answered in a low voice: "Yes, Your Honor, I understand."

"Then, Mr. Wellington, I would ask you," continued the judge stridently, "on the charge of manslaughter, how do you plead?"

Suddenly a voice could be heard from the corridor just outside the courtroom.

"Wait, wait, Tommy, wait." It was Jack's voice.

The courtroom doors burst open. Chief Hanrahan entered, followed by Anne and Jack. The chief walked up to the railing, leaned over, and spoke to the prosecutor.

"Your honor, the prosecution asks for a short recess..." said Mr. Randal.

"The court shall be in recess for twenty minutes."

Anne rushed to her mother and hugged her, then whispered in her ear. Mrs. Wellington began to cry. Jack leaned over the rail and spoke to Tom who sat looking confused. Then Jack spoke to Mr. Wentworth who stood expressionless. Just then the courtroom door opened. Two officers held the door as Mr. Wellington entered in a wheelchair pushed by Bromley. Helen gasped, stood, and ran to her husband.

Soon the judge re-entered the courtroom. "Mr. Randal, do you wish to speak?"

"Yes, Your Honor. In light of new information that has just come to our attention, the Commonwealth wishes to drop all charges against the defendant."

Murmurs could be heard from the gallery. Then the courtroom was silent once again.

"Mr. Wellington, you are free to go. This court is adjourned."

"All rise."

As the judge left the courtroom, cheers and shouts rang out. Tom turned; Mr. Wentworth opened the gate in the railing and Tom stepped through it. He hugged his mother who had dissolved in tears. As she held her son and sobbed, Tom looked over her shoulder at Anne and drew her to him as well. Then Helen and Anne stepped back and Bromley pushed Mr. Wellington's chair up to Tom. He shook his father's hand.

"Thank you, Father."

"Don't thank me, Son. Thank these two," said Mr. Wellington, pointing to Anne and Jack.

Jack was standing beside Anne as Tom extended his hand to him. But Jack grabbed his friend and gave him a bear hug.

"I know it's a little late in the season, Jack," said Tom. "But maybe we could go fishing, just the two of us? Up at Hampton Ponds?"

"That would be swell, Tommy. Probably nothing's biting, but it's not about the fish anyway, right? It never was about the fish."

Anne took Tom's hand. "Let's go home, Tommy...and start living again!"

Anne and Jack chose to ride the trolley back to Springfield together. "I still don't understand why they didn't arrest Tommy right away...after Donovan reported seeing him," offered Jack.

"Chief Hanrahan admitted to Father that he never really believed Tommy started the fire. It was the shirt that made him suspicious. O'Malley's claim that he found the shirt in a garbage can several days after the fire was a little hard for him to believe. Especially since the chief knew O'Malley and Donovan were friends and that they had made their hatred of Frenchmen pretty well known."

"He told Father that the district attorney wanted to arrest Tommy right away after the shirt was turned in, but he resisted. Then when the fire marshal's report came in, the DA put the pressure on to arrest Tommy. He said he thinks the DA was actually trying to protect the two cops. We're just lucky Father and the chief were friends or Tommy might have been forced to plead guilty."

CHAPTER 41

# Star-gazing
*November 1916*

T he entire Wellington household staff stood around the front door smiling and cheering as the Reo carrying Tom and Mrs. Wellington pulled under the portico followed momentarily by the Pierce Arrow with Mr. Wellington and his nurse. Hanna spoke on behalf of all the staff. Helen thanked her officially, then hugged her warmly. Tears glinted in their eyes.

The Wellington home was a bee hive of activity for the rest of the day. Friends and family members visited and called to congratulate Mr. and Mrs. Wellington and Tom. At one point several dozen well-wishers were gathered in the grand parlor. Anne was surprised and very happy to see Carolyn and her mother. The three were involved in a long conversation and Jack excused himself to make a telephone call in the library. He knew Marie would be home from school by now and he wanted to give her the good news about Tom. He promised to be home for dinner.

When Jack returned to the grand parlor he saw Tom standing alone in the glasshouse and their eyes met. Jack walked through the tall glass doors and smiled at his old friend. Tom was looking younger and much happier than he had in a long time.

"I was just thinking of the night of Mother and Father's anniversary. Remember? You and Anne out on the lawn...looking at the stars...in the fog?" They both laughed.

"Yeh, that was quite a night, wasn't it, Tommy?" answered Jack, gazing on the lush greenery. He sensed that

Tom wanted to say something but was having difficulty finding the words.

Finally Tom spoke. "Jack...you know...you didn't have to...Why did you even bother to help me? After everything? I don't know why, but you believed in me...you and Annie...when even I had lost faith in myself."

"Listen, Tommy, it wasn't that big a deal...it's just what a friend does for a friend..." Jack laughed. "Where have I heard that before? Oh, yeh, you were going to give me lessons about the fairer sex." They both laughed again.

"I guess that's what you'd call the blind leading the blind, huh?" admitted Tom.

Finally Jack turned, looked his friend in the eye, and spoke with forced casualness. "So what now, Tommy? Back to Harvard?"

There was a long silence. Jack looked away, thinking he was putting too much pressure on his friend by asking that question. "I'm sorry, Tommy, I shouldn't..."

"No, Jack," said Tom softly, his voice low and tentative. "You should...I want you to...to keep asking. The truth is, I don't know...but I have to do something for myself. There's a clinic in Williamstown that Annie found out about. They say they can help people like me. You know, people always say that a drinking problem is a sign of weakness or a character flaw. To be honest, sometimes I think that's my problem, I don't know. But this place, they treat it like a sickness...a disease...they claim they can cure drinking. Sounds a little crazy, I know, but I'm willing to give it a try."

"That's great, Tommy. That's really swell."

"You, Jack, you're the reason, really. I look at you, how you've done so much in school, in work, and all you've done for your father and sisters. I guess I wish I could be more like you."

After the last of the well-wishers had departed, the Wellington family sat together by the fireplace. It was the first time, thought Jack, that he had been with all four of them since Tommy's accident.

"Jack," said Mr. Wellington. "This family owes you a great deal. What you did for Tommy, well, it was very impressive, young man, very impressive. Maybe you should consider a career in law, or as a private investigator. Ever think of that?"

Jack smiled. "It wasn't all my doing." He was standing next to Anne who was seated by the fire. He put his hand on her shoulder. "This young lady was amazing. You should have heard her putting the squeeze on Donovan. She's good. It reminded me of the way she once interrogated Tommy and me about... eh... well...let's just say she's tough. She could be a lawyer someday, maybe a prosecutor, right Tommy?"

"I pity the poor defendant!" replied Tom. Everyone laughed as Anne smiled and blushed.

Jack was preparing to leave for home. He and Anne stood looking out one of the library windows at the lights of the city twinkling below.

"With all that's been going on I forgot to tell you, Anne, I got a letter yesterday. I've been accepted to Worcester Polytechnic Institute for next fall. And they've offered me a full scholarship."

Anne beamed. "Oh, Jackie, that's wonderful news. I'm so happy for you." She hugged and kissed him. "What did your father have to say about that? And your sisters?"

"Oh, Dad and Marie are excited for me." Jack chuckled. "Claire says she's mad at me in advance for going away, but I think she'll get used to the idea."

Anne laughed for a moment at the thought of Claire scolding her big brother. Then she looked squarely into Jack's eyes, her eyes filling with tears of joy. "Your mom would be so proud of you...so proud of you, Jackie. And so am I." She paused. "And how do you feel about it, young man?"

"A little scared, I guess, but also excited. I want to study mechanical engineering. And I want to come back to Holyoke after I graduate and design better looms and spinning rigs, make them quieter and cleaner and safer so mill workers won't have to suffer the way they do." Jack looked out across the city that he knew so well. "Maybe make life in this town a little better, you know?" He thought about that for a moment, then continued. "But I want to be able to help Dad with the farm, too. I don't know - farming is just in my blood, I guess."

"You have a lot of dreams, Jack Bernard," offered Anne.

"Yes, I guess I do, now that you mention it," responded Jack.

Anne hugged him tightly, kissed him, and looked into his eyes. "I like a man with dreams."

Thanksgiving at the Bernards was celebrated in the usual fashion, a huge turkey, mashed potatoes, stewed beets, Brussels' sprouts, onions in cream sauce, sweet turnips. A special prayer of Thanksgiving was offered for Tom and the entire Wellington family.

After dinner the family sat in the parlor by the fireplace. Charles looked up from the evening paper. "Mr. Wilson refuses to support extending the vote to women. That's one thing he and I agree on. I'm just not sure that the women of this nation are ready to vote."

"But Daddy," said Claire, "the real question is not whether the women of America are ready to vote. The real question is whether the men of America are ready for the women to vote!"

Charles looked startled as he raised his eyes from the newspaper.

"I agree with Claire," interjected Marie.

Charles turned to his son, smiling: "Jack, are you going to support your father on this?"

Jack shook his head. "I don't know, Dad. If Claire and Marie are on the side of women's suffrage, I think we oppose it at our peril!"

Jack had promised to visit the Wellingtons later that afternoon. Before leaving he went to the barn to tend to the animals. Claire was already feeding the chickens when Jack appeared and the two stood side-by-side watching the birds scramble for their feed.

"You know what I'm most thankful for, Jackie?"

"What?"

"That you and Anne are friends again. I don't know why you two took so long to make up; I guess you're both just stubborn."

"I suppose you're right, Claire, I suppose you're right." The two exchanged amused gazes. But Jack could tell that his little sister was not quite through with him and he waited for her next parry.

"One more question, Jackie...are you and Anne gonna get married?"

"Why Claire Hélène Bernard," scolded Marie who had just appeared through the barn door. "When will you learn not to be impertinent?" She glared briefly at her sister, then turned and looked up into Jack's eyes as if awaiting his reply.

Jack looked at each of his sisters with a twinkle in his eye. "You know, you are both impertinent, each in your own way. And I honestly don't know which of you is worse." Then he turned and headed for the house.

When Jack arrived at the Wellingtons' home, Mrs. Wellington greeted him and showed him into the library. Mr. Wellington was seated by the fire. Anne and Tom, they explained, had gone for an after-dinner walk and would no doubt be back soon. Mr. Wellington asked about the Bernards' Thanksgiving. Soon Anne appeared and sat next to Jack. The four talked casually for a few minutes, then Mr. and Mrs. Wellington excused themselves.

"So, you and Tommy went for a walk...trying to digest that turkey and all those fixings, I suspect?"

"In part, yes, a brisk walk is known to aid digestion," explained Anne. Then she paused. "Actually, we went to Forestdale Cemetery."

Jack nodded slowly. "Matthew?"

Anne looked into Jack's eyes. "It was something we needed to do...together...you know what I mean."

"And how did it go?"

"Well, I'm not sure Tommy sees the connection...I mean between losing Matthew and his personal problems...at least, not yet. But we talked about it...at least we started talking about it, right?"

"A young lady once told me 'It takes time.' She was very wise...and very pretty as I recall!" said Jack with a smile.

Anne nodded and grinned: "Well, whoever she was, she was right." Then she looked intently into Jack's eyes and took his hand. "Tommy talked a lot about you, Jackie, you and your family. He said he thought maybe your family's faith helped you get through times of sadness and loss. 'There's something there,' he kept saying, 'I'm not sure exactly what it is, but there's something there, Annie, something we don't have, something maybe we need.'"

"I don't know about that, Annie," replied Jack. "When Mom died...I'm not sure how I could have gotten through that without you. Faith helps, sure...but it takes more..." He squeezed her hand gently.

The couple stood before a tall window looking out at the darkening sky, a few evening stars just beginning to appear overhead. Then Jack turned to Anne.

"By the way, those dreams I told you about the other day?" He paused.

Anne looked deep into his eyes.

"Yes, Jack?"

"You're in every one, Anne Wellington. I thought you should know."

Anne looked up at Jack and smiled.

"I hope that's okay with you," added Jack hopefully.

"Jack Bernard," replied Anne, "there's nowhere else on earth I would rather be."

Just then Tom entered the library. Seeing the couple at the window, he cleared his throat loudly: "Ahem...ahem...hello. I hate to interrupt. What's going on? Did I miss anything?"

"Annie and I were just looking at the stars," said Jack. "They really are out tonight, Tommy!" They all laughed.

Anne wrapped her arms around the two young men and the three gazed up at the sky. "My boys," she whispered, "My favorite boys."

### T H E  E N D

# Acknowledgments

*Trolley Days* is dedicated to the memory of my father, Robert W. McMaster, who was a boy in the nineteen-teens when trolleys still plied the streets of most of New England's cities and towns. It was his stories of riding the streetcars of Southbridge, Massachusetts, that first whetted my interest in the days of trolleys.

I am indebted to many friends and family members who read earlier versions of this manuscript and encouraged me to see the project through to completion: Susan Milsom, John Burk, Amy Morris, Martha McMaster, Lynn Bosman, Barbara Podosek, and James Bosman. I thank Julie Dupuis for her memories and insights. Benjamin Martins deserves a special note of gratitude for his cover design.

Meekins Library in Williamsburg, Massachusetts, and the Holyoke History Room Collections of the Holyoke Public Library at Holyoke Community College were invaluable resources for this project. Wistariahurst Museum in Holyoke, the Lowell National Historical Park, and the American Textile History Museum in Lowell, Massachusetts, were important sources of inspiration.

Finally, I thank my wife, Susan Milsom, for her advice, support, and encouragement throughout this project.

# Bibliography

Brault, G. J. 1986. *The French-Canadian Heritage in New England.* University Press of New England, Hanover, NH 03755 USA.

Cummings, O. R. 1972. *Berkshire Street Railway.* National Railway Historical Society, Warehouse Point, CT 06088 USA.

DiCarlo, Ella Merkel. 1982. *Holyoke - Chicopee: a Perspective.* Transcript-Telegram, Holyoke, MA 01040 USA.

Dublin, Thomas, 1992. *Lowell : the Story of an Industrial City.* Nat'l. Park Service, U.S. Dept. of the Interior, Washington, DC 20240 USA.

Ducharme, Jay. 2008. *Mountain Park.* Arcadia Publications, Charleston, SC 29401 USA.

Myers, Andrew H. [undated]. *The Charlottesville Woolen Mills: Working Life, Wartime, and the Walkout of 1918.* [www.historicwoolenmills.org].

Rivard, Paul E. 2002. *A New Order of Things: How the Textile Industry Transformed New England.* University Press of New England, Hanover, NH 03755 USA.

## Illustrations

The author is indebted to Benjamin Christopher Martins, creator of the cover design (also on page 128). Interior illustrations originally appeared in books, periodicals, and postal cards of the period:

Facing page 1: Trolley Centre, Westfield, postcard, ca 1905
Page 18: Pocket watch, artist unknown
Page 44: *Harper's Round Table*, Vol. 16, 1895, by C. W. Breck
Page 56: *St. Nicholas Magazine*, Vol. 36, 1909, by Charles M. Relyea
Page 58: Mountain Park Pavilion, Holyoke, postcard, ca 1910
Page 70: A Holyoke Canal, *Picturesque Hampden*, 1892, by Walter Cox
Page 94: *St. Nicholas Magazine*, Vol. 25, 1898, by Charles M. Relyea
Page 106: Tower on Poet's Seat, Greenfield, artist unknown
Page 184: Mt. Tom cable car, Holyoke, artist unknown
Page 190: "David" by Michelangelo
Page 196: *St. Nicholas Magazine*, Vol. 27, 1900, by B. J. Rosenmeyer
Page 208: Letter from Buenos Aires
Page 248: *St. Nicholas Magazine*, Vol. 30, 1903, by Verna E. Clark
Page 276: Holyoke City Hall, *Bay State Monthly*, Vol. 3, 1885
Page 302: Main Street, Springfield, postcard, ca 1905
Page 309: Star-gazers, artist unknown

# About the Author

**Robert T. McMaster** grew up in Southbridge, Massachusetts, a New England mill town. He holds a B.A. from Clark University and graduate degrees from Boston College, Smith College, and the University of Massachusetts. He taught biology at Holyoke Community College in Massachusetts from 1994 to 2014. His parents' reminiscences of growing up in early 20th century America were the inspiration for his first two novels, *Trolley Days* (2012) and *The Dyeing Room* (2014).

For more information on the author, his books, and that era, visit **www.TrolleyDays.net**.

CPSIA information can be obtained at www.ICGtesting.com
Printed in the USA
LVOW11s1538080515

437779LV00001B/124/P